The Red Cockade

by

Stanley John Weyman

Double9
BOOKS

The Red Cockade
by Stanley John Weyman

Copyright © 2024

All Rights reserved.

ISBN: 978-93-63050-95-2

Published by

DOUBLE 9 BOOKS

2/13-B, Ansari Road
Daryaganj, New Delhi – 110002
info@double9books.com
www.double9books.com
Tel. 011-40042856

ABOUT THE AUTHOR

Stanley John Weyman 7 August 1855 – 10 April 1928) was an English historical romance writer. His most successful novels, written between 1890 and 1895, were set in late 16th and early 17th-century France. They were quite successful at the time, but are now largely forgotten. Stanley John Weyman was born on August 7, 1855, in Ludlow, Shropshire, as the second son of an attorney. He attended Shrewsbury School and Christ Church, Oxford, and graduated in 1877 with a degree in Modern History. Following a year of teaching at the King's School in Chester, he returned to Ludlow in December 1879 to live with his widowed mother. Weyman was called to the law in 1881 but struggled as a barrister due to his shyness, nervousness, and soft-spokenness. However, the lack of briefs provided him time to write. His short story "King Pippin and Sweet Clive" was published in the Cornhill Magazine, but its editor, James Payn, a novelist himself, advised Weyman that it would be simpler to make a career by writing novels. Weyman saw himself as a historian, so he was particularly pleased by excellent feedback on an article he wrote about Oliver Cromwell that appeared in the English Historical Review.

CONTENTS

CHAPTER I
THE MARQUIS DE ST. ALAIS

When we reached the terraced walk, which my father made a little before his death, and which, running under the windows at the rear of the Château, separates the house from the new lawn, St. Alais looked round with eyes of scarcely-veiled contempt.

"What have you done with the garden?" he asked, his lip curling.

"My father removed it to the other side of the house," I answered.

"Out of sight?"

"Yes," I said; "it is beyond the rose garden."

"English fashion!" he answered with a shrug and a polite sneer. "And you prefer to see all this grass from your windows?"

"Yes," I said, "I do."

"Ah! And that plantation? It hides the village, I suppose, from the house?"

"Yes."

He laughed. "Yes," he said. "I notice that that is the way of all who prate of the people, and freedom, and fraternity. They love the people; but they love them at a distance, on the farther side of a park or a high yew hedge. Now, at St. Alais I like to have my folks under my eye, and then, if they do not behave, there is the *carcan*. By the way, what have you done with yours, Vicomte? It used to stand opposite the entrance."

"I have burned it," I said, feeling the blood mount to my temples.

"Your father did, you mean?" he answered, with a glance of surprise.

"No," I said stubbornly, hating myself for being ashamed of that before St. Alais of which I had been proud enough when alone. "I did. I burned it last winter. I think the day of such things is past."

The Marquis was not my senior by more than five years; but those five years, spent in Paris and Versailles, gave him a wondrous advantage, and I felt his look of contemptuous surprise as I should have felt a blow. However, he did not say anything at the moment, but after a short pause changed the subject and began to speak of my father; recalling him and things in connection with him in a tone of respect and affection that in a moment disarmed my resentment.

"The first time that I shot a bird on the wing I was in his company!" he said, with the wonderful charm of manner that had been St. Alais' even in boyhood.

"Twelve years ago," I said.

"Even so, Monsieur," he replied with a laughing bow. "In those days there was a small boy with bare legs, who ran after me, and called me Victor, and thought me the greatest of men. I little dreamed that he would ever live to expound the rights of man to me. And, *Dieu!* Vicomte, I must keep Louis from you, or you will make him as great a reformer as yourself. However," he continued, passing from that subject with a smile and an easy gesture, "I did not come here to talk of him, but of one, M. le Vicomte, in whom you should feel even greater interest."

I felt the blood mount to my temples again, but for a different reason. "Mademoiselle has come home?" I said.

"Yesterday," he answered. "She will go with my mother to Cahors to-morrow, and take her first peep at the world. I do not doubt that among the many new things she will see, none will interest her more than the Vicomte de Saux."

"Mademoiselle is well?" I said clumsily.

"Perfectly," he answered with grave politeness, "as you will see for yourself to-morrow evening, if we do not meet on the road. I daresay that you will like a week or so to commend yourself to her, M. le Vicomte? And after that, whenever Madame la Marquise and you can settle the date, and so forth, the match had better come off--while I am here."

I bowed. I had been expecting to hear this for a week past; but from Louis, who was on brotherly terms with me, not from Victor. The latter had indeed been my boyish idol; but that was years ago, before Court life and a long stay at Versailles and St. Cloud had changed him into the splendid-looking man I saw before me, the raillery of whose eye I found it as difficult to meet as I found it impossible to match the aplomb of his manner. Still, I strove to make such acknowledgments as became me; and to adopt that nice mixture of self-respect, politeness, and devotion which I knew that the occasion, formally treated, required. But my tongue stumbled, and in a moment he relieved me.

"Well, you must tell that to Denise," he said pleasantly; "doubtless you will find her a patient listener. At first, of course," he continued, pulling on his gauntlets and smiling faintly, "she will be a little shy. I have no doubt that the good sisters have brought her up to regard a man in much the same light as a wolf; and a suitor as something worse. But, *eh bien, mon ami!* women are women after all, and in a week or two you will commend yourself. We may hope, then, to see you to-morrow evening--if not before?"

"Most certainly, M. le Marquis."

"Why not Victor?" he answered, laying his hand on my arm with a touch of the old *bonhomie*. "We shall soon be brothers, and then, doubtless, shall hate one another. In the meantime, give me your company to the gates. There was one other thing I wanted to name to you. Let me see--what was it?"

But either he could not immediately remember, or he found a difficulty in introducing the subject, for we were nearly half-way down the avenue of walnut trees that leads to the village when he spoke again. Then he plunged into the matter abruptly.

"You have heard of this protest?" he said.

"Yes," I answered reluctantly and with a foresight of trouble.

"You will sign it, of course?"

He had hesitated before he asked the question; I hesitated before I answered it. The protest to which he referred--how formal the phrase now sounds, though we know that under it lay the beginning of trouble and a new world--was one which it was proposed to move in the coming meeting of the *noblesse* at Cahors; its aim, to condemn the conduct of our representatives at Versailles, in consenting to sit with the Third Estate.

Now, for myself, whatever had been my original views on this question--and, as a fact, I should have preferred to see reform following the English model, the nobles' house remaining separate--I regarded the step, now it was taken, and legalised by the King, as irrevocable; and protest as useless. More, I could not help knowing that those who were moving the protest desired also to refuse all reform, to cling to all privileges, to balk all hopes of better government; hopes, which had been rising higher, day by day, since the elections, and which it might not now be so safe or so easy to balk. Without swallowing convictions, therefore, which were pretty well known, I could not see my way to supporting it. And I hesitated.

"Well?" he said at last, finding me still silent.

"I do not think that I can," I answered, flushing.

"Can support it?"

"No," I said.

He laughed genially. "Pooh!" he said. "I think that you will. I want your promise, Vicomte. It is a small matter; a trifle, and of no importance; but we must be unanimous. That is the one thing necessary."

I shook my head. We had both come to a halt under the trees, a little within the gates. His servant was leading the horses up and down the road.

"Come," he persisted pleasantly: "you do not think that anything is going to come of this chaotic States General, which his Majesty was mad enough to let Neckar summon? They met on the 4th of May; this is the 17th of July; and to this date they have done nothing but wrangle! Nothing! Presently they will be dismissed, and there will be an end of it!"

"Why protest, then?" I said rather feebly.

"I will tell you, my friend," he answered, smiling indulgently and tapping his boot with his whip. "Have you heard the latest news?"

"What is it?" I replied cautiously. "Then I will tell you if I have heard it."

"The King has dismissed Neckar!"

"No!" I cried, unable to hide my surprise.

"Yes," he answered; "the banker is dismissed. In a week his States General or National Assembly, or whatever he pleases to call it, will go too, and we shall be where we were before. Only, in the meantime, and to strengthen the King in the wise course he is at last pursuing, we must show that we are alive. We must show our sympathy with him. We must act. We must protest."

"But, M. le Marquis," I said, a little heated, perhaps, by the news, "are you sure that the people will quietly endure this? Never was so bitter a winter as last winter; never a worse harvest, or such pinching. On the top of these, their hopes have been raised, and their minds excited by the elections, and----

"Whom have we to thank for that?" he said, with a whimsical glance at me. "But, never fear, Vicomte; they will endure it. I know Paris; and I can assure you that it is not the Paris of the Fronde, though M. de Mirabeau would play the Retz. It is a peaceable, sensible Paris, and it will not rise. Except a bread riot or two, it has seen no rising to speak of for a century and a half: nothing that two companies of Swiss could not deal with as easily as D'Argenson cleared the Cour des Miracles. Believe me, there is no danger of that kind: with the least management, all will go well!"

But his news had roused my antagonism. I found it more easy to resist him now.

"I do not know," I said coldly; "I do not think that the matter is so simple as you say. The King must have money, or be bankrupt; the people have no money to pay him. I do not see how things can go back to the old state."

M. de St. Alais looked at me with a gleam of anger in his eyes.

"You mean, Vicomte," he said, "that you do not wish them to go back?"

"I mean that the old state was impossible," I said stiffly. "It could not last. It cannot return."

For a moment he did not answer, and we stood confronting one another--he just without, I just within, the gateway--the cool foliage stretching over us, the dust and July sunshine in the road beyond him; and if my face reflected his, it was flushed, and set, and determined. But in a twinkling his changed; he broke into an easy, polite laugh, and shrugged his shoulders with a touch of contempt.

"Well," he said, "we will not argue; but I hope that you will sign. Think it over, M. le Vicomte, think it over. Because"--he paused, and looked at me gaily--"we do not know what may be depending upon it."

"That is a reason," I answered quickly, "for thinking more before I----"

"It is a reason for thinking more before you refuse," he said, bowing very low, and this time without smiling. Then he turned to his horse, and his servant held the stirrup while he mounted. When he was in the saddle and had gathered up the reins, he bent his face to mine.

"Of course," he said, speaking in a low voice, and with a searching look at me, "a contract is a contract, M. le Vicomte; and the Montagues and Capulets, like your *carcan*, are out of date. But, all the same, we must go one way--*comprenez-vous?*--we must go one way--or separate! At least, I think so."

And nodding pleasantly, as if he had uttered in these words a compliment instead of a threat, he rode off; leaving me to stand and fret and fume, and finally to stride back under the trees with my thoughts in a whirl, and all my plans and hopes jarring one another in a petty copy of the confusion that that day prevailed, though I guessed it but dimly, from one end of France to the other.

For I could not be blind to his meaning; nor ignorant that he had, no matter how politely, bidden me choose between the alliance with his family, which my father had arranged for me, and the political views in which my father had brought me up, and which a year's residence in England had not failed to strengthen. Alone in the Château since my father's death, I had lived a good deal in the future--in day-dreams of Denise de St. Alais, the fair girl who was to be my wife, and whom I had not seen since she went to her convent school; in day-dreams, also, of work to be done in spreading round me the prosperity I had seen in England. Now, St. Alais' words menaced one or other of these prospects; and that was bad enough. But, in truth, it was not that, so much as his presumption, that stung me; that made me swear one moment and laugh the next, in a kind of irritation not difficult to understand. I was twenty-two, he was twenty-seven; and he dictated to me! We were country bumpkins, he of the *haute politique*, and he had come from Versailles or from Paris to drill us! If I went his way I might marry his sister; if not, I might not! That was the position.

No wonder that before he had left me half an hour I had made up my mind to resist him; and so spent the rest of the day composing sound and unanswerable reasons for the course I intended to take; now conning over a letter in which M. de Liancourt set forth his plan of reform, now summarising the opinions with which M. de Rochefoucauld had favoured me on his last journey to Luchon. In half an hour and the heat of temper! thinking no more than ten thousand others, who that week chose one of two courses, what I was doing. Gargouf, the St. Alais' steward, who doubtless heard that day the news of Neckar's fall, and rejoiced, had no foresight of what it meant to him. Father Benôit, the cure, who supped with me that evening, and heard the tidings with sorrow--he, too, had no special vision. And the innkeeper's son at La Bastide, by Cahors--probably he, also, heard the news; but no shadow of a sceptre fell across his path, nor any of a *bâton* on that of the notary at the other La Bastide. A notary, a *bâton*! An innkeeper, a sceptre! *Mon Dieu!* what conjunctions they would have seemed in those days! We should have been wiser than Daniel, and more prudent than Joseph, if we had foreseen such things under the old *régime*--in the old France, in the old world, that died in that month of July, 1789!

And yet there were signs, even then, to be read by those with eyes, that foretold something, if but a tithe of the inconceivable future; of which signs I myself remarked sufficient by the way next day to fill my mind with other thoughts than private resentment; with some nobler aims than self-assertion. Riding to Cahors, with Gil and André at my back, I saw not only the havoc caused by the great frosts of the winter and spring, not only walnut trees blackened and withered, vines stricken, rye killed, a huge proportion of the land fallow, desert, gloomy and unsown: not only those common signs of poverty to which use had accustomed me--though on my first return from England I had viewed them with horror--mud cabins, I mean, and unglazed windows, starved cattle, and women bent double, gathering weeds. But I saw other things more ominous; a strange herding of men at cross-roads and bridges, where they waited for they knew not what; a something lowering in these men's silence, a something expectant in their faces; worst of all, a something dangerous in their scowling eyes and sunken cheeks. Hunger had pinched them; the elections had roused them. I trembled to think of the issue, and that in the hint of danger I had given St. Alais, I had been only too near the mark.

A league farther on, where the woodlands skirt Cahors, I lost sight of these things; but for a time only. They reappeared presently in another form. The first view of the town, as, girt by the shining Lot, and protected by ramparts and towers, it nestles under the steep hills, is apt to take the eye; its matchless bridge, and time-worn Cathedral, and great palace seldom failing to rouse the admiration even of those who know them. But that day I saw none of these things. As I passed down towards the market-place they were selling grain under a guard of soldiers with fixed bayonets; and the starved faces of the waiting crowd that filled all that side of the square, their shrunken, half-naked figures, and dark looks, and the sullen muttering, which seemed so much at odds with the sunshine, occupied me, to the exclusion of everything else.

Or not quite. I had eyes for one other thing, and that was the astonishing indifference with which those whom curiosity, or business, or habit had brought to the spot, viewed this spectacle. The inns were full of the gentry of the province, come to the Assembly; they looked on from the windows, as at a show, and talked and jested as if at home in their châteaux. Before the doors of the Cathedral a group of ladies and clergymen walked to and fro, and now and then they turned a listless eye on what was passing; but for the most part they seemed to be unconscious of it, or, at the best, to have no concern with it. I have heard it said since, that in those days we had two worlds in France, as far apart as hell and heaven; and what I saw that evening went far to prove it.

In the square a shop at which pamphlets and journals were sold was full of customers, though other shops in the neighbourhood were closed, their owners fearing mischief. On the skirts of the crowd, and a little aloof from it,

I saw Gargouf, the St. Alais' steward. He was talking to a countryman; and, as I passed, I heard him say with a gibe, "Well, has your National Assembly fed you yet?"

"Not yet," the clown answered stupidly, "but I am told that in a few days they will satisfy everybody."

"Not they!" the agent answered brutally. "Why, do you think that they will feed you?"

"Oh, yes, by your leave; it is certain," the man said. "And, besides, every one is agreed----"

But then Gargouf saw me, saluted me, and I heard no more. A moment later, however, I came on one of my own people, Buton, the blacksmith, in the middle of a muttering group. He looked at me sheepishly, finding himself caught; and I stopped, and rated him soundly, and saw him start for home before I went to my quarters.

These were at the Trois Rois, where I always lay when in town; Doury, the innkeeper, providing a supper ordinary for the gentry at eight o'clock, at which it was the custom to dress and powder.

The St. Alais had their own house in Cahors, and, as the Marquis had forewarned me, entertained that evening. The greater part of the company, indeed, repaired to them after the meal. I went myself a little late, that I might avoid any private talk with the Marquis; I found the rooms already full and brilliantly lighted, the staircase crowded with valets, and the strains of a harpsichord trickling melodiously from the windows. Madame de St. Alais was in the habit of entertaining the best company in the province; with less splendour, perhaps, than some, but with so much ease, and taste, and good breeding, that I look in vain for such a house in these days.

Ordinarily, she preferred to people her rooms with pleasant groups, that, gracefully disposed, gave to a *salon* an air elegant and pleasing, and in character with the costume of those days, the silks and laces, powder and diamonds, the full hoops and red-heeled shoes. But on this occasion the crowd and the splendour of the entertainment apprised me, as soon as I crossed the threshold, that I was assisting at a party of more than ordinary importance; nor had I advanced far before I guessed that it was a political rather than a social gathering. All, or almost all, who would attend the Assembly next day were here; and though, as I wound my way through the glittering crowd, I heard very little serious talk--so little, that I marvelled to think that people could discuss the respective merits of French and Italian opera, of Grétry and Bianchi, and the like, while so much hung in the balance--of the effect intended I had no doubt; nor that Madame, in assembling all the wit and beauty of the province, was aiming at things higher than amusement.

With, I am bound to confess, a degree of success. At any rate it was difficult to mix with the throng which filled her rooms, to run the gauntlet of bright eyes and witty tongues, to breathe the atmosphere laden with perfume and music, without falling under the spell, without forgetting. Inside the door M. de Gontaut, one of my father's oldest friends, was talking with the two Harincourts. He greeted me with a sly smile, and pointed politely inwards.

"Pass on, Monsieur," he said. "The farthest room. Ah! my friend, I wish I were young again!"

"Your gain would be my loss, M. le Baron," I said civilly, and slid by him. Next, I had to speak to two or three ladies, who detained me with wicked congratulations of the same kind; and then I came on Louis. He clasped my hand, and we stood a moment together. The crowd elbowed us; a simpering fool at his shoulder was prating of the social contract. But as I felt the pressure of Louis' hand, and looked into his eyes, it seemed to me that a breath of air from the woods penetrated the room, and swept aside the heavy perfumes.

Yet there was trouble in his look. He asked me if I had seen Victor.

"Yesterday," I said, understanding him perfectly, and what was amiss. "Not to-day."

"Nor Denise?"

"No. I have not had the honour of seeing Mademoiselle."

"Then, come," he answered. "My mother expected you earlier. What did you think of Victor?"

"That he went Victor, and has returned a great personage!" I said, smiling.

Louis laughed faintly, and lifted his eyebrows with a comical air of sufferance.

"I was afraid so," he said. "He did not seem to be very well pleased with you. But we must all do his bidding--eh, Monsieur? And, in the meantime, come. My mother and Denise are in the farthest room."

He led the way thither as he spoke; but we had first to go through the card-room, and then the crowd about the farther doorway was so dense that we could not immediately enter; and so I had time--while outwardly smiling and bowing--to feel a little suspense. At last we slipped through and entered a smaller room, where were only Madame la Marquise--who was standing in the middle of the floor talking with the Abbé Mesnil--two or three ladies, and Denise de St. Alais.

Mademoiselle had her seat on a couch by one of the ladies; and naturally my eyes went first to her. She was dressed in white, and it struck me with the force of a blow how small, how childish she was! Very fair, of the purest complexion, and perfectly formed, she seemed to derive an extravagant, an absurd, air of dignity from the formality of her dress, from the height of the powdered hair that strained upwards from her forehead, from the stiffness of her brocaded petticoat. But she was very small. I had time to note this, to feel a little disappointment, and to fancy that, cast in a larger mould, she would have been supremely handsome; and then the lady beside her, seeing me, spoke to her, and the child--she was really little more--looked up, her face grown crimson. Our eyes met--thank God! she had Louis' eyes--and she looked down again, blushing painfully.

I advanced to pay my respects to Madame, and kissed the hand, which, without at once breaking off her conversation, she extended to me.

"But such powers!" the Abbé, who had something of the reputation of a *philosophe*, was saying to her. "Without limit! Without check! Misused, Madame----"

"But the King is too good!" Madame la Marquise answered, smiling.

"When well advised, I agree. But then the deficit?"

The Marquise shrugged her shoulders. "His Majesty must have money," she said.

"Yes--but whence?" the Abbé asked, with answering shrug.

"The King was too good at the beginning," Madame replied, with a touch of severity. "He should have made them register the edicts. However, the Parliament has always given way, and will do so again."

"The Parliament--yes," the Abbé retorted, smiling indulgently. "But it is no longer a question of the Parliament; and the States General----"

"States General pass," Madame responded grandly. "The King remains!"

"Yet if trouble comes?"

"It will not," Madame answered with the same grand air. "His Majesty will prevent it." And then with a word or two more she dismissed the Abbé and turned to me. She tapped me on the shoulder with her fan. "Ah! truant," she said, with a glance in which kindness and a little austerity were mingled. "I do not know what I am to say to you! Indeed, from the account Victor gave me yesterday, I hardly knew whether to expect you this evening or not. Are you sure that it is you who are here?"

"I will answer for my heart, Madame," I answered, laying my hand upon it.

Her eyes twinkled kindly.

"Then," she said, "bring it where it is due, Monsieur." And she turned with a fine air of ceremony, and led me to her daughter. "Denise," she said, "this is M. le Vicomte de Saux, the son of my old, my good friend. M. le Vicomte--my daughter. Perhaps you will amuse her while I go back to the Abbé."

Probably Mademoiselle had spent the evening in an agony of shyness, expecting this moment; for she curtsied to the floor, and then stood dumb and confused, forgetting even to sit down, until I covered her with fresh blushes by begging her to do so. When she had complied, I took my stand before her, with my hat in my hand; but between seeking for the right compliment, and trying to trace a likeness between her and the wild, brown-faced child of thirteen, whom I had known four years before--and from the dignified height of nineteen immeasurably despised--I grew shy myself.

"You came home last week, Mademoiselle?" I said at last.

"Yes, Monsieur," she answered, in a whisper, and with downcast eyes.

"It must be a great change for you!"

"Yes, Monsieur."

Silence: then, "Doubtless the Sisters were good to you?" I suggested.

"Yes, Monsieur."

"Yet, you were not sorry to leave?"

"Yes, Monsieur."

But on that the meaning of what she had last said came home to her, or she felt the banality of her answers; for, on a sudden, she looked swiftly up at me, her face scarlet, and, if I was not mistaken, she was within a little of bursting into tears. The thought appalled me. I stooped lower.

"Mademoiselle!" I said hurriedly, "pray do not be afraid of me. Whatever happens, you shall never have need to fear me. I beg of you to look on me as a friend--as your brother's friend. Louis is my----"

Crash! While the name hung on my lips, something struck me on the back, and I staggered forward, almost into her arms; amid a shiver of broken glass, a flickering of lights, a rising chorus of screams and cries. For a moment I could not think what was happening, or had happened; the blow had taken away my breath. I was conscious only of Mademoiselle clinging terrified to my arm, of her face, wild with fright, looking up to me, of the sudden cessation of the music. Then, as people pressed in on us, and I began to recover, I turned and saw that the window behind me had been driven in, and the lead and panes shattered; and that among the *débris* on the floor lay a great stone. It was that which had struck me.

CHAPTER II
THE ORDEAL

It was wonderful how quickly the room filled--filled with angry faces, so that almost before I knew what had happened, I found a crowd round me, asking what it was; M. de St. Alais foremost. As all spoke at once, and in the background where they could not see, ladies were screaming and chattering, I might have found it difficult to explain. But the shattered window and the great stone on the floor spoke for themselves, and told more quickly than I could what had taken place.

On the instant, with a speed which surprised me, the sight blew into a flame passions already smouldering. A dozen voices cried, "Out on the *canaille!*" In a moment some one in the background followed this up with "Swords, Messieurs, swords!" Then, in a trice half the gentlemen were elbowing one another towards the door, St. Alais, who burned to avenge the insult offered to his guests, taking the lead. M. de Gontaut and one or two of the elders tried to restrain him, but their remonstrances were in vain, and in a moment the room was almost emptied of men. They poured out into the street, and began to scour it with drawn blades and raised voices. A dozen valets, running out officiously with flambeaux, aided in the search; for a few minutes the street, as we who remained viewed it from the windows, seemed to be alive with moving lights and figures.

But the rascals who had flung the stone, whatever the motive which inspired them, had fled in time; and presently our party returned, some a little ashamed of their violence, others laughing as they entered, and bewailing their silk stockings and spattered shoes; while a few, less fashionable or more impetuous, continued to denounce the insult, and threaten vengeance. At another time, the act might have seemed trivial, a childish insult; but in the strained state of public feeling it had an unpleasant and menacing air which was not lost on the more thoughtful. During the absence of the street party, the draught from the broken window had blown a curtain against some candles and set it alight; and though the stuff had been torn down with little damage, it still smoked among the *débris* on the floor. This, with the startled faces of the ladies, and the shattered glass, gave a look of disorder and ruin to the room, where a few minutes before all had worn so seemly and festive an air.

It did not surprise me, therefore, that St. Alais' face, stern enough at his entrance, grew darker as he looked round.

"Where is my sister?" he said abruptly, almost rudely.

"Here," Madame la Marquise answered. Denise had flown long before to her side, and was clinging to her.

"She is not hurt?"

"No," Madame answered, playfully tapping the girl's cheek. "M. de Saux had most reason to complain."

"Save me from my friends, eh, Monsieur?" St. Alais said, with an unpleasant smile.

I started. The words were not much in themselves, but the sneer underlying them was plain. I could scarcely pass it by. "If you think, M. le Marquis," I said sharply, "that I knew anything of this outrage----"

"That you knew anything? *Ma foi,* no!" he replied lightly, and with a courtly gesture of deprecation. "We have not fallen to that yet. That any gentleman in this company should sink to play the fellow to those--is not possible! But I think we may draw a useful lesson from this, Messieurs," he continued, turning from me and addressing the company. "And that is a lesson to hold our own, or we shall soon lose all."

A hum of approbation ran round the room.

"To maintain privileges, or we shall lose rights."

Twenty voices were raised in assent.

"To stand now," he continued, his colour high, his hand raised, "or never!"

"Then now! Now!"

The cry rose suddenly not from one, but from a hundred throats--of men and women; in a moment the room catching his tone seemed to throb with enthusiasm, with the pulse of resolve. Men's eyes grew bright under the candles, they breathed quickly, and with heightened colour. Even the weakest felt the influence; the fool who had prated of the social contract and the rights of man was as loud as any. "Now! Now!" they cried with one voice.

What followed on that I have never completely fathomed; nor whether it was a thing arranged, or merely an inspiration, born of the common enthusiasm. But while the windows still shook with that shout, and every eye was on him, M. de Alais stepped forward, the most gallant and perfect figure, and with a splendid gesture drew his sword.

"Gentlemen!" he cried, "we are of one mind, of one voice. Let us be also in the fashion. If, while all the world is fighting to get and hold, we alone stand still and on the defensive--we court attack, and, what is worse, defeat! Let us unite then, while it is still time, and show that, in Quercy at least, our Order will stand or fall together. You have heard of the oath of the Tennis Court and the 20th of June. Let us, too, take an oath--this 22nd of July; not with uplifted hands like a club of wordy debaters, promising all things to all men; but with uplifted swords. As nobles and gentlemen, let us swear to stand by the rights, the privileges, and the exemptions of our Order!"

A shout that made the candles flicker and jump, that filled the street, and was heard even in the distant market-place, greeted the proposal. Some drew their swords at once, and flourished them above their heads; while ladies waved their fans or kerchiefs. But the majority cried, "To the larger room! To the larger room!" And on the instant, as if in obedience to an order, the company turned that way, and flushed, and eager, pressed through the narrow doorway into the next room.

There may have been some among them less enthusiastic than others; some more earnest in show than at heart; none, I am sure, who, on this, followed so slowly, so reluctantly, with so heavy a heart, and sure a presage of evil as I did. Already I foresaw the dilemma before me; but angry, hot-faced, and uncertain, I could discern no way out of it.

If I could have escaped, and slipped clear from the room, I would have done so without scruple; but the stairs were on the farther side of the great room which we were entering, and a dense crowd cut me off from them; moreover, I felt that St. Alais' eye was upon me, and that, if he had not framed the ordeal to meet my case, and extort my support, he was at least determined, now that his blood was fired, that I should not evade it.

Still I would not hasten the evil day, and I lingered near the inner door, hoping; but the Marquis, on reaching the middle of the room, mounted a chair and turned round; and so contrived still to face me. The mob of gentlemen formed themselves round him, the younger and more tumultuous uttering cries of "Vive la Noblesse!" And a fringe of ladies encircled all. The lights, the brilliant dresses and jewels on which they shone, the impassioned faces, the waving kerchiefs and bright eyes, rendered the scene one to be remembered, though at the moment I was conscious only of St. Alais' gaze.

"Messieurs," he cried, "draw your swords, if you please!"

They flashed out at the word, with a steely glitter which the mirrors reflected; and M. de St. Alais passed his eye slowly round, while all waited for the word. He stopped; his eye was on me.

"M. de Saux," he said politely, "we are waiting for you."

Naturally all turned to me. I strove to mutter something, and signed to him with my hand to go on. But I was too much confused to speak clearly; my only hope was that he would comply, out of prudence.

But that was the last thing he thought of doing. "Will you take your place, Monsieur?" he said smoothly.

Then I could escape no longer. A hundred eyes, some impatient, some merely curious, rested on me. My face burned.

"I cannot do so," I answered.

There fell a great silence from one end of the room to the other.

"Why not, Monsieur, if I may ask?" St. Alais said still smoothly.

"Because I am not--entirely at one with you," I stammered, meeting all eyes as bravely as I could. "My opinions are known, M. de St. Alais," I went on more steadfastly. "I cannot swear."

He stayed with his hand a dozen who would have cried out upon me.

"Gently, Messieurs," he said, with a gesture of dignity, "gently, if you please. This is no place for threats. M. de Saux is my guest; and I have too great a respect for him not to respect his scruples. But I think that there is another way. I shall not venture to argue with him myself. But--Madame," he continued, smiling as he turned with an inimitable air to his mother, "I think that if you would permit Mademoiselle de St. Alais to play the recruiting-sergeant--for this one time--she could not fail to heal the breach."

A murmur of laughter and subdued applause, a flutter of fans and women's eyes greeted the proposal. But, for a moment, Madame la Marquise, smiling and sphinx-like, stood still, and did not speak. Then she turned to her daughter, who, at the mention of her name, had cowered back, shrinking from sight.

"Go, Denise," she said simply. "Ask M. de Saux to honour you by becoming your recruit."

The girl came forward slowly, and with a visible tremor; nor shall I ever forget the misery of that moment, or the shame and obstinacy that alternately surged through my brain as I awaited her. Thought, quicker than lightning, showed me the trap into which I had fallen, a trap far more horrible than the dilemma I had foreseen. Nor was the poor girl herself, as she stood before me, tortured by shyness, and stammering her little petition in words barely intelligible, the least part of my pain.

For to refuse her, in face of all those people, seemed a thing impossible. It seemed a thing as brutal as to strike her; an act as cruel, as churlish, as unworthy of a gentleman as to trample any helpless sensitive thing under foot! And I felt that; I felt it to the utmost. But I felt also that to assent was to turn my back on consistency, and my life; to consent to be a dupe, the victim of a ruse; to be a coward, though every one there might applaud me. I saw both these things, and for a moment I hesitated between rage and pity; while lights and fair faces, inquisitive or scornful, shifted mazily before my eyes. At last--

"Mademoiselle, I cannot," I muttered. "I cannot."

"Monsieur!"

It was not the girl's word, but Madame's, and it rang high and sharp through the room; so that I thanked God for the intervention. It cleared in a moment the confusion from my brain. I became myself. I turned to her; I bowed.

"No, Madame, I cannot," I said firmly, doubting no longer, but stubborn, defiant, resolute. "My opinions are known. And I will not, even for Mademoiselle's sake, give the lie to them."

As the last word fell from my lips, a glove, flung by an unseen hand, struck me on the cheek; and then for a moment the room seemed to go mad. Amid a storm of hisses, of *"Vaurien!"* and *"A bas le traître!"* a dozen blades were brandished in my face, a dozen challenges were flung at my head. I had not learned at that time how excitable is a crowd, how much less merciful than any member of it; and surprised and deafened by the tumult, which the shrieks of the ladies did not tend to diminish, I recoiled a pace.

M. de St. Alais took advantage of the moment. He sprang down, and thrusting aside the blades which threatened me, flung himself in front of me.

"Messieurs, listen!" he cried, above the uproar. "Listen, I beg! This gentleman is my guest. He is no longer of us, but he must go unharmed. A way! A way, if you please, for M. le Vicomte de Saux."

They obeyed him reluctantly, and falling back to one side or the other, opened a way across the room to the door. He turned to me, and bowed low--his courtliest bow.

"This way, Monsieur le Vicomte, if you please," he said. "Madame la Marquise will not trespass on your time any longer."

I followed him with a burning face, down the narrow lane of shining parquet, under the chandelier, between the lines of mocking eyes; and not a man interposed. In dead silence I followed him to the door. There he stood aside, and bowed to me, and I to him; and I walked out mechanically--walked out alone.

I passed through the lobby. The crowd of peeping, grinning lackeys that filled it stared at me, all eyes; but I was scarcely conscious of their impertinence or their presence. Until I reached the street, and the cold air revived me, I went like a man stunned, and unable to think. The blow had fallen on me so suddenly, so unexpectedly.

When I did come a little to myself, my first feeling was rage. I had gone into M. de St. Alais' house that evening, possessing everything; I came out, stripped of friends, reputation, my betrothed! I had gone in, trusting to his friendship, the friendship that was a tradition in our families; he had worsted me by a trick. I stood in the street, and groaned as I thought of it; as I pictured the sorry figure I had cut amongst them, and reflected on what was before me.

For, presently, I began to think that I had been a fool--that I should have given way. I could not, as I stood in the street there, foresee the future; nor know for certain that the old France was passing, and that even now, in Paris, its death-knell had gone forth. I had to live by the opinions of the people round me; to think, as I paced the streets, how I should face the company to-morrow, and whether I should fly, or whether I should fight. For in the meeting on the morrow----

Ah! the Assembly. The word turned my thoughts into a new channel. I could have my revenge there. That I might not raise a jarring note *there*, they had cajoled me, and when cajolery failed, had insulted me. Well, I would show them that the new way would succeed no better than the old, and that where they had thought to suppress a Saux they had raised a Mirabeau. From this point I passed the night in a fever. Resentment spurred ambition; rage against my caste, a love of the people. Every sign of misery and famine that had passed before my eyes during the day recurred now, and was garnered for use. The early daylight found me still pacing my room, still thinking, composing, reciting; when André, my old body-servant, who had been also my father's, came at seven with a note in his hand, I was still in my clothes.

Doubtless he had heard downstairs a garbled account of what had occurred, and my cheek burned. I took no notice of his gloomy looks, however, but, without speaking, I opened the note. It was not signed, but the handwriting was Louis'.

"Go home," it ran, "and do not show yourself at the Assembly. They will challenge you one by one; the event is certain. Leave Cahors at once, or you are a dead man."

That was all! I smiled bitterly at the weakness of the man who could do no more for his friend than this.

"Who gave it to you?" I asked André.

"A servant, Monsieur."

"Whose?"

But he muttered that he did not know; and I did not press him. He assisted me to change my dress; when I had done, he asked me at what hour I needed the horses.

"The horses! For what?" I said, turning and staring at him.

"To return, Monsieur."

"But I do not return to-day!" I said in cold displeasure. "Of what are you speaking? We came only yesterday."

"True, Monsieur," he muttered, continuing to potter over my dressing things, and keeping his back to me. "Still, it is a good day for returning."

"You have been reading this note!" I cried wrathfully. "Who told you that----"

"All the town knows!" he answered, shrugging his shoulders coolly. "It is, 'André, take your master home!' and, 'André, you have a hot-pate for a master,' and André this, and André that, until I am fairly muddled! Gil has a bloody nose, fighting a Harincourt lad that called Monsieur a fool; but for me, I am too old for fighting. And there is one other thing I am too old for," he continued, with a sniff.

"What is that, impertinent?" I cried.

"To bury another master."

I waited a minute. Then I said: "You think that I shall be killed?"

"It is the talk of the town!"

I thought a moment. Then: "You served my father, André," I said.

"Ah! Monsieur."

"Yet you would have me run away?"

He turned to me, and flung up his hands in despair.

"*Mon Dieu!*" he cried, "I don't know what I would have! We are ruined by these *canaille*. As if God made them to do anything but dig and work; or we could do without poor! If you had never taken up with them, Monsieur----"

"Silence, man!" I said sternly. "You know nothing about it. Go down now, and another time be more careful. You talk of the *canaille* and the poor! What are you yourself?"

"I, Monsieur?" he cried, in astonishment.

"Yes--you!"

He stared at me a moment with a face of bewilderment. Then slowly and sorrowfully he shook his head, and went out. He began to think me mad.

When he was gone I did not at once move. I fancied it likely that if I showed myself in the streets before the Assembly met, I should be challenged, and forced to fight. I waited, therefore, until the hour of meeting was past; waited in the dull upper room, feeling the bitterness of isolation, and thinking, sometimes of Louis St. Alais, who had let me go, and spoken no word in my behalf, sometimes of men's unreasonableness; for in some of the provinces half of the nobility were of my way of thinking. I thought of Saux, too; and I will not say that I felt no temptation to adopt the course which André had suggested--to withdraw quietly thither, and then at some later time, when men's minds were calmer, to vindicate my courage. But a certain stubbornness, which my father had before me, and which I have heard people say comes of an English strain in the race, conspired with resentment to keep me in the way I had marked out. At a quarter past ten, therefore, when I thought that the last of the Members would have preceded me to the Assembly, I went downstairs, with hot cheeks, but eyes that were stern enough; and finding André and Gil waiting at the door, bade them follow me to the Chapter House beside the Cathedral, where the meetings were held.

Afterwards I was told that, had I used my eyes, I must have noticed the excitement which prevailed in the streets; the crowd, dense, yet silent, that filled the Square and all the neighbouring ways; the air of expectancy, the closed shops, the cessation of business, the whispering groups in alleys and at doors. But I was wrapped up in myself, like one going on a forlorn hope;

and of all remarked only one thing--that as I crossed the Square a man called out, "God bless you, Monsieur!" and another, "*Vive Saux!*" and that thereon a dozen or more took off their caps. This I did notice; but mechanically only. The next moment I was in the entry which leads alongside one wall of the Cathedral to the Chapter House, and a crowd of clerks and servants, who blocked it almost from wall to wall, were making way for me to pass; not without looks of astonishment and curiosity.

Threading my way through them, I entered the empty vestibule, kept clear by two or three ushers. Here the change from sunshine to shadow, from the life and light and stir which prevailed outside, to the silence of this vaulted chamber, was so great that it struck a chill to my heart. Here, in the greyness and stillness, the importance of the step I was about to take, the madness of the challenge I was about to fling down, in the teeth of my brethren, rose before me; and if my mind had not been braced to the utmost by resentment and obstinacy, I must have turned back. But already my feet rang noisily on the stone pavement, and forbade retreat. I could hear a monotonous voice droning in the Chamber beyond the closed door; and I crossed to that door, setting my teeth hard, and preparing myself to play the man, whatever awaited me.

Another moment, and I should have been inside. My hand was already on the latch, when some one, who had been sitting on the stone bench in the shadow under the window, sprang up, and hurried to stop me. It was Louis de St. Alais. He reached me before I could open the door, and, thrusting himself in front of me, set his back against the panels.

"Stop, man! for God's sake, stop!" he cried passionately, yet kept his voice low. "What can one do against two hundred? Go back, man, go back, and I will----"

"*You will!*" I answered with fierce contempt, yet in the same low tone--the ushers were staring curiously at us from the door by which I had entered. "You will? You will do, I suppose, as much as you did last night, Monsieur."

"Never mind that now!" he answered earnestly; though he winced, and the colour rose to his brow. "Only go! Go to Saux, and----"

"Keep out of the way!"

"Yes," he said, "and keep out of the way. If you will do that----"

"Keep out of the way?" I repeated savagely.

"Yes, yes; then everything will blow over."

"Thank you!" I said slowly; and I trembled with rage. "And how much, may I ask, are you to have, M. le Comte, for ridding the Assembly of me?"

He stared at me. "Adrien!" he cried.

But I was ruthless. "No, Monsieur le Comte--not Adrien!" I said proudly; "I am that only to my friends."

"And I am no longer one?"

I raised my eyebrows contemptuously. "*After last night?*" I said. "After last night? Is it possible, Monsieur, that you fancy you played a friendly part? I came into your house, your guest, your friend, your all but relative; and you laid a trap for me, you held me up to ridicule and odium, you----"

"I did?" he exclaimed.

"Perhaps not with your own voice. But you stood by and saw it done! You stood by and said no word for me! You stood by and raised no finger for me! If you call that friendship----"

He stopped me with a gesture full of dignity. "You forget one thing, M. le Vicomte," he said, in a tone of proud reticence.

"Name it!" I answered disdainfully.

"That Mademoiselle de St. Alais is my sister!"

"Ah!"

"And that, whether the fault was yours or not, you last evening treated her lightly--before two hundred people! You forget that, M. le Vicomte."

"I treated her lightly?" I replied, in a fresh excess of rage. We had moved, as if by common consent, a little from the door, and by this time were glaring into one another's eyes. "And with whom lay the fault if I did? With whom lay the fault, Monsieur? You gave me the choice--nay, you forced me to make choice between slighting her and giving up opinions and convictions which I hold, in which I have been bred, in which----"

"*Opinions!*" he said more harshly than he had yet spoken. "And what are, after all, opinions? Pardon me, I see that I annoy you, Monsieur. But I am not philosophic; I have not been to England; and I cannot understand a man----"

"Giving up anything for his opinions!" I cried, with a savage sneer. "No, Monsieur, I daresay you cannot. If a man will not stand by his friends he will not stand by his opinions. To do either the one or the other, M. le Comte, a man must not be a coward."

He grew pale, and looked at me strangely. "Hush, Monsieur!" he said--involuntarily, it seemed to me. And a spasm crossed his face, as if a sharp pain shot through him.

But I was beside myself with passion. "A coward!" I repeated. "Do you understand me, M. le Comte? Or do you wish me to go inside and repeat the word before the Assembly?"

"There is no need," he said, growing as red as he had before been pale.

"There should be none," I answered, with a sneer. "May I conclude that you will meet me after the Assembly rises?"

He bowed without speaking; and then, and not till then, something in his silence and his looks pierced the armour of my rage; and on a sudden I grew sick at heart, and cold. It was too late, however; I had said that which could never be unsaid. The memory of his patience, of his goodness, of his forbearance, came after the event. I saluted him formally; he replied; and I turned grimly to the door again.

But I was not to pass through it yet.

A second time when I had the latch in my grasp, and the door an inch open, a hand plucked me back; so forcibly, that the latch rattled as it fell, and I turned in a rage. To my astonishment it was Louis again, but with a changed face--a face of strange excitement. He retained his hold on me.

"No," he said, between his teeth. "You have called me a coward, M. le Vicomte, and I will not wait! Not an hour. You shall fight me now. There is a garden at the back, and----"

But I had grown as cold as he hot. "I shall do nothing of the kind," I said, cutting him short. "After the Assembly----"

He raised his hand and deliberately struck me with his glove across the face.

"Will that persuade you, then?" he said, as I involuntarily recoiled. "After that, Monsieur, if you are a gentleman, you will fight me. There is a garden at the back, and in ten minutes----"

"In ten minutes the Assembly may have risen," I said.

"I will not keep you so long!" he answered sternly. "Come, sir! Or must I strike you again?"

"I will come," I said slowly. "After you, Monsieur."

CHAPTER III
IN THE ASSEMBLY

The blow, and the insult with which he accompanied it, put an end for the moment to my repentance. But short as was the distance across the floor from the one door to the other, it gave me time to think again; to remember that this was Louis; and that whatever cause I had had to complain of him, whatever grounds to suspect that he was the tool of others, no friend could have done more to assuage my wrath, nor the most honest more to withhold me from entering on an impossible task. Melting quickly, melting almost instantly, I felt with a kind of horror that if kindness alone had led him to interpose, I had made him the worst return in the world; in fine, before the outer door could be opened to us, I repented anew. When the usher held it for me to pass, I bade him close it, and, to Louis' surprise, turned, and, muttering something, ran back. Before he could do more than utter a cry I was across the vestibule; a moment, and I had the door of the Assembly open.

Instantly I saw before me--I suppose that my hand had raised the latch noisily--tiers of surprised faces all turned my way. I heard a murmur of mingled annoyance and laughter. The next moment I was threading my way to my place with the monotonous voice of the President in my ears, and the scene round me so changed--from that low-toned altercation outside, to this Chamber full of light and life, and thronged with starers--that I sank into my seat, dazzled and abashed; and almost forgetful for the time of the purpose which brought me thither.

A little, and my face grew hotter still; and with good reason. Each of the benches on which we sat held three. I shared mine with one of the Harincourts and M. d'Aulnoy, my place being between them. I had scarcely taken it five seconds, when Harincourt rose slowly, and, without turning his face to me, moved away down the gangway, and, fanning himself delicately with his hat, assumed a leaning position against a desk with his gaze on the President. Half a minute, and D'Aulnoy followed his example. Then the three behind me rose, and quietly and without looking at me found other places. The three before me followed suit. In two minutes I sat alone, isolated, a mark for all eyes; a kind of leper in the Assembly!

I ought to have been prepared for some such demonstration. But I was not, and my cheeks burned, as if the curious looks to which I was exposed were a hot fire. It was impossible for me, taken by surprise, to hide my embarrassment; for, wherever I gazed, I met sneering eyes and contemptuous glances; and pride would not let me hang my head. For many minutes, therefore, I was unconscious of everything but that scorching gaze. I could not hear what was going forward. The President's voice was a dull, meaningless drawl to me.

Yet all the while anger and resentment were hardening me in my resolve; and, presently, the cloud passed from my mind, and left me exulting. The monotonous reading, to which I had listened without understanding it, came to an end, and was followed by short, sharp interrogations--a question and an answer, a name and a reply. It was that awoke me. The drawl had been the reading of the cahier; now they were voting on it.

Presently it would be my turn; it was coming to my turn now. With each vote--I need not say that all were affirmative--more faces, and yet more, were turned to the place where I sat; more eyes, some hostile, some triumphant, some merely curious, were directed to my face. Under other circumstances this might have cowed me; now it did not. I was wrought up to face it. The unfriendly looks of so many who had called themselves my friends, the scornful glances of new men of ennobled families, who had been glad of my father's countenance, the consciousness that all had deserted me merely because I maintained in practice opinions which half of them had proclaimed in words--these things hardened me to a pitch of scorn no whit below that of my opponents; while the knowledge that to blench now must cover me with lasting shame closed the door to thoughts of surrender.

The Assembly, on the other hand, felt the novelty of its position. Men were not yet accustomed to the war of the Senate; to duels of words more deadly than those of the sword: and a certain doubt, a certain hesitation, held the majority in suspense, watching to see what would happen. Moreover, the leaders, both M. de St. Alais, who headed the hotter and prouder party of the Court, and the nobles of the Robe and Parliament, who had only lately discovered that their interest lay in the same direction, found themselves embarrassed by the very smallness of the opposition; since a substantial majority must have been accepted as a fact, whereas one man--one man only standing in the way of unanimity--presented himself as a thing to be removed, if the way could be discovered.

"M. le Comte de Cantal?" the President cried, and looked, not at the person he named, but at me.

"Content!"

"M. le Vicomte de Marignac?"

"Content!"

The next name I could not hear, for in my excitement it seemed that all in the Chamber were looking at me, that voice was failing me, that when the moment came I should sit dumb and paralysed, unable to speak, and for ever disgraced. I thought of this, not of what was passing; then, in a moment, self-control returned; I heard the last name before mine, that of M. d'Aulnoy, heard the answer given. Then my own name, echoing in hollow silence.

"M. le Vicomte de Saux?"

I stood up. I spoke, my voice sounding harsh, and like another man's. "I dissent from this cahier!" I cried.

I expected an outburst of wrath; it did not come. Instead, a peal of laughter, in which I distinguished St. Alais' tones, rang through the room, and brought the blood to my cheeks. The laughter lasted some time, rose and fell, and rose again; while I stood pilloried. Yet this had one effect the laughers did not anticipate. On occasions the most taciturn become eloquent. I forgot the periods from Rochefoucauld and Liancourt, which I had so carefully prepared; I forgot the passages from Turgot, of which I had made notes, and I broke out in a strain I had not foreseen or intended.

"Messieurs!" I cried, hurling my voice through the Chamber, "I dissent from this cahier because it is effete and futile; because, if for no other reason, the time when it could have been of service is past. You claim your privileges; they are gone! Your exemptions; they are gone! You protest against the union of your representatives with those of the people; but they have sat with them! They have sat with them, and you can no more undo that by a protest than you can set back the tide! The thing is done. The dog is hungry, you have given it a bone. Do you think to get the bone back, unmouthed, whole, without loss? Then you are mad. But this is not all, nor the principal of my objections to this cahier. France to-day stands naked, bankrupt, without treasury, without money. Do you think to help her, to clothe her, to enrich her, by maintaining your privileges, by maintaining your exemptions, by standing out for the last jot and tittle of your rights? No, Messieurs. In the old days those exemptions, those rights, those privileges, wherein our ancestors gloried, and gloried well, were given to them because they were the buckler of France. They maintained and armed and led men; the commonalty did the rest. But now the people fight, the people pay, the people do all. Yes, Messieurs, it is true; it is true that which we have all heard, '*Le manant paye pour tout!*'"

I paused; expecting that now, at last, the long-delayed outburst of anger would come. Instead, before any in the Chamber could speak, there rose through the windows, which looked on the market-place, and had been widely opened on account of the heat, a great cry of applause; the shout of the street, that for the first time heard its wrongs voiced. It was full of assent and rejoicing, yet no attack could have disconcerted me more completely. I stood astonished, and silenced.

The effect which it had on me was slight, however, in comparison with that which it had on my opponents. The cries of dissent they were about to utter died stillborn at the portent; and, for a moment, men stared at one another as if they could not believe their ears. For that moment a silence of rage, of surprise, prevailed through the whole Chamber. Then M. de St. Alais sprang to his feet.

"What is this?" he cried, his handsome face dark with excitement. "Has the King ordered us, too, to sit with the third estate? Has he so humiliated us? If not, M. le President--if not, I say," he continued, sternly putting down an attempt at applause, "and if this be not a conspiracy between some of our body and the *canaille* to bring about another Jacquerie----"

The President, a weak man of a Robe family, interrupted him. "Have a care, Monsieur," he said. "The windows are still open."

"Open?"

The President nodded.

"And what if they are? What of it?" St. Alais answered harshly. "What of it, Monsieur?" he continued, looking round him with an eye which seemed to collect and express the scorn of the more fiery spirits. "If so, let it be so! Let them be open. Let the people hear both sides, and not only those who flatter them; those who, by building on their weakness and ignorance, and canting about their rights and our wrongs, think to exalt themselves into Retzs and Cromwells! Yes, Monsieur le President," he continued, while I strove in vain to interrupt him, and half the Assembly rose to their feet in confusion, "I repeat the phrase--who, to the ambition of a Cromwell or a Retz add their violence, not their parts!"

The injustice of the reproach stung me, and I turned on him. "M. le Marquis!" I cried hotly, "if, by that phrase, you refer to me----"

He laughed scornfully. "As you please, Monsieur," he said.

"I fling it back! I repudiate it!" I cried. "M. de St. Alais has called me a Retz--a Cromwell----"

"Pardon me," he interposed swiftly; "a would-be Retz!"

"A traitor, either way!" I answered, striving against the laughter, which at his repartee flashed through the room, bringing the blood rushing to my face. "A traitor either way! But I say that he is the traitor who to-day advises the King to his hurt."

"And not he who comes here with a mob at his back?" St. Alais retorted, with heat almost equal to my own. "Who, one man, would brow-beat a hundred, and dictate to this Assembly?"

"Monsieur repeats himself," I cried, cutting him short in my turn, though no laughter followed my gibe. "I deny what he says. I fling back his accusations; I retort upon him! And, for the rest, I object to this cahier, I dissent from it, I----"

But the Assembly was at the end of its patience. A roar of "Withdraw! withdraw!" drowned my voice, and, in a moment, the meeting so orderly a few minutes before, became a scene of wild uproar. A few of the elder men continued to keep their seats, but the majority rose; some had already sprung to the windows, and closed them, and still stood with their feet on the ledge, looking down on the confusion. Others had gone to the door and taken their stand there, perhaps with the idea of resisting intrusion. The President in vain cried for silence. His voice, equally with mine, was lost in the persistent clamour, which swelled to a louder pitch whenever I offered to speak, and sank only when I desisted.

At length M. de St. Alais raised his hand, and with little difficulty procured silence. Before I could take advantage of it, the President interposed. "The Assembly of the noblesse of Quercy," he said hurriedly, "is in favour of this cahier, maintaining our ancient rights, privileges, and exemptions. The Vicomte de Saux alone protests. The cahier will be presented."

"I protest!" I cried weakly.

"I have said so," the President answered, with a sneer. And a peal of derisive laughter, mingled with shouts of applause, ran round the Chamber. "The cahier will be presented. The matter is concluded."

Then, in a moment, magically, as it seemed to me, the Chamber resumed its ordinary aspect. The Members who had risen returned to their seats, those who had closed the windows descended, a few retired, the President proceeded with some ordinary business. Every trace of the storm disappeared. In a twinkling all was as it had been.

Even where I sat; for no isolation, no division from my fellows could exceed that in which I had sat before. But whereas before I had had my weapon in reserve and my revenge in prospect, that was no longer so. I had shot my bolt, and I sat miserable, fettered by the silence and the strange glances that hemmed me in, and growing each moment more depressed and more self-conscious; longing to escape, yet shrinking from moving, even from looking about me.

In this condition not the least of my misery lay in the reflection that I had done no good; that I had suffered for a quixotism, and shown myself stubborn and obstinate to no purpose. Too late, I considered that I might have maintained my principles and yet conformed; I might have stated my convictions and waived them in deference to the majority. I might have----

But alas! whatever I might have done, I had not done it; and the die was cast. I had declared myself against my order; I had forfeited all I could claim from my order. Henceforth, I was not of it. It was no fancy that already men who had occasion to pass before me drew their skirts aside and bowed formally as to one of another class!

How long I should have endured this penance--these veiled insults and the courtesy that stung deeper--before I plucked up spirit to withdraw, I cannot say. It was an interposition from without that broke the spell. An usher came to me with a note. I opened it with clumsy fingers under a fire of hostile eyes, and found that it was from Louis.

"If you have a spark of honour"--it ran--"you will meet me, without a moment's delay, in the garden at the back of the Chapter House. Do so, and you may still call yourself a gentleman. Refuse, or delay even for ten minutes, and I will publish your shame from one end of Quercy to the other. He cannot call himself Adrien du Pont de Saux, who puts up with a blow!"

I read it twice while the usher waited. The words had a cruel, heartless ring in them; the taunting challenge was brutal in its directness. Yet my heart grew soft as I read, and I had much ado to keep the tears from my eyes--under all those eyes. For Louis did not deceive me this time. This note, so unlike him, this desperate attempt to draw me out, and save me from opponents more ruthless, were too transparent to delude me; and, in a moment, the icy bands which had been growing over me melted. I still sat alone; but I was not quite deserted. I could hold up my head again, for I had a friend. I remembered that, after all, through all, I was Adrien du Pont de Saux, guiltless of aught worse than holding in Quercy opinions which the Lameths and Mirabeaus, the Liancourts and Rochefoucaulds held in their provinces; guiltless, I told myself, of aught besides standing for right and justice.

But the usher waited. I took from the desk before me a scrap of paper, and wrote my answer. "Adrien does not fight with Louis because St. Alais struck Saux."

I wrapped it up and gave it to the usher; then I sat back a different man, able to meet all eyes, with a heart armed against all misfortunes. Friendship, generosity, love, still existed, though the gentry of Quercy, the Gontauts, and Marignacs, sat aloof. Life would still hold sweets, though the grass should grow in the walnut avenue, and my shield should never quarter the arms of St. Alais.

So I took courage, stood up, and moved to go out. But the moment I did so, a dozen Members sprang to their feet also; and, as I walked down one gangway towards the door, they crowded down another parallel with it; offensively, openly, with the evident intention of intercepting me before I could escape. The commotion was so great that the President paused in his reading to watch the result; while the mass of Members who kept their places, rose that they might have a better view. I saw that I was to be publicly insulted, and a fierce joy took the place of every other feeling. If I went slowly, it was not through fear; the pent-up passions of the last hour inspired me, and I would not have hastened the climax for the world. I reached the foot of the gangway, in another moment we must have come into collision, when an abrupt explosion of voices, a great roar in the street, that penetrated through the closed windows, brought us to a halt. We paused, listening and glaring, while the few who had not stood up before, rose hurriedly, and the President, startled and suspicious, asked what it was.

For answer the sound rose again--dull, prolonged, shaking the windows; a hoarse shout of triumph. It fell--not ceasing, but passing away into the distance--and then once more it swelled up. It was unlike any shout I had ever heard.

Little by little articulate words grew out of it, or succeeded it; until the air shook with the measured rhythm of one stern sentence. "*A bas la Bastille! A bas la Bastille!*"

We were to hear many such cries in the time to come, and grow accustomed to such alarms; to the hungry roar in the street, and the loud knocking at the door that spelled fate. But they were a new thing then, and the Assembly, as much outraged as alarmed by this second trespass on its dignity, could only look at its President, and mutter wrathful threats against the *canaille*. The *canaille* that had crouched for a century seemed in some unaccountable way to be changing its posture!

One man cried out one thing, and one another; that the streets should be cleared, the regiment sent for, or complaint made to the Intendant. They were still speaking when the door opened and a Member came in. It was Louis de St. Alais, and his face was aglow with excitement. Commonly the most modest and quiet of men, he stood forward now, and raised his hand imperatively for silence.

"Gentlemen," he said, in a loud, ringing voice, "there is strange news! A courier with letters for my brother, M. de St. Alais, has spoken in the street. He brings strange tidings."

"What?" two or three cried.

"The Bastille has fallen!"

No one understood--how should they?--but all were silent. Then, "What do you mean, M. St. Alais?" the President asked, in bewilderment; and he raised his hand that the silence might be preserved. "The Bastille has fallen? How? What is it?"

"It was captured on Tuesday by the mob of Paris," Louis answered distinctly, his eyes bright, "and M. de Launay, the Governor, murdered in cold blood."

"The Bastille captured? By the mob?" the President exclaimed incredulously. "It is impossible, Monsieur. You must have misunderstood."

Louis shook his head. "It is true, I fear," he said.

"And M. de Launay?"

"That too, I fear, M. le President."

Then, indeed, men looked at one another; startled, pale-faced, asking each mute questions of his fellows; while in the street outside the hum of disorder and rejoicing grew moment by moment more steady and continuous. Men looked at each other alarmed, and could not believe. The Bastille which had stood so many centuries, captured? The Governor killed? Impossible, they muttered, impossible. For what, in that case, was the King doing? What the army? What the Governor of Paris?

Old M. de Gontaut put the thought into words. "But the King?" he said, as soon as he could get a hearing. "Doubtless his Majesty has already punished the wretches?"

The answer came from an unexpected quarter, in words as little expected. M. de St. Alais, to whom Louis had handed a letter, rose from his seat with an open paper in his hand. Doubtless, if he had taken time to consider, he would have seen the imprudence of making public all he knew; but the surprise and mortification of the news he had received--news that gave the lie to his confident assurances, news that made the most certain doubt the ground on which they stood, swept away his discretion. He spoke.

"I do not know what the King was doing," he said, in mocking accents, "at Versailles; but I can tell you how the army was employed in Paris. The Garde Française were foremost in the attack. Besenval, with such troops as have not deserted, has withdrawn. The city is in the hands of the mob. They have shot Flesselles, the Provost, and elected Bailly, Mayor. They have raised a Militia and armed it. They have appointed Lafayette, General. They have adopted a badge. They have----"

"But, *mon Dieu!*" the President cried aghast. "This is a revolt!"

"Precisely, Monsieur," St. Alais answered.

"And what does the King?"

"He is so good--that he has done nothing," was the bitter answer.

"And the States General?--the National Assembly at Versailles?"

"Oh, they? They too have done nothing."

"It is Paris, then?" the President said.

"Yes, Monsieur, it is Paris," the Marquis answered. "But Paris?" the President exclaimed helplessly. "Paris has been quiet so many years."

To this, however, the thought in every one's mind, there seemed to be no answer. St. Alais sat down again, and, for a moment, the Assembly remained stunned by astonishment, prostrate under these new, these marvellous facts. No better comment on the discussions in which it had been engaged a few minutes before could have been found. Its Members had been dreaming of their rights, their privileges, their exemptions; they awoke to find Paris in flames, the army in revolt, order and law in the utmost peril.

But St. Alais was not the man to be long wanting to his part, nor one to abdicate of his free will a leadership which vigour and audacity had secured for him. He sprang to his feet again, and in an impassioned harangue called upon the Assembly to remember the Fronde.

"As Paris was then, Paris is now!" he cried. "Fickle and seditious, to be won by no gifts, but always to be overcome by famine. Best assured that the fat bourgeois will not long do without the white bread of Gonesse, nor the tippler without the white wine of Arbois! Cut these off, the mad will grow sane, and the traitor loyal. Their National Guards, and their Badges, and their Mayors, and their General? Do you think that these will long avail against the forces of order, of loyalty, against the King, the nobility, the clergy, against France? No, gentlemen, it is impossible," he continued, looking round him with warmth. "Paris would have deposed the great Henry and exiled Mazarin; but in the result it licked their shoes. It will be so again, only we must stand together, we must be firm. We must see that these disorders spread no farther. It is the King's to govern, and the people's to obey. It has been so, and it will be so to the end!"

His words were not many, but they were timely and vigorous; and they served to reassure the Assembly. All that large majority, which in every gathering of men has no more imagination than serves to paint the future in the colours of the past, found his arguments perfectly convincing; while the few who saw more clearly, and by the light of instinct, or cold reason, discerned that the state of France had no precedent in its history, felt, nevertheless, the infection of his confidence. A universal shout of applause greeted his last sentence, and, amid tumultuous cries, the concourse, which had remained on its feet, poured into the gangways, and made for the door; a desire to see and hear what was going forward moving all to get out as quickly as possible, though it was not likely that more could be learned than was already known.

I shared this feeling myself, and, forgetting in the excitement of the moment my part in the day's debate, I pressed to the door. The Bastille fallen? The Governor killed? Paris in the hands of the mob? Such tidings were enough to set the brain in a whirl, and breed forgetfulness of nearer matters. Others, in the preoccupation of the moment, seemed to be equally oblivious, and I forced my way out with the rest.

But in the doorway I happened, by a little clumsiness, to touch one of the Harincourts. He turned his head, saw who it was had touched him, and tried to stop. The pressure was too great, however, and he was borne on in front of me, struggling and muttering something I could not hear. I guessed what it was, however, by the manner in which others, abreast of him, and as helpless, turned their heads and sneered at me; and I was considering how I could best encounter what was to come, when the sight which met our gaze, as we at last issued from the narrow passage and faced the market-place-- two steps below us--drove their existence for a moment from my mind.

CHAPTER IV
L'AMI DU PEUPLE

There were others who stood also; impressed by a sight which, in the light of the news we had just heard, that astonishing, that amazing news, seemed to have especial significance. We had not yet grown accustomed in France to crowds. For centuries the one man, the individual, King, Cardinal, Noble, or Bishop, had stood forward, and the many, the multitude, had melted away under his eye; had bowed and passed.

But here, within our view, rose the cold lowering dawn of a new day. Perhaps, if we had not heard what we had heard--that news, I mean--or if the people had not heard it, the effect on us, the action on their part, might have been different. As it was, the crowd that faced us in the Square as we came out, the great crowd that faced us and stretched from wall to wall, silent, vigilant, menacing, showed not a sign of flinching; and we did. We stood astonished, each halting as he came out, and looking, and then consulting his neighbour's eyes to learn what he thought.

We had over our heads the great Cathedral, from the shadow of which we issued. We had among us many who had been wont to see a hundred peasants tremble at their frown. But in a moment, in a twinkling, as if that news from Paris had shaken the foundations of Society, we found these things in question. The crowd in the Square did not tremble. In a silence that was grimmer than howling it gave back look for look. Nor only that; but as we issued, they made no way for us, and those of the Assembly who had already gone down, had to walk along the skirts of the press to get to the inn. We who came later saw this, and it had its weight with us. We were Nobles of the province; but we were only two hundred, and between us and the Trois Rois, between us and our horses and servants, stretched this line of gloomy faces, these thousands of silent men.

No wonder that the sight, and something that underlay the sight, diverted my mind for a moment from M. Harincourt and his purpose, and that I looked abroad; while he, too, stood gaping and frowning, and forgot me. Perforce we had to go down; one by one reluctantly, a meagre string winding across the face of the crowd; sullen defiance on one side, scorn on the other. In Cahors it came to be remembered as the first triumph of the people, the first step in the degradation of the privileged. A word had brought it about. A word, *the Bastille fallen*, had combined the floating groups, and formed of them this which we saw--the people.

Under such circumstances it needed only the slightest spark to bring about an explosion; and that was presently supplied. M. de Gontaut, a tall, thin, old man, who could remember the early days of the late King, walked a little way in front of me. He was lame, and used a cane, and as a rule a servant's arm. This morning, the lackey was not forthcoming, and he felt the inconvenience of skirting instead of crossing the square. Nevertheless he was not foolish enough to thrust himself into the crowd; and all might have gone well, if a rogue in the front rank of the throng had not, perhaps by accident, tripped up the cane with his foot. M. le Baron turned in a flash, every hair of his eyebrows on end, and struck the fellow with his stick.

"Stand back, rascal!" he cried, trembling, and threatening to repeat the blow. "If I had you, I would soon----"

The man spat at him.

M. de Gontaut uttered an oath, and in ungovernable rage struck the wretch two or three blows--how many I could not see, though I was only a few paces behind. Apparently the man did not strike back, but shrank, cowed by the old noble's fury. But those behind flung him forward, with cries of "Shame! *A bas la Noblesse!*" and he fell against M. de Gontaut. In a moment the Baron was on the ground.

It was so quickly done that only those in the immediate neighbourhood, St. Alais, the Harincourts, and myself, saw the fall. Probably the mob meant no great harm; they had not yet lost all reverence. But at the time, with the tale of De Launay in my ears, and my imagination inflamed, I thought that they intended M. de Gontaut's death, and as I saw his old head fall, I sprang forward to protect him.

St. Alais was before me, however. Bounding forward, with rage not less than Gontaut's, he hurled the aggressor back with a blow which sent him into the arms of his supporters. Then dragging M. de Gontaut to his feet, the Marquis whipped out his sword, and darting the bright point hither and thither with the skill of a practised fencer, in a twinkling he cleared a space round him, and made the nearest give back with shrieks and curses.

Unfortunately he touched one man; the fellow was not hurt, but at the prick he sank down screaming, and in a second the mood of the crowd changed. Shrieks, half-playful, gave way to a howl of rage. Some one flung a stick, which struck the Marquis on the chest, and for a moment stopped him. The next instant he sprang at the man who had thrown it, and would have run him through, but the fellow fled, and the crowd, with a yell of triumph, closed over his path. This stopped St. Alais in mid course, and left him only the choice between retreating, or wounding people who were innocent.

He fell back with a sneering word, and sheathed his sword. But the moment his back was turned a stone struck him on the head, and he staggered forward. As he fell the crowd uttered a yell, and half a dozen men dashed at him to trample on him.

Their blood was up; this time I made no mistake, I read mischief in their eyes. The scream of the man whom he had wounded, though the fellow was more frightened than hurt, was in their ears. One of the Harincourts struck down the foremost, but this only enraged without checking them. In a moment he was swept aside and flung back, stunned and reeling; and the crowd rushed upon their victim.

I threw myself before him. I had just time to do that, and cry "Shame! shame!" and force back one or two; and then my intervention must have come to nothing, it must have fared as ill with me as with him, if in the nick of time, with a ring of grimy faces threatening us, and a dozen hands upraised, I had not been recognised. Buton, the blacksmith of Saux--one of the foremost--screamed out my name, and turning with outstretched arms, forced back his neighbours. A man of huge strength, it was as much as he could do to stem the torrent; but in a moment his frenzied cries became heard and understood. Others recognised me, the crowd fell back. Some one raised a cry of "*Vive Saux!* Long live the friend of the people!" and the shout being taken up first in one place and then in another, in a trice the Square rang with the words.

I had not then learned the fickleness of the multitude, or that from *A bas* to *vive* is the step of an instant; and despite myself, and though I despised myself for the feeling, I felt my heart swell on the wave of sound. "*Vive Saux! Vive l'ami du peuple!*" My equals had scorned me, but the people--the people whose faces wore a new look to-day, the people to whom this one word, the Bastille fallen, had given new life--acclaimed me. For a moment, even while I cried to them, and shook my hands to them to be silent, there flashed me the things it meant; the things they had to give, power and tribuneship! "*Vive Saux!* long live the friend of the people!" The air shook with the sound; the domes above me gave it back. I felt myself lifted up on it; I felt myself for the minute another and a greater man!

Then I turned and met St. Alais' eye, and I fell to earth. He had risen, and, pale with rage, was wiping the dust from his coat with a handkerchief. A little blood was flowing from the wound in his head, but he paid no heed to it, in the intentness with which he was staring at me, as if he read my thoughts. As soon as something like silence was obtained, he spoke.

"Perhaps if your friends have quite done with us, M. de Saux--we may go home?" he said, his voice trembling a little.

I stammered something in answer to the sneer, and turned to accompany him; though my way to the inn lay in the opposite direction. Only the two Harincourts and M. de Gontaut were with us. The rest of the Assembly had either got clear, or were viewing the fracas from the door of the Chapter House, where they stood, cut off from us by a wall of people. I offered my arm to M. de Gontaut, but he declined it with a frigid bow, and took Harincourt's; and M. le Marquis, when I turned to him, said, with a cold smile, that they need not trouble me.

"Doubtless we shall be safe," he sneered, "if you will give orders to that effect."

I bowed, without retorting on him; he bowed; and he turned away. But the crowd had either read his attitude aright, or gathered that there was an altercation between us, for the moment he moved they set up a howl. Two or three stones were thrown, notwithstanding Buton's efforts to prevent it; and before the party had retired ten yards the rabble began to press on them savagely. Embarrassed by M. de Gontaut's presence and helplessness, the other three could do nothing. For an instant I had a view of St. Alais standing gallantly at bay with the old noble behind him, and the blood trickling down his cheek. Then I followed them, the crowd made instant way for me, again the air rang with cheers, and the Square in the hot July sunshine seemed a sea of waving hands.

M. de St. Alais turned to me. He could still smile, and with marvellous self-command, in one and the same instant he recovered from his discomfiture and changed his tactics.

"I am afraid that after all we must trouble you," he said politely. "M. le Baron is not a young man, and your people, M. de Saux, are somewhat obstreperous."

"What can I do?" I said sullenly. I had not the heart to leave them to their fortunes; at the same time I was as little disposed to accept the onus he would lay on me.

"Accompany us home," he said pleasantly, drawing out his snuff-box and taking a pinch.

The people had fallen silent again, but watched us heedfully. "If you think it will serve?" I answered.

"It will," he said briskly. "You know, M. le Vicomte, that a man is born and a man dies every minute? Believe me no King dies--but another King is born."

I winced under the sarcasm, under the laughing contempt of his eye. Yet I saw nothing for it but to comply, and I bowed and turned to go with them. The crowd opened before us; amid mingled cheers and yells we moved away. I intended only to accompany them to the outskirts of the throng, and then to gain the inn by a by-path, get my horses and be gone. But a party of the crowd continued to follow us through the streets, and I found no opportunity. Almost before I knew it, we were at the St. Alais' door, still with this rough attendance at our heels.

Madame and Mademoiselle, with two or three women, were on the balcony, looking and listening; at the door below stood a group of scared servants. While I looked, however, Madame left her place above and in a moment appeared at the door, the servants making way for her. She stared in wonder at us, and from us to the rabble that followed; then her eye caught the bloodstains on M. de St. Alais' cravat, and she cried out to know if he was hurt.

"No, Madame," he said lightly. "But M. de Gontaut has had a fall."

"What has happened?" she asked quickly. "The town seems to have gone mad! I heard a great noise a while ago, and the servants brought in a wild tale about the Bastille."

"It is true."

"What? That the Bastille----"

"Has been taken by the mob, Madame; and M. de Launay murdered."

"Impossible!" Madame cried with flashing eyes. "That old man?"

"Yes," M. de St. Alais answered with treacherous suavity. "Messieurs the Mob are no respecters of persons. Fortunately, however," he went on, smiling at me in a way that brought the blood to my cheeks, "they have leaders more prudent and sagacious than themselves."

But Madame had no ears for his last words, no thought save of this astonishing news from Paris. She stood, her cheeks on fire, her eyes full of tears; she had known De Launay. "Oh, but the King will punish them!" she cried at last. "The wretches! The ingrates! They should all be broken on the wheel! Doubtless the King has already punished them."

"He will, by-and-by, if he has not yet," St. Alais answered. "But for the moment, you will easily understand, Madame, that things are out of joint. Men's heads are turned, and they do not know themselves. We have had a little trouble here. M. de Gontaut has been roughly handled, and I have not entirely escaped. If M. de Saux had not had his people well in hand," he continued, turning to me with a laughing eye, "I am afraid that we should have come off worse."

Madame stared at me, and, beginning slowly to comprehend, seemed to freeze before me. The light died out of her haughty face. She looked at me grimly. I had a glimpse of Mademoiselle's startled eyes behind her, and of the peeping servants; then Madame spoke. "Are these some of--M. de Saux's people?" she asked, stepping forward a pace, and pointing to the crew of ruffians who had halted a few paces away, and were watching us doubtfully.

"A handful," M. de St. Alais answered lightly. "Just his bodyguard, Madame. But pray do not speak of him so harshly; for, being my mother, you must be obliged to him. If he did not quite save my life, at least he saved my beauty."

"With those?" she said scornfully.

"With those or from those," he answered gaily. "Besides, for a day or two we may need his protection. I am sure that, if you ask him, Madame, he will not refuse it."

I stood, raging and helpless, under the lash of his tongue; and Madame de St. Alais looked at me. "Is it possible," she said at last, "that M. de Saux has thrown in his lot with wretches such as those?" And she pointed with magnificent scorn to the scowling crew behind me. "With wretches who----"

"Hush, Madame," M. le Marquis said in his gibing fashion. "You are too bold. For the moment they are our masters, and M. de Saux is theirs. We must, therefore----"

"We must not!" she answered impetuously, raising herself to her full height and speaking with flashing eyes. "What? Would you have me palter with the scum of the streets? With the dirt under our feet? With the sweepings of the gutter? Never! I and mine have no part with traitors!"

"Madame!" I cried, stung to speech by her injustice. "You do not know what you say! If I have been able to stand between your son and danger, it has been through no vileness such as you impute to me."

"Impute?" she exclaimed. "What need of imputation, Monsieur, with those wretches behind you? Is it necessary to cry 'A bas le roi!' to be a traitor? Is not that man as guilty who fosters false hopes, and misleads the ignorant? Who hints what he dare not say, and holds out what he dares not promise? Is he not the worst of traitors? For shame, Monsieur, for shame!" she continued. "If your father----"

"Oh!" I cried. "This is intolerable!"

She caught me up with a bitter gibe. "It is!" she retorted. "It *is* intolerable--that the King's fortresses should be taken by the rabble, and old men slain by scullions! It is intolerable that nobles should forget whence they are sprung, and stoop to the kennel! It is intolerable that the King's name should be flouted, and catchwords set above it! All these things are intolerable; but they are not of our doing. They are your acts. And for you," she continued--and suddenly stepping by me, she addressed the group of rascals who lingered, listening and scowling, a few paces away--"for you, poor fools, do not be deceived. This gentleman has told you, doubtless, that there is no longer a King of France! That there are to be no more taxes nor *corvées*; that the poor will be rich, and everybody noble! Well, believe him if you please. There have been poor and rich, noble and simple, spenders and makers, since the world began, and a King in France. But believe him if you please. Only now go! Leave my house. Go, or I will call out my servants, and whip you through the streets like dogs! To your kennels, I say!"

She stamped her foot, and to my astonishment, the men, who must have known that her threat was an empty one, sneaked away like the dogs to which she had compared them. In a moment--I could scarcely believe it--the street was empty. The men who had come near to killing M. de Gontaut, who had stoned M. de St. Alais, quailed before a woman! In a twinkling the last man was gone, and she turned to me, her face flushed, her eyes gleaming with scorn.

"There, sir," she said, "take that lesson to heart. That is your brave people! And now, Monsieur, do you go too! Henceforth my house is no place for you. I will have no traitors under my roof--no, not for a moment."

She signed to me to go with the same insolent contempt which had abashed the crowd; but before I went I said one word. "You were my father's friend, Madame," I said before them all.

She looked at me harshly, but did not answer.

"It would have better become you, therefore," I continued, "to help me than to hurt me. As it is, were I the most loyal of his Majesty's subjects, you have done enough to drive me to treason. In the future, Madame la Marquise, I beg that you will remember that."

And I turned and went, trembling with rage.

The crowd in the Square had melted by this time, but the streets were full of those who had composed it; who now stood about in eager groups, discussing what had happened. The word Bastille was on every tongue; and, as I passed, way was made for me, and caps were lifted. "God bless you, M. de Saux," and, "You are a good man," were muttered in my ear. If there seemed to be less noise and less excitement than in the morning, the air of purpose that everywhere prevailed was not to be mistaken.

This was so clear that, though noon was barely past, shopkeepers had closed their shops and bakers their bakehouses; and a calm, more ominous than the storm that had preceded it, brooded over the town. The majority of the Assembly had dispersed in haste, for I saw none of the Members, though I heard that a large body had gone to the barracks. No one molested me--the fall of the Bastille served me so far--and I mounted, and rode out of town, without seeing any one, even Louis.

To tell the truth, I was in a fever to be at home; in a fever to consult the only man who, it seemed to me, could advise me in this crisis. In front of me, I saw it plainly, stretched two roads; the one easy and smooth, if perilous, the other arid and toilsome. Madame had called me the Tribune of the People, a would-be Retz, a would-be Mirabeau. The people had cried my name, had hailed me as a saviour. Should I fit on the cap? Should I take up the *rôle*? My own caste had spurned me. Should I snatch at the dangerous honour offered to me, and stand or fall with the people?

With the people? It sounded well, but, in those days, it was a vaguer phrase than it is now; and I asked myself who, that had ever taken up that cause, had stood? A bread riot, a tumult, a local revolt--such as this which had cost M. de Launay his life--of things of that size the people had shown themselves capable; but of no lasting victory. Always the King had held his own, always the nobles had kept their privileges. Why should it be otherwise now?

There were reasons. Yes, truly; but they seemed less cogent, the weight of precedent against them heavier, when I came to think, with a trembling heart, of acting on them. And the odium of deserting my order was no small matter to face. Hitherto I had been innocent; if they had put out the lip at me, they had done it wrongfully. But if I accepted this part, the part they assigned to me, I must be prepared to face not only the worst in case of failure, but in success to be a pariah. To be Tribune of the People, and an outcast from my kind!

I rode hard to keep pace with these thoughts; and I did not doubt that I should be the first to bring the tale to Saux. But in those days nothing was more marvellous than the speed with which news of this kind crossed the country. It passed from mouth to mouth, from eye to eye; the air seemed to carry it. It went before the quickest traveller.

Everywhere, therefore, I found it known. Known by people who had stood for days at cross-roads, waiting for they knew not what; known by scowling men on village bridges, who talked in low voices and eyed the towers of the Château; known by stewards and agents, men of the stamp of Gargouf, who smiled incredulously, or talked, like Madame St. Alais, of the King, and how good he was, and how many he would hang for it. Known, last of all, by Father Benôit, the man I would consult. He met me at the gate of the Château, opposite the place where the *carcan* had stood. It was too dark to see his face, but I knew the fall of his *soutane* and the shape of his hat. I sent on Gil and André, and he walked beside me up the avenue, with his hand on the withers of my horse.

"Well, M. le Vicomte, it has come at last," he said.

"You have heard?"

"Buton told me."

"What? Is he here?" I said in surprise. "I saw him at Cahors less than three hours ago."

"Such news gives a man wings," Father Benôit answered with energy. "I say again, it has come. It has come, M. le Vicomte."

"Something," I said prudently.

"Everything," he answered confidently. "The mob took the Bastille, but who headed them? The soldiers; the Garde Française. Well, M. le Vicomte, if the army cannot be trusted, there is an end of abuses, an end of exemptions, of extortions, of bread famines, of Foulons and Berthiers, of grinding the faces of the poor, of----"

The Curé's list was not half exhausted when I cut it short. "But if the army is with the mob, where will things stop?" I said wearily.

"We must see to that," he answered.

"Come and sup with me," I said, "I have something to tell you, and more to ask you."

He assented gladly. "For there will be no sleep for me to-night," he said, his eye sparkling. "This is great news, glorious news, M. le Vicomte. Your father would have heard it with joy."

"And M. de Launay?" I said as I dismounted.

"There can be no change without suffering," he answered stoutly, though his face fell a little. "His fathers sinned, and he has paid the penalty. But God rest his soul! I have heard that he was a good man."

"And died in his duty," I said rather tartly.

"Amen," Father Benôit answered.

Yet it was not until we were sat down in the Chestnut Parlour (which the servants called the English Room), and, with candles between us, were busy with our cheese and fruit, that I appreciated to the full the impression which the news had made on the Curé. Then, as he talked, as he told and listened, his long limbs and lean form trembled with excitement; his thin face worked. "It is the end," he said. "You may depend upon it, M. le Vicomte, it is the end. Your father told me many times that in money lay the secret of power. Money, he used to say, pays the army, the army secures all. A while ago the money failed. Now the army fails. There is nothing left."

"The King?" I said, unconsciously quoting Madame la Marquise.

"God bless his Majesty!" the Curé answered heartily. "He means well, and now he will be able to do well, because the nation will be with him. But without the nation, without money or an army--a name only. And the name did not save the Bastille."

Then, beginning with the scene at Madame de St. Alais' reception, I told him all that had happened to me; the oath of the sword, the debate in the Assembly, the tumult in the Square--last of all, the harsh words with which Madame had given me my *congé*; all. As he listened he was extraordinarily moved. When I described the scene in the Chamber, he could not be still, but in his enthusiasm, walked about the parlour, muttering. And, when I told him how the crowd had cried "*Vive Saux!*" he repeated the words softly and looked at me with delighted eyes. But when I came--halting somewhat in my speech, and colouring and playing with my bread to hide my disorder--to tell him my thoughts on the way home, and the choice that, as it seemed to me, was offered to me, he sat down, and fell also to crumbling his bread and was silent.

CHAPTER V
THE DEPUTATION

He sat silent so long, with his eyes on the table, that presently I grew nettled; wondering what ailed him, and why he did not speak and say the things that I expected. I had been so confident of the advice he would give me, that, from the first, I had tinged my story with the appropriate colour. I had let my bitterness be seen; I had suppressed no scornful word, but supplied him with all the ground he could desire for giving me the advice I supposed to be upon his lips.

And yet he did not speak. A hundred times I had heard him declare his sympathy with the people, his hatred of the corruption, the selfishness, the abuses of the Government; within the hour I had seen his eye kindle as he spoke of the fall of the Bastille. It was at his word I had burned the *carcan*; at his instance I had spent a large sum in feeding the village during the famine of the past year. Yet now--now, when I expected him to rise up and bid me do my part, he was silent!

I had to speak at last. "Well?" I said irritably. "Have you nothing to say, M. le Curé?" And I moved one of the candles so as to get a better view of his features. But he still looked down at the table, he still avoided my eye, his thin face thoughtful, his hand toying with the crumbs.

At last, "M. le Vicomte," he said softly, "through my mother's mother I, too, am noble."

I gasped; not at the fact with which I was familiar, but at the application I thought he intended. "And for that," I said amazed, "you would----"

He raised his hand to stop me. "No," he said gently, "I would not. Because, for all that, I am of the people by birth, and of the poor by my calling. But----"

"But what?" I said peevishly.

Instead of answering me he rose from his seat, and, taking up one of the candles, turned to the panelled wall behind him, on which hung a full-length portrait of my father, framed in a curious border of carved foliage.

He read the name below it. "Antoine du Pont, Vicomte de Saux," he said, as if to himself. "He was a good man, and a friend to the poor. God keep him."

He lingered a moment, gazing at the grave, handsome face, and doubtless recalling many things; then he passed, holding the candle aloft, to another picture which flanked the table: each wall boasted one. "Adrien du Pont, Vicomte de Saux," he read, "Colonel of the Regiment Flamande. He was killed, I think, at Minden. Knight of St. Louis and of the King's Bedchamber. A handsome man, and doubtless a gallant gentleman. I never knew him."

I answered nothing, but my face began to burn as he passed to a third picture behind me. "Antoine du Pont, Vicomte de Saux," he read, holding up the candle, "Marshal and Peer of France, Knight of the King's Orders, a Colonel of the Household and of the King's Council. Died of the plague at Genoa in 1710. I think I have heard that he married a Rohan."

He looked long, then passed to the fourth wall, and stood a moment quite silent. "And this one?" he said at last. "He, I think, has the noblest face of all. Antoine, Seigneur du Pont de Saux, of the Order of St. John of Jerusalem, Preceptor of the French tongue. Died at Valetta in the year after the Great Siege--of his wounds, some say; of incredible labours and exertions, say the Order. A Christian soldier."

It was the last picture, and, after gazing at it a moment, he brought the candle back and set it down with its two fellows on the shining table; that, with the panelled walls, swallowed up the light, and left only our faces white and bright, with a halo round them, and darkness behind them. He bowed to me. "M. le Vicomte," he said at last, in a voice which shook a little, "you come of a noble stock."

I shrugged my shoulders. "It is known," I said. "And for that?"

"I dare not advise you."

"But the cause is good!" I cried.

"Yes," he answered slowly. "I have been saying so all my life. I dare not say otherwise now. But--the cause of the people is the people's. Leave it to the people."

"*You* say that!" I answered, staring at him, angry and perplexed. "You, who have told me a hundred times that I am of the people! that the nobility are of the people; that there are only two things in France, the King and the people."

He smiled somewhat sadly; tapping on the table with his fingers. "That was theory," he said. "I try to put it into practice, and my heart fails me. Because I, too, have a little nobility, M. le Vicomte, and know what it is."

"I don't understand you," I said in despair. "You blow hot and cold, M. le Curé. I told you just now that I spoke for the people at the meeting of the noblesse, and you approved."

"It was nobly done."

"Yet now?"

"I say the same thing," Father Benôit answered, his fine face illumined with feeling. "It was nobly done. Fight for the people, M. le Vicomte, but among your fellows. Let your voice be heard there, where all you will gain for yourself will be obloquy and black looks. But if it comes, if it has come, to a struggle between your class and the commons, between the nobility and the vulgar; if the noble must side with his fellows or take the people's pay, then"--Father Benôit's voice trembled a little, and his thin white hand tapped softly on the table--"I would rather see you ranked with your kind."

"Against the people?"

"Yes, against the people," he answered, shrinking a little.

I was astonished. "Why, great heaven," I said, "the smallest logic----"

"Ah!" he answered, shaking his head sadly, and looking at me with kind eyes. "There you beat me; logic is against me. Reason, too. The cause of the people, the cause of reform, of honesty, of cheap grain, of equal justice, *must* be a good one. And who forwards it must be in the right. That is so, M. le Vicomte. Nay, more than that. If the people are left to fight their battle alone the danger of excesses is greater. I see that. But instinct does not let me act on the knowledge."

"Yet, M. de Mirabeau?" I said. "I have heard you call him a great man."

"It is true," Father Benôit answered, keeping his eyes on mine, while he drummed softly on the table with his fingers.

"I have heard you speak of him with admiration."

"Often."

"And of M. de Lafayette?"

"Yes."

"And the Lameths?"

M. le Curé nodded.

"Yet all these," I said stubbornly, "all these are nobles--nobles leading the people!"

"Yes," he said.

"And you do not blame them?"

"No, I do not blame them."

"Nay, you admire them! You admire them, Father," I persisted, glowering at him.

"I know I do," he said. "I know that I am weak and a fool. Perhaps worse, M. le Vicomte, in that I have not the courage of my convictions. But, though I admire those men, though I think them great and to be admired, I have heard men speak of them who thought otherwise; and--it may be weak--but I knew you as a boy, and I would not have men speak so of you. There are things we admire at a distance," he continued, looking at me a little drolly, to hide the affection that shone in his eyes, "which we, nevertheless, do not desire to find in those we love. Odium heaped on a stranger is nothing to us; on our friends, it were worse than death."

He stopped, his voice trembling; and we were both silent for a while. Still, I would not let him see how much his words had touched me; and by-and-by----

"But my father?" I said. "He was strongly on the side of reform!"

"Yes, by the nobles, for the people."

"But the nobles have cast me out!" I answered. "Because I have gone a yard, I have lost all. Shall I not go two, and win all back?"

"Win all," he said softly--"but lose how much?"

"Yet if the people win? And you say they will?"

"Even then, Tribune of the People," he answered gently, "and an outcast!"

They were the very words I had applied to myself as I rode; and I started. With sudden vividness I saw the picture they presented; and I understood why Father Benôit had hesitated so long in my case. With the purest intentions and the most upright heart, I could not make myself other than what I was; I should rise, were my efforts crowned with success, to a point of splendid isolation; suspected by the people, whose benefactor I had been, hated and cursed by the nobles whom I had deserted.

Such a prospect would have been far from deterring some; and others it might have lured. But I found myself, in this moment of clear vision, no hero. Old prejudices stirred in the blood, old traditions, born of centuries of precedence and privilege, awoke in the memory. A shiver of doubt and mistrust--such as, I suppose, has tormented reformers from the first, and caused all but the hardiest to flinch--passed through me, as I gazed across the candles at the Curé. I feared the people--the unknown. The howl of exultation, that had rent the air in the Market-place at Cahors, the brutal cries that had hailed Gontaut's fall, rang again in my ears. I shrank back, as a man shrinks who finds himself on the brink of an abyss, and through the wavering mist, parted for a brief instant by the wind, sees the cruel rocks and jagged points that wait for him below.

It was a moment of extraordinary prevision, and though it passed, and speedily left me conscious once more of the silent room and the good Curé--who affected to be snuffing one of the long candles--the effect it produced on my mind continued. After Father Benôit had taken his leave, and the house was closed, I walked for an hour up and down the walnut avenue; now standing to gaze between the open iron gates that gave upon the road; now turning my back on them, and staring at the grey, gaunt, steep-roofed house with its flanking tower and round *tourelles*.

Henceforth, I made up my mind, I would stand aside. I would welcome reform, I would do in private what I could to forward it; but I would not a second time set myself against my fellows. I had had the courage of my opinions. Henceforth, no man could say that I had hidden them, but after this I would stand aside and watch the course of events.

A cock crowed at the rear of the house--untimely; and across the hushed fields, through the dusk, came the barking of a distant dog. As I stood listening, while the solemn stars gazed down, the slight which St. Alais had put upon me dwindled--dwindled to its true dimensions. I thought of Mademoiselle Denise, of the bride I had lost, with a faint regret that was almost amusement. What would she think of this sudden rupture? I wondered. Of this strange loss of her *fiancé*? Would it awaken her curiosity, her interest? Or would she, fresh from her convent school, think that things in the world went commonly so--that *fiancés* came and passed, and receptions found their natural end in riot?

I laughed softly, pleased that I had made up my mind. But, had I known, as I listened to the rustling of the poplars in the road, and the sounds that came out of the darkened world beyond them, what was passing there-- had I known that, I should have felt even greater satisfaction. For this was Wednesday, the 22nd of July; and that night Paris still palpitated after viewing strange things. For the first time she had heard the horrid cry, "*A la lanterne!*" and seen a man, old and white-headed, hanged, and tortured, until death freed him. She had seen another, the very Intendant of the City, flung down, trampled and torn to pieces in his own streets--publicly, in full day, in the presence of thousands. She had seen these things, trembling; and other things also--things that had made the cheeks of reformers grow pale, and betrayed to all thinking men that below Lafayette, below Bailly, below the Municipality and the Electoral Committee, roared and seethed the awakened forces of the Faubourgs, of St. Antoine, and St. Marceau!

What could be expected, what was to be expected, but that such outrages, remaining unpunished, should spread? Within a week the provinces followed the lead of Paris. Already, on the 21st the mob of Strasbourg had sacked the Hôtel de Ville and destroyed the Archives; and during the same week, the Bastilles at Bordeaux and Caen were taken and destroyed. At Rouen, at Rennes, at Lyons, at St. Malo, were great riots, with fighting; and nearer Paris, at Poissy, and St. Germain, the populace hung the millers. But, as far as Cahors was concerned, it was not until the astonishing tidings of the King's surrender reached us, a few days later--tidings that on the 17th of July he had entered insurgent Paris, and tamely acquiesced in the destruction of the Bastille--it was not until that news reached us, and hard on its heels a rumour of the second rising on the 22nd, and the slaughter of Foulon and Berthier--it was not until then, I say, that the country round us began to be moved. Father Benôit, with a face of astonishment and doubt, brought me the tidings, and we walked on the terrace discussing it. Probably reports, containing more or less of the truth, had reached the city before, and, giving men something else to think of, had saved me from challenge or molestation. But, in the country where I had spent the week in moody unrest, and not unfrequently reversing in the morning the decision at which I had arrived in the night, I had heard nothing until the Curé came--I think on the morning of the 29th of July.

"And what do you think now?" I said thoughtfully, when I had listened to his tale.

"Only what I did before," he answered stoutly. "It has come. Without money, and therefore without soldiers who will fight, with a starving people, with men's minds full of theories and abstractions, that all tend towards change, what can a Government do?"

"Apparently it can cease to govern," I said tartly; "and that is not what any one wants."

"There must be a period of unrest," he replied, but less confidently. "The forces of order, however, the forces of the law have always triumphed. I don't doubt that they will again."

"After a period of unrest?"

"Yes," he answered. "After a period of unrest. And, I confess, I wish that we were through that. But we must be of good heart, M. le Vicomte. We must trust the people; we must confide in their good sense, their capacity for government, their moderation----"

I had to interrupt him. "What is it, Gil?" I said with a gesture of apology. The servant had come out of the house and was waiting to speak to me.

"M. Doury, M. le Vicomte, from Cahors," he answered.

"The inn-keeper?"

"Yes, Monsieur; and Buton. They ask to see you."

"Together?" I said. It seemed a strange conjunction.

"Yes, Monsieur."

"Well, show them here," answered, after consulting my companion's face. "But Doury? I paid my bill. What can he want?"

"We shall see," Father Benôit answered, his eyes on the door. "Here they come. Ah! Now, M. le Vicomte," he continued in a lower tone, "I feel less confident."

I suppose he guessed something akin to the truth; but for my part I was completely at a loss. The innkeeper, a sleek, complaisant man, of whom, though I had known him some years, I had never seen much beyond the crown of his head, nor ever thought of him as apart from his guests and his ordinary, wore, as he advanced, a strange motley of dignity and subservience; now strutting with pursed lips, and an air of extreme importance, and now stooping to bow in a shame-faced and half-hearted manner. His costume was as great a surprise as his appearance, for, instead of his citizen's suit of black, he sported a blue coat with gold buttons, and a canary waistcoat, and he carried a gold-headed cane; sober splendours, which, nevertheless, paled before two large bunches of ribbons, white, red, and blue, which he wore, one on his breast, and one in his hat.

His companion, who followed a foot or two behind, his giant frame and sun-burned face setting off the citizen's plumpness, was similarly bedizened. But though be-ribboned and in strange company, he was still Baton, the smith. His face reddened as he met my eyes, and he shielded himself as well as he could behind Doury's form.

"Good-morning, Doury," I said. I could have laughed at the awkward complaisance of the man's manner, if something in the gravity of the Curé's face had not restrained me. "What brings you to Saux?" I continued. "And what can I do for you?"

"If it please you, M. le Vicomte," he began. Then he paused, and straightening himself--for habit had bent his back--he continued abruptly, "Public business, Monsieur, with you on it."

"With me?' I said, amazed. On public business?"

He smiled in a sickly way, but stuck to his text. "Even so, Monsieur," he said. "There are such great changes, and--and so great need of advice."

"That I ought not to wonder at M. Doury seeking it at Saux?"

"Even so, Monsieur."

I did not try to hide my contempt and amusement; but shrugged my shoulders, and looked at the Curé.

"Well," I said, after a moment of silence, "and what is it? Have you been selling bad wine? Or do you want the number of courses limited by Act of the States General? Or----"

"Monsieur," he said, drawing himself up with an attempt at dignity, "this is no time for jesting. In the present crisis inn-keepers have as much at stake as, with reverence, the noblesse; and deserted by those who should lead them----"

"What, the inn-keepers?" I cried.

He grew as red as a beetroot. "M. le Vicomte understands that I mean the people," he said stiffly. "Who deserted, I say, by their natural leaders----"

"For instance?"

"M. le Duc d'Artois, M. le Prince de Condé, M. le Duc de Polignac, M.----"

"Bah!" I said. "How have they deserted?"

"*Pardieu*, Monsieur! Have you not heard?"

"Have I not heard what?"

"That they have left France? That on the night of the 17th, three days after the capture of the Bastille, the princes of the blood left France by stealth, and----"

"Impossible!" I said. "Impossible! Why should they leave?"

"That is the very question, M. le Vicomte," he answered, with eager forwardness, "that is being asked. Some say that they thought to punish Paris by withdrawing from it. Some that they did it to show their disapproval of his most gracious Majesty's amnesty, which was announced on that day. Some that they stand in fear. Some even that they anticipated Foulon's fate----"

"Fool!" I cried, stopping him sternly--for I found this too much for my stomach--"you rave! Go back to your menus and your bouillis! What do you know about State affairs? Why, in my grandfather's time," I continued wrathfully, "if you had spoken of princes of the blood after that fashion, you would have tasted bread and water for six months, and been lucky had you got off unwhipped!"

He quailed before me, and forgetting his new part in old habits, muttered an apology. He had not meant to give offence, he said. He had not understood. Nevertheless, I was preparing to read him a lesson when, to my astonishment, Buton intervened.

"But, Monsieur, that is thirty years back," he said doggedly.

"What, villain?" I exclaimed, almost breathless with astonishment, "what do you in this *galère?*"

"I am with him," he answered, indicating his companion by a sullen gesture.

"On State business?"

"Yes, Monsieur."

"Why, *mon Dieu*," I cried, staring at them between amusement and incredulity, "if this is true, why did you not bring the watch-dog as well! And Farmer Jean's ram? And the good-wife's cat? And M. Doury's turnspit? And----"

M. le Curé touched my arm. "Perhaps you had better hear what they have to say," he observed softly. "Afterwards, M. le Vicomte----"

I nodded sulkily. "What is it, then?" I said. "Ask what you want to ask."

"The Intendant has fled," Doury answered, recovering something of his lost dignity, "and we are forming, in pursuance of advice received from Paris, and following the glorious example of that city, a Committee; a Committee to administer the affairs of the district. From that Committee, I, Monsieur, with my good friend here, have the honour to be a deputation."

"With him?" I said, unable to control myself longer. "But, in heaven's name, what has he to do with the Committee? Or the affairs of the district?"

And I pointed with relentless finger at Buton, who reddened under his tan, and moved his huge feet uneasily, but did not speak.

"He is a member of it," the inn-keeper answered, regarding his colleague with a side glance, which seemed to express anything but liking. "This Committee, to be as perfect as possible, Monsieur le Vicomte will understand, must represent all classes."

"Even mine, I suppose," I said, with a sneer.

"It is on that business we have come," he answered awkwardly. "To ask, in a word, M. le Vicomte, that you will allow yourself to be elected a member, and not only a member----"

"What elevation!"

"But President of the Committee."

After all--it was no more than I had been foreseeing! It had come suddenly, but in the main it was only that in sober fact which I had foreseen in a dream. Styled the mandate of the people, it had sounded well; by the mouth of Doury, the inn-keeper, Buton assessor, it jarred every nerve in me. I say, it should not have surprised me; while such things were happening in the world, with a King who stood by and saw his fortress taken, and his servants killed, and pardoned the rebels; with an Intendant of Paris slaughtered in his own streets; with rumours and riots in every province, and flying princes, and swinging millers, there was really nothing wonderful in the invitation. And now, looking back, I find nothing surprising in it. I have lived to see men of the same trade as Doury, stand by the throne, glittering in stars and orders; and a smith born in the forge sit down to dine with Emperors. But that July day on the terrace at Saux, the offer seemed of all farces the wildest, and of all impertinences the most absurd.

"Thanks, Monsieur," I said, at last, when I had sufficiently recovered from my astonishment. "If I understand you rightly, you ask me to sit on the same Committee with that man?" And I pointed grimly to Buton. "With the peasant born on my land, and subject yesterday to my justice? With the serf whom my fathers freed? With the workman living on my wages?"

Doury glanced at his colleague. "Well, M. le Vicomte," he said, with a cough, "to be perfect, you understand, a Committee must represent all."

"A Committee!" I retorted, unable to repress my scorn. "It is a new thing in France. And what is the perfect Committee to do?"

Doury on a sudden recovered himself, and swelled with importance. "The Intendant has fled," he said, "and people no longer trust the magistrates. There are rumours of brigands, too; and corn is required. With all this the Committee must deal. It must take measures to keep the peace, to supply the city, to satisfy the soldiers, to hold meetings, and consider future steps. Besides, M. le Vicomte," he continued, puffing out his cheeks, "it will correspond with Paris; it will administer the law; it will----"

"In a word," I said quietly, "it will govern. The King, I suppose, having abdicated."

Doury shrank bodily, and even lost some of his colour. "God forbid!" he said, in a whining tone. "It will do all in his Majesty's name."

"And by his authority?"

The inn-keeper stared at me, startled and nonplussed; and muttered something about the people.

"Ah!" I said. "It is the people who invite me to govern, then, is it? With an inn-keeper and a peasant? And other inn-keepers and peasants, I suppose? To govern! To usurp his Majesty's functions? To supersede his magistrates; to bribe his forces? In a word, friend Doury," I continued suavely, "to commit treason. Treason, you understand?"

The inn-keeper did; and he wiped his forehead with a shaking hand, and stood, scared and speechless, looking at me piteously. A second time the blacksmith took it on himself to answer.

"Monseigneur," he muttered, drawing his great black hand across his beard.

"Buton," I answered suavely, "permit me. For a man who aspires to govern the country, you are too respectful."

"You have omitted one thing it is for the Committee to do," the smith answered hoarsely, looking--like a timid, yet sullen, dog--anywhere but in my face.

"And that is?"

"To protect the Seigneurs."

I stared at him, between anger and surprise. This was a new light. After a pause, "From whom?" I said curtly.

"Their people," he answered.

"Their Butons," I said. "I see. We are to be burned in our beds, are we?"

He stood sulkily silent.

"Thank you, Buton," I said. "And that is your return for a winter's corn. Thanks! In this world it is profitable to do good!"

The man reddened through his tan, and on a sudden looked at me for the first time. "You know that you lie, M. le Vicomte!" he said.

"Lie, sirrah?" I cried.

"Yes, Monsieur," he answered. "You know that I would die for the seigneur, as much as if the iron collar were round my neck! That before fire touched the house of Saux it should burn me! That I am my lord's man, alive and dead. But, Monseigneur," and, as he continued, he lowered his tone to one of earnestness, striking in a man so rough, "there are abuses, and there must be an end of them. There are tyrants, and they must go. There are men and women and children starving, and there must be an end of that. There is grinding of the faces of the poor, Monseigneur--not here, but everywhere round us--and there must be an end of that. And the poor pay taxes and the rich go free; the poor make the roads, and the rich use them; the poor have no salt, while the King eats gold. To all these things there is now to be an end--quietly, if the seigneurs will--but an end. An end, Monseigneur, though we burn châteaux," he added grimly.

CHAPTER VI
A MEETING IN THE ROAD

The unlooked-for eloquence which rang in the blacksmith's words, and the assurance of his tone, no less than this startling disclosure of thoughts with which I had never dreamed of crediting him, or any peasant, took me so aback for a moment that I stood silent. Doury seized the occasion, and struck in.

"You see now, M. le Vicomte," he said complacently, "the necessity for such a Committee. The King's peace must be maintained."

"I see," I answered harshly, "that there are violent men abroad, who were better in the stocks. Committee? Let the King's officers keep the King's peace! The proper machinery----"

"It is shattered!"

The words were Doury's. The next moment he quailed at his presumption. "Then let it be repaired!" I thundered. "*Mon Dieu!* that a set of tavern cooks and base-born rascals should go about the country prating of it, and prating to me! Go, I will have nothing to do with you or your Committee. Go, I say!"

"Nevertheless--a little patience, M. le Vicomte," he persisted, chagrin on his pale face--"nevertheless, if any of the nobility would give us countenance, you most of all----"

"There would then be some one to hang instead of Doury!" I answered bluntly. "Some one behind whom he could shield himself, and lesser villains hide. But I will not be the stalking-horse."

"And yet, in other provinces," he answered desperately, his disappointment more and more pronounced, "M. de Liancourt and M. de Rochefoucauld have not disdained to----"

"Nevertheless, I disdain!" I retorted. "And more, I tell you, and I bid you remember it, you will have to answer for the work you are doing. I have told you it is treason. It is treason; I will have neither act nor part in it. Now go."

"There will be burning," the smith muttered.

"Begone!" I said sternly. "If you do not----"

"Before the morn is old the sky will be red," he answered. "On your head, Seigneur, be it!"

I aimed a blow at him with my cane; but he avoided it with a kind of dignity, and stalked away, Doury following him with a pale, hang-dog face, and his finery sitting very ill upon him. I stood and watched them go, and then I turned to the Curé to hear what he had to say.

But I found him gone also. He, too, had slipped away; through the house, to intercept them at the gates, perhaps, and dissuade them. I waited for him, querulously tapping the walk with my stick, and watching the corner of the house. Presently he came round it, holding his hat an inch or two above his head, his lean, tall figure almost shadowless, for it was noon. I noticed that his lips moved as he came towards me; but, when I spoke, he looked up cheerfully.

"Yes," he said in answer to my question, "I went through the house, and stopped them."

"It would be useless," I said. "Men so mad as to think that they could replace his Majesty's Government with a Committee of smiths and pastrycooks----"

"I have joined it," he answered, smiling faintly.

"The Committee?" I ejaculated, breathless with surprise.

"Even so."

"Impossible!"

"Why?" he said quietly. "Have I not always predicted this day? Is not this what Rousseau, with his *Social Contract*, and Beaumarchais, with his 'Figaro,' and every philosopher who ever repeated the one, and every fine lady who ever applauded the other, have been teaching? Well, it has come, and I have advised you, M. le Vicomte, to stand by your order. But I, a poor man, I stand by mine. And for the Committee of what seems to you, my friend, impossible people, is not any kind of government"--this more warmly, and as if he were arguing with himself--"better than none? Understand, Monsieur, the old machinery has broken down. The Intendant has fled. The people defy the magistrates. The soldiers side with the people. The *huissiers* and tax collectors are--the Good God knows where!"

"Then," I said indignantly, "it is time for the gentry to----"

"Take the lead and govern?" he rejoined. "By whom? A handful of servants and game-keepers? Against the people? against such a mob as you saw in the Square at Cahors? Impossible, Monsieur."

"But the world seems to be turning upside down," I said helplessly.

"The greater need of a strong unchanging holdfast--not of the world," he answered reverently; and he lifted his hat a moment from his head and stood in thought. Then he continued: "However, the matter is this. I hear from Doury that the gentry are gathering at Cahors, with the view of combining, as you suggest, and checking the people. Now, it must be useless, and it may be worse. It may lead to the very excesses they would prevent."

"In Cahors?"

"No, in the country. Buton, be sure, did not speak without warrant. He is a good man, but he knows some who are not, and there are lonely châteaux in Quercy, and dainty women who have never known the touch of a rough hand, and--and children."

"But," I cried aghast, "do you fear a Jacquerie?"

"God knows," he answered solemnly. "The fathers have eaten sour grapes, and the children's teeth are set on edge. How many years have men spent at Versailles the peasant's blood, life, bone, flesh! To pay back at last, it may be, of their own! But God forbid, Monsieur, God forbid. Yet, if ever--it comes now."

When he was gone I could not rest. His words had raised a fever in me. What might not be afoot, what might not be going on, while I lay idle? And, presently, to quench my thirst for news, I mounted and rode out on the way to Cahors. The day was hot, the time for riding ill-chosen; but the exercise did me good. I began to recover from the giddiness of thought into which the Curé's fears, coming on the top of Buton's warning, had thrown me. For a while I had seen things with their eyes; I had allowed myself to be carried away by their imaginations; and the prospect of a France ruled by a set of farriers and postillions had not seemed so bizarre as it began to look, now that I had time, mounting the long hill, which lies one league from Saux and two from Cahors, to consider it calmly. For a moment, the wild idea of a whole gentry fleeing like hares before their peasantry, had not seemed so very wild.

Now, on reflection, beginning to see things in their normal sizes, I called myself a simpleton. A Jacquerie? Three centuries and more had passed since France had known the thing in the dark ages. Could any, save a child alone in the night, or a romantic maiden solitary in her rock castle, dream of its recurrence? True, as I skirted St. Alais, which lies a little aside from the road, at the foot of the hill, I saw at the village-turning a sullen group of faces that should have been bent over the hoe; a group, gloomy, discontented, waiting--waiting, with shock heads and eyes glittering under low brows, for God knows what. But I had seen such a gathering before; in bad times, when seed was lacking, or when despair, or some excessive outrage on the part of the *fermier*, had driven the peasants to fold their hands and quit the fields. And always it had ended in nothing, or a hanging at most. Why should I suppose that anything would come of it now, or that a spark in Paris must kindle a fire here?

In fact, I as good as made up my mind; and laughed at my simplicity. The Curé had let his predictions run away with him, and Buton's ignorance and credulity had done the rest. What, I now saw, could be more absurd than to suppose that France, the first, the most stable, the most highly civilised of States, wherein for two centuries none had resisted the royal power and stood, could become in a moment the theatre of barbarous excesses? What more absurd than to conceive it turned into the *Petit Trianon* of a gang of *rôturiers* and *canaille*?

At this point in my thoughts I broke off, for, as I reached it, a coach came slowly over the ridge before me and began to descend the road. For a space it hung clear-cut against the sky, the burly figure of the coachman and the heads of the two lackeys who swung behind it visible above the hood. Then it began to drop down cautiously towards me. The men behind sprang down and locked the wheels, and the lumbering vehicle slid and groaned downwards, the wheelers pressing back, the leading horses tossing their heads impatiently. The road there descends not in *lacets*, but straight, for nearly half a mile between poplars; and on the summer air the screaming of the wheels and the jingling of the harness came distinctly to the ear.

Presently I made out that the coach was Madame St. Alais'; and I felt inclined to turn and avoid it. But the next moment pride came to my aid, and I shook my reins and went on to meet it.

I had scarcely seen a person except Father Benôit since the affair at Cahors, and my cheek flamed at the thought of the *rencontre* before me. For the same reason the coach seemed to come on very slowly; but at last I came abreast of it, passed the straining horses, and looked into the carriage with my hat in my hand, fearing that I might see Madame, hoping I might see Louis, ready with a formal salute at least. Politeness required no less.

But sitting in the place of honour, instead of M. le Marquis, or his mother, or M. le Comte, was one little figure throned in the middle of the seat; a little figure with a pale inquiring face that blushed scarlet at sight of me, and eyes that opened wide with fright, and lips that trembled piteously. It was Mademoiselle!

Had I known a moment earlier that she was in the carriage and alone, I should have passed by in silence; as was doubtless my duty after what had happened. I was the last person who should have intruded on her. But the men, grinning, I dare say, at the encounter--for probably Madame's treatment of me was the talk of the house--had drawn up, and I had reined up instinctively; so that before I quite understood that she was alone, save for two maids who sat with their backs to the horses, we were gazing at one another--like two fools!

"Mademoiselle!" I said.

"Monsieur!" she answered mechanically.

Now, when I had said that, I had said all that I had a right to say. I should have saluted, and gone on with that. But something impelled me to add--"Mademoiselle is going--to St. Alais?"

Her lips moved, but I heard no sound. She stared at me like one under a spell. The elder of her women, however, answered for her, and said briskly:----

"Ah, *oui*, Monsieur."

"And Madame de St. Alais?"

"Madame remains at Cahors," the woman answered in the same tone, "with M. le Marquis, who has business."

Then, at any rate, I should have gone on; but the girl sat looking at me, silent and blushing; and something in the picture, something in the thought of her arriving alone and unprotected at St. Alais, taken with a memory of the lowering faces I had seen in the village, impelled me to stand and linger; and finally to blurt out what I had in my mind.

"Mademoiselle," I said impulsively, ignoring her attendants, "if you will take my advice--you will not go on."

One of the women muttered "*Ma foi!*" under her breath. The other said "Indeed!" and tossed her head impertinently. But Mademoiselle found her voice.

"Why, Monsieur?" she said clearly and sweetly, her eyes wide with a surprise that for the moment overcame her shyness.

"Because," I answered diffidently--I repented already that I had spoken--"the state of the country is such--I mean that Madame la Marquise scarcely understands perhaps that--that----"

"What, Monsieur?" Mademoiselle asked primly.

"That at St. Alais," I stammered, "there is a good deal of discontent, Mademoiselle, and----"

"At St. Alais?" she said.

"In the neighbourhood, I should have said," I answered awkwardly. "And--and in fine," I continued very much embarrassed, "it would be better, in my poor opinion, for Mademoiselle to turn and----"

"Accompany Monsieur, perhaps?" one of the women said; and she giggled insolently.

Mademoiselle St. Alais flashed a look at the offender, that made me wink. Then with her cheeks burning, she said:----

"Drive on!"

I was foolish and would not let ill alone. "But, Mademoiselle," I said, "a thousand pardons, but----"

"Drive on!" she repeated; this time in a tone, which, though it was still sweet and clear, was not to be gainsaid. The maid who had not offended--the other looked no little scared--repeated the order, the coach began to move, and in a moment I was left in the road, sitting on my horse with my hat in my hand, and looking foolishly at nothing.

The straight road running down between lines of poplars, the descending coach, lurching and jolting as it went, the faces of the grinning lackeys as they looked back at me through the dust--I well remember them all. They form a picture strangely vivid and distinct in that gallery where so many more important have faded into nothingness. I was hot, angry, vexed with myself; conscious that I had trespassed beyond the becoming, and that I more than deserved the repulse I had suffered. But through all ran a thread of a new feeling--a quite new feeling. Mademoiselle's face moved before my eyes--showing through the dust; her eyes full of dainty surprise, or disdain as delicate, accompanied me as I rode. I thought of her, not of Buton or Doury, the Committee or the Curé, the heat or the dull road. I ceased to speculate except on the chances of a peasant rising. That, that alone assumed a new and more formidable aspect; and became in a moment imminent and probable. The sight of Mademoiselle's childish face had given a reality to Buton's warnings, which all the Curé's hints had failed to impart to them.

So much did the thought now harass me, that to escape it I shook up my horse, and cantered on, Gil and André following, and wondering, doubtless, why I did not turn. But, wholly taken up with the horrid visions which the blacksmith's words had called up, I took no heed of time until I awoke to find myself more than half-way on the road to Cahors, which lies three leagues and a mile from Saux. Then I drew rein and stood in the road, in a fit of excitement and indecision. Within the half-hour I might be at Madame St. Alais' door in Cahors, and, whatever happened then, I should have no need to reproach myself. Or in a little more I might be at home, ingloriously safe.

Which was it to be? The moment, though I did not know it, was fateful. On the one hand, Mademoiselle's face, her beauty, her innocence, her helplessness, pleaded with me strangely, and dragged me on to give the warning. On the other, my pride urged me to return, and avoid such a reception as I had every reason to expect.

In the end I went on. In less than half an hour I had crossed the Valaridré bridge.

Yet it must not be supposed that I decided without doubt, or went forward without misgiving. The taunts and sneers to which Madame had treated me were too recent for that; and a dozen times pride and resentment almost checked my steps, and I turned and went home again. On each occasion, however, the ugly faces and brutish eyes I had seen in the village rose before me; I remembered the hatred in which Gargouf, the St. Alais' steward, was held; I pictured the horrors that might be enacted before help could come from Cahors; and I went on.

Yet with a mind made up to ridicule; which even the crowded streets, when I reached them, failed to relieve, though they wore an unmistakable air of excitement. Groups of people, busily conversing, were everywhere to be seen; and in two or three places men were standing on stools--in a fashion then new to me--haranguing knots of idlers. Some of the shops were shut, there were guards before others, and before the bakehouses. I remarked a great number of journals and pamphlets in men's hands, and that where these were, the talk rose loudest. In some places, too, my appearance seemed to create excitement, but this was of a doubtful character, a few greeting me respectfully, while more stared at me in silence. Several asked me, as I passed, if I brought news, and seemed disappointed when I said I did not; and at two points a handful of people hooted me.

This angered me a little, but I forgot it in a thing still more surprising. Presently, as I rode, I heard my name called; and turning, found M. de Gontaut hurrying after me as fast as his dignity and lameness would permit. He leaned, as usual, on the arm of a servant, his other hand holding a cane and snuff-box; and two stout fellows followed him. I had no reason to suppose that he would appreciate the service I had done him more highly, or acknowledge it more gratefully, than on the day of the riot; and my surprise was great when he came up, his face all smiles.

"Nothing, for months, has given me so much pleasure as this," he said, saluting me with overwhelming cordiality. "By my faith, M. le Vicomte, you have outdone us all! You will have such a reception yonder! and you have brought two good knaves, I see. It is not fair," he continued, nodding his head with senile jocularity. "I declare it is not fair. But you know the text? 'There is more joy in heaven over one sinner that repenteth than----' Ha! ha! Well, we must not be jealous. You have taught them a lesson; and now we are united."

"But, M. le Baron," I said in amazement, as, obeying his gesture, I moved on, while he limped jauntily beside me, "I do not understand you in the least!"

"You don't?"

"No!" I said.

"Ah! you did not think that we should hear it so soon," he replied, shaking his head sagely. "Oh, I can tell you we are well provided. The campaign has begun, and the information department has not been neglected. Little escapes us, and we shall soon set these rogues right. But, for the fact, that damned rascal Doury let it out. I hear you told them some fine home-truths. A Committee, the insolents! And in our teeth! But you gave them a sharp set-back, I hear, M. le Vicomte. If you had joined it, now----"

He stopped abruptly. A man crossing the street had slightly jostled him. The old noble lost his temper, and on the instant raised his stick with a passionate oath, and the man cowered away begging his pardon. But M. de Gontaut was not to be appeased.

"Vagabond!" he cried after him, in a voice trembling with rage, "you would throw me down again, would you? We will put you in your place by-and-by. We will; why, *Dieu!* when I was young----"

"But, M. le Baron," I said to divert his attention, for two or three bystanders were casting ugly looks at us, and I saw that it needed little to bring about a fracas, "are you quite sure that we shall be able to keep them in check?"

The old noble still trembled, but he drew himself up with a gesture of pathetic gallantry.

"You shall see!" he cried. "When it comes to hard knocks, you shall see, Monsieur. But here we are; and there is Madame St. Alais on the balcony with some of her bodyguard." He paused to kiss his hand, with the air of a Polignac. "Up there, M. le Vicomte, you will see what you will see," he continued. "And I--I shall be in luck, too, for I have brought you."

It seemed to me more like a dream than a reality. A fortnight before, I had been spurned from this house with insults; I had been bidden never to enter it again. Now, on the balconies, from which pretty faces and powdered heads looked down, handkerchiefs fluttered to greet me. On the stairs, which, crowded with servants and lackeys, shook under the constant stream of comers and goers, I was received with a hum of applause. In every corner snuff-boxes were being tapped and canes handled; the flashing of roguish eyes behind fans vied with the glitter of mirrors. And through all a lane was made for me. At the door Louis met me. A little farther on, Madame came half-way across the room to me. It was a triumph--a triumph which I found inexplicable, unintelligible, until I learned that the rebuff which I had administered to the deputation had been exaggerated a dozen times, nay, a hundred times, until it met even the wishes of the most violent; while the sober and thoughtful were too glad to hail in my adhesion the proof of that reaction, which the Royalist party, from the first day of the troubles, never ceased to expect.

No wonder that, taken by surprise and intoxicated with incense, I let myself go. To have declared in that company and with Madame's gracious words in my ears, that I had not come to join them, that I had come on a different errand altogether, that though I had repelled the deputation I had no intention of acting against it, would have required a courage and a hardness I could not boast; while the circumstances of the deputation, Doury's presumption and Buton's hints, to say nothing of the violence of the Parisian mob, had not failed to impress me unfavourably. With a thousand others who had prepared themselves to welcome reform, I recoiled when I saw the lengths to which it was tending; and, though nothing had been farther from my mind when I entered Cahors than to join myself to the St. Alais faction, I found it impossible to reject their apologies on the spot, or explain on the instant the real purpose with which I had come to them.

I was, in fact, the sport of circumstances; weak, it will be said, in the wrong place and stubborn in the wrong; betraying a boy's petulance at one time, and a boy's fickleness at another; and now a tool and now a churl. Perhaps truly. But it was a time of trial; nor was I the only man or the oldest man who, in those days, changed his opinions, and again within the week went back; or who found it hard to find a cockade, white, black, red or tricolour, to his taste.

Besides, flattery is sweet, and I was young; moreover, I had Mademoiselle in my head and nothing could exceed Madame's graciousness. I think she valued me the more for my late revolt, and prided herself on my reduction in proportion as I had shown myself able to resist.

"Few words are better, M. le Vicomte," she said, with a dignity which honoured me equally with herself. "Many things have happened since I saw you. We are neither of us quite of the same opinion. Forgive me. A woman's word and a man's sword do no dishonour."

I bowed, blushing with pleasure. After a fortnight spent in solitude these moving groups, bowing, smiling, talking in low, earnest tones of the one purpose, the one aim, had immense influence with me. I felt the contagion. I let Madame take me into her confidence.

"The King"--it was always the King with her--"in a week or two the King will assert himself. As yet his ear has been abused. It will pass; in the meantime we must take our proper places. We must arm our servants and keepers, repress disorder and resist encroachment."

"And the Committee, Madame?"

She tapped me, smiling, with the ends of her dainty fingers.

"We will treat it as you treated it," she said.

"You think that you will be strong enough?"

"We," she answered.

"We?" I said, correcting myself with a blush.

"Why not? How can it be otherwise?" she replied, looking proudly round her. "Can you look round and doubt it, M. le Vicomte?"

"But France?" I said.

"We are France," she retorted with a superb gesture.

And certainly the splendid crowd that filled her rooms was almost warrant for the words; a crowd of stately men and fair women such as

I have only seen once or twice since those days. Under the surface there may have been pettiness and senility; the exhaustion of vice; jealousy and lukewarmness and dissension; but the powder and patches, the silks and velvets of the old *régime*, gave to all a semblance of strength, and at least the appearance of dignity. If few were soldiers, all wore swords and could use them. The fact that the small sword, so powerful a weapon in the duel, is useless against a crowd armed with stones and clubs had not yet been made clear. Nothing seemed more easy than for two or three hundred swordsmen to rule a province.

At any rate I found nothing but what was feasible in the notion; and with little real reluctance, if no great enthusiasm, I pinned on the white cockade. Putting all thoughts of present reform from my mind, I agreed that order--order was the one pressing need of the country.

On that all were agreed, and all were hopeful. I heard no misgivings, but a good deal of vapouring, in which poor M. de Gontaut, with the palsy almost upon him, had his part. No one dropped a hint of danger in the country, or of a revolt of the peasants. Even to me, as I stood in the brilliant crowd, the danger grew to seem so remote and unreal, that, delicacy as well as the fear of ridicule, kept me silent. I could not speak of Mademoiselle without awkwardness, and so the warning which I had come to give died on my lips. I saw that I should be laughed at, I fancied myself deceived, and I was silent.

It was only when, after promising to return next day, I stood at the door prepared to leave, and found myself alone with Louis, that I let a word fall. Then I asked him with a little hesitation if he thought that his sister was quite safe at St. Alais.

"Why not?" he said easily, with his hand on my shoulder.

"The 'trouble is not in the town only," I hinted. "Nor perhaps the worst of the trouble."

He shrugged his shoulders. "You think too much of it, *mon cher*," he answered. "Believe me, now that we are at one the trouble is over."

And that was the evening of the 4th of August, the day on which the Assembly in Paris renounced at a single sitting all immunities, exemptions, and privileges, all feudal dues, and fines, and rights, all tolls, all tithes, the salt tax, the game laws, *capitaineries!* At one sitting, on that evening; and Louis thought that the trouble was over!

CHAPTER VII
THE ALARM

At that time, a brazier in the market-place, and three or four lanterns at street crossings, made up the most of the public lighting. When I paused, therefore, to breathe my horse on the brow of the slope, beyond the Valandré bridge, and looked back on Cahors, I saw only darkness, broken here and there by a blur of yellow light; that still, by throwing up a fragment of wall or eaves, told in a mysterious way of the sleeping city.

The river, a faint, shimmering line, conjectured rather than seen, wound round all. Above, clouds were flying across the sky, and a wind, cold for the time of year--cold, at least, after the heat of the day--chilled the blood, and slowly filled the mind with the solemnity of night.

As I stood listening to the breathing of the horses, the excitement in which I had passed the last few hours died away, and left me wondering--wondering, and a little regretful. The exaltation gone, I found the scene I had just left flavourless; I even presently began to find it worse. Some false note in the cynical, boastful voices and the selfish--the utterly selfish--plans, to which I had been listening for hours, made itself heard in the stillness. Madame's "We are France," which had sounded well amid the lights and glitter of the *salon*, among laces and *fripons* and rose-pink coats, seemed folly in the face of the infinite night, behind which lay twenty-five millions of Frenchmen.

However, what I had done, I had done. I had the white cockade on my breast; I was pledged to order--and to my order. And it might be the better course. But, with reflection, enthusiasm faded; and, by some strange process, as it faded, and the scene in which I had just taken part lost its hold, the errand that had brought me to Cahors recovered importance. As Madame St. Alais' influence grew weak, the memory of Mademoiselle, sitting lonely and scared in her coach, grew vivid, until I turned my horse fretfully, and endeavoured to lose the thought in rapid movement.

But it is not so easy to escape from oneself at night, as in the day. The soughing of the wind through the chestnut trees, the drifting clouds, and the sharp ring of hoofs on the road, all laid as it were a solemn finger on the pulses and stilled them. The men behind me talked in sleepy voices, or rode silently. The town lay a hundred leagues behind. Not a light appeared on the upland. In the world of night through which we rode, a world of black, mysterious bulks rising suddenly against the grey sky, and as suddenly sinking, we were the only inhabitants.

At last we reached the hill above St. Alais, and I looked eagerly for lights in the valley; forgetting that, as it wanted only an hour of midnight, the village would have retired hours before. The disappointment, and the delay--for the steepness of the hill forbade any but a walking pace--fretted me; and when I heard, a moment later, a certain noise behind me, a noise I knew only too well, I flared up.

"Stay, fool!" I cried, reining in my horse, and turning in the saddle. "That mare has broken her shoe again, and you are riding on as if nothing were the matter! Get down--and see. Do you think that I----"

"Pardon, Monsieur," Gil muttered. He had been sleeping in his saddle.

He scrambled down. The mare he rode, a valuable one, had a knack of breaking her hind shoe; after which she never failed to lame herself at the first opportunity. Buton had tried every method of shoeing, but without success.

I sprang to the ground while he lifted the foot. My ear had not deceived me; the shoe was broken. Gil tried to remove the jagged fragment left on the hoof, but the mare was restive, and he had to desist.

"She cannot go to Saux in that state," I said angrily.

The men were silent for a moment, peering at the mare. Then Gil spoke.

"The St. Alais forge is not three hundred yards down the lane, Monsieur," he said. "And the turn is yonder. We could knock up Petit Jean, and get him to bring his pincers here. Only----"

"Only what?" I said peevishly.

"I quarrelled with him at Cahors Fair, Monsieur," Gil answered sheepishly; "and he might not come for us."

"Very well," I said gruffly, "I will go. And do you stay here, and keep the mare quiet."

André held the stirrup for me to mount. The smithy, the first hovel in the village, was a quarter of a mile away, and, in reason, I should have ridden to it. But, in my irritation, I was ready to do anything they did not propose, and, roughly rejecting his help, I started on foot. Fifty paces brought me to the branch road that led to St. Alais, and, making out the turning with a little difficulty, I plunged into it; losing, in a moment, the cheerful sound of jingling bits and the murmur of the men's voices.

Poplars rose on high banks on either side of the lane, and made the place as dark as a pit, and I had almost to grope my way. A stumble added to my irritation, and I cursed the St. Alais for the ruts, and the moon for its untimely setting. The ceaseless whispering of the poplar leaves went with me, and, in some unaccountable way, annoyed me. I stumbled again, and swore at Gil, and then stopped to listen. I was in the road, and yet I heard the jingling of bits again, as if the horses were following me.

I stopped angrily to listen, thinking that the men had disobeyed my orders. Then I found that the sound came from the front, and was heavier and harder than the ringing of bit or bridle. I groped my way forward, wondering somewhat, until a faint, ruddy light, shining on the darkness and the poplars, prepared me for the truth--welcome, though it seemed of the strangest--that the forge was at work.

As I took this in, I turned a corner, and came within sight of the smithy; and stood in astonishment. The forge was in full blast. Two hammers were at work; I could see them rising and falling, and hear, though they seemed to be muffled, the rhythmical jarring clang as they struck the metal. The ruddy glare of the fire flooded the road and burnished the opposite trees, and flung long, black shadows on the sky.

Such a sight filled me with the utmost astonishment, for it was nearly midnight. Fortunately something else I saw astonished me still more, and stayed my foot. Between the point where I stood by the hedge and the forge a number of men were moving, and flitting to and fro; men with bare arms and matted heads, half-naked, with skins burned black. It would have been hard to count them, they shifted so quickly; and I did not try. It was enough for me that one half of them carried pikes and pitchforks, that one man seemed to be detailing them into groups, and giving them directions; and that, notwithstanding the occasional jar of the hammers, an air of ferocious stealth marked their movements.

For a moment I stood rooted to the spot. Then, instinctively, I stepped aside into the shadow of the hedge, and looked again. The man who acted as the leader carried an axe on his shoulder, the broad blade of which, as it caught the glow of the furnace, seemed to be bathed in blood. He was never still--this man. One moment he moved from group to group, gesticulating, ordering, encouraging. Now he pulled a man out of one troop and thrust him forcibly into another; now he made a little speech, which was dumb play to me, a hundred paces away; now he went into the forge, and his huge bulk for a moment intercepted the light. It was Petit Jean, the smith.

I made use of the momentary darkness which he caused on one of these occasions, and stole a little nearer. For I knew now what was before me. I knew perfectly that all this meant blood, fire, outrage, flames rising to heaven, screams startling the stricken night! But I must know more, if I would do anything. I went nearer therefore, creeping along the hedge, and crouching in the ditch, until no more than twelve yards separated me from the muster. Then I stood still, as Petit Jean came out again, to distribute another bundle of weapons, clutched instantly and eagerly by grimy hands. I could hear now, and I shuddered at what I heard. Gargouf was in every mouth. Gargouf, the St. Alais' steward, coupled with grisly tortures and slow deaths, with old sins, and outrages, and tyrannies, now for the first time voiced, now to be expiated!

At last, one man laid the torch by crying aloud, "To the Château! To the Château!" and in an instant the words changed the feelings with which I had hitherto stared into immediate horror. I started forward. My impulse, for a moment, was to step into the light and confront them--to persuade, menace, cajole, turn them any way from their purpose. But, in the same moment, reflection showed me the hopelessness of the attempt. These were no longer peasants, dull, patient clods, such as I had known all my life; but maddened beasts; I read it in their gestures and the growl of their voices. To step forward would be only to sacrifice myself; and with this thought I crept back, gained the deeper shadow, and, turning on my heel, sped down the lane. The ruts and the darkness were no longer anything to me. If I stumbled, I did not notice it. If I fell, it was no matter. In less than a minute I was standing, breathless, by the astonished servants, striving to tell them quickly what they must do.

"The village is rising!" I panted. "They are going to burn the Château, and Mademoiselle is in it! Gil, ride, gallop, lose not a minute, to Cahors, and tell M. le Marquis. He must bring what forces he can. And do you, André, go to Saux. Tell Father Benôit. Bid him do his utmost--bring all he can."

For answer, they stared, open-mouthed, through the dusk. "And the mare, Monsieur?" one asked at last dully.

"Fool! let her go!" I cried. "The mare? Do you understand? The Château is----"

"And you, Monsieur?"

"I am going to the house by the garden wing. Now go! Go, men!" I continued'. "A hundred livres to each of you if the house is saved!"

I said the house because I dared not speak what was really in my mind; because I dared not picture the girl, young, helpless, a woman, in the hands of those monsters. Yet it was that which goaded me now, it was that which gave me such strength that, before the men had ridden many yards, I had forced my way through the thick fence, as if it had been a mass of cobwebs. Once on the other side, in the open, I hastened across one field and a second, skirted the village, and made for the gardens which abutted on the east wing of the Château. I knew these well; the part farthest from the house, and most easy of entrance, was a wilderness, in which I had often played as a child. There was no fence round this, except a wooden paling, and none between it and the more orderly portion; while a side door opened from the latter into a passage leading to the great hall of the Château. The house, a long, regular building, reared by the Marquis's father, was composed of two wings and a main block. All faced the end of the village street at a distance of a hundred paces; a wide, dusty, ill-planted avenue leading from the iron gates, which stood always open, to the state entrance.

The rioters had only a short distance to go, therefore, and no obstacle between them and the house; none when they reached it of greater consequence than ordinary doors and shutters, should the latter be closed. As I ran, I shuddered to think how defenceless all lay; and how quickly the wretches, bursting in the doors, would overrun the shining parquets, and sweep up the spacious staircase.

The thought added wings to my feet. I had farther to go than they had, and over hedges, but before the first sounds of their approach reached the house I was already in the wilderness, and forcing my way through it, stumbling over stumps and bushes, falling more than once, covered with dust and sweat, but still pushing on.

At last I sprang into the open garden, with its shadowy walks, and nymphs, and fauns; and looked towards the village. A dull red light was beginning to show among the trunks of the avenue; a murmur of voices sounded in the distance. They were coming! I wasted no more than a single glance; then I ran down the walk, between the statues. In a moment I passed into the darker shadow under the house, I was at the door. I thrust my shoulder against it. It resisted; it resisted! and every moment was precious. I could no longer see the approaching lights nor hear the voices of the crowd--the angle of the house intervened; but I could imagine only too vividly how they were coming on; I fancied them already at the great door.

I hammered on the panels with my fist; then I fumbled for the latch, and found it. It rose, but the door held. I shook it. I shook it again in a frenzy; at last, forgetting caution, I shouted--shouted more loudly. Then, after an age, as it seemed to me, standing panting in the darkness, I heard halting footsteps come along the passage, and saw a line of light grow, and brighten under the door. At last a quavering voice asked:----

"Who is it?"

"M. de Saux," I answered impatiently. "M. de Saux! Let me in. Let me in, do you hear?" And I struck the panels wrathfully.

"Monsieur," the voice answered, quavering more and more, "is there anything the matter?"

"Matter? They are going to burn the house, fool!" I cried. "Open! open! if you do not wish to be burned in your beds!"

For a moment I fancied that the man still hesitated. Then he unbarred. In a twinkling I was inside, in a narrow passage, with dingy, stained walls. An old man, lean-jawed and feeble, an old valet whom I had often seen at worsted work in the ante-room, confronted me, holding an iron candlestick. The light shook in his hands, and his jaw fell as he looked at me. I saw that I had nothing to expect from him, and I snatched the bar from his hands, and set it back in its place myself. Then I seized the light.

"Quick!" I said passionately. "To your mistress."

"Monsieur?"

"Upstairs! Upstairs!"

He had more to say, but I did not wait to hear it. Knowing the way, and having the candle, I left him, and hurried along the passage. Stumbling over three or four mattresses that lay on the floor, doubtless for the servants, I reached the hall. Here my taper shone a mere speck in a cavern of blackness; but it gave me light enough to see that the door was barred, and I turned to the staircase. As I set my foot on the lowest step the old valet, who was following me as fast as his trembling legs would carry him, blundered against a spinning-wheel that stood in the hall. It fell with a clatter, and in a moment a chorus of screams and cries broke out above. I sprang up the stairs three at a stride, and on the lobby came on the screamers--a terrified group, whose alarm the doubtful light of a tallow candle, that stood beside them on the floor, could not exaggerate. Nearest to me stood an old footman and a boy--their terror-stricken eyes met mine as I mounted the last stairs. Behind them, and crouching against a tapestry-covered seat that ran along the wall, were the rest; three or four women, who shrieked and hid their faces in one another's garments. They did not look up or take any heed of me; but continued to scream steadily.

The old man with a quavering oath tried to still them.

"Where is Gargouf?" I asked him.

"He has gone to fasten the back doors, Monsieur," he answered.

"And Mademoiselle?"

"She is yonder."

He turned as he spoke; and I saw behind him a heavy curtain hiding the oriel window of the lobby. It moved while I looked, and Mademoiselle emerged from its folds, her small, childish face pale, but strangely composed. She wore a light, loose robe, hastily arranged, and had her hair hanging free at her back. In the gloom and confusion, which the feeble candles did little to disperse, she did not at first see me.

"Has Gargouf come back?" she asked.

"No, Mademoiselle, but----"

The man was going to point me out; she interrupted him with a sharp cry of anger.

"Stop these fools," she said. "Oh, stop these fools! I cannot hear myself speak. Let some one call Gargouf! Is there no one to do anything?"

One of the old men pottered off to do it, leaving her standing in the middle of the terror-stricken group; a white pathetic little figure, keeping fear at bay with both hands. The dark curtains behind threw her face and form into high relief; but admiration was the last thought in my mind.

"Mademoiselle," I said, "you must fly by the garden door."

She started and stared at me, her eyes dilating.

"Monsieur de Saux," she muttered. "Are you here? I do not--I do not understand. I thought----"

"The village is rising," I said. "In a moment they will be here."

"They are here already," she answered faintly.

She meant only that she had seen their approach from the window; but a dull murmur that at the moment rose on the air outside, and penetrating the walls, grew each instant louder and more sinister, seemed to give another significance to her words. The women listened with white faces, then began to scream afresh. A reckless movement of one of them dashed out the nearer of the two lights. The old man who had admitted me began to whimper.

"O *mon Dieu!*" I cried fiercely, "can no one still these cravens?" For the noise almost robbed me of the power of thought, and never had thought been more necessary. "Be still, fools," I continued, "no one will hurt *you*. And do you, Mademoiselle, please to come with me. There is not a moment to be lost. The garden by which I entered----"

But she looked at me in such a way that I stopped.

"Is it necessary to go?" she said doubtfully. "Is there no other way, Monsieur?"

The noise outside was growing louder. "What men have you?" I said.

"Here is Gargouf," she answered promptly. "He will tell you."

I turned to the staircase and saw the steward's face, at all times harsh and grim, rising out of the well of the stairs. He had a candle in one hand and a pistol in the other; and his features as his eyes met mine wore an expression of dogged anger, the sight of which drew fresh cries from the women. But I rejoiced to see him, for he at least betrayed no signs of flinching. I asked him what men he had.

"You see them," he answered drily, betraying no surprise at my presence.

"Only these?"

"There were three more," he said. "But I found the doors unbarred, and the men gone. I am keeping this," he continued, with a dark glance at his pistol, "for one of them."

"Mademoiselle must go!" I said.

He shrugged his shoulders with an indifference that maddened me. "How?" he asked.

"By the garden door."

"They are there. The house is surrounded."

I cried out at that in despair; and on the instant, as if to give point to his words, a furious blow fell on the great doors below, and awakening every echo in the house, proclaimed that the moment was come. A second shock followed; then a rain of blows. While the maids shrieked and clung to one another, I looked at Mademoiselle, and she at me.

"We must hide you," I muttered.

"No," she said.

"There must be some place," I said, looking round me desperately, and disregarding her answer. The noise of the blows was deafening. "In the----"

"I will not hide, Monsieur," she answered. Her cheeks were white, and her eyes seemed to flicker with each blow. But the maiden who had been dumb before me a few days earlier was gone; in her place I saw Mademoiselle de St. Alais, conscious of a hundred ancestors. "They are our people. I will meet them," she continued, stepping forward bravely, though her lip trembled. "Then if they dare----"

"They are mad," I answered. "They are mad! Yet it is a chance; and we have few! If I can get to them before they break in, I may do something. One moment, Mademoiselle; screen the light, will you?"

Some one did so, and I turned feverishly and caught hold of the curtain. But Gargouf was before me. He seized my arm, and for the moment checked me.

"What is it? What are you going to do?" he growled.

"Speak to them from the window."

"They will not listen."

"Still I will try. What else is there?"

"Lead and iron," he answered in a tone that made me shiver. "Here are M. le Marquis's sporting guns; they shoot straight. Take one, M. le Vicomte; I will take the other. There are two more, and the men can shoot. We can hold the staircase, at least."

I took one of the guns mechanically, amid a dismal uproar; wailing and the thunder of blows within, outside the savage booing of the crowd. No help could come for another hour; and for a moment in this desperate strait my heart failed me. I wondered at the steward's courage.

"You are not afraid?" I said. I knew how he had trampled on the poor wretches outside; how he had starved them and ground them down, and misused them through long years.

He cursed the dogs.

"You will stand by Mademoiselle?" I said feverishly. I think it was to hearten myself by his assurance.

He squeezed my hand in a grip of iron, and I asked no more. In a moment, however, I cried aloud.

"Ah, but they will burn the house!" I said. "What is the use of holding the staircase, when they can burn us like rats?"

"We shall die together," was his only answer. And he kicked one of the weeping, crouching women. "Be still, you whelp!" he said. "Do you think that will help you?"

But I heard the door below groan, and I sprang to the window and dragged aside the curtain, letting in a ruddy glow that dyed the ceiling the colour of blood. My one fear was that I might be too late; that the door would yield or the crowd break in at the back before I could get a hearing. Luckily, the casement gave to the hand, and I thrust it open, and, meeting a cold blast of air, in a twinkling was outside, on the narrow ledge of the window over the great doors, looking down on such a scene as few châteaux in France had witnessed since the days of the third Henry--God be thanked!

A little to one side the great dovecot was burning, and sending up a trail of smoke that, blown across the avenue, hid all beyond in a murky reek, through which the flames now and again flickered hotly. Men, busy as devils, black against the light, were plying the fire with straw. Beyond the dovecot, an outhouse and a stack were blazing; and nearer, immediately before the house, a crowd of moving figures were hurrying to and fro, some battering the doors and windows, others bringing fuel, all moving, yelling, laughing--laughing the laughter of fiends to the music of crackling flames and shivering glass.

I saw Petit Jean in the forefront giving orders; and men round him. There were women, too, hanging on the skirts of the men; and one woman, in the midst of all, half-naked, screaming curses, and brandishing her arms. It was she who added the last touch of horror to the scene; and she, too, who saw me first, and pointed me out with dreadful words, and cursed me, and the house, and cried for our blood.

CHAPTER VIII
GARGOUF

Some called for silence, while others stared at me stupidly, or pointed me out to their fellows; but the greater part took up the woman's cry, and, enraged by my presence, shook their fists at me, and shouted vile threats and viler abuse. For a minute the air rang with "*A bas les Seigneurs! A bas les tyrans!*" And I found this bad enough. But, presently, whether they caught sight of the steward, or merely returned to their first hatred, from which my appearance had only for the moment diverted them, the cry changed to a sullen roar of "Gargouf! Gargouf!" A roar so full of the lust for blood, and coupled with threats so terrible, that the heart sickened and the cheek grew pale at the sound.

"Gargouf! Gargouf! Give us Gargouf!" they howled. "Give us Gargouf! and he shall eat hot gold! Give us Gargouf, and he shall need no more of our daughters!"

I shuddered to think that Mademoiselle heard; shuddered to think of the peril in which she stood. The wretches below were no longer men; under the influence of this frenzied woman they were mad brute beasts, drunk with fire and licence. As the smoke from the burning building eddied away for a moment across the crowd and hid it, and still that hoarse cry came out of the mirk, I could believe that I heard not men, but maddened hounds raving in the kennel.

Again the smoke drifted away; and some one in the rear shot at me. I heard the glass splinter beside me. Another, a little nearer, flung up a burning fragment that, alighting on the ledge, blazed and spluttered by my foot. I kicked it down.

The act, for the moment, stilled the riot, and I seized the opportunity. "You dogs!" I said, striving to make my voice heard above the hissing of the flames. "Begone! The soldiers from Cahors are on the road. I sent for them this hour back. Begone, before they come, and I will intercede for you. Stay, and do further mischief, and you shall hang, to the last man!"

Some answered with a yell of derision, crying out that the soldiers were with them. More, that the nobles were abolished, and their houses given to the people. One, who was drunk, kept shouting, *"A bas la Bastille! A bas la Bastille!"* with a stupid persistence.

A moment more and I should lose my chance. I waved my hand! "What do you want?" I cried.

"Justice!" one shouted, and another, "Vengeance!" A third, "Gargouf!" And then all, "Gargouf! Gargouf!" until Petit Jean stilled the tumult.

"Have done!" he cried to them, in his coarse, brutal voice. "Have we come here only to yell? And do you, Seigneur, give up Gargouf, and you shall go free. Otherwise, we will burn the house, and all in it."

"You villain!" I said. "We have guns, and----"

"The rats have teeth, but they burn! They burn!" he answered, pointing triumphantly, with the axe he held, to the flaming buildings. "They burn! Yet listen, Seigneur," he continued, "and you shall have a minute to make up your minds. Give up Gargouf to us to do with as we please, and the rest shall go."

"All?"

"All."

I trembled. "But Gargouf, man?" I said. "Will you--what will you do with him?"

"Roast him!" the smith cried, with a fearful oath; and the wretches round him laughed like fiends. "Roast him, when we have plucked him bare."

I shuddered. From Cahors help could not come for another hour. From Saux it might not come at all. The doors below me could not stand long, and these brutes were thirty to one, and mad with the lust of vengeance. With the wrongs, the crimes, the vices of centuries to avenge, they dreamed that the day of requital was come; and the dream had turned clods into devils. The very flames they had kindled gave them assurance of it. The fire was in their blood. *A bas la Bastille! A bas les tyrans!*

I hesitated.

"One minute!" the smith cried, with a boastful gesture--"one minute we give you! Gargouf or all."

"Wait!"

I turned and went in--turned from the smoky glare, the circling pigeons, the grotesque black figures, and the terror and confusion of the night, and went in to that other scene scarcely less dreadful to me; though only two candles, guttering in tin sockets, lit the landing, and it borrowed from the outside no more than the ruddy reflection of horror. The women had ceased to scream and sob, and crowded together silent and panic-stricken. The old men and the lad moistened their lips, and looked furtively from the arms they handled to one another's faces. Mademoiselle alone stood erect, pale, firm. I shot a glance at the slender little figure in the white robe, then I looked away. I dared not say what I had in my mind. I knew that she had heard, and----

She said it! "You have answered them?" she muttered, her eyes meeting mine.

"No," I said, looking away again. "They have given us a minute to decide, and----"

"I heard them," she answered shivering. "Tell them."

"But, Mademoiselle----"

"Tell them never! Never!" she cried feverishly. "Be quick, or they will think that we are dreaming of it."

Yet I hesitated--while the flames crackled outside. What, after all, was this rascal's life beside hers? What his tainted existence, who all these years had ground the faces of the poor and dishonoured the helpless, beside her youth? It was a dreadful moment, and I hesitated. "Mademoiselle," I muttered at last, avoiding her eyes, "you have not thought, perhaps. But to refuse this offer may be to sacrifice all--and not save him."

"I have thought!" she answered, with a passionate gesture. "I have thought. But he was my father's steward, Monsieur, and he is my brother's; if he has sinned, it was for them. It is for them to pay the penalty. And--after all, it may not come to that," she continued, her face changing, and her eyes seeking mine, full of sudden terror. "They will not dare, I think. They will never dare to----"

"Where is he?" I asked hoarsely.

She pointed to the corner behind her. I looked, and could scarcely believe my eyes. The man whom I had left full of a desperate courage, prepared to sell his life dearly, now crouched a huddled figure in the darkest angle of the tapestry seat. Though I had spoken of him in a low voice, and without naming him, he heard me, and looked up, and showed a face to match his attitude; a face pallid and sweating with fear; a face that, vile at the best and when redeemed by hardihood, looked now the vilest thing on earth. *Ciel!* that fear should reduce a man to that! He tried to speak as his eyes met mine, but his lips moved inaudibly, and he only crouched lower, the picture of panic and guilt.

I cried out to the others to know what had happened to him. "What is it?" I said.

No one answered; and then I seemed to know. While he had thought all in danger, while he had felt himself only one among many, the common courage of a man had supported him. But God knows what voices, only too well known to him, what accents of starving men and wronged women, had spoken in that fierce cry for his life! What plaints from the dead, what curses of babes hanging on dry breasts! At any rate, whatever he had heard in that call for his blood, *his* blood--it had unmanned him. In a moment, in a twinkling, it had dashed him back into this corner, a trembling craven, holding up his hands for his life.

Such fear is infectious, and I strode to him in a rage and shook him.

"Get up, hound!" I said. "Get up and strike a blow for your life; or, by heaven, no one else will!"

He stood up. "Yes, yes, Monsieur," he muttered. "I will! I will stand up for Mademoiselle. I will----"

But I heard his teeth chatter, and I saw that his eyes wandered this way and that, as do a hare's when the dogs close on it; and I knew that I had nothing to expect from him. A howl outside warned me at the same moment that our respite was spent; and I flung him off and turned to the window.

Too late, however; before I could reach it, a thundering blow on the doors below set the candles flickering and the women shrieking; then for an instant I thought that all was over. A stone came through the window; another followed it, and another. The shattered glass fell over us; the draught put out one light, and the women, terrified beyond control, ran this way and that with the other, shrieking dismally. This, the yelling of the crowd outside, the sombre light and more sombre glare, the utter confusion and panic, so distracted me, that for a moment I stood irresolute, inactive, looking wildly about me; a poltroon waiting for some one to lead. Then a touch fell on my arm, and I turned and found Mademoiselle at my side, and saw her face upturned to mine.

It was white, and her eyes were wide with the terror she had so long repressed. Her hold on me grew heavier; she swayed against me, clinging to me.

"Oh!" she whispered in my ear in a voice that went to my heart. "Save me! Save me! Can nothing be done? Can nothing be done, Monsieur? Must we die?"

"We must gain time," I said. My courage returned wonderfully, as I felt her weight on my arm. "All is not over yet," I said. "I will speak to them."

And setting her on the seat, I sprang to the window and passed through it. Outside, things at a first glance seemed unchanged. The wavering flames, the glow, the trail of smoke and sparks, all were there. But a second glance showed that the rioters no longer moved to and fro about the fire, but were massed directly below me in a dense body round the doors, waiting for them to give way. I shouted to them frantically, hoping still to delay them. I called Petit Jean by name. But I could not make myself heard in the uproar, or they would not heed; and while I vainly tried, the great doors yielded at last, and with a roar of triumph the crowd burst in.

Not a moment was to be lost. I sprang back through the window, clutching up as I did so the gun Gargouf had given me; and then I stood in amazement. The landing was empty! The rush of feet across the hall below shook the house. Ten seconds and the mob, whose screams of triumph already echoed through the passages, would be on us. But where was Mademoiselle? Where was Gargouf? Where were the servants, the waiting-maids, the boy, whom I had left here?

I stood an instant paralysed, like a man in a nightmare; brought up short in that supreme moment. Then, as the first crash of heavy feet sounded on the stairs, I heard a faint scream, somewhere to my right, as I stood. On the instant I sprang to the door which, on that side, led to the left wing. I tore it open and passed through it--not a moment too soon. The slightest delay, and the foremost rioters must have seen me. As it was I had time to turn the key, which, fortunately, was on the inside.

Then I hurried across the room, making my way to an open door at the farther end, from which light issued; I passed through the room beyond, which was empty, then into the last of the suite.

Here I found the fugitives; who had fled so precipitately that they had not even thought of closing the doors behind them. In this last refuge-- Madame's boudoir, all white and gold--I found them crouching among gilt-backed chairs and flowered cushions. They had brought only one candle with them; and the silks and gew-gaws and knick-knacks on which its light shone dimly, gave a peculiar horror to their white faces and glaring eyes, as, almost mad with terror, they huddled in the farthest corner and stared at me.

They were such cowards that they put Mademoiselle foremost; or it was she who stood out to meet me. She knew me before they did, therefore, and quieted them. When I could hear my own voice, I asked where Gargouf was.

They had not discovered that he was not with them, and they cried out, saying that he had come that way.

"You followed him?"

"Yes, Monsieur."

This explained their flight, but not the steward's absence. What matter where he had gone, however, since his help could avail little. I looked round--looked round in despair; the very simpering Cupids on the walls seemed to mock our danger. I had the gun, I could fire one shot, I had one life in my hands. But to what end? In a moment, at any moment, within a minute or two at most, the doors would be forced, and the horde of mad brutes would pour in upon us, and----

"Ah, Monsieur, the closet staircase! He has gone by the closet staircase!"

It was the boy who spoke. He alone of them had his wits about him.

"Where is it?" I said.

The lad sprang forward to show me, but Mademoiselle was before him with the candle. She flew back into the passage, a passage of four or five feet only between that room and the second of the suite; in the wall of this she flung open a door, apparently of a closet. I looked in and saw the beginning of a staircase. My heart leapt at the sight.

"To the floor above?" I said.

"No, Monsieur, to the roof!"

"Up, up, then!" I cried in a frenzy of impatience. "It will give us time. Quick. They are coming."

For I heard the door at the end of the suite, the door I had locked, creak and yield. They were forcing it, at any moment it might give; where I stood waiting to bring up the rear, their hoarse cries and curses came to my ears. But the good door held; it held, long enough at any rate. Before it gave way we were on the stairs and I had shut the door of the closet behind me. Then, holding to the skirts of the woman before me, I groped my way up quickly--up and up through darkness with a close smell of bats in my nostrils--and almost before I could believe it, I stood with the panting, trembling group on the roof. The glare of the burning outhouses below shone on a great stack of chimneys beside us and reddened the sky above, and burnished the leaves of the chestnut trees that rose on a level with our eyes. But all the lower part of the steep roofs round us, and the lead gutters that ran between them, lay in darkness, the denser for the contrast. The flames crackled below, and a thick reek of smoke swept up past the coping, but the noise alike of fire and riot was deadened here. The night wind cooled our brows, and I had a minute in which to think, to breathe, to look round.

"Is there any other way to the roof?" I asked anxiously.

"One other, Monsieur!"

"Where? Or do you stay here, and guard this door," I said, pressing my gun on the man who had answered. "And let the boy come and show me. Mademoiselle, stay there if you please."

The boy ran before me to the farther end of the roof, and in a lead walk, between two slopes, showed me a large trap-door. It had no fastening on the outside, and for a moment I stood nonplussed; then I saw, a few feet away, a neat pile of bricks, left there, I learned afterwards, in the course of some repairs. I began to remove them as fast as I could to the trap-door, and the boy saw and followed my example; in two minutes we had stacked a hundred and more on the door. Telling him to add another hundred to the number, I left him at the task and flew back to the women.

They might burn the house under us; that always, and for certain, and it meant a dreadful death. Yet I breathed more freely here. In the white and gold room below, among Madame's mirrors and Cupids, and silken cushions, and painted Venuses, my heart had failed me. The place, with its heavy perfumes, had stifled me. I had pictured the brutish peasants bursting in on us there--on the screaming women, crouching vainly behind chairs and couches; and the horror of the thought overcame me. Here, in the open, under the sky, we could at least die fighting. The depth yawned beyond the coping; the weakest had here no more to fear than death. Besides we had a respite, for the house was large, and the fire could not lick it up in a moment.

And help might come. I shaded my eyes from the light below, and looked into the darkness in the direction of the village and the Cahors road. In an hour, at furthest, help might come. The glare in the sky must be visible for miles; it would spur on the avengers. Father Benôit, too, if he could get help--he might be here at any time. We were not without hope.

Suddenly, while we stood together, the women sobbing and whimpering, the old man-servant spoke.

"Where is M. Gargouf?" he muttered under his breath.

"Ah!" I exclaimed; "I had forgotten him."

"He came up," the man continued, peering about him. "This door was open, M. le Vicomte, when we came to it."

"Ah! then where is he?"

I looked round too. All the roof, I have said, was dark, and not all of it was on the same level; and here and there chimneys broke the view. In the obscurity, the steward might be lurking close to us without our knowledge; or he might have thrown himself down in despair. While I looked, the boy whom I had left by the bricks came flying to us.

"There is some one there!" he said. And he clung to the old man in terror.

"It must be Gargouf!" I answered. "Wait here!" And, disregarding the women's prayers that I would stay with them, I went quickly along the leads to the other trap-door, and peered about me through the gloom. For a moment I could see no one, though the light shining on the trees made it easy to discern figures standing nearer the coping. Presently, however, I caught the sound of some one moving; some one who was farther away still, at the very edge of the roof. I went on cautiously, expecting I do not know what; and close to a stack of chimneys I found Gargouf.

He was crouching on the coping in the darkest part, where the end wall of the east wing overlooked the garden by which I had entered. This end wall had no windows, and the greater part of the garden below it lay it darkness; the angle of the house standing between it and the burning buildings. I supposed that the steward had sneaked hither, therefore, to hide; and set it down to the darkness that he did not know me, but, as I approached, he rose on his knees on the ledge, and turned on me, snarling like a dog.

"Stand back!" he said, in a voice that was scarcely human. "Stand back, or I will----"

"Steady, man," I answered quietly, beginning to think that fear had unhinged him. "It is I, M. de Saux."

"Stand back!" was his only answer; and, though he cowered so low that I could not get his figure against the shining trees, I saw a pistol-barrel gleam as he levelled it. "Stand back! Give me a minute! a minute only"--and his voice quavered--"and I will cheat the devils yet! Come nearer, or give the alarm, and I will not die alone! I will not die alone! Stand back!"

"Are you mad?" I said.

"Back, or I shoot!" he growled. "I will not die alone."

He was kneeling on the very edge, with his left hand against the chimney. To rush upon him in that posture was to court death; and I had nothing to gain by it. I stepped back a pace. As I did so, at the moment I did so, he slid over the edge, and was gone!

I drew a deep breath and listened, flinching and drawing back involuntarily. But I heard no sound of a fall; and in a moment, with a new idea in my mind, I stepped forward to the edge, and looked over.

The steward hung in mid-air, a dozen feet below me. He was descending; descending foot by foot, slowly, and by jerks; a dim figure, growing dimmer. Instinctively I felt about me; and in a second laid my hand on the rope by which he hung. It was secured round the chimney. Then I understood. He had conceived this way of escape, perhaps had stored the rope for it beforehand, and, like the villain he was, had kept the thought to himself, that his chance might be the better, and that he might not have to give the first place to Mademoiselle and the women. In the first heat of the discovery, I almost found it in my heart to cut the rope, and let him fall; then I remembered that if he escaped, the way would lie open for others; and then, even as I thought this, into the garden below me, there shone a sudden flare of light, and a stream of a dozen rioters poured round the corner, and made for the door by which I had entered the house.

I held my breath. The steward, hanging below me, and by this time half-way to the ground, stopped, and moved not a limb. But he still swung a little this way and that, and in the strong light of the torches which the new-comers carried, I could see every knot in the rope, and even the trailing end, which, as I looked, moved on the ground with his motion.

The wretches, making for the door, had to pass within a pace of the rope, of that trailing end; yet it was possible that, blinded by the lights they carried, and their own haste and excitement, they might not see it. I held my breath as the leader came abreast of it; I fancied that he must see it. But he passed, and disappeared in the doorway. Three others passed the rope together. A fifth, then three more, two more; I began to breathe more freely. Only one remained--a woman, the same whose imprecations had greeted me on my appearance at the window. It was not likely that she would see it. She was running to overtake the others; she carried a flare in her right hand, so that the blaze came between her and the rope. And she was waving the light in a mad woman's frenzy, as she danced along, hounding on the men to the sack.

But, as if the presence of the man who had wronged her had over her some subtle influence--as if some sense, unowned by others, warned her of his presence, even in the midst of that babel and tumult--she stopped short under him, with her foot almost on the threshold. I saw her head turn slowly. She raised her eyes, holding the torch aside. She saw him!

With a scream of joy, she sprang to the foot of the rope, and began to haul at it as if in that way she might get to him sooner; while she filled the air with her shrieks and laughter. The men, who had gone into the house, heard her, and came out again; and after them others. I quailed, where I knelt on the parapet, as I looked down and met the wolfish glare of their upturned eyes; what, then, must have been the thoughts of the wretched man taken in his selfishness--hanging there helpless between earth and heaven? God knows.

He began to climb upwards, to return; and actually ascended hand over hand a dozen feet. But he had been supporting himself for some minutes, and at that point his strength failed him. Human muscles could do no more. He tried to haul himself up to the next knot, but sank back with a groan. Then he looked at me. "Pull me up!" he gasped in a voice just audible. "For God's sake! For God's sake, pull me up!"

But the wretches below had the end of the rope, and it was impossible to raise him, even had I possessed the strength to do it. I told him so, and bade him climb--climb for his life. In a moment it would be too late.

He understood. He raised himself with a jerk to the next knot, and hung there. Another desperate effort, and he gained the next; though I could almost hear his muscles crack, and his breath came in gasps. Three more knots--they were about a foot apart--and he would reach the coping.

But as he turned up his face to me, I read despair in his eyes. His strength was gone; and while he hung there, the men began, with shouts of laughter, to shake the rope this way and that. He lost his grip, and, with a groan, slid down three or four feet; and again got hold and hung there--silent.

By this time the group below had grown into a crowd--a crowd of maddened beings, raving and howling, and leaping up at him as dogs leap at food; and the horror of the sight, though the doomed man's features were now in shadow, and I could not read them, overcame me. I rose to draw back--shuddering, listening for his fall. Instead, before I had quite retreated, a hot flash blinded me, and almost scorched my face, and, as the sharp report of a pistol rang out, the steward's body plunged headlong down--leaving a little cloud of smoke where I stood.

He had balked his enemies.

CHAPTER IX
THE TRICOLOUR

It was known afterwards that they fell upon the body and tore it, like the dogs they were; but I had seen enough. I reeled back, and for a few moments leaned against the chimney, trembling like a woman, sick and faint. The horrid drama had had only one spectator--myself; and the strange solitude from which I had viewed it, kneeling at the edge of the roof of the Château, with the night wind on my brow and the tumult far below me, had shaken me to the bottom of my soul. Had the ruffians come upon me then I could not have lifted a finger; but, fortunately, though the awakening came quickly, it came by another hand. I heard the rustle of feet behind me, and, turning, found Mademoiselle de St. Alais at my shoulder, her small face grey in the gloom.

"Monsieur," she said, "will you come?"

I sprang up, ashamed and conscience-stricken. I had forgotten her, all, in the tragedy. "What is it?" I said.

"The house is burning."

She said it so calmly, in such a voice, that I could not believe her, or that I understood; though it was the thing I had told myself must happen. "What, Mademoiselle? This house?" I said stupidly.

"Yes," she replied, as quietly as before. "The smoke is rising through the closet staircase. I think that they have set the east wing on fire."

I hastened back with her, but before I reached the little door by which we had ascended I saw that it was true. A faint, whitish eddy of smoke, scarcely visible in the dusk, was rising through the crack between door and lintel. When we came up the women were still round it watching it; but while I looked, dazed and wondering what we were to do, the group melted away, and Mademoiselle and I were left alone beside the stream of smoke that grew each moment thicker and darker.

A few moments before, immediately after my escape from the rooms below, I had thought that I could face this peril; anything, everything, had then seemed better than to be caught with the women, in the confinement of those luxurious rooms, perfumed with *poudre de rose*, and heavy with jasmine--to be caught there by the brutes who were pursuing us. Now the danger that showed itself most pressing seemed the worst. "We must take off the bricks!" I cried. "Quick, and open that door! There is nothing else for it. Come, Mademoiselle, if you please!"

"They are doing it," she answered.

Then I saw whither the women and the servants had gone. They were already beside the other door, the trap-door, labouring frantically to remove the bricks we had piled on it. In a moment I caught the infection of their haste.

"Come, Mademoiselle! come!" I cried, advancing involuntarily a step towards the group. "Very likely the rogues below will be plundering now, and we may pass safely. At any rate, there is nothing else for it."

I was still flurried and shaken--I say it with shame--by Gargouf's fate; and when she did not answer at once, I looked round impatiently. To my astonishment, she was gone. In the darkness, it was not easy to see any one at a distance of a dozen feet, and the reek of the smoke was spreading. Still, she had been at my elbow a moment before, she could not be far off. I took a step this way and that, and looked again anxiously; and then I found her. She was kneeling against a chimney, her face buried in her hands. Her hair covered her shoulders, and partly hid her white robe.

I thought the time ill-chosen, and I touched her angrily. "Mademoiselle!" I said. "There is not a moment to be lost! Come! they have opened the door!"

She looked up at me, and the still pallor of her face sobered me. "I am not coming," she said, in a low voice. "Farewell, Monsieur!"

"You are not coming?" I cried.

"No, Monsieur; save yourself," she answered firmly and quietly. And she looked up at me with her hands still clasped before her, as if she were fain to return to her prayers, and waited only for me to go.

I gasped.

"But, Mademoiselle!" I cried, staring at the white-robed figure, that in the gloom--a gloom riven now and again by hot flashes, as some burning spark soared upwards--seemed scarcely earthly--"But, Mademoiselle, you do not understand. This is no child's play. To stay here is death! death! The house is burning under us. Presently the roof, on which we stand, will fall in, and then----"

"Better that," she answered, raising her head with heaven knows what of womanly dignity, caught in this supreme moment by her, a child--"Better that, than that I should fall into their hands. I am a St. Alais, and I can die," she continued firmly. "But I must not fall into their hands. Do you, Monsieur, save yourself. Go now, and I will pray for you."

"And I for you, Mademoiselle," I answered, with a full heart. "If you stay, I stay."

She looked at me a moment, her face troubled. Then she rose slowly to her feet. The servants had disappeared, the trap-door lay open; no one had yet come up. We had the roof to ourselves. I saw her shudder as she looked round; and in a second I had her in my arms--she was no heavier than a child--and was half-way across the roof. She uttered a faint cry of remonstrance, of reproach, and for an instant struggled with me. But I only held her the tighter, and ran on. From the trap-door a ladder led downwards; somehow, still holding her with one hand, I stumbled down it, until I reached the foot, and found myself in a passage, which was all dark. One way, however, a light shone at the end of it.

I carried her towards this, her hair lying across my lips, her face against my breast. She no longer struggled, and in a moment I came to the head of a staircase. It seemed to be a servant's staircase, for it was bare, and mean, and narrow, with white-washed walls that were not too clean. There were no signs of fire here, even the smoke had not yet reached this part; but half-way down the flight a candle, overturned, but still burning, lay on a step, as if some one had that moment dropped it. And from all the lower part of the house came up a great noise of riot and revelry, coarse shrieks, and shouts, and laughter. I paused to listen.

Mademoiselle lifted herself a little in my arms. "Put me down, Monsieur," she whispered.

"You will come?"

"I will do what you tell me."

I set her down in the angle of the passage, at the head of the stairs; and in a whisper I asked her what was beyond the door, which I could see at the foot of the flight.

"The kitchen," she answered.

"If I had any cloak to cover you," I said, "I think that we could pass. They are not searching for us. They are robbing and drinking."

"Will you get the candle?" she whispered, trembling. "In one of these rooms we may find something."

I went softly down the bare stairs, and, picking it up, returned with it in my hand. As I came back to her, our eyes met, and a slow blush, gradually deepening, crept over her face, as dawn creeps over a grey sky. Having come, it stayed; her eyes fell, and she turned a little away from me, confused and frightened. We were alone; and for the first time that night, I think, she remembered her loosened hair and the disorder of her dress--that she was a woman and I a man.

It was a strange time to think of such things; when at any instant the door at the foot of the stairs before us might open, and a dozen ruffians stream up, bent on plunder, and worse. But the look and the movement warmed my heart, and set my blood running as it had never run before. I felt my courage return in a flood, and with it twice my strength. I felt capable of holding the staircase against a hundred, a thousand, as long as she stood at the top. Above all, I wondered how I could have borne her in my arms a minute before, how I could have held her head against my breast, and felt her hair touch my lips, and been insensible! Never again should I carry her so with an even pulse. The knowledge of that came to me as I stood beside her at the head of the bare stairs, affecting to listen to the noises below, that she might have time to recover herself.

A moment, and I began to listen seriously; for the uproar in the kitchen through which we must pass to escape, was growing louder; and at the same time that I noticed this, a smell of burning wood, with a whiff of smoke, reached my nostrils, and warned me that the fire was extending to the wing in which we stood. Behind us, as we stood, looking down the stairs, was a door; along the passage to the left by which we had come were other doors. I thrust the candle into Mademoiselle's hands, and begged her to go and look in the rooms.

"There may be a cloak, or something!" I said eagerly. "We must not linger. If you will look, I will----"

No more; for as the last word trembled on my lips the door at the foot of the stairs flew open, and a man blundered through it and began to ascend towards us, two steps at a time. He carried a candle before him, and a large bar in his right hand; and a savage roar of voices came with him through the doorway.

He appeared so suddenly that we had no time to move. I had a side glimpse of Mademoiselle standing spell-bound with horror, the light drooping in her hand. Then I snatched the candle from her and quenched it; and, plucking it from the iron candlestick, stood waiting, with the latter in my hand--waiting, stooping forward, for the man. I had left my sword in the farther wing, and had no other weapon; but the stairs were narrow, the sloping ceiling low, and the candlestick might do. If his comrades did not follow him, it might do.

He came up rapidly, two-thirds of the way, holding the light high in front of him. Only four or five steps divided him from us! Then on a sudden, he stumbled, swore, and fell heavily forwards. The light in his hand went out, and we were in darkness!

Instinctively I gripped Mademoiselle's hand in my left hand to stay the scream that I knew was on her lips; then we stood like two statues, scarcely daring to breathe. The man, so near us, and yet unconscious of our presence, got up swearing; and, after a terrible moment of suspense, during which I think he fumbled for the candle, he began to clatter down the stairs again. They had closed the door at the bottom, and he could not for a moment find the string of the latch. But at last he found it, and opened the door. Then I stepped back, and under cover of the babel that instantly poured up the staircase I drew Mademoiselle into the room behind us, and, closing the door which faced the stairs, stood listening.

I fancied that I could hear her heart beating. I could certainly hear my own. In this room we seemed for the moment safe; but how were we, without a light, to find anything to disguise her? How were we to pass through the kitchen? And in a moment I began to regret that I had left the stairs. We were in perfect darkness here and could see nothing in the room, which had a close, unused smell, as of mice; but even as I noticed this the fumes of burning wood, which had doubtless entered with us, grew stronger and overcame the other smell. The rushing wind-like sound of the fire, as it caught hold of the wing, began to be audible, and the distant crackling of flames. My heart sank.

"Mademoiselle," I said softly. I still held her hand.

"Yes, Monsieur," she murmured faintly. And she seemed to lean against me.

"Are there no windows in this room?"

"I think that they are shuttered," she murmured.

With a new thought in my mind, that the way of the kitchen being hopeless we might escape by the windows, I moved a pace to look for them.

I would have loosed her hand to do this, that my own might be free to grope before me, but to my surprise she clung to me and would not let me go. Then in the darkness I heard her sigh, as if she were about to swoon; and she fell against me.

"Courage, Mademoiselle, courage!" I said, terrified by the mere thought.

"Oh, I am frightened!" she moaned in my ear. "I am frightened! Save me, Monsieur, save me!"

She had been so brave before that I wondered; not knowing that the bravest woman's courage is of this quality. But I had short time for wonder. Her weight hung each instant more dead in my arms, and my heart beating wildly as I held her I looked round for help, for a thought, for an idea. But all was dark. I could not remember even where the door stood by which we had entered. I peered in vain, for the slightest glimmer of light that might betray the windows. I was alone with her and helpless, our way of retreat cut off, the flames approaching. I felt her head fall back and knew that she had swooned; and in the dark I could do no more than support her, and listen and listen for the returning steps of the man, or what else would happen next.

For a long time, a long time it seemed to me, nothing happened. Then a sudden burst of sound told me that the door at the foot of the stairs had been opened again; and on that followed a clatter of wooden shoes on the bare stairs. I could judge now where the door of the room was, and I quickly but tenderly laid Mademoiselle on the floor a little behind it, and waited myself on the threshold. I still had my candlestick, and I was desperate.

I heard them pass, my heart beating; and then I heard them pause and I clutched my weapon; and then a voice I knew gave an order, and with a cry of joy I dragged open the door of the room and stood before them--stood before them, as they told me afterwards, with the face of a ghost or a man risen from the dead.

There were four of them, and the nearest to us was Father Benôit.

The good priest fell on my neck and kissed me. "You are not hurt?" he cried.

"No," I said dully. "You have come then?"

"Yes," he said. "In time to save you, God be praised! God be praised! And Mademoiselle? Mademoiselle de St. Alais?" he added eagerly, looking at me as if he thought I was not quite in my senses. "Have you news of her?"

I turned without a word, and went back into the room. He followed with a light, and the three men, of whom Buton was one, pressed in after him.

They were rough peasants, but the sight made them give back, and uncover themselves. Mademoiselle lay where I had left her, her head pillowed on a dark carpet of hair; from the midst of which her child's face, composed and white as in death, looked up with solemn half-closed eyes to the ceiling. For myself, I stared down at her almost without emotion, so much had I gone through. But the priest cried out aloud.

"*Mon Dieu!*" he said, with a sob in his voice. "Have they killed her?"

"No," I answered. "She has only fainted. If there is a woman here----"

"There is no woman here that I dare trust," he answered between his teeth. And he bade one of the men go and get some water, adding a few words which I did not hear.

The man returned almost immediately, and Father Benôit, bidding him and his fellows stand back a little, moistened her lips with water, afterwards dashing some in her face; doing it with an air of haste that puzzled me until I noticed that the room was grown thick with smoke, and on going myself to the door saw the red glow of the fire at the end of the passage, and heard the distant crash of falling stones and timbers. Then I thought that I understood the men's attitude, and I suggested to Father Benôit that I should carry her out.

"She will never recover here," I said, with a sob in my throat. "She will be suffocated if we do not get her into the air."

A thick volume of smoke swept along the passage as I spoke, and gave point to my words.

"Yes," the priest said slowly, "I think so, too, my son, but----"

"But what?" I cried. "It is not safe to stay!"

"You sent to Cahors?"

"Yes," I answered. "Has M. le Marquis come?"

"No; and you see, M. le Vicomte, I have only these four men," he explained. "Had I stayed to gather more I might have been too late. And with these only I do not know what to do. Half the poor wretches who have done this mischief are mad with drink. Others are strangers, and----"

"But I thought--I thought that it was all over," I cried in astonishment.

"No," he answered gravely. "They let us pass in after an altercation; I am of the Committee, and so is Buton there. But when they see you, and especially Mademoiselle de St. Alais--I do not know how they may act, my friend."

"But, *mon Dieu!*" I cried. "Surely they will not dare----"

"No, Monseigneur, have no fear, they shall not dare!"

The words came out of the smoke. The speaker was Buton. As he spoke, he stepped forward, swinging the ponderous bar he carried, his huge hairy arms bare to the elbow. "Yet there is one thing you must do," he said.

"What?"

"You must put on the tricolour. They will not dare to touch that."

He spoke with a simple pride, which at the moment I found unintelligible. I understand it better now. Nay, on the morrow, it was no riddle to me, though an abiding wonder.

The priest sprang at the idea. "Good," he said. "Buton has hit it! They will respect that."

And before I could speak he had detached the large rosette which he wore on his *soutane*, and was pinning it on my breast.

"Now yours, Buton," he continued; and taking the smith's--it was not too clean--he fixed it on Mademoiselle's left shoulder. "There," he said eagerly, when it was done. "Now, M. le Vicomte, take her up. Quick, or we shall be stifled. Buton and I will go before you, and our friends here will follow you."

Mademoiselle was beginning to come to herself with sighs and sobs, when I raised her in my arms; and we were all coughing with the smoke. This in the passage outside was choking; had we delayed a minute longer we could not have passed out safely, for already the flames were beginning to lick the door of the next room, and dart out angry tongues towards us. As it was, we stumbled down the stairs in some fashion, one helping another; and checked for an instant by the closed door at the bottom, were glad to fall when it was opened pell-mell in the kitchen, where we stood with smarting eyes, gasping for breath.

It was the grand kitchen of the Château that had seen many a feast prepared, and many a quarry brought home; but for Mademoiselle's sake I was glad that her face was against my breast, and that she could not see it now. A great fire, fed high with fat and hams, blazed on the hearth, and before it, instead of meat, the carcases of three dogs hung from the jack, and tainted the air with the smell of burning flesh. They were M. le Marquis' favourite hounds, killed in pure wantonness. Below them the floor, strewn with bottles, ran deep in wasted wine, out of which piles of shattered furniture and staved casks rose like islands. All that the rioters had not taken they had spoiled; even now in one corner a woman was filling her apron with salt from a huge trampled heap, and at the battered *dressoir* three or four men were plundering. The main body of the peasants, however, had retired outside, where they could be heard fiercely cheering on the flames, shouting when a chimney fell or a window burst, and flinging into the fire every living thing unlucky enough to fall into their hands. The plunderers, on seeing us, sneaked out with grim looks like wolves driven from the prey. Doubtless, they spread the news; for while we paused, though it was only for a moment, in the middle of the floor, the uproar outside ceased, and gave place to a strange silence in the midst of which we appeared at the door.

The glare of the burning house threw a light as strong as that of day on the scene before us; on the line of savage frenzied faces that confronted us, and the great pile of wreckage that stood about and bore witness to their fury. But for a moment the light failed to show us to them; we were in the shadow of the wall, and it was not until we had advanced some paces that the ominous silence was broken, and the mob, with a howl of rage, sprang forward, like bloodhounds slipped from the leash. Low-browed and shock-headed, half-naked, and black with smoke and blood, they seemed more like beasts than men; and like beasts they came on, snapping the teeth and snarling, while from the rear--for the foremost were past speech--came screams of "*Mort aux Tyrans! Mort aux Accapareurs!*" that, mingling with the tumult of the fire, were enough to scare the stoutest.

Had my escort blenched for an instant our fate was sealed. But they stood firm, and before their stern front all but one man quailed and fell back--fell back snarling and crying for our blood. That one came on, and aimed a blow at me with a knife. On the instant Buton raised his iron bar, and with a stentorian cry of "Respect the Tricolour!" struck him to the ground, and strode over him.

"Respect the Tricolour!" he shouted again, with the voice of a bull; and the effect of the words was magical. The crowd heard, fell back, and fell aside, staring stupidly at me and my burden.

"Respect the Tricolour!" Father Benôit cried, raising his hand aloft; and he made the sign of the cross. On that in an instant a hundred voices took it up; and almost before I could apprehend the change, those who a moment earlier had been gaping for our blood were thrusting one another back, and shouting as with one voice, "Way, way for the Tricolour!"

There was something unutterably new, strange, formidable in this reverence; this respect paid by these savages to a word, a ribbon, an idea. It made an impression on me that was never quite effaced. But at the moment I was scarcely conscious of this. I heard and saw things dully. Like a man in a dream, I walked through the crowd, and, stumbling under my burden, passed down the lane of brutish faces, down the avenue, down to the gate. There Father Benôit would have taken Mademoiselle from me, but I would not let him.

"To Saux! To Saux!" I said feverishly; and then, I scarcely knew how, I found myself on a horse holding her before me. And we were on the road to Saux, lighted on our way by the flames of the burning Château.

CHAPTER X
THE MORNING AFTER THE STORM

Father Benôit had the forethought, when we reached the cross-roads, to leave a man there to await the party from Cahors, and warn them of Mademoiselle's safety; and we had not ridden more than half a mile before the clatter of hoofs behind us announced that they were following. I was beginning to recover from the stupor into which the excitement of the night had thrown me, and I reined up to deliver over my charge, should M. de St. Alais desire to take her.

But he was not of the party. The leader was Louis, and his company consisted, to my surprise, of no more than six or seven servants, old M. de Gontaut, one of the Harincourts, and a strange gentleman. Their horses were panting and smoking with the speed at which they had come, and the men's eyes glittered with excitement. No one seemed to think it strange that I carried Mademoiselle; but all, after hurriedly thanking God that she was safe, hastened to ask the number of the rioters.

"Nearly a hundred," I said. "As far as I could judge. But where is M. le Marquis?"

"He had not returned when the alarm came."

"You are a small party?"

Louis swore with vexation. "I could get no more," he said. "News came at the same time that Marignac's house was on fire, and he carried off a dozen. A score of others took fright, and thought it might be the same with them; and they saddled up in haste, and went to see. In fact," he continued bitterly, "it seemed to me to be every one for himself. Always excepting my good friends here."

M. de Gontaut began to chuckle, but choked for want of breath. "Beauty in distress!" he gasped. Poor fellow, he could scarcely sit his horse.

"But you will come on to Saux?" I said. They were turning their horses in a cloud of steam that mistily lit up the night.

"No!" Louis answered, with another oath; and I did not wonder that he was not himself, that his usual good nature had deserted him. "It is now or never! If we can catch them at this work----"

I did not hear the rest. The trampling of their horses, as they drove in the spurs and started down the road, drowned the words. In a moment they were fifty paces away; all but one, who, detaching himself at the last moment, turned his horse's head, and rode up to me. It was the stranger, the only one of the party, not a servant, whom I did not know.

"How are they armed, if you please?" he asked.

"They have at least one gun," I said, looking at him curiously. "And by this time probably more. The mass of them had pikes and pitchforks."

"And a leader?"

"Petit Jean, the smith, of St. Alais, gave orders."

"Thank you, M. le Vicomte," he said, and saluted. Then, touching his horse with the spur, he rode off at speed after the others.

I was in no condition to help them, and I was anxious to put Mademoiselle, who lay in my arms like one dead, in the women's care. The moment they were gone, therefore, we pursued our way, Father Benôit and I silent and full of thought, the others chattering to one another without pause or stay. Mademoiselle's head lay on my right shoulder. I could feel the faint beating of her heart; and in that slow, dark ride had time to think of many things: of her courage and will and firmness--this poor little convent-bred one, who a fortnight before had not found a word to throw at me; last, but not least, of the womanly weakness, dear to my man's heart, that had sapped her reserve at last, and brought her arms to my neck and her cry to my ear. The faint perfume of her hair was in my nostrils; I longed to kiss the half-shrouded head. But, if in an hour I had learned to love her, I had learned to honour her more; and I repressed the impulse, and only held her more gently, and tried to think of other things until she should be out of my arms.

If I did not find that so easy, it was not for want of food for thought. The glow of the fire behind us reddened all the sky at our backs; the murmur of the mob pursued us; more than once, as we went, a figure sneaked by us in the blackness, and fled, as if to join them. Father Benôit fancied that there was a second fire a league to the east; and in the tumult and upheaval of all things on this night, and the consequent confusion of thought into which I had fallen, it would scarcely have surprised me if flames had broken out before us also, and announced that Saux was burning.

But I was spared that. On the contrary, the whole village came out to meet us, and accompanied us, cheering, from the gates to the door of the Château, where, in the glare of the lights they carried, and amid a great silence of curiosity and expectation, Mademoiselle was lifted from my saddle and carried into the house. The women who pressed round the door to see, stooped forward to follow her with their eyes; but none as I followed her.

Much that passes for fair at night wears a foul look by day; and things tolerable in the suffering have a knack of seeming fantastically impossible in the retrospect. When I awoke next morning, in the great chair in the hall--wherein, tradition had it, Louis the Thirteenth had once sat--and, after three hours of troubled sleep, found André standing over me, and the sun pouring in through door and window, I fancied for a moment that the events of the night, as I remembered them, were a dream. Then my eyes fell on a brace of pistols, which I had placed by my side over night, and on the tray at which Father Benôit and I had refreshed ourselves; and I knew that the things had happened. I sprang up.

"Is M. de St. Alais here?" I said.

"No, Monsieur."

"Nor M. le Comte?"

"No, Monsieur."

"What!" I said. "Have none of the party come?" For I had gone to sleep expecting to be called up to receive them within the hour.

"No, M. le Vicomte," the old man answered, "except--except one gentleman who was with them, and who is now walking with M. le Curé in the garden. And for him----"

"Well?" I said sharply, for André, who had got on his most gloomy and dogmatic air, stopped with a sniff of contempt.

"He does not seem to be a man for whom M. le Vicomte should be roused," he answered obstinately. "But M. le Curé would have it; and in these days, I suppose, we must tramp for a smith, let alone an officer of excise."

"Buton is here, then?"

"Yes, Monsieur; and walking on the terrace, as if of the family. I do not know what things are coming to," André continued, grumbling, and raising his voice as I started to go out, "or what they would be at. But when M. le

Vicomte took away the *carcan* I knew what was likely to happen. Oh! yes," he went on still more loudly, while he stood holding the tray, and looking after me with a sour face, "I knew what would happen! I knew what would happen!"

And, certainly, if I had not been shaken completely out of the common rut of thought, I should have found something odd, myself, in the combination of the three men whom I found on the terrace. They were walking up and down, Father Benôit, with downcast eyes and his hands behind him, in the middle. On one side of him moved Buton, coarse, heavy-shouldered, and clumsy, in his stained blouse; on the other side paced the stranger of last night, a neat, middle-sized man, very plainly dressed, with riding boots and a sword. Remembering that he had formed one of Louis' party, I was surprised to see that he wore the tricolour; but I forgot this in my anxiety to know what had become of the others. Without standing on ceremony, I asked him.

"They attacked the rioters, lost one man, and were beaten off," he answered with dry precision.

"And M. le Comte?"

"Was not hurt. He returned to Cahors, to raise more men. I, as my advice seemed to be taken in ill part, came here."

He spoke in a blunt, straightforward way, as to an equal; and at once seemed to be, and not to be, a gentleman. The Curé, seeing that he puzzled me, hastened to introduce him.

"This, M. le Vicomte," he said, "is M. le Capitaine Hugues, late of the American Army. He has placed his services at the disposal of the Committee."

"For the purpose," the Captain went on, before I had made up my mind how to take it, "of drilling and commanding a body of men to be raised in Quercy to keep the peace. Call them militia; call them what you like."

I was a good deal taken aback. The man, alert, active, practical, with the butt of a pistol peeping from his pocket, was something new to me.

"You have served his Majesty?" I said at last, to gain time to think.

"No," he answered. "There are no careers in that army, unless you have so many quarterings. I served under General Washington."

"But I saw you last night with M. de St. Alais?"

"Why not, M. le Vicomte?" he answered, looking at me plainly. "I heard that a house was being burned. I had just arrived, and I placed myself at M. le Comte's disposal. But they had no method, and would take no advice."

"Well," I said, "these seem to me to be rather extreme steps. You know---"

"M. de Marignac's house was burned last night," the Curé said softly.

"Oh!"

"And I fear that we shall hear of others. I think that we must look matters in the face, M. le Vicomte."

"It is not a question of thinking or looking, but of doing!" the Captain said, interrupting him harshly. "We have a long summer's day before us, but if by to-night we have not done something, there will be a sorry dawning in Quercy to-morrow."

"There are the King's troops," I said.

"They refuse to obey orders. Therefore, they are worse than useless."

"Their officers?"

"They are staunch; but the people hate them. A knight of St. Louis is to the mob what a red rag is to a bull. I can answer for it that they have enough to do to keep their men in barracks, and guard their own heads."

I resented his familiarity, and the impatience with which he spoke; but, resent it as I might, I could not return to the tone I had used yesterday. Then it had seemed an outrageous thing that Buton should stand by and listen. To-day the same thing had an ordinary air. And this, moreover, was a different man from Doury; arguments that had crushed the one would have no weight with the other. I saw that, and, rather helplessly, I asked Father Benôit what he would have.

He did not answer. It was the Captain who replied. "We want you to join the Committee," he said briskly.

"I discussed that yesterday," I answered with some stiffness. "I cannot do so. Father Benôit will tell you so."

"It is not Father Benôit's answer I want," the Captain replied. "It is yours, M. le Vicomte."

"I answered yesterday," I said haughtily--"and refused."

"Yesterday is not to-day," he retorted. "M. de St. Alais' house stood yesterday; it is a smoking ruin today. M. de Marignac's likewise. Yesterday much was conjecture. To-day facts speak for themselves. A few hours' hesitation, and the province will be in a blaze from one end to the other."

I could not gainsay this; at the same time there was one other thing I could not do, and that was change my views again. Having solemnly put on the white cockade in Madame St. Alais' drawing-room, I had not the courage to execute another *volte-face*. I could not recant again.

"It is impossible--impossible in my case," I stammered at last peevishly, and in a disjointed way. "Why do you come again to me? Why do you not go to some one else? There are two hundred others whose names----"

"Would be of no use to us," M. le Capitaine answered brusquely; "whereas yours would reassure the fearful, attach some moderate men to the cause and not disgust the masses. Let me be frank with you, M. le Vicomte," he continued in a different tone. "I want your co-operation. I am here to take risks, but none that are unnecessary; and I prefer that my commission should issue from above as well as from below. Add your name to the Committee and I accept their commission. Without doubt I could police Quercy in the name of the Third Estate, but I would rather hang, draw, and quarter in the name of all three."

"Still, there are others----"

"You forget that I have got to rule the *canaille* in Cahors," he answered impatiently, "as well as these mad clowns, who think that the end of the world is here. And those others you speak of----"

"Are not acceptable," Father Benôit said gently, looking at me with yearning in his kind eyes. The light morning air caught the skirts of his cassock as he spoke, and lifted them from his lean figure. He held his shovel hat in his hand, between his face and the sun. I knew that there was a conflict in his mind as in mine, and that he would have me and would have me not; and the knowledge strengthened me to resist his words.

"It is impossible," I said.

"Why?"

I was spared the necessity of answering. I had my face to the door of the house, and as the last word was spoken saw André issue from it with M. de St. Alais. The manner in which the old servant cried, "M. le Marquis de St. Alais, to see M. le Vicomte!" gave us a little shock, it was so full of sly triumph; but nothing on M. de St. Alais' part, as he approached, betrayed that he noticed this. He advanced with an air perfectly gay, and saluted me with good humour. For a moment I fancied that he did not know what had happened in the night; his first words, however, dispelled the idea.

"M. le Vicomte," he said, addressing me with both ease and grace, "we are for ever grateful to you. I was abroad on business last night, and could do nothing; and my brother must, I am told, have come too late, even if, with so small a force, he could effect anything. I saw Mademoiselle as I passed through the house, and she gave me some particulars."

"She has left her room?" I cried in surprise. The other three had drawn back a little, so that we enjoyed a kind of privacy.

"Yes," he answered, smiling slightly at my tone. "And I can assure you, M. le Vicomte, has spoken as highly of you as a maiden dare. For the rest, my mother will convey the thanks of the family to you more fitly than I can. Still, I may hope that you are none the worse."

I muttered that I was not; but I hardly knew what I said. St. Alais' demeanour was so different from that which I had anticipated, his easy calmness and gaiety were so unlike the rage and heat which seemed natural in one who had just heard of the destruction of his house and the murder of his steward, that I was completely nonplussed. He appeared to be dressed with his usual care and distinction, though I was bound to suppose that he had been up all night; and, though the outrages at St. Alais and Marignac's had given the lie to his most confident predictions, he betrayed no sign of vexation.

All this dazzled and confused me; yet I must say something. I muttered a hope that Mademoiselle was not greatly shaken by her experiences.

"I think not," he said. "We St. Alais are not made of sugar. And after a night's rest--- But I fear that I am interrupting you?" And for the first time he let his eyes rest on my companions.

"It is to Father Benôit and to Buton here, that your thanks are really due, M. le Marquis," I said. "For without their aid----"

"That is so, is it?" he said coldly. "I had heard it."

"But not all?" I exclaimed.

"I think so," he said. Then, continuing to look at them, though he spoke to me, he continued: "Let me tell you an apologue, M. le Vicomte. Once upon a time there was a man who had a grudge against a neighbour because the good man's crops were better than his. He went, therefore, secretly and by night, and not all at once--not all at once, Messieurs, but little by little-- he let on to his neighbour's land the stream of a river that flowed by both their farms. He succeeded so well that presently the flood not only covered the crops, but threatened to drown his neighbour, and after that his own crops and himself! Apprised too late of his folly---- But how do you like the apologue, M. le Curé?"

"It does not touch me," Father Benôit answered with a wan smile.

"I am no man's servant, as the slave boasted," St. Alais answered with a polite sneer.

"For shame! for shame, M. le Marquis!" I cried, losing patience. "I have told you that but for M. le Curé and the smith here, Mademoiselle and I----"

"And I have told you," he answered, interrupting me with grim good humour, "what I think of it, M. le Vicomte! That is all."

"But you do not know what happened?" I persisted, stung to wrath by his injustice. "You are not, you cannot be, aware that when Father Benôit and his companions arrived, Mademoiselle de St. Alais and I were in the most desperate plight? that they saved us only at great risk to themselves? and that for our safety at last you have to thank rather the tricolour, which those wretches respected, than any display of force which we were able to make."

"That, too, is so, is it?" he said, his face grown dark. "I shall have something to say to it presently. But, first, may I ask you a question, M. le Vicomte? Am I right in supposing that these gentlemen are waiting on you from--pardon me if I do not get the title correctly--the Honourable the Committee of Public Safety?"

I nodded.

"And I presume that I may congratulate them on your answer?"

"No, you may not!" I replied, with satisfaction. "This gentleman"--and I pointed to the Capitaine Hugues--"has laid before me certain proposals and certain arguments in favour of them."

"But he has not laid before you the most potent of all arguments," the Captain said, interposing, with a dry bow. "I find it, and you, M. le Vicomte, will find it, too, in M. le Marquis de St. Alais!"

The Marquis stared at him coldly. "I am obliged to you," he said contemptuously. "By-and-by, perhaps, I shall have more to say to you. For the present, however, I am speaking to M. le Vicomte." And he turned and addressed me again. "These gentlemen have waited on you. Do I understand that you have declined their proposals?"

"Absolutely!" I answered. "But," I continued warmly, "it does not follow that I am without gratitude or natural feeling."

"Ah!" he said. Then, turning, with an easy air, "I see your servant there," he said. "May I summon him one moment?"

"Certainly."

He raised his hand, and André, who was watching us from the doorway, flew to take his orders.

He turned to me again. "Have I your permission?"

I bowed, wondering.

"Go, my friend, to Mademoiselle de St. Alais," he said. "She is in the hall. Beg her to be so good as to honour us with her presence."

André went, with his most pompous air; and we remained, wondering. No one spoke. I longed to consult Father Benôit by a look, but I dared not do so, lest the Marquis, who kept his eyes on my face, his own wearing an enigmatical smile, should take it for a sign of weakness. So we stood until Mademoiselle appeared in the doorway, and, after a momentary pause, came timidly along the terrace towards us.

She wore a frock which I believe had been my mother's, and was too long for her; but it seemed to my eyes to suit her admirably. A kerchief covered her shoulders, and she had another laid lightly on her unpowdered hair, which, knotted up loosely, strayed in tiny ringlets over her neck and ears. To this charming disarray, her blushes, as she came towards us, shading her eyes from the sun, added the last piquancy. I had not seen her since the women lifted her from my saddle, and, seeing her now, coming along the terrace in the fresh morning light, I thought her divine! I wondered how I could have let her go. An insane desire to defy her brother and whirl her off, out of this horrid imbroglio of parties and politics, seized upon me.

But she did not look towards me, and my heart sank. She had eyes only for M. le Marquis; approaching him as if he had a magnet which drew her to him.

"Mademoiselle," he said gravely, "I am told that your escape last night was due to your adoption of an emblem, which I see that you are still wearing. It is one which no subject of his Majesty can wear with honour. Will you oblige me by removing it?"

Pale and red by turns, she shot a piteous glance at us. "Monsieur?" she muttered, as if she did not understand.

"I think I have spoken plainly," he said. "Be good enough to remove it."

Wincing under the rebuke, she hesitated, looking for a moment as if she would burst into tears. Then, with her lip trembling, and with trembling fingers, she complied, and began to unfasten the tricolour, which the servants--without her knowledge, it may be--had removed from the robe she had worn to that which she now wore. It took her a long time to remove it, under our eyes, and I grew hot with indignation. But I dared not interfere, and the others looked on gravely.

"Thank you," M. de Alais said, when, at last, she had succeeded in unpinning it. "I know, Mademoiselle, that you are a true St. Alais, and would die rather than owe your life to disloyalty. Be good enough to throw that down, and tread upon it."

She started violently at the words. I think we all did. I know that I took a step forward, and, but for M. le Marquis' raised hand, must have intervened. But I had no right; we were spectators, it was for her to act. She stood a moment with all our eyes upon her, stood staring breathless and motionless at her brother; then, still looking at him, with a shivering sigh, she slowly and mechanically lifted her hand, and dropped the ribbon. It fluttered down.

"Tread upon it!" the Marquis said ruthlessly.

She trembled; her face, her child's face, grown quite white. But she did not move.

"Tread upon it!" he said again.

And then, without looking down, she moved her foot forward, and touched the ribbon.

CHAPTER XI
THE TWO CAMPS

"Thank you, Mademoiselle; now you can go," he said.

But he need not have spoken, for the moment his sister had done his bidding she turned from us; before two words had passed his lips she was hurrying back to the house in a passion of grief, her face covered, and her slight figure shaken by sobs that came back to us on the summer air.

The sight stung me to rage; yet for a moment, and by a tremendous effort I restrained myself. I would hear him out.

But he either did not, or would not see the effect he had produced. "There, Messieurs," he said, his face somewhat pale. "I am obliged to your patience. Now you know what I think of your tricolour and your services. It shall shelter neither me nor mine! I hold no parley with assassins."

I sprang forward, I could contain myself no longer. "And I!" I cried, "I, M. le Marquis, have something to say, too! I have something to declare! A moment ago I refused that tricolour! I rejected the overtures of those who brought it to me. I was resolved to stand by you and by my brethren against my better judgment. I was of your party, though I did not believe in it; and you might have tied me to it. But this gentleman is right, you are yourself the strongest argument against yourself. And I do this! I do this!" I repeated passionately. "See, M. le Marquis, and know that it is your doing!"

With the word I snatched up the ribbon, on which Mademoiselle had trodden, and with fingers that trembled scarcely less than hers had trembled, when she unfastened it, I pinned it on my breast.

He bowed, with a sardonic smile. "A cockade is easily changed," he said. But I could see that he was livid with rage; that he could have slain me for the rebuke.

"You mean," I said hotly, "that I am easily turned."

"You put on the cap, M. le Vicomte," he retorted.

The other three had withdrawn a little--not without open signs of disgust--and left us face to face on the spot on which we had stood three weeks before on the eve of his mother's reception. Still raging with anger on Mademoiselle's account, and minded to wound him, I recalled that to him, and the prophecies he had then uttered, prophecies which had been so ill-fulfilled.

He took me up at the second word. "Ill-fulfilled?" he said grimly. "Yes, M. le Vicomte, but why? Because those who should support me, those who from one end of France to the other should support the King, are like you--waverers who do not know their own minds! Because the gentlemen of France are proving themselves churls and cravens, unworthy of the names they bear! Yes, ill-fulfilled," he continued bitterly, "because you, M. de Saux, and men like you, are for this to-day, and for that to-morrow, and cry one hour, 'Reform,' and the next, 'Order!'"

The denial stuck in my throat, and my passion dying down I could only glower at him. He saw this, and taking advantage of my momentary embarrassment, "But enough," he continued in a tone of dignity very galling to me, since it was he who had behaved ill, not I. "Enough of this. While it was possible I courted your aid, M. de Saux; and I acknowledge, I still acknowledge, and shall be the last to disclaim, the obligation under which you last night placed us. But there can never be true fellowship between those who wear that"--and he pointed to the tricolour I had assumed--"and those who serve the King as we serve him. You will pardon me, therefore, if I take my leave, and without delay withdraw my sister from a house in which her presence may be misunderstood, as mine, after what has passed, must be unwelcome."

He bowed again with that, and led the way into the house; while I followed, tongue-tied and with a sudden chill at my heart. There was no one in the hall except André, who was hovering about the farther door; but in the avenue beyond were three or four mounted servants waiting for M. de St. Alais, and half-way down the avenue a party of three were riding towards the gates. It needed but a glance to show me that the foremost of these was Mademoiselle, and that she rode low in the saddle, as if she still wept. And I turned in a hot fit to M. de St. Alais.

But I found his eye fixed on me in such a fashion that the words died on my lips. He coughed drily. "Ah!" he said. "So Mademoiselle has herself felt the propriety of leaving. You will permit me, then, to make her acknowledgments, M. de Saux, and to take leave for her."

He saluted me with the words and turned. He already had his foot raised to the stirrup when I muttered his name.

He looked round. "Pardon!" he said. "Is there anything----"

I beckoned to the servants to stand back. I was in misery between rage and shame, the hot fit gone. "Monsieur," I said, "there is one more thing to be said. This does not end all between Mademoiselle and me. For Mademoiselle----"

"We will not speak of her!" he exclaimed.

But I was not to be put down. "For Mademoiselle, I do not know her sentiments," I continued, doggedly disregarding his interruption, "nor whether I am agreeable to her. But for myself, M. de St. Alais, I tell you frankly that I love her; nor shall I change because I wear one tricolour or another. Therefore----"

"I have only one thing to say," he cried, raising his hand to stay me.

I gave way, breathing hard. "What is it?" I said.

"That you make love like a bourgeois!" he answered, laughing insolently. "Or a mad Englishman! And as Mademoiselle de St. Alais is not a baker's daughter, to be wooed after that fashion, I find it offensive. Is that enough or shall I say more, M. le Vicomte?"

"That will not be enough to turn me from my path!" I answered. "You forget that I carried Mademoiselle hither in my arms last night. But I do not forget it, and she will not forget it. We cannot be henceforth as we were, M. le Marquis."

"You saved her life and base a claim upon it?" he said scornfully. "That is generous and like a gentleman!"

"No, I do not!" I answered passionately. "But I have held Mademoiselle in my arms, and she has laid her head on my breast, and you can undo neither the one nor the other. Henceforth I have a right to woo her, and I shall win her."

"While I live you never shall!" he answered fiercely. "I swear that, as she trod on that ribbon--at my word, at my word, Monsieur!--so she shall tread on your love. From this day seek a wife among your friends. Mademoiselle de St. Alais is not for you."

I trembled with rage. "You know, Monsieur, that I cannot fight you!" I said.

"Nor I you," he answered. "I know it. Therefore," he continued, pausing an instant and reverting with marvellous ease to his former politeness, "I will fly from you. Farewell, Monsieur--I do not say, until we meet again; for I do not think that we shall meet much in future."

I found nothing wherewith to answer that, and he turned and moved' away down the avenue. Mademoiselle and her escort had disappeared; his servants, obeying my gesture, were almost at the gates. I watched his figure as he rode under the boughs of the walnuts, that meeting low over his head let the sun fall on him through spare rifts; and, sore and miserable at heart myself, I marvelled at the gallant air he maintained, and the careless grace of his bearing.

Certainly he had force. He had the force his fellows lacked; and he had it so abundantly, that as I gazed after him the words I had used to him seemed weak and foolish, the resolution I had flung in his teeth childish. After all, he was right; this, to which my feelings had impelled me on the spur of anger and love and the moment, was no French or proper way of wooing, nor one which I should have relished in my sister's case. Why then had I degraded Mademoiselle by it, and exposed myself? Men wooed mistresses that way, not wives!

So that I felt very wretched as I turned to go into the house. But there my eye alighted on the pistols which still lay on the table in the hall, and with a sudden revulsion of feeling I remembered that others' affairs were out of order too; that the Châteaux of St. Alais and Marignac lay in ashes, that last night I had saved Mademoiselle from death, that beyond the walnut avenue with its cool, long shade and dappled floor, beyond the quiet of this summer day, lay the seething, brawling world of Quercy and of France--the world of maddened peasants and frightened townsfolk, and soldiers who would not fight, and nobles who dared not.

Then, *Vive le Tricolor!* the die was cast. I went through the house to find Father Benôit and his companions, meaning to throw in my lot and return with them. But the terrace was empty; they were nowhere to be seen. Even of the servants I could only find André, who came pottering to me with his lips pursed up to grumble. I asked him where the Curé was.

"Gone, M. le Vicomte."

"And Buton?"

"He too. With half the servants, for the matter of that."

"Gone?" I exclaimed. "Whither?"

"To the village to gossip," he answered churlishly. "There is not a turnspit now but must hear the news, and take his own leave and time to gather it. The world is turned upside down, I think. It is time his Majesty the King did something."

"Did not M. le Curé leave a message?"

The old servant hesitated. "Well, he did," he said grudgingly. "He said that if M. le Vicomte would stay at home until the afternoon, he should hear from him."

"But he was going to Cahors!" I said. "He is not returning to-day?"

"He went by the little alley to the village," André answered obstinately. "I do not know anything about Cahors."

"Then go to the village now," I said, "and learn whether he took the Cahors road."

The old man went grumbling, and I remained alone on the terrace. An abnormal quietness, as of the afternoon, lay on the house this summer morning. I sat down on a stone seat against the wall, and began to go over the events of the night, recalling with the utmost vividness things to which at the time I had scarcely given a glance, and shuddering at horrors that in the happening had barely moved me. Gradually my thoughts passed from these things which made my pulses beat; and I began to busy myself with Mademoiselle. I saw her again sitting low in the saddle and weeping as she went. The bees hummed in the warm air, the pigeons cooed softly in the dovecot, the trees on the lawn below me shaped themselves into an avenue over her head, and, thinking of her, I fell asleep.

After such a night as I had spent it was not unnatural. But when I awoke, and saw that it was high noon, I was wild with vexation. I sprang up, and darting suspicious glances round me, caught André skulking away under the house wall. I called him back, and asked him why he had let me sleep.

"I thought that you were tired, Monsieur," he muttered, blinking in the sun. "M. le Vicomte is not a peasant that he may not sleep when he pleases."

"And M. le Curé? Has he not returned?"

"No, Monsieur."

"And he went--which way?"

He named a village half a league from us; and then said that my dinner waited.

I was hungry, and for a moment asked no more, but went in and sat down to the meal. When I rose it was nearly two o'clock. Expecting Father Benôit every moment, I bade them saddle the horses that I might be ready to go; and then, too restless to remain still, I went into the village. Here I found all in turmoil. Three-fourths of the inhabitants were away at St. Alais inspecting the ruins, and those who remained thought of nothing so little as doing their ordinary work; but, standing in groups at their doors, or at the cross-roads, or the church gates, were discussing events. One asked me timidly if it was true that the King had given all the land to the peasants; another, if there were to be any more taxes; a third, a question still more simple. Yet with this, I met with no lack of respect; and few failed to express their joy that I had escaped the ruffians *là-bas*. But as I approached each group a subtle shade of expectation, of shyness and suspicion seemed to flit across faces the most familiar to me. At the moment I did not understand it, and even apprehended it but dimly. Now, after the event, now that it is too late, I know that it was the first symptom of the social poison doing its sure and deadly work.

With all this, I could hear nothing of M. le Curé; one saying that he was here, another there, a third that he had gone to Cahors; and, in the end, I returned to the Château in a state of discomfort and unrest hard to describe. I would not again leave the front of the house lest I should miss him; and for hours I paced the avenue, now listening at the gates or looking up the road, now walking quickly to and fro under the walnuts. In time evening fell, and night; and still I was here awaiting the Curé's coming, chained to the silent house; while my mind tortured me with pictures of what was going forward outside. The restless demon of the time had hold of me; the thought that I lay here idle, while the world heaved, made me miserable, filled me with shame. When André came at last to summon me to supper, I swore at him; and the moment I had done, I went up to the roof of the Château and watched the night, expecting to see again a light in the sky, and the far-off glare of burning houses.

I saw nothing, however, and the Curé did not come; and, after a wakeful night, seven in the morning saw me in the saddle and on the road to Cahors. André complained of illness and I took Gil only. The country round St. Alais seemed to be deserted; but, half a league farther on, over the hill, I came on a score of peasants trudging sturdily forward. I asked them whither they were going, and why they were not in the fields.

"We are going to Cahors, Monseigneur, for arms," they said.

"For arms! Whom are you going to fight?"

"The brigands, Monseigneur. They are burning and murdering on every side. By the mercy of God they have not yet visited us. And to-night we shall be armed."

"Brigands!" I said. "What brigands?"

But they could not answer that; and I left them in wonder at their simplicity and rode on. I had not yet done with these brigands, however. Half a league short of Cahors I passed through a hamlet where the same idea prevailed. Here they had raised a rough barricade at the end of the street towards the country, and I saw a man on the church tower keeping watch. Meanwhile every one in the place who could walk had gone to Cahors.

"Why?" I asked. "For what?"

"To hear the news."

Then I began to see that my imagination had not led me astray. All the world was heaving, all the world was astir. Every one was hurrying to hear and to learn and to tell; to take arms if he had never used arms before, to advise if all his life he had obeyed orders, to do anything and everything but his daily work. After this, that I should find Cahors humming like a hive of bees about to swarm, and the Valandré bridge so crowded that I could scarcely force my way through its three gates, and the *queue* of people waiting for rations longer, and the rations shorter than ever before--after this, I say, all these things seemed only natural.

Nor was I much surprised to find that as I rode through the streets, wearing the tricolour, I was hailed here and there with cheers. On the other hand, I noticed that wearers of white cockades were not lacking. They kept the wall in twos and threes, and walked with raised chins, and hands on sword-knots, and were watched askance by the commonalty. A few of them were known to me, more were strangers; and while I blushed under the scornful looks of the former, knowing that I must seem to them a renegade, I wondered who the latter were. Finally I was glad to escape from both by alighting at Doury's, over whose door a huge tricolour flag hung limp in the sunshine.

M. le Curé de Saux? Yes, he was even then sitting with the Committee upstairs. Would M. le Vicomte walk up?

I did so, through a press of noisy people, who thronged the stairs and passages and lobbies, and talked, and gesticulated, and seemed to be settled there for the day. I worked my way through these at last, the door was opened, a fresh gust of noise came out to meet me, and I entered the room. In it, seated round a long table, I found a score of men, of whom some rose to meet me, while more kept their seats; three or four were speaking at once and did not stop on my entrance. I recognised at the farther end Father Benôit and Buton, who came to meet me, and Capitaine Hugues, who rose, but continued to speak. Besides these there were two of the smaller noblesse, who left their chairs, and came to me in an ecstasy, and Doury, who rose and sat down half a dozen times; and one or two Curés and others of that rank, known to me by sight. The uproar was great, the confusion equal to it. Still, somehow, and after a moment of tumult, I found myself received and welcomed and placed in a chair at the end of the table, with M. le Capitaine on one side of me and a notary of Cahors on the other. Then, under cover of the noise, I stole a few words with Father Benôit, who lingered a moment beside me.

"You could not join us yesterday?" he muttered, with a pathetic look that only I understood.

"But you left a message, bidding me wait for you!" I answered.

"I did?" he said. "No; I left a message asking you to follow us--if it pleased you."

"Then I never got it," I replied. "André told me----"

"Ah! André," he answered softly. And he shook his head.

"The rascal!" I said; "then he lied to me! And----"

But some one called the Curé to his place, and we had to part. At the same instant most of the talkers ceased; a moment, and only two were left speaking, who, without paying the least regard to one another, continued to hold forth to their neighbours, haranguing, one on the social contract; the other on the brigands--the brigands who were everywhere burning the corn and killing the people!

At last M. le Capitaine, after long waiting to speak, attacked the former speaker. "Tut, Monsieur!" he said. "This is not the time for theory. A halfpennyworth of fact----

"Is worth a pound of theory!" the man of the brigands--he was a grocer, I believe--cried eagerly; and he brought his fist down on the table.

"But now is the time!--the God-sent time, to frame the facts to the theory!" the other combatant screamed. "To form a perfect system! To regenerate the world, I say! To----"

"To regenerate the fiddlestick!" his opponent answered, with equal heat. "When brigands are at our very doors! when our crops are being burned and our houses plundered! when----"

"Monsieur," the Captain said harshly, commanding silence by the gravity of his tone--"if you please!"

"Yes."

"Then, to be plain, I do not believe any more in your brigands than in M. l'Avoué's theories."

This time it was the grocer's turn to scream. "What?" he cried. "When they have been seen at Figeac, and Cajarc, and Rodez, and----"

"By whom?" the soldier asked sharply, interrupting him.

"By hundreds."

"Name one."

"But it is notorious!"

"Yes, Monsieur--it is a notorious lie!" M. le Capitaine answered bluntly. "Believe me, the brigands with whom we have to deal are nearer home. Allow us to arrange with them first, and do not deafen M. le Vicomte with your chattering."

"Hear! hear!" the lawyer cried.

But this insult proved too much for the man of the brigands. He began again, and others joined in, for him and against him; to my despair, it seemed as if the quarrel were only beginning--as if peace would have to be made afresh.

How all this noise, tumult, and disputation, this absence of the politeness to which I had been accustomed all my life, this vulgar jostling and brawling depressed me I need not say. I sat deafened, lost in the scramble; of no more account, for the moment, than Buton. Nay of less; for while I gazed about me and listened, sunk in wonder at my position at a table with people of a class with whom I had never sat down before--save at the chance table of an inn, where my presence kept all within bounds--it was Buton who, by coming to the officer's aid, finally gained silence.

"Now you have had your say, perhaps you will let me have mine," the Captain said, with acerbity, taking advantage of the hearing thus gained for him. "It is very well for you, M. l'Avoué, and you, Monsieur--I have forgotten your name--you are not fighting men, and my difficulty does not affect you. But there are half a dozen at this table who are placed as I am, and they understand. You may organise; but if your officers are carried off every morning, you will not go far."

"How carried off?" the lawyer cried, puffing out his thin cheeks. "Members of the Committee of----"

"How?" M. le Capitaine rejoined, cutting him short without ceremony--"by the prick of a small sword! You do not understand; but, for some of us, we cannot go three paces from this door without risk of an insult and a challenge."

"That is true!" the two gentlemen at the foot of the table cried with one voice.

"It is true, and more," the Captain continued, warming as he spoke. "It is no chance work, but a plan. It is their plan for curbing us. I have seen three men in the streets to-day, who, I can swear, are fencing-masters in fine clothes."

"Assassins!" the lawyer cried pompously. "That is all very well," Hugues said more soberly. "You can call them what you please. But what is to be done? If we cannot move abroad without a challenge and a duel, we are helpless. You will have all your leaders picked off."

"The people will avenge you!" the lawyer said, with a grand air.

M. le Capitaine shrugged his shoulders. "Thank you for nothing," he said.

Father Benôit interposed. "At present," he said anxiously, "I think that there is only one thing to be done. You have said, M. le Capitaine, that some of the committee are not fighting men. Why, I would ask, should any fight, and play into our opponents' hands?"

"*Par Dieu!* I think that you are right!" Hugues answered frankly. And he looked round as if to collect opinions. "Why should we? I am sure that I do not wish to fight. I have given my proofs."

There was a short pause, during which we looked at one another doubtfully. "Well, why not?" the Captain said at last. "This is not play, but business. We are no longer gentlemen at large, but soldiers under discipline."

"Yes," I said stiffly, for I found all looking at me. "But it is difficult, M. le Capitaine, for men of honour to divest themselves of certain ideas. If we are not to protect ourselves from insult, we sink to the level of beasts."

"Have no fear, M. le Vicomte!" Buton cried abruptly. "The people will not suffer it!"

"No, no; the people will not suffer it!" one or two echoed; and for a moment the room rang with cries of indignation.

"Well, at any rate," the Captain said at last, "all are now warned. And if, after this, they fight lightly, they do it with full knowledge that they are playing their adversaries' game. I hope all understand that. For my part," he continued, shrugging his shoulders with a dry laugh, "they may cane me; I shall not fight them! I am no fool!"

CHAPTER XII
THE DUEL

I have said already how all this weighed me down; with what misgivings I looked along the table, from the pale, pinched features of the lawyer to the smug grin of the grocer, or Buton's coarse face; with what sinkings of heart I found myself on a sudden the equal of these men, addressed now with rude abruptness, and now with servility; last, but not least, with what despondency I listened to the wrangling which followed, and which it needed all the exertions of the Captain to control. Fortunately, the sitting did not last long. After half an hour of debate and conversation, during which I did what I could to aid the few who knew anything of business, the meeting broke up; and while some went out on various missions, others remained to deal with such affairs as arose. I was one of those appointed to stay, and I drew Father Benôit into a corner, and, hiding for a moment the feeling of despair which possessed me, I asked him if any further outbreaks had occurred in the country round.

"No," he answered, secretly pressing my hand. "We have done so much good, I think." Then, in a different tone, which showed how clearly he read my mind, he continued, under his breath, "Ah! M. le Vicomte, let us only keep the peace! Let us do what lies to our hands. Let us protect the innocent, and then, no matter what happens. Alas, I foresee more than I predicted. More than I dreamed of is in peril. Let us only cling to----"

He stopped, and turned, startled by the noisy entrance of the Captain; who came in so abruptly that those who remained at the table sprang to their feet. M. Hugues' face was flushed, his eyes were gleaming with anger. The lawyer, who stood nearest to the door, turned a shade paler, and stammered out a question. But the Captain passed by him with a glance of contempt, and came straight to me. "M. le Vicomte," he said out loud, blurting out his words in haste, "you are a gentleman. You will understand me. I want your help."

I stared at him. "Willingly," I said. "But what is the matter?"

"I have been insulted!" he answered, his moustaches curling.

"How?"

"In the street! And by one of those puppies! But I will teach him manners! I am a soldier, sir, and I----"

"But, stay, M. le Capitaine," I said, really taken aback. "I understood that there was to be no fighting. And that you in particular----"

"Tut! tut!"

"Would be caned before you would go out."

"*Sacré Nom!*" he cried, "what of that? Do you think that I am not a gentleman because I have served in America instead of in France?"

"No," I said, scarcely able to restrain a smile. "But it is playing into their hands. So you said yourself, a minute ago, and----"

"Will you help me, or will you not, sir?" he retorted angrily. And then, as the lawyer tried to intervene, "Be silent, you!" he continued, turning on him so violently that the scrivener jumped back a pace. "What do you know of these things? You miserable pettifogger! you----"

"Softly, softly, M. le Capitaine," I said, startled by this outbreak, and by the prospect of further brawling which it disclosed. "M. l'Avoué is doing merely his duty in remonstrating. He is in the right, and----

"I have nothing to do with him! And for you--you will not assist me?"

"I did not say that."

"Then, if you will, I crave your services at once! At once," he said more calmly; but he still kept his shoulder to the lawyer. "I have appointed a meeting behind the Cathedral. If you will honour me, I must ask you to do so immediately."

I saw that it was useless to say more; that he had made up his mind; and for answer I took up my hat. In a moment we were moving towards the door. The lawyer, the grocer, half a dozen cried out on us, and would have stopped us. But Father Benôit remained silent, and I went on down the stairs, and out of the house. Outside it was easy to see that the quarrel and insult had had spectators; a gloomy crowd, not compact, but made up of watching groups, filled all the sunny open part of the square. The pavement, on the other hand, along which we had to pass to go to the Cathedral, had for its only occupants a score or more of gentlemen, who, wearing white cockades, walked up and down in threes and fours. The crowd eyed them silently; they affected to see nothing of the crowd. Instead, they talked and smiled carelessly, and with half-opened eyes; swung their canes, and saluted one another, and now and then stopped to exchange a word or a pinch of snuff. They wore an air of insolence, ill-hidden, which the silent, almost cowed looks of the multitude, as it watched them askance, seemed to justify.

We had to run the gauntlet of these; and my face burned with shame, as we passed. Many of the men, whom I met now, I had met two days before at Madame St. Alais', where they had seen me put on the white cockade; they saw me now in the opposite camp, they knew nothing of my reasons, and I read in their averted eyes and curling lips what they thought of the change. Others--and they looked at me insolently, and scarcely gave me room to pass--were strangers, wearing military swords, and the cross of St. Louis.

Fortunately the passage was as short as it was painful. We passed under the north wall of the Cathedral, and through a little door into a garden, where lime trees tempered the glare of the sun, and the town, with its crowd and noise, seemed to be in a moment left behind. On the right rose the walls of the apse and the heavy eastern domes of the Cathedral; in front rose the ramparts; on the left an old, half-ruined tower of the fourteenth century lifted a frowning ivy-covered head. In the shadow, at its foot, on a piece of smooth sward, a group of four persons were standing waiting for us.

One was M. de St. Alais, one was Louis; the others were strangers. A sudden thought filled me with horror. "Whom are you going to fight?" I muttered.

"M. de St. Alais," the Captain answered, in the same tone. And then, being within earshot of the others, I could say no more. They stepped forward, and saluted us.

"M. le Vicomte?" Louis said. He was grave and stern. I scarcely knew him.

I assented mechanically, and we stepped aside from the others. "This is not a case that admits of intervention, I believe?" he said, bowing.

"I suppose not," I answered huskily.

In truth, I could scarcely speak for horror. I was waking slowly to the consciousness of the dilemma in which I had placed myself. Were St. Alais to fall by the Captain's sword, what would his sister say to me, what would she think of me, how would she ever touch my hand? And yet could I wish ill to my own principal? Could I do so in honour, even if something sturdy and practical, something of plain gallantry in the man, whom I was here to second, had not already and insensibly won my heart?

Yet one of the two must fall. The great clock above my head, slowly telling out the hour of noon, beat the truth into my brain. For a moment I grew dizzy; the sun dazzled me, the trees reeled before me, the garden swam. The murmur of the crowd outside filled my ears. Then out of the mist Louis' voice, unnaturally steady, gripped my attention, and my brain grew clear again.

"Have you any objection to this spot?" he said. "The grass is dry, and not slippery. They will fight in shadow, and the light is good."

"It will do," I muttered.

"Perhaps you will examine it? There is, I think, no trip or fault."

I affected to do so. "I find none," I said hoarsely.

"Then we had better place our men?"

"I think so."

I had no knowledge of the skill of either combatant, but, as I turned to join Hugues, I was startled by the contrast which the two presented as they stood a little apart, their upper clothes removed. The Captain was the shorter by a head, and stiff and sturdy, with a clear eye and keen visage. M. le Marquis, on the other hand, was tall and lithe, and long in the arm, with a reach which threatened danger, and a smile almost as deadly. I thought that if his skill and coolness were on a par with his natural gifts, M. Hugues--But then again my head reeled. What did I wish?

"We are ready," M. Louis said impatiently; and I noticed that he glanced past me towards the gate of the garden. "Will you measure the swords, M. le Vicomte?"

I complied, and was about to place my man, when M. le Capitaine indicated by a sign that he wished to speak to me, and, disregarding the frowns of the other side, I led him apart.

His face had lost the glow of passion which had animated it a few minutes before, and was pale and stern. "This is a fool's trick," he said curtly, and under his breath. "It will serve me right if that puppy goes through me. You will do me a favour, M. le Vicomte?"

I muttered that I would do him any in my power.

"I borrowed a thousand francs to fit myself out for this service," he continued, avoiding my eye, "from a man in Paris whose name you will find in my valise at the inn. Should anything happen to me, I should be glad if you will send him what is left. That is all."

"He shall be paid in full," I said. "I will see to it."

He wrung my hand, and went to his station; and Louis and I placed ourselves on either side of the two, ready, with our swords drawn, to interfere should need arise. The signal was given, the principals saluted, and fell on guard, and in a moment the grinding and clicking of the blades began, while the pigeons of the Cathedral flew in eddies above us, and in the middle of the garden a little fountain tinkled softly in the sunshine.

They had not made three passes before the great diversity of their styles became apparent. While Hugues played vigorously with his body, stooping, and moving, and stepping aside, but keeping his arm stiff, and using his wrist much, M. le Marquis held his body erect and still, but moved his arm, and, fencing with a school correctness, as if he held a foil, disdained all artifices save those of the weapon. It was clear that he was the better fencer, and that, of the two, the Captain must tire first, since he was never still, and the wrist is more quickly fatigued that the arm; but, in addition to this, I soon perceived that the Marquis was not putting forth his full strength, but, depending on his defence, was waiting to tire out his opponent. My eyes grew hot, my throat dry, as I watched breathlessly, waiting for the stroke that must finish all--waiting and flinching. And then, on a sudden, something happened. The Captain seemed to slip, yet did not slip, but in a moment, stooping almost prone, his left hand on the ground, was under the other's guard. His point was at the Marquis's breast, when the latter sprang back--sprang back, and just saved himself. Before the Captain could recover his footing, Louis dashed his sword aside.

"Foul play!" he cried passionately. "Foul play! A stroke *dessous!* It is not *en règle.*"

The Captain stood breathing quickly, his point to the ground. "But why not, Monsieur?" he said. Then he looked to me.

"I scarcely understand, M. de St. Alais," I said stiffly. "The stroke----"

"Is not allowed."

"In the schools," I said. "But this is a duel."

"I have never seen it used in a duel," he said.

"No matter," I answered warmly. "To interfere on such provocation is absurd."

"Monsieur!"

"Is absurd!" I repeated firmly. "After such treatment I have no resource but to withdraw M. le Capitaine from the field."

"Perhaps you will take his place," some one behind me said with a sneer.

I turned sharply. One of the two persons whom we had found with St. Alais was the speaker. I saluted him. "The surgeon?" I said.

"No," he answered angrily. "I am M. du Marc, and very much at your service."

"But not a second," I rejoined. "And, therefore, you have no right to be standing where you are, nor to be here. I must request you to withdraw."

"I have at least as much right as those," he answered, pointing to the roof of the Cathedral, over the battlements of which a number of heads could be seen peering down at us.

I stared.

"Our friends have at least as much right as yours," he continued, taunting me.

"But they do not interfere," I answered firmly. "Nor shall you. I request you to withdraw."

He still refused, and even tried to bluster; but this proved too much for Louis' stomach; he intervened sharply, and at a word from him the bully shrugged his shoulders and moved away. Then we four looked at one another.

"We had better proceed," the Captain said bluntly. "If the stroke was irregular, this gentleman was right to interfere. If not----"

"I am willing," M. de St. Alais said. And in a moment the two fell on guard, and to it again; but more fiercely now, and with less caution, the Captain more than once using a rough, sweeping parry, in greater favour with practical fighters than in the fencing school. This, though it left him exposed to a *riposte*, seemed to disconcert M. le Marquis, who fenced, I thought, less skilfully than before, and more than once seemed to be flurried by the Captain's attack. I began to feel doubtful of the result, my heart began to beat more quickly, the glitter of the blades as they slid up and down one another confused my sight. I looked for one moment across at Louis--and in that moment the end came. M. le Capitaine used again his sweeping parry, but this time the circle was too wide; St. Alais' blade darted serpent-like under his. The Captain staggered back. His sword dropped from his hand.

Before he could fall I caught him in my arms, but blood was gushing already from a wound in the side of his neck. He just turned his eyes to my face, and tried once to speak. I caught the words, "You will----" and then blood choked his voice, and his eyes slowly closed. He was dead, or as good as dead, before the surgeon could reach him, before I could lay him on the grass.

I knelt a moment beside him perfectly stunned by the suddenness of the catastrophe; watching in a kind of fascination the surgeon feeling pulse and heart, and striving with his thumb to stop the bleeding. For a moment or two my world was reduced to the sinking grey face, the quivering eyelids before me, and I saw nothing, heeded nothing, thought of nothing else. I could not believe that the valiant spirit had fled already; that the stout man who had so quickly yet insensibly won my liking was in this moment dead; dead and growing livid, while the pigeons still circled overhead, and the sparrows chirped, and the fountain tinkled in the sunshine.

I cried out in my agony. "Not dead?" I said. "Not dead so soon?"

"Yes, M. le Vicomte, it was bad luck," the surgeon answered, letting the passive head fall on the stained grass. "With such a wound nothing can be done."

He rose as he spoke; but I remained on my knees, wrapt and absorbed; staring at the glazing eyes that a few minutes before had been full of life and keenness. Then with a shudder I turned my look on myself. His blood covered me; it was on my breast, my arm, my hands, soaking into my coat. From it my thoughts turned to St. Alais, and at the moment, as I looked instinctively round to see where he was, or if he had gone, I started. The deep boom of a heavy bell, tolled once, shook the air; while its solemn burden still hung mournfully on the ear, quick footsteps ran towards me, and I heard a harsh cry at my elbow. "But, *mon Dieu!* This is murder! They are murdering us!"

I looked behind me. The speaker was Du Marc, the bully who had vainly tried to provoke me. The two St. Alais and the surgeon were with him, and all four came from the direction of the door by which we had entered. They passed me with averted eyes, and hurried towards a little postern which flanked the old tower, and opened on the ramparts. As they went out of sight behind a buttress that intervened the bell boomed out again above my head, its dull note full of menace.

Then I awoke and understood; understood that the noise which filled my ears was not the burden of the bell carried on from one deep stroke to another, but the roar of angry voices in the square, the babel of an approaching crowd crying: "*A la lanterne! A la lanterne!*" From the battlements of the Cathedral, from the louvres of the domes, from every window of the great gloomy structure that frowned above me, men were making signs, and pointing with their hands, and brandishing their fists--at me, I thought at first, or at the body at my feet. But then I heard footsteps again, and I turned and found the other four behind me, close to me; the two St. Alais pale and stern, with bright eyes, the bully pale, too, but with a look which shot furtively here and there, and white lips.

"Curse them, they are at that door, too!" he cried shrilly. "We are beset. We shall be murdered. By God, we shall be murdered, and by these *canaille!* By these--I call all here to witness that it was a fair fight! I call you to witness, M. le Vicomte, that----"

"It will help us much," St. Alais said with a sneer, "if he does. If I were once at home----"

"Ay, but how are we to get there?" Du Marc cried. He could not hide his terror. "Do you understand," he continued querulously, addressing me, "that we shall be murdered? Is there no other door? Speak, some one. Speak!"

His fears appealed to me in vain. I would scarcely have stirred a finger to save him. But the sight of the two St. Alais standing there pale and irresolute, while that roar of voices grew each moment louder and nearer, moved me. A moment, and the mob would break in; perhaps finding us by Hugues' side, it might in its fury sacrifice all indifferently. It might; and then I heard, to give point to the thought, the crash of one of the doors of the garden as it gave way; and I cried out almost involuntarily that there was another door--another door, if it was open. I did not look to see if they followed, but, leaving the dead, I took the lead, and ran across the sward towards the wall of the Cathedral.

The crowd were already pouring into the garden, but a clump of shrubs hid us from them as we fled; and we gained unseen a little door, a low-browed postern in the wall of the apse, that led, I knew--for not long before I had conducted an English visitor over the Cathedral--to a sacristy connected with the crypt. My hope of finding the door open was slight; if I had stayed to weigh the chances I should have thought them desperate. But to my joy as I came up to it, closely followed by the others, it opened of itself, and a priest, showing his tonsured head in the aperture, beckoned to us to hasten. He had little need to do so; in a moment we had obeyed, were by his side, and panting, heard the bolts shoot home behind us. For the moment we were safe.

Then we breathed again. We stood in the twilight of a long narrow room with walls and roof of stone, and three loopholes for windows. Du Marc was the first to speak. "*Mon Dieu*, that was close," he said, wiping his brow, which in the cold light wore an ugly pallor. "We are----"

"Not out of the wood yet," the surgeon answered gravely, "though we have good grounds for thanking M. le Vicomte. They have discovered us! Yes, they are coming!"

Probably the people on the roof had watched us enter and denounced our place of refuge; for as he spoke, we heard a rush of feet, the door shook under a storm of blows, and a score of grimy savage faces showed at the slender arrow-slits, and glaring down, howled and spat curses upon us. Luckily the door was of oak, studded and plated with iron, fashioned in old, rough days for such an emergency, and we stood comparatively safe. Yet it was terrible to hear the cries of the mob, to feel them so close, to gauge their hatred, and know while they beat on the stone as though they would tear the walls with their naked hands, what it would be to fall into their power!

We looked at one another, and--but it may have been the dim light--I saw no face that was not pale. Fortunately the pause was short. The Curé who had admitted us, unlocked as quickly as he could an inner door. "This way," he said--but the snarling of the beasts outside almost drowned his voice--"if you will follow me, I will let you out by the south entrance. But, be quick, gentlemen, be quick," he continued, pushing us out before him, "or they may guess what we are about, and be there before us."

It may be imagined that after that we lost no time. We followed him as quickly as we could along a narrow subterranean passage, very dimly lit, at the end of which a flight of six steps brought us into a second passage. We almost ran along this, and though a locked door delayed us a moment--which seemed a minute, and a long one--the key was found and the door opened. We passed through it, and found ourselves in a long narrow room, the counterpart of that we had first entered. The curé opened the farther door of this; I looked out. The alley outside, the same which led beside the Cathedral to the Chapter House, was empty.

"We are in time," I said, with a sigh of relief; it was pleasant to breathe the fresh air again. And I turned, still panting with the haste we had made, to thank the good Curé who had saved us.

M. de St. Alais, who followed me, and had kept silence throughout, thanked him also. Then M. le Marquis stood hesitating on the threshold, while I looked to see him hurry away. At last he turned to me. "M. de Saux," he said, speaking with less aplomb than was usual with him--but we were all agitated--"I should thank you also. But perhaps the situation in which we stand towards one another----"

"I think nothing of that," I answered harshly. "But that in which we have just stood----"

"Ah," he rejoined, shrugging his shoulders, "if you take it that way----"

"I do take it that way," I answered--the Captain's blood was not yet dry on the man's sword, and he spoke to me! "I do take it that way. And I warn you, M. le Marquis," I continued sternly, "that if you pursue your plan further, a plan that has already cost one brave man his life, it will recoil on yourselves, and that most terribly."

"At least I shall not ask you to shield me," he answered proudly. And he walked carelessly away, sheathing his sword as he went. The passage was still empty. There was no one to stop him.

Louis followed him; Du Marc and the surgeon had already disappeared. I fancied that as Louis passed me he hung a moment on his heel; and that he would have spoken to me, would have caught my eye, would have taken my hand, had I given him an opening. But I saw before me Hugues' dead face and sunken eyes, and I set my own face like a stone, and turned away.

CHAPTER XIII
A LA LANTERNE

For, of all the things that had happened since I left the Committee Room, the Captain's death remained the one most real and most deeply bitten into my mind. He had shared with me the walk from the inn to the garden, and the petty annoyances that had then filled my thoughts. He had faced them with me, and bravely; and this late association, and the picture of him as he walked beside me, full of life and coarse wrath, rose up now and cried out against his death; cried out that it was impossible. So that it seemed horrible to me, and I shook with fear, and loathed the man whose hand had done it.

Nor was that all. I had known Hugues barely forty-eight hours, my liking for him was only an hour born; but I had his story. I could follow him going about to borrow the small sum of money he had possessed. I could trace the hopes he had built on it. I could see him coming here full of honest courage, believing that he had found an opening; a man strong, confident, looking forward, full of plans. And then of all, this was the end! He had hoped, he had purposed; and on the other side of the Cathedral, he lay stark--stark and dead on the grass.

It seemed so sad and pitiful, I had the man so vividly in my mind, that I scarcely gave a thought to the St. Alais' danger and escape; that, and our hasty flight, had passed like a dream. I was content to listen a moment beside the church door; and then satisfied that the murmur of the crowd was dying in the distance, and that the city was quiet, I thanked the Vicar again, and warmly, and, taking leave of him, in my turn walked up the passage.

It was so still that it echoed my footsteps; and presently I began to think the silence odd. I began to wonder why the mob, which a few minutes before had shown itself so vindictive, had not found its way round; why the neighbourhood had become on a sudden so quiet. A few paces would show, however; I hastened on, and in a moment stood in the market-place.

To my astonishment it lay sunny, tranquil, utterly deserted; a dog ran here and there with tail high, nosing among the garbage; a few old women were at the stalls on the farther side; about as many people were busy, putting up shutters and closing shops. But the crowd which had filled the place so short a time before, the *queue* about the corn measures, the white cockades, all were gone; I stood astonished.

For a moment only, however. Then, in place of the silence which had prevailed between the high walls of the passage, a dull sound, distant and heavy, began to speak to me; a sullen roar, as of breakers falling on the beach. I started and listened. A moment more, and I was across the Square, and at the door of the inn. I darted into the passage, and up the stairs, my heart beating fast.

Here, too, I had left a crowd in the passages, and on the stairs. Not a man remained. The house seemed to be dead; at noon-day with the sun shining outside. I saw no one, heard no one, until I reached the door of the room in which I had left the Committee and entered. Here, at last, I found life; but the same silence.

Round the table were seated some dozen of the members of the Committee. On seeing me they started, like men detected in an act of which they were ashamed, some continuing to sit, sullen and scowling, with their elbows on the table, others stooping to their neighbours' ears to whisper, or listen. I noticed that many were pale and all gloomy; and though the room was light, and hot noon poured in through three windows, a something grim in the silence, and the air of expectation which prevailed, struck a chill to my heart.

Father Benôit was not of them, but Baton was, and the lawyer, and the grocer, and the two gentlemen, and one of the Curés, and Doury--the last-named pale and cringing, with fear sitting heavily on him. I might have thought, at a first glance round, that nothing which had happened outside was known to them; that they were ignorant alike of the duel and the riot; but a second glance assured me that they knew all, and more than I did; so many of them, when they had once met my eyes, looked away.

"What has happened?" I asked, standing half-way between the door and the long table.

"Don't you know, Monsieur?"

"No," I muttered, staring at them. Even here that distant murmur filled the air.

"But you were at the duel, M. le Vicomte?" The speaker was Buton.

"Yes," I said nervously. "But what of that? I saw M. le Marquis safe on his way home, and I thought that the crowd had separated. Now--" and I paused, listening.

"You fancy that you still hear them?" he said, eying me closely and smiling.

"Yes; I fear that they are at mischief."

"We are afraid of that, too," the smith answered drily, setting his elbows on the table, and looking at me anew. "It is not impossible."

Then I understood. I caught Doury's eye--which would fain have escaped mine--and read it there. The hooting of the distant crowd rose more loudly on the summer stillness; as it did so, faces round the table grew graver, lips grew longer, some trembled and looked down; and I understood. "My God!" I cried in excitement, trembling myself. "Is no one going to do anything, then? Are you going to sit here, while these demons work their will? While houses are sacked and women and children----"

"Why not?" Buton said curtly.

"Why not?" I cried.

"Ay, why not?" he answered sternly--and I began to see that he dominated the others; that he would not and they dared not. "We went about to keep the peace, and see that others kept it. But your white cockades, your gentlemen bullies, your soldierless officers, M. le Vicomte--I speak without offence--would not have it. They undertook to bully us; and unless they learn a lesson now, they will bully us again. No, Monsieur," he continued, looking round with a hard smile--already power had changed him wondrously--"let the people have their way for half an hour, and----"

"The people?" I cried. "Are the rascals and sweepings of the streets, the gaol-birds, the beggars and *forçats* of the town--are they the people?"

"No matter," he said frowning.

"But this is murder!"

Two or three shivered, and some looked sullenly from me, but the blacksmith only shrugged his shoulders. Still I did not despair, I was going to say more--to try threats, even prayers; but before I could speak, the man nearest to the windows raised his hand for silence, and we heard the distant riot sink, and in the momentary quiet which followed the sharp report of a gun ring out, succeeded by another and another. Then a roar of rage-- distinct, articulate, full of menace.

"Oh, *mon Dieu!*" I cried, looking round, while I trembled with indignation, "I cannot stand this! Will no one act? Will no one do anything? There must be some authority. There must be some one to curb this *canaille*; or presently, I warn you, I warn you all, that they will cut your throats also; yours, M. l'Avoué, and yours, Doury!"

"There was some one; and he is dead," Buton answered. The rest of the Committee fidgeted gloomily.

"And was he the only one?"

"They've killed him," the smith said bluntly. "They must take the consequences."

"They?" I cried, in a passion of wrath and pity. "Ay, and you! And you! I tell you that you are using this scum of the people to crush your enemies! But presently they will crush you too!"

Still no one spoke, no one answered me; no eyes met mine; then I saw how it was; that nothing I could say would move them; and I turned without another word, and I ran downstairs. I knew already, or could guess, whither the crowd had gone, and whence came the shouting and the shots; and the moment I reached the Square I turned in the direction of the St. Alais' house, and ran through the streets; through quiet streets under windows from which women looked down white and curious, past neat green blinds of modern houses, past a few staring groups; ran on, with all about me smiling, but always with that murmur in my ears, and at my heart grim fear.

They were sacking the St. Alais' house! And Mademoiselle! And Madame!

The thought of them came to me late; but having come it was not to be displaced. It gripped my heart and seemed to stop it. Had I saved Mademoiselle only for this? Had I risked all to save her from the frenzied peasants, only that she might fall into the more cruel hands of these maddened wretches, these sweepings of the city?

It was a dreadful thought; for I loved her, and knew, as I ran, that I loved her. Had I not known it I must have known it now, by the very measure of agony which the thought of that horror caused me. The distance from the Trois Rois to the house was barely four hundred yards, but it seemed infinite to me. It seemed an age before I stopped breathless and panting on the verge of the crowd, and strove to see, across the plain of heads, what was happening in front.

A moment, and I made out enough to relieve me; and I breathed more freely. The crowd had not yet won its will. It filled the street on either side of the St. Alais' house from wall to wall; but in front of the house itself, a space was still kept clear by the fire of those within. Now and again, a man or a knot of men would spring out of the ranks of the mob, and darting across this open space to the door, would strive to beat it in with axes and bars, and even with naked hands; but always there came a puff of smoke from the shuttered and loop-holed windows, and a second and a third, and the men fell back, or sank down on the stones, and lay bleeding in the sunshine.

It was a terrible sight. The wild beast rage of the mob, as they watched their leaders fall, yet dared not make the rush *en masse* which must carry the place, was enough, of itself, to appal the stoutest. But when to this and their fiendish cries were added other sounds as horrid--the screams of the wounded and the rattle of musketry--for some of the mob had arms, and were firing from neighbouring houses at the St. Alais' windows--the effect was appalling. I do not know why, but the sunshine, and the tall white houses which formed the street, and the very neatness of the surroundings, seemed to aggravate the bloodshed; so that for a while the whole, the writhing crowd, the open space with its wounded, the ugly cries and curses and shots, seemed unreal. I, who had come hot-foot to risk all, hesitated; if this was Cahors, if this was the quiet town I had known all my life, things had come to a pass indeed. If not, I was dreaming.

But this last was a thought too wild to be entertained for more than a few seconds; and with a groan I thrust myself into the press, bent desperately on getting through and reaching the open space; though what I should do when I got there, or how I could help, I had not considered. I had scarcely moved, however, when I felt my arm gripped, and some one clinging obstinately to me, held me back. I turned to resent the action with a blow,--I was beside myself; but the man was Father Benôit, and my hand fell. I caught hold of him with a cry of joy, and he drew me out of the press.

His face was pale and full of grief and consternation; yet by a wonderful chance I had found him, and I hoped. "You can do something!" I cried in his ear, gripping his hand hard. "The Committee will not act, and this is murder! Murder, man! Do you see?"

"What can I do?" he wailed; and he threw up his other hand with a gesture of despair.

"Speak to them."

"Speak to them?" he answered. "Will mad dogs stand when you speak to them? Or will mad dogs listen? How can you get to them? Where can you speak to them? It is impossible. It is impossible, Monsieur. They would kill their fathers to-day, if they stood between them and vengeance."

"Then, what will you do?" I cried passionately. "What will you do?"

He shook his head; and I saw that he meant nothing, that he could do nothing. And then my soul revolted. "You must! You shall!" I cried fiercely. "You have raised this devil, and you must lay him! Are these the liberties about which you have talked to us? Are these the people for whom you have pleaded? Answer, answer me, what you will do!" I cried. And I shook him furiously.

He covered his face with his hand. "God forgive us!" he said. "God help us!"

I looked at him for the first and only time in my life with contempt--with rage. "God help you?" I cried--I was beside myself. "God helps those who help themselves! You have brought this about! You! You! You have preached this! Now mend it!"

He trembled, and was silent. Unsupported by the passion which animated me, in face of the brute rage of the people, his courage sank.

"Now mend it!" I repeated furiously.

"I cannot get to them," he muttered.

"Then I will make a way for you!" I answered madly, recklessly. "Follow me! Do you hear that noise? Well, we will play a part in it!"

A dozen guns had gone off, almost in a volley. We could not see the result, nor what was passing; but the hoarse roar of the mob intoxicated me. I cried to him to follow, and rushed into the press.

Again he caught and stayed me, clinging to me with a stubbornness which would not be denied. "If you will go, go through the houses! Go through the opposite houses!" he muttered in my ear.

I had sense enough, when he had spoken twice, to understand him and comply. I let him lead me aside, and in a moment we were out of the press, and hurrying through an alley at the back of the houses that faced the St. Alais' mansion. We were not the first to go that way; some of the more active of the rioters had caught the idea before us, and gone by this path to the windows, whence they were firing. We found two or three of the doors open, therefore, and heard the excited cries and curses of the men who had taken possession. However, we did not go far. I chose the first door, and, passing quickly by a huddled, panic-stricken group of women and children--probably the occupants of the house--who were clustered about it, I went straight through to the street door.

Two or three ruffianly men with smoke-grimed faces were firing through a window on the ground floor, and one of these, looking behind him as I passed, saw me. He called to me to stop, adding with an oath that if I went into the street I should be shot by the aristocrats. But in my excitement I took no heed; in a second I had the door open, and was standing in the street--

alone in the sunny, cleared space. On either side of me, fifty paces distant, were the close ranks of the mob; in front of me rose the white blind face of the St. Alais' house, from which, even as I appeared, there came a little spit of smoke and the bang of a musket.

The crowd, astonished to see me there alone and standing still, fell silent, and I held up my hand. A gun went off above my head, and another; and a splinter flew from one of the green shutters opposite. Then a voice from the crowd cried out to cease firing; and for a moment all was still. I stood in the midst of a hot breathless hush, my hand raised. It was my opportunity--I had got it by a miracle; but for a moment I was silent, I could find no words.

At last, as a low murmur began to make itself heard, I spoke.

"Men of Cahors!" I cried. "In the name of the Tricolour, stand!" And trembling with agitation, acting on the impulse of the instant, I walked slowly across the street to the door of the besieged house, and under the eyes of all I took the Tricolour from my bosom, and hung it on the knocker of the door. Then I turned. "I take possession," I cried hoarsely, at the top of my voice, that all might hear, "I take possession of this house and all that are in it in the name of the Tricolour, and the Nation, and the Committee of Cahors. Those within shall be tried, and justice done upon them. But for you, I call upon you to depart, and go to your homes in peace, and the Committee----"

I got no farther. With the word a shot whizzed by my ear, and struck the plaster from the wall; and then, as if the sound released all the passions of the people, a roar of indignation shook the air. They hissed and swore at me, yelled "*A la lanterne!*" and "*A bas le traître!*" and in an instant burst their bounds. As if invisible floodgates gave way, the mob on either side rushed suddenly forward, and, rolling towards the door in a solid mass, were in an instant upon me.

I expected that I should be torn to pieces, but instead I was only buffeted and flung aside and forgotten, and in a moment was lost in the struggling, writhing mass of men, who flung themselves pell-mell upon the door, and fell over one another, and wounded one another in the fury with which they attacked it. Men, injured earlier, were trodden under foot now; but no one stayed for their cries. Twice a gun was fired from the house, and each shot took effect; but the press was so great, and the fury of the assailants, as they swarmed about the door, so blind, that those who were hit sank down unobserved, and perished under their comrades' feet.

Thrust against the iron railings that flanked the door, I clung to them, and protected from the pressure by a pillar of the porch, managed with some difficulty to keep my place. I could not move, however; I had to stand there while the crowd swayed round me, and I waited in dizzy, sickening horror for the crisis. It came at last. The panels of the door, riven and shattered, gave way; the foremost assailants sprang at the gap. Yet still the frame, held by one hinge, stood, and kept them out. As that yielded at length under their blows, and the door fell inward with a crash, I flung myself into the stream, and was carried into the house among the foremost, fortunately--for several fell--on my feet.

I had the thought that I might outpace the others, and, getting first to the rooms upstairs, might at least fight for Mademoiselle if I could not save her. For I had caught the infection of the mob, my blood was on fire. There was no one in all the crowd more set to kill than I was. I raced in, therefore, with the rest; but when I reached the foot of the stairs I saw, and they saw, that which stopped us all.

It was M. de Gontaut, lifted, in that moment of extreme danger, above himself. He stood alone on the stairs, looking down on the invaders, and smiling--smiling, with everything of senility and frivolity gone from his face, and only the courage of his caste left. He saw his world tottering, the scum and rabble overwhelming it, everything which he had loved, and in which he had lived, passing; he saw death waiting for him seven steps below, and he smiled. With his slender sword hanging at his wrist, he tapped his snuff-box and looked down at us; no longer garrulous, feeble, almost--with his stories of stale intrigues and his pagan creed--contemptible; but steady and proud, with eyes that gleamed with defiance.

"Well, dogs," he said, "will you earn the gallows?"

For a second no one moved. For a second the old noble's presence and fearlessness imposed on the vilest; and they stared at him, cowed by his eye. Then he stirred. With a quiet gesture, as of a man saluting before a duel, he caught up the hilt of his sword, and presented the lower point. "Well," he said with bitter scorn in his tone, "you have come to do it. Which of you will go to hell for the rest? For I shall take one."

That broke the spell. With a howl, a dozen ruffians sprang up the stairs. I saw the bright steel flash once, twice; and one reeled back, and rolled down under his fellows' feet. Then a great bar swept up and fell on the smiling face, and the old noble dropped without a cry or a groan, under a storm of blows that in a moment beat the life out of his body.

It was over in a moment, and before I could interfere. The next, a score of men leaped over the corpse and up the stairs, with horrid cries--I after them. To the right and left were locked doors, with panels Wätteau-painted; they dashed these in with brutal shouts, and, in a twinkling, flooded the splendid rooms, sweeping away, and breaking, and flinging down in wanton mischief, everything that came to hand--vases, statues, glasses, miniatures. With shrieks of triumph, they filled the *salon* that had known for generations only the graces and beauty of life; and clattered over the shining parquets that had been swept so long by the skirts of fair women. Everything they could not understand was snatched up and dashed down; in a moment the great Venetian mirrors were shattered, the pictures pierced and torn, the books flung through the windows into the street.

I had a glimpse of the scene as I paused on the landing. But a glance sufficed to convince me that the fugitives were not in these rooms, and I sprang on, and up the next flight. Here, short as had been my delay, I found others before me. As I turned the corner of the stairs I came on three men, listening at a door; before I could reach them one rose. "Here they are!" he cried. "That is a woman's voice! Stand back!" And he lifted a crowbar to beat in the door.

"Hold!" I cried in a voice that shook him, and made him lower his weapon. "Hold! In the name of the Committee, I command you to leave that door. The rest of the house is yours. Go and plunder it."

The men glared at me. "*Sacré ventre!*" one of them hissed. "Who are you?"

"The Committee!" I answered.

He cursed me, and raised his hand. "Stand back!" I cried furiously, "or you shall hang!"

"Ho! ho! An aristocrat!" he retorted; and he raised his voice. "This way, friends--this way! An aristocrat! An aristocrat!" he cried.

At the word a score of his fellows came swarming up the stairs. I saw myself in an instant surrounded by grimy, pocked faces and scowling eyes,--by haggard creatures sprung from the sewers of the town. Another second and they would have laid hands on me; but desperate and full of rage I rushed instead on the man with the bar, and, snatching it from him before he guessed my intention, in a twinkling laid him at my feet.

In the act, however, I lost my balance, and stumbled. Before I could recover myself one of his comrades struck me on the head with his wooden shoe. The blow partially stunned me; still I got to my feet again and hit out wildly, and drove them back, and for a moment cleared the landing round me. But I was dizzy; I saw all now through a red haze, the figures danced before me; I could no longer think or aim, but only hear taunts and jeers on every side. Some one plucked my coat. I turned blindly. In a moment another struck me a crushing blow--how, or with what, I never knew--and I fell senseless and as good as dead.

CHAPTER XIV
IT GOES ILL

It was August, and the leaves of the chestnuts were still green, when they sacked the St. Alais' house at Cahors, and I fell senseless on the stairs. The ash trees were bare, and the oaks clad only in russet, when I began to know things again; and, looking sideways from my pillow into the grey autumnal world, took up afresh the task of living. Even then many days had to elapse before I ceased to be merely an animal--content to eat, and drink, and sleep, and take Father Benôit kneeling by my bed for one of the permanent facts of life. But the time did come at last, in late November, when the mind awoke, as those who watched by me had never thought to see it awake; and, meeting the good Curé's eyes with my eyes, I saw him turn away and break into joyful weeping.

A week from that time I knew all--the story, public and private, of that wonderful autumn, during which I had lain like a log in my bed. At first, avoiding topics that touched me too nearly, Father Benôit told me of Paris; of the ten weeks of suspicion and suspense which followed the Bastille riots--weeks during which the Fauxbourgs, scantly checked by Lafayette and his National Guards, kept jealous watch on Versailles, where the Assembly sat in attendance on the King; of the scarcity which prevailed through this trying time, and the constant rumours of an attack by the Court; of the Queen's unfortunate banquet, which proved to be the spark that fired the mine; last of all, of the great march of the women to Versailles, on the 5th of October, which, by forcing the King and the Assembly to Paris, and making the King a prisoner in his own palace, put an end to this period of uncertainty.

"And since then?" I said in feeble amazement. "This is the 20th of November, you tell me?"

"Nothing has happened," he answered, "except signs and symptoms."

"And those?"

He shook his head gravely. "Every one is enrolled in the National Guards--that, for one. Here in Quercy, the corps which M. Hugues took it in hand to form numbers some thousands. Every one is armed, therefore. Then, the game laws being abolished, every one is a sportsman. And so many nobles have emigrated, that either there are no nobles or all are nobles."

"But who governs?"

"The Municipalities. Or, where there are none, Committees."

I could not help smiling. "And your Committee, M. le Curé?" I said.

"I do not attend it," he answered, wincing visibly. "To be plain, they go too fast for me. But I have worse yet to tell you!"

"What?"

"On the Fourth of August the Assembly abolished the tithes of the Church; early in this month they proposed to confiscate the estates of the Church! By this time it is probably done."

"What! And the clergy are to starve?" I cried in indignation.

"Not quite," he answered, smiling sadly. "They are to be paid by the State--as long as they please the State!"

He went soon after he had told me that; and I lay in amazement, looking through the window, and striving to picture the changed world that existed round me. Presently André came in with my broth. I thought it weak, and said so; the strong gust of outside life, which the news had brought into my chamber, had roused my appetite, and given me a distaste for *tisanes* and slops.

But the old fellow took the complaint very ill. "Well," he grumbled, "and what else is to be expected, Monsieur? With little rent paid, and half the pigeons in the cot slaughtered, and scarcely a hare left in the country side? With all the world shooting and snaring, and smiths and tailors cocked up on horses--ay, and with swords by their sides--and the gentry gone, or hiding their heads in beds, it is a small thing if the broth is weak! If M. le Vicomte liked strong broth, he should have been wise enough to keep the cow himself, and not----"

"Tut, tut, man!" I said, wincing in my turn. "What of Buton?"

"Monsieur means M. le Capitaine Buton?" the old man answered with a sneer. "He is at Cahors."

"And was any one punished for--for the affair at St. Alais?"

"No one is punished now-a-days," André replied tartly. "Except sometimes a miller, who is hung because corn is dear."

"Then even Petit Jean----"

"Petit Jean went to Paris. Doubtless he is now a Major or a Colonel."

With this shot the old man left me--left me writhing. For through all I had not dared to ask the one thing I wished to know; the one thing that, as my strength increased, had grown with it, from a vague apprehension of evil, which the mind, when bidden do its duty, failed to grasp, to a dreadful anxiety only too well understood and defined; a brooding fear that weighed upon me like an evil dream, and in spite of youth sapped my life, and retarded my recovery.

I have read that a fever sometimes burns out love; and that a man rises cured not only of his illness, but of the passion which consumed him, when he succumbed to it. But this was not my fate; from the moment when that dull anxiety about I knew not what took shape and form, and I saw on the green curtains of my bed a pale child's face--a face that now wept and now gazed at me in sad appeal--from that moment Mademoiselle was never out of my waking mind for an hour. God knows, if any thought of me on her part, if any silent cry of her heart to me in her troubles, had to do with this; but it was the case.

However, on the next day the fear and the weight were removed. I suppose that Father Benôit had made up his mind to broach the subject, which hitherto he had shunned with care; for his first question, after he had learned how I did, brought it up. "You have never asked what happened after you were injured, M. le Vicomte?" he said with a little hesitation. "Do you remember?"

"I remember all," I said with a groan.

He drew a breath of relief. I think he had feared that there was still something amiss with the brain. "And yet you have never asked?" he said.

"Man! cannot you understand why--why I have not asked?" I cried hoarsely, rising, and sinking back in my seat in uncontrollable agitation. "Cannot you understand that until I asked I had hope? But now, torture me no longer! Tell me, tell me all, man, and then----"

"There is nothing but good to tell," he answered cheerfully, endeavouring to dispel my fears at the first word. "You know the worst. Poor M. de Gontaut was killed on the stairs. He was too infirm to flee. The rest, to the meanest servant, got away over the roofs of the neighbouring houses."

"And escaped?"

"Yes. The town was in an uproar for many hours, but they were well hidden. I believe that they have left the country."

"You do not know where they are, then?"

"No," he answered, "I never saw any of them after the outbreak. But I heard of them being in this or that château--at the Harincourts', and elsewhere. Then the Harincourts left--about the middle of October, and I think that M. de St. Alais and his family went with them."

I lay for a while too full of thankfulness to speak. Then, "And you know nothing more?"

"Nothing," the Curé answered.

But that was enough for me. When he came again I was able to walk with him on the terrace, and after that I gained strength rapidly. I remarked, however, that as my spirits rose, with air and exercise, the good priest's declined. His kind, sensitive face grew day by day more sombre, his fits of silence longer. When I asked him the reason, "It goes ill, it goes ill," he said. "And, God forgive me, I had to do with it."

"Who had not?" I said soberly.

"But I should have foreseen!" he answered, wringing his hands openly. "I should have known that God's first gift to man was Order. Order, and to-day, in Cahors, there is no tribunal, or none that acts: the old magistrates are afraid, and the old laws are spurned, and no man can even recover a debt! Order, and the worst thing a criminal, thrown into prison, has now to fear is that he may be forgotten. Order, and I see arms everywhere, and men who cannot read teaching those who can, and men who pay no taxes disposing of the money of those who do! I see famine in the town, and the farmers and the peasants killing game or folding their hands; for who will work when the future is uncertain? I see the houses of the rich empty, and their servants starving; I see all trade, all commerce, all buying and selling, except of the barest necessaries, at an end! I see all these things, M. le Vicomte, and shall I not say, 'Mea Culpa, Mea Culpa'?"

"But liberty," I said feebly. "You once said yourself that a certain price must----"

"Is liberty licence to do wrong?" he answered with passion--seldom had I seen him so moved. "Is liberty licence to rob and blaspheme, and move your neighbour's landmark? Does tyranny cease to be tyranny, when the tyrants are no longer one, but a thousand? M. le Vicomte, I know not what to do, I know not what to do," he continued. "For a little I would go out into the world, and at all costs unsay what I have said, undo what I have done! I would! I would indeed!"

"Something more has happened?" I said, startled by this outbreak. "Something I have not heard?"

"The Assembly took away our tithes and our estates!" he answered bitterly. "That you know. They denied our existence as a Church. That you know. They have now decreed the suppression of all religious houses. Presently they will close also our churches and cathedrals. And we shall be pagans!"

"Impossible!" I said.

"But it is true."

"The suppression, yes. But for the churches and cathedrals----"

"Why not?" he answered despondently. "God knows there is little faith abroad. I fear it will come. I see it coming. The greater need--that we who believe should testify."

I did not quite understand at the time what he meant or would be at, or what he had in his mind; but I saw that his scrupulous nature was tormented by the thought that he had hastened the catastrophe; and I felt uneasy when he did not appear next day at his usual time for visiting me. On the following day he came; but was downcast and taciturn, taking leave of me when he went with a sad kindness that almost made me call him back. The next day again he did not appear; nor the day after that. Then I sent for him, but too late; I sent, only to learn from his old housekeeper that he had left home suddenly, after arranging with a neighbouring curé to have his duties performed for a month.

I was able by this time to go abroad a little, and I walked down to his cottage; I could learn no more there, however, than that a Capuchin monk had been his guest for two nights, and that M. le Curé had left for Cahors a few hours after the monk. That was all; I returned depressed and dissatisfied. Such villagers as I met by the way greeted me with respect, and even with sympathy--it was the first time I had gone into the hamlet; but the shadow of suspicion which I had detected on their faces some months before had grown deeper and darker with time. They no longer knew with certainty their places or mine, their rights or mine; and shy of me and doubtful of themselves, were glad to part from me.

Near the gates of the avenue I met a man whom I knew; a wine-dealer from Aulnoy. I stayed to ask him if the family were at home.

He looked at me in surprise. "No, M. le Vicomte," he said. "They left the country some weeks ago--after the King was persuaded to go to Paris."

"And M. le Baron?"

"He too."

"For Paris?"

The man, a respectable bourgeois, grinned at me. "No, Monsieur, I fancy not," he said. "You know best, M. le Vicomte; but if I said Turin, I doubt I should be little out."

"I have been ill," I said. "And have heard nothing."

"You should go into Cahors," he answered; with rough good-nature. "Most of the gentry are there--if they have not gone farther. It is safer than the country in these days. Ah, if my father had lived to see----"

He did not finish the sentence in words, but raised his eyebrows and shoulders, saluted me, and rode away. In spite of his surprise it was easy to see that the change pleased him, though he veiled his satisfaction out of civility.

I walked home feeling lonely and depressed. The tall stone house, the seigneurial tower and turret and dovecot, stripped of the veil of foliage that in summer softened their outlines, stood up bare and gaunt at the end of the avenue; and seemed in some strange way to share my loneliness and to speak to me of evil days on which we had alike fallen. In losing Father Benôit I had lost my only chance of society just when, with returning strength, the desire for companionship and a more active life was awakening. I thought of this gloomily; and then was delighted to see, as I approached the door, a horse tethered to the ring beside it. There were holsters on the saddle, and the girths were splashed.

André was in the hall, but to my surprise, instead of informing me that there was a visitor, he went on dusting a table, with his back to me.

"Who is here?" I said sharply.

"No one," he answered.

"No one? Then whose is that horse?"

"The smith's, Monsieur."

"What? Buton's?"

"Ay, Buton's! It is a new thing hanging it at the front door," he added, with a sneer.

"But what is he doing? Where is he?"

"He is where he ought to be; and that is at the stables," the old fellow answered doggedly. "I'll be bound that it is the first piece of honest work he has done for many a day."

"Is he shoeing?"

"Why not? Does Monsieur want him to dine with him?" was the ill-tempered retort.

I took no notice of this, but went to the stables. I could hear the bellows heaving; and turning the corner of the building I came on Buton at work in the forge with two of his men. The smith was stripped to his shirt, and with his great leather apron round him, and his bare, blackened arms, looked like the Buton of six months ago. But outside the forge lay a little heap of clothes neatly folded, a blue coat with red facings, a long blue waistcoat, and a hat with a huge tricolour; and as he released the horse's hoof on which he was at work, and straightened himself to salute me, he looked at me with a new look, that was something between appeal and defiance.

"Tut, tut!" I said, fleering at him. "This is too great an honour, M. le Capitaine! To be shod by a member of the Committee!"

"Has M. le Vicomte anything of which to complain?" he said, reddening under the deep tan of his face.

"I? No, indeed. I am only overwhelmed by the honour you do me."

"I have been here to shoe once a month," he persisted stubbornly. "Does Monsieur complain that the horses have suffered?"

"No. But----"

"Has M. le Vicomte's house suffered? Has so much as a stack of his corn been burned, or a colt taken from the fields, or an egg from the nest?"

"No," I said.

Buton nodded gloomily. "Then if Monsieur has no fault to find," he replied, "perhaps he will let me finish my work. Afterwards I will deliver a message I have for him. But it is for his ear, and the forge----"

"Is not the place for secrets, though the smith is the man!" I answered, with a parting gibe, fired over my shoulders. "Well, come to me on the terrace when you have finished."

He came an hour later, looking hugely clumsy in his fine clothes; and with a sword--heaven save us!--a sword by his side. Presently the murder came out; he was the bearer of a commission appointing me Lieutenant-Colonel in the National Guard of the Province. "It was given at my request," he said, with awkward pride. "There were some, M. le Vicomte, who thought that you had not behaved altogether well in the matter of the riot, but I rattled their heads together. Besides I said, 'No Lieutenant-Colonel, no Captain!' and they cannot do without me. I keep this side quiet."

What a position it was! Ah, what a position it was! And how for a moment the absurdity of it warred in my mind with the humiliation! Six months before I should have torn up the paper in a fury, and flung it in his face, and beaten him out of my presence with my cane. But much had happened since then; even the temptation to break into laughter, into peal upon peal of gloomy merriment, was not now invincible. I overcame it by an effort, partly out of prudence, partly from a better motive--a sense of the man's rough fidelity amid circumstances, and in face of anomalies, the most trying. I thanked him instead, therefore--though I almost choked; and I said I would write to the Committee.

Still he lingered, rubbing one great foot against another; and I waited with mock politeness to hear his business. At length, "There is another thing I wish to say, M. le Vicomte," he growled. "M. le Curé has left Saux."

"Yes?"

"Well, he is a good man; or he was a good man," he continued grudgingly. "But he is running into trouble, and you would do well to let him know that."

"Why?" I said. "Do you know where he is?"

"I can guess," he answered. "And where others are, too; and where there will presently be trouble. These Capuchin monks are not about the country for nothing. When the crows fly home there will be trouble. And I do not want him to be in it."

"I have not the least idea where he is," I said coldly. "Nor what you mean." The smith's tone had changed and grown savage and churlish.

"He has gone to Nîmes," he answered.

"To Nîmes?" I cried in astonishment. "How do you know? It is more than I know."

"I do know," he answered. "And what is brewing there. And so do a great many more. But this time the St. Alais and their bullies, M. le Vicomte--ay, they are all there--will not escape us. We will break their necks. Yes, M. le Vicomte, make no mistake," he continued, glaring at me, his eyes red with suspicion and anger, "mix yourselves up with none of this. We are the people! The people! Woe to the man or thing that stands in our way!"

"Go!" I said. "I have heard enough. Begone!"

He looked at me a moment as if he would answer me. But old habits overcame him, and with a sullen word of farewell he turned, and went round the house. A minute later I heard his horse trot down the avenue.

I had cut him short; nevertheless the instant he was gone I wished him back, that I might ask him more. The St. Alais at Nîmes? Father Benôit at Nîmes? And a plot brewing there in which all had a hand? In a moment the news opened a window, as it were, into a wider world, through which I looked, and no longer felt myself shut in by the lonely country round me and the lack of society. I looked and saw the great white dusty city of the south, and trouble rising in it, and in the middle of the trouble, looking at me wistfully, Denise de St. Alais.

Father Benôit had gone thither. Why might not I?

I walked up and down in a flutter of spirits, and the longer I considered it, the more I liked it; the longer I thought of the dull inaction in which I must spend my time at home, unless I consented to rub shoulders with Buton and his like, the more taken I was with the idea of leaving.

And after all why not? Why should I not go?

I had my commission in my pocket, wherein I was not only appointed to the National Guards, but described as *ci-devant* "President of the Council of Public Safety in the Province of Quercy"; and this taking the place of papers or passport would render travelling easy. My long illness would serve as an excuse for a change of air; and explain my absence from home; I had in the house as much money as I needed. In a word, I could see no difficulty, and nothing to hinder me, if I chose to go. I had only to please myself.

So the choice was soon made. The following day I mounted a horse for the first time, and rode two-thirds of a league on the road, and home again very tired.

Next morning I rode to St. Alais, and viewed the ruins of the house and returned; this time I was less fatigued.

Then on the following day, Sunday, I rested; and on the Monday I rode half-way to Cahors and back again. That evening I cleaned my pistols and overlooked Gil while he packed my saddle-bags, choosing two plain suits, one to pack and one to wear, and a hat with a small tricolour rosette. On the following morning, the 6th of March, I took the road; and parting from André on the outskirts of the village, turned my horse's head towards Figeac with a sense of freedom, of escape from difficulties and embarrassments, of hope and anticipation, that made that first hour delicious; and that still supported me when the March day began to give place to the chill darkness of evening--evening that in an unknown, untried place is always sombre and melancholy.

CHAPTER XV
AT MILHAU

I met with many strange things on that journey. I found it strange to see, as I went, armed peasants in the fields; to light in each village on men drilling; to enter inns and find half a dozen rustics seated round a table with glasses and wine, and perhaps an inkpot before them, and to learn that they called themselves a Committee. But towards evening of the third day I saw a stranger thing than any of these. I was beginning to mount the valley of the Tarn which runs up into the Cevennes at Milhau; a north wind was blowing, the sky was overcast, the landscape grey and bare; a league before me masses of mountain stood up gloomily blue. On a sudden, as I walked wearily beside my horse, I heard voices singing in chorus; and looked about me. The sound, clear and sweet as fairy's music, seemed to rise from the earth at my feet.

A few yards farther, and the mystery explained itself. I found myself on the verge of a little dip in the ground, and saw below me the roofs of a hamlet, and on the hither side of it a crowd of a hundred or more, men and women. They were dancing and singing round a great tree, leafless, but decked with flags: a few old people sat about the roots inside the circle, and but for the cold weather and the bleak outlook, I might have thought that I had come on a May-day festival.

My appearance checked the singing for a moment; then two elderly peasants made their way through the ring and came to meet me, walking hand in hand. "Welcome to Vlais and Giron!" cried one. "Welcome to Giron and Vlais!" cried the other. And then, before I could answer, "You come on a happy day," cried both together.

I could not help smiling. "I am glad of that," I said. "May I ask what is the reason of your meeting?"

"The Communes of Giron and Vlais, of Vlais and Giron," they answered, speaking alternately, "are today one. To-day, Monsieur, old boundaries disappear; old feuds die. The noble heart of Giron, the noble heart of Vlais, beat as one."

I could scarcely refrain from laughing at their simplicity; fortunately, at that moment, the circle round the tree resumed their song and dance, which had even in that weather a pretty effect, as of a Watteau *fête*. I congratulated the two peasants on the sight.

"But, Monsieur, this is nothing," one of them answered with perfect gravity. "It is not only that the boundaries of communes are disappearing; those of provinces are of the past also. At Valence, beyond the mountains, the two banks of the Rhone have clasped hands and sworn eternal amity. Henceforth all Frenchmen are brothers; all Frenchmen are of all provinces!"

"That is a fine idea," I said.

"No son of France will again shed French blood!" he continued.

"So be it."

"Catholic and Protestant, Protestant and Catholic will live at peace! There will be no law-suits. Grain will circulate freely, unchecked by toils or dues. All will be free, Monsieur. All will be rich."

They said more in the same sanguine simple tone, and with the same naïve confidence; but my thoughts strayed from them, attracted by a man, who, seated among the peasants at the foot of the tree, seemed to my eyes to be of another class. Tall and lean, with lank black hair, and features of a stern, sour cast, he had nothing of outward show to distinguish him from those round him. His dress, a rough hunting suit, was old and patched; the spurs on his brown, mud-stained boots were rusty and bent. Yet his carriage possessed an ease the others lacked; and in the way he watched the circling rustics I read a quiet scorn.

I did not notice that he heeded or returned my gaze, but I had not gone on my way a hundred paces, after taking leave of the two mayors and the revellers, before I heard a step, and looking round, saw the stranger coming after me. He beckoned, and I waited until he overtook me.

"You are going to Milhau?" he said, speaking abruptly, and with a strong country accent; yet in the tone of one addressing an equal.

"Yes, Monsieur," I said. "But I doubt if I shall reach the town to-night."

"I am going also," he answered. "My horse is in the village."

And without saying more he walked beside me until we reached the hamlet. There--the place was deserted--he brought from an outhouse a sorry mare, and mounted. "What do you think of that rubbish?" he said suddenly as we took the road again. I had watched his proceedings in silence.

"I fear that they expect too much," I answered guardedly.

He laughed; a horse-laugh full of scorn. "They think that the millennium has come," he said. "And in a month they will find their barns burned and their throats cut."

"I hope not," I said.

"Oh, I hope not," he answered cynically. "I hope not, of course. But even so *Vive la Nation! Vive la Revolution!*"

"What? If that be its fruit?" I asked.

"Ay, why not?" he answered, his gloomy eyes fixed on me. "It is every one for himself, and what has the old rule done for me that I should fear to try the new? Left me to starve on an old rock and a dovecot; sheltered by bare stones, and eating out of a black pot! While women and bankers, scented fops and lazy priests prick it before the King! And why? Because I remain, sir, what half the nation once were."

"A Protestant?" I hazarded.

"Yes, Monsieur. And a poor noble," he answered bitterly. "The Baron de Géol, at your service."

I gave him my name in return.

"You wear the tricolour," he said; "yet you think me extreme? I answer, that that is all very well for you; but we are different people. You are doubtless a family man, M. le Vicomte, with a wife----"

"On the contrary, M. le Baron."

"Then a mother, a sister?"

"No," I said, smiling. "I have neither. I am quite alone."

"At least with a home," he persisted, "means, friends, employment, or the chance of employment?"

"Yes," I said, "that is so."

"Whereas I--I," he answered, growing guttural in his excitement, "have none of these things. I cannot enter the army--I am a Protestant! I am shut off from the service of the State--I am a Protestant! I cannot be a lawyer or a judge--I am a Protestant! The King's schools are closed to me--I am a Protestant! I cannot appear at Court--I am a Protestant! I--in the eyes of the law I do not exist! I--I, Monsieur," he continued more slowly, and with an air not devoid of dignity, "whose ancestors stood before Kings, and whose grandfather's great-grandfather saved the fourth Henry's life at Coutras--I do not exist!"

"But now?" I said, startled by his tone of passion.

"Ay, now," he answered grimly, "it is going to be different. Now, it is going to be otherwise, unless these black crows of priests put the clock back again. That is why I am on the road."

"You are going to Milhau?"

"I live near Milhau," he answered. "And I have been from home. But I am not going home now. I am going farther--to Nîmes."

"To Nîmes?" I said in surprise.

"Yes," he said. And he looked at me askance and a trifle grimly, and did not say any more. By this time it was growing dark; the valley of the Tarn, along which our road lay, though fertile and pleasant to the eye in summer, wore at this season, and in the half-light, a savage and rugged aspect. Mountains towered on either side; and sometimes, where the road drew near the river, the rushing of the water as it swirled and eddied among the rocks below us, added its note of melancholy to the scene. I shivered. The uncertainty of my quest, the uncertainty of everything, the gloom of my companion, pressed upon me. I was glad when he roused himself from his brooding, and pointed to the lights of Milhau glimmering here and there on a little plain, where the mountains recede from the river.

"You are doubtless going to the inn?" he said, as we entered the outskirts. I assented. "Then we part here," he continued. "To-morrow, if you are going to Nîmes---- But you may prefer to travel alone."

"Far from it," I said.

"Well, I shall be leaving the east gate--about eight o'clock," he answered grudgingly. "Good-night, Monsieur."

I bade him good-night, and leaving him there, rode into the town: passing through narrow, mean streets, and under dark archways and hanging lanterns, that swung and creaked in the wind, and did everything but light the squalid obscurity. Though night had fallen, people were moving briskly to and fro, or standing at their doors; the place, after the solitude through which I had ridden, had the air of a city; and presently I became aware that a little crowd was following my horse. Before I reached the inn, which stood in a dimly-lit square, the crowd had grown into a great one, and was beginning to press upon me; some who marched nearest to me staring up inquisitively into my face, while others, farther off, called to their neighbours, or to dim forms seen at basement windows, that it was he!

I found this somewhat alarming. Still they did not molest me; but when I halted they halted too, and I was forced to dismount almost in their arms. "Is this the inn?" I said to those nearest to me; striving to appear at my ease.

"Yes! yes!" they cried with one voice, "that is the inn!"

"My horse——"

"We will take the horse! Enter! Enter!"

I had little choice, they flocked so closely round me; and, affecting carelessness, I complied, thinking that they would not follow, and that inside I should learn the meaning of their conduct. But the moment my back was turned they pressed in after me and beside me, and, almost sweeping me off my feet, urged me along the narrow passage of the house, whether I would or no. I tried to turn and remonstrate; but the foremost drowned my words in loud cries for "M. Flandre! M. Flandre!"

Fortunately the person addressed was not far off. A door towards which I was being urged opened, and he appeared. He proved to be an immensely stout man, with a face to match his body; and he gazed at us for a moment, astounded by the invasion. Then he asked angrily what was the matter. "*Ventre de Ciel!*" he cried. "Is this my house or yours, rascals? Who is this?"

"The Capuchin! The Capuchin!" cried a dozen voices.

"Ho! ho!" he answered, before I could speak. "Bring a light."

Two or three bare-armed women whom the noise had brought to the door of the kitchen fetched candles, and raising them above their heads gazed at me curiously. "Ho! ho!" he said again. "The Capuchin is it? So you have got him."

"Do I look like one?" I cried angrily, thrusting back those who pressed on me most closely. "*Nom de Dieu!* Is this the way you receive guests, Monsieur? Or is the town gone mad?"

"You are not the Capuchin monk?" he said, somewhat taken aback, I could see, by my boldness.

"Have I not said that I am not? Do monks in your country travel in boots and spurs?" I retorted.

"Then your papers!" he answered curtly. "Your papers! I would have you to know," he continued, puffing out his cheeks, "that I am Mayor here as well as host, and I keep the jail as well as the inn. Your papers, Monsieur, if you prefer the one to the other."

"Before your friends here?" I said contemptuously.

"They are good citizens," he answered.

I had some fear, now I had come to the pinch, that the commission I carried might fail to produce all the effects with which I had credited it. But I had no choice, and ultimately nothing to dread; and after a momentary hesitation I produced it. Fortunately it was drawn in complimentary terms and gave the Mayor, I know not how, the idea that I was actually bound at the moment on an errand of state. When he had read it, therefore, he broke into a hundred apologies, craved leave to salute me, and announced to the listening crowd that they had made a mistake.

It struck me at the time as strange, that they, the crowd, were not at all embarrassed by their error. On the contrary, they hastened to congratulate me on my acquittal, and even patted me on the shoulder in their good humour; some went to see that my horse was brought in, or to give orders on my behalf, and the rest presently dispersed, leaving me fain to believe that they would have hung me to the nearest *lanterne* with the same stolid complaisance.

When only two or three remained, I asked the Mayor for whom they had taken me.

"A disguised monk, M. le Vicomte," he said. "A very dangerous fellow, who is known to be travelling with two ladies--all to Nîmes; and orders have been sent from a high quarter to arrest him."

"But I am alone!" I protested. "I have no ladies with me."

He shrugged his shoulders. "Just so, M. le Vicomte," he answered. "But we have got the two ladies. They were arrested this morning, while attempting to pass through the town in a carriage. We know, therefore, that he is now alone."

"Oh," I said. "So now you only want him? And what is the charge against him?" I continued, remembering with a languid stirring of the pulses that a Capuchin monk had visited Father Benôit before his departure. It seemed to be strange that I should come upon the traces of another here.

"He is charged," M. Flandre answered pompously, "with high treason against the nation, Monsieur. He has been seen here, there, and everywhere, at Montpellier, and Cette, and Albi, and as far away as Auch; and always preaching war and superstition, and corrupting the people."

"And the ladies?" I said smiling. "Have they too been corrupting----"

"No, M. le Vicomte. But it is believed that wishing to return to Nîmes, and learning that the roads were watched, he disguised himself and joined himself to them. Doubtless they are *dévotes*."

"Poor things!" I said, with a shudder of compassion; every one seemed to be so good-tempered, and yet so hard. "What will you do with them?"

"I shall send for orders," he answered. "In his case," he continued airily, "I should not need them. But here is your supper. Pardon me, M. le Vicomte, if I do not attend on you myself. As Mayor I have to take care that I do not compromise--but you understand?"

I said civilly that I did; and supper being laid, as was then the custom in the smaller inns, in my bedroom, I asked him to take a glass of wine with me, and over the meal learned much of the state of the country, and the fermentation that was at work along the southern seaboard, the priests stirring up the people with processions and sermons. He waxed especially eloquent upon the excitement at Nîmes, where the masses were bigoted Romanists, while the Protestants had a following, too, with the hardy peasants of the mountains behind them. "There will be trouble, M. le Vicomte, there will be trouble there," he said with meaning. "Things are going too well for the people *la bas*. They will stop them if they can."

"And this man?"

"Is one of their missionaries."

I thought of Father Benôit, and sighed. "By the way," the Mayor said abruptly, gazing at me in moony thoughtfulness, "that is curious now!"

"What?" I said.

"You come from Cahors, M. le Vicomte?"

"Well?"

"So do these women; or they say they do. The prisoners."

"From Cahors?"

"Yes. It is odd now," he continued, rubbing his chin, "but when I read your commission I did not think of that."

I shrugged my shoulders impatiently. "It does not follow that I am in the plot," I said. "For goodness sake, M. le Maire, do not let us open the case again. You have seen my papers, and----"

"Tut! tut!" he said. "That is not my meaning. But you may know these persons."

"Oh!" I said; and then I sat a moment, staring at him between the candles, my hand raised, a morsel on my fork. A wild extravagant thought had flashed into my mind. Two ladies from Cahors? From Cahors, of all places? "How do they call themselves?" I asked.

"Corvas," he answered.

"Oh! Corvas," I said, falling to eating again, and putting the morsel into my mouth. And I went on with my supper.

"Yes. A merchant's wife, she says she is. But you shall see her."

"I don't remember the name," I answered.

"Still, you may know them," he rejoined, with the dull persistence of a man of few ideas. "It is just possible that we have made a mistake, for we found no papers in the carriage, and only one thing that seemed suspicious."

"What was that?"

"A red cockade."

"A *red* cockade?"

"Yes," he answered. "The badge of the old Leaguers, you know."

"But," I said, "I have not heard of any party adopting that."

He rubbed his bald head a little doubtfully. "No," he said, "that is true. Still, it is a colour we don't like here. And two ladies travelling alone--alone, Monsieur! Then their driver, a half-witted fellow, who said that they had engaged him at Rodez, though he denied stoutly that he had seen the Capuchin, told two or three tales. However, if you will eat no more, M. le Vicomte, I will take you to see them. You may be able to speak for or against them."

"If you do not think that it is too late?" I said, shrinking somewhat from the interview.

"Prisoners must not be choosers," he answered, with an unpleasant chuckle. And he called from the door for a lantern and his cloak.

⹀ "The ladies are not here, then?" I said.

"No," he answered, with a wink. "Safe bind, safe find! But they have nothing to cry about. There are one or two rough fellows in the clink, so Babet, the jailer, has given them room in his house."

At this moment the lantern came, and the Mayor having wrapped his portly person in a cloak, we passed out of the house. The square outside was utterly dark, such lights as had been burning when I arrived had been extinguished, perhaps by the wind, which was rising, and now blew keenly across the open space. The yellow glare of the lantern was necessary, but though it showed us a few feet of the roadway, and enabled us to pick our steps, it redoubled the darkness beyond; I could not see even the line of the roofs, and had no idea in what direction we had gone or how far, when M. Flandre halted abruptly, and, raising the lantern, threw its light on a greasy stone wall, from which, set deep in the stone-work, a low iron-studded door frowned on us. About the middle of the door hung a huge knocker, and above it was a small *grille*.

"Safe bind, safe find!" the Mayor said again with a fat chuckle; but, instead of raising the knocker, he drew his stick sharply across the bars of the *grille*.

The summons was understood and quickly answered. A face peered a moment through the grating; then the door opened to us. The Mayor took the lead, and we passed in, out of the night, into a close, warm air reeking of onions and foul tobacco, and a hundred like odours. The jailer silently locked the door behind us, and, taking the Mayor's lantern from him, led the way down a grimy, low-roofed passage barely wide enough for one man. He halted at the first door on the left of the passage, and threw it open.

M. Flandre entered first, and, standing while he removed his hat, for an instant filled the doorway. I had time to hear and note a burst of obscene singing, which came from a room farther down the passage; and the frequent baying of a prison-dog, that, hearing us, flung itself against its chain, somewhere in the same direction. I noted, too, that the walls of the passage in which I stood were dingy and trickling with moisture, and then a voice, speaking in answer to M. Flandre's salutation, caught my ear and held me motionless.

The voice was Madame's--Madame de St. Alais'!

It was fortunate that I had entertained, though but a second, the wild, extravagant thought that had occurred to me at supper; for in a measure it had prepared me. And I had little time for other preparation, for thought, or decision. Luckily the room was thick with vile tobacco smoke, and the steam from linen drying by the fire; and I took advantage of a fit of coughing, partly assumed, to linger an instant on the threshold after M. Flandre had gone in. Then I followed him.

There were four people in the room besides the Mayor, but I had no eyes for the frowsy man and woman who sat playing with a filthy pack of cards at a table in the middle of the floor. I had only eyes for Madame and Mademoiselle, and them I devoured. They sat on two stools on the farther side of the hearth; the girl with her head laid wearily back against the wall, and her eyes half-closed; the mother, erect and watchful, meeting the Mayor's look with a smile of contempt. Neither the prison-house, nor danger, nor the companionship of this squalid hole had had power to reduce her fine spirit; but as her eyes passed from the Mayor and encountered mine, she started to her feet with a gasping cry, and stood staring at me.

It was not wonderful that for a second, peering through the reek, she doubted. But one there was there who did not doubt. Mademoiselle had sprung up in alarm at the sound of her mother's cry, and for the briefest moment we looked at one another. Then she sank back on her stool, and I heard her break into violent crying.

"Hallo!" said the Mayor. "What is this?"

"A mistake, I fear," I said hoarsely, in words I had already composed. "I am thankful, Madame," I continued, bowing to her with distant ceremony, and as much indifference as I could assume, "that I am so fortunate as to be here."

She muttered something and leaned against the wall. She had not yet recovered herself.

"You know the ladies?" the Mayor said, turning to me and speaking roughly; even with a tinge of suspicion in his voice. And he looked from one to the other of us sharply.

"Perfectly," I said.

"They are from Cahors?"

"From that neighbourhood."

"But," he said, "I told you their names, and you said that you did not know them, M. le Vicomte?"

For a moment I held my breath; gazing into Madame's face and reading there anxiety, and something more--a sudden terror. I took the leap--I could do nothing else. "You told me Corvas--that the lady's name was Corvas," I muttered.

"Yes," he said.

"But Madame's name is Corréas."

"Corréas?" he repeated, his jaw falling.

"Yes, Corréas. I dare say that the ladies," I continued with assumed politeness, "did not in their fright speak very clearly."

"And their name is Corréas?"

"I told you that it was," Madame answered, speaking for the first time, "and also that I knew nothing of your Capuchin monk. And this last," she continued earnestly, her eyes fixed on mine in passionate appeal--in appeal that this time could not be mistaken--"I say again, on my honour!"

I knew that she meant this for me; and I responded to the cry. "Yes, M. le Maire," I said, "I am afraid that you have made a mistake. I can answer for Madame as for myself."

The Mayor rubbed his head.

CHAPTER XVI
THREE IN A CARRIAGE

"Of course, if Madame--if Madame knows nothing of the monk," he said, looking vacantly about the dirty room, "it is clear that--it seems clear that there has been a mistake."

"And only one thing remains to be done," I suggested.

"But--but," he continued, with a resumption of his former importance, "there is still one point unexplained--that of the red cockade, Monsieur? What of that, M. le Vicomte?"

"The red cockade?" I said.

"Ay, what of that?" he asked briskly.

I had not expected this, and I looked desperately at Madame. Surely her woman's wit would find a way, whatever the cockade meant. "Have you asked Madame Corréas?" I said at last, feebly shifting the burden. "Have you asked her to explain it?"

"No," he answered.

"Then I would ask her," I said.

"Nay, do not ask me; ask M. le Vicomte," she answered lightly. "Ask him of what colour are the facings of the National Guards of Quercy?"

"Red!" I cried, in a burst of relief. "Red!" I knew, for had I not seen Buton's coat lying by the forge? But how Madame de St. Alais knew I have no idea.

"Ah!" M. Flandre said, with the air of one still a little doubtful. "And Madame wears the cockade for that reason?"

"No, M. le Maire," she answered, with a roguish smile; I saw that it was her plan to humour him. "I do not--my daughter does. If you wish to ask further, or the reason, you must ask her."

M. Flandre had the curiosity of the true bourgeois, and the love of the sex. He simpered. "If Mademoiselle would be so good," he said.

Denise had remained up to this point hidden behind her mother, but at the word she crept out, and reluctantly and like a prisoner brought to the bar, stood before us. It was only when she spoke, however, nay, it was not until she had spoken some words that I understood the full change that I saw in her; or why, instead of the picture of pallid weariness which she had presented a few minutes before, she now showed, as she stood forward, a face covered with blushes, and eyes shining and suffused.

"It is simple, Monsieur," she said in a low voice. "My *fiancé*, M. le Maire, is in that regiment."

"And you wear it for that reason?" the Mayor cried, delighted.

"I love him," she said softly. And for a moment--for a moment her eyes met mine.

Then I know not which was the redder, she or I; or which found that vile and filthy room more like a palace, its tobacco-laden air more sweet! I had not dreamed what she was going to say, least of all had I dreamed what her eyes said, as for that instant they met mine and turned my blood to fire! I lost the Mayor's blunt answer and his chuckling laugh; and only returned to a sense of the present when Mademoiselle slipped back to hide her burning face behind her mother, and I saw in her place Madame, facing me, with her finger to her lip, and a glance of warning in her eyes.

It was a warning not superfluous, for in the flush of my first enthusiasm I might have said anything. And the Mayor was in better hands than mine. The little touch of romance and sentiment which Mademoiselle's avowal had imported into the matter, had removed his last suspicion and won his heart. He ogled Madame, he beamed on the girl with fatherly gallantry. He made a jest of the monk.

"A mistake, and yet one I cannot deplore, Madame," he protested, with clumsy civility. "For it has given me the pleasure of seeing you."

"Oh, M. le Maire!" Madame simpered.

"But the state of the country is really such," he continued, "that for the beautiful sex to be travelling alone is not safe. It exposes them----"

"To worse *rencontres* than this, I fear," Madame said, darting a look from her fine eyes. "If this were the worst we poor women had to fear!" And she looked at him again.

"Ah, Madame!" he said, delighted.

"But, alas, we have no escort."

The fat Mayor sighed, I think that he was going to offer himself. Then a thought struck him. "Perhaps this gentleman," and he turned to me. "You go to Nîmes, M. le Vicomte?"

"Yes," I said. "And, of course, if Madame Corréas----"

"Oh, it would be troubling M. le Vicomte," Madame said; and she went a step farther from me and a step nearer to M. Flandre, as if he must understand her hesitation.

"I am sure it could be no trouble to any one!" he answered stoutly. "But for the matter of that, if M. le Vicomte perceives any difficulty," and he laid his hand on his heart, "I will find some one----"

"Some one?" Madame said archly.

"Myself," the Mayor answered.

"Ah!" she cried, "if you----"

But I thought that now I might safely step in. "No, no," I said. "M. le Maire is taking all against me. I can assure you, Madame, I shall be glad to be of service to you. And our roads lie together. If, therefore----"

"I shall be grateful," Madame answered with a delightful little courtesy. "That is, if M. le Maire will let out his poor prisoners. Who, as he now knows, have done nothing worse than sympathise with National Guards."

"I will take it on myself, Madame," M. Flandre said, with vast importance. He had been brought to the desired point. "The case is quite clear. But----" he paused and coughed slightly, "to avoid complications, you had better leave early. When you are gone, I shall know what explanations to give. And if you would not object to spending the night here," he continued, looking round him, with a touch of sheepishness, "I think that----"

"We shall mind it less than before," Madame said, with a look and a sigh. "I feel safe since you have been to see us." And she held out a hand that was still white and plump.

The Mayor kissed it.

As I walked, a few minutes later, across the square, picking my steps by the yellow light of M. Flandre's lantern, and at times enveloped in the flying skirt of his cloak--for the good man had his own visions and for a hundred yards together forgot his company--I could have thought all that had passed a dream; so unreal seemed the squalid prison-lodging I had just left, so marvellous the ladies' presence in it, so incredible Mademoiselle's blushing avowal made to my face. But a wheezing clock overhead struck the hour before midnight, and I counted the strokes; a watchman, not far from me, cried, after the old fashion, that it was eleven o'clock and a fine night; and I stumbled over a stone. No, I was not dreaming.

But if I had to stumble then, to persuade myself that I was awake, how was it with me next morning, when, with the first glimmer of light, I walked beside the carriage from the inn to the prison, and saw, before I reached the gloomy door, Madame and Mademoiselle standing shivering under the wall beside it? How was it with me when I held Mademoiselle's hand in mine, as I helped her in, and then followed her in and sat opposite to her- -sat opposite to her with the knowledge that I was so to sit for days, that I was to be her fellow-traveller, that we were to go to Nîmes together?

Ah, how was it, indeed? But there is nothing quite perfect; there is no hour in which a man says that he is quite happy; and a shadow of fear and stealth darkened my bliss that morning. The Mayor was there to see us start, and I fancy that it was his face of apprehension that lay at the bottom of this feeling. A moment, however, and the face was gone from the window; another, and the carriage began to roll quickly through the dim streets, while we lay back, each in a corner, hidden by the darkness even from one another. Still, we had the gates to pass, and the guard; or the watch might stop us, or some early-rising townsman, or any one of a hundred accidents. My heart beat fast.

But all went well. Within five minutes we had passed the gates and left them behind us, and were rolling in safety along the road. The dawn was no more than grey, the trees showed black against the sky, as we crossed the Tarn by the great bridge, and began to climb the valley of the Dourbie.

I have said that we could not see one another. But on a sudden Madame laughed out of the darkness of her corner. "O Richard, O *mon Roi!*" she hummed. Then "The fat fool!" she cried; and she laughed again.

I thought her cruel, and almost an ingrate; but she was Mademoiselle's mother, and I said nothing. Mademoiselle was opposite to me, and I was happy. I was happy, thinking what she would say to me, and how she would look at me, when the day came and she could no longer escape my eyes; when the day came and the dainty, half-shrouded face that already began to glimmer in the roomy corner of the old berlin should be mine to look on, to feast my eyes on, to question and read through long days and hours of a journey, a journey through heaven!

Already it was growing light; I had but a little longer to wait. A rosy flush began to tinge one half the sky; the other half, pale blue and flecked with golden clouds, lay behind us. A few seconds, and the mountain tips caught the first rays of the sun, and floated far over us, in golden ether. I cast one greedy glance at Mademoiselle's face, saw there the dawn out-blushed,

I met for one second her eyes and saw the glory of the ether outshone--and then I looked away, trembling. It seemed sacrilege to look longer.

Suddenly Madame laughed again, out of her corner; a laugh that made me wince, and grow hot. "She is not made for a nun, M. le Vicomte, is she?" she said.

I bounced in my seat. The speaker's tone, gay, insulting, flicked, not me, but the girl, like a whip.

"You really, Denise, must have had practice," Madame continued smoothly. "I love, you love, we love--you are quite perfect. Did you practise with M. le Directeur? Or with the big boys over the wall?"

"Madame!" I cried. The girl had drawn her hood over her face, but I could fancy her shame.

But Madame was inexorable. "Really, Denise, I do not know that I ever told even your father 'I love you,'" she said. "At any rate, until he had kissed me on the lips. But I suppose that you reverse the order----"

"Madame," I stammered. "This is infamous!"

"What, Monsieur?" she answered, this time heeding me. "May I not punish my daughter in my own way?"

"Not before me," I retorted, full of wrath. "It is cruel! It is----"

"Oh, before you, M. le Vicomte?" Madame answered, mocking me. "And why not before you? I cannot degrade her lower than she has herself stooped!"

"It is false!" I cried, in hot rage. "It is a cruel falsehood!"

"Oh, I can? Then if I please, I shall!" Madame answered, with ruthless pleasantry. "And you, Monsieur, will sit by and listen, if I please. Though, make no mistake, M. le Vicomte," she continued, leaning forward, and gazing keenly into my face. "Because I punish her before you, do not think that you are, or ever shall be, of the family. Or that this unmaidenly, immodest----"

Mademoiselle uttered a cry of pain, and shrank lower in her corner.

"Little fool," Madame continued coolly, "who, when she was primed with a cock-and-bull story about the cockade, must needs add, 'I love him'--I love him, and she a maiden!--will ever be anything to you! That link was broken long ago. It was broken when your friends burned our house at St. Alais; it was broken when they sacked our house in Cahors; it was broken when they made our king a prisoner, when they murdered our friends, when they dragged our Church a slave at the chariot wheels of their triumph; ay, and broken once for all, beyond mending by mock heroics! Understand that fully, M. le Vicomte," Madame continued pitilessly. "But as you saw her stoop, you shall see her punished. She is the first St. Alais that ever wooed a lover!"

I knew that of the family which would have given the lie to that statement; but it was not a tale for Mademoiselle's ears, and instead I rose. "At least, Madame," I said, bowing, "I can free Mademoiselle from the embarrassment of my presence. And I shall do so."

"No, you will not do even that," Madame answered unmoved. "If you will sit down, I will tell you why."

I sat down, compelled by her tone.

"You will not do it," Madame continued, looking me coolly in the face, "because I am bound to admit, though I no longer like you, that you are a gentleman."

"And therefore should leave you."

"On the contrary, for that reason you will continue to travel with us."

"Outside," I said.

"No, inside," she answered quietly. "We have no passport nor papers; without your company we should be stopped in each town through which we pass. It is unfortunate," Madame continued, shrugging her shoulders; "--I did not know that the country was in so bad a state, or I would have taken precautions--it is unfortunate. But as it is we must put up with it and travel together."

I felt a warm rush of joy, of triumph, of coming vengeance. "Thank you, Madame," I said, and I bowed to her, "for telling me that. It seems, then, that you are in my power."

"Ah?"

"And that to requite you for the pain you have just caused Mademoiselle, I have only to leave you."

"Well?"

"I see even now a little town before us; in three minutes we shall enter it. Very well, Madame. If you say another word to your daughter, if you insult her again in my presence by so much as a syllable, I leave you and go my way."

To my surprise Madame St. Alais broke into a silvery laugh. "You will not, Monsieur," she said. "And yet I shall treat my daughter as I please."

"I shall do so!"

"You will not."

"Why, then? Why shall I not?" I cried.

"Because," she answered, laughing softly, "you are a gentleman, M. le Vicomte, and can neither leave us nor endanger us. That is all."

I sank back in my seat, and glared at her in speechless indignation; seeing in a flash my impotence and her power. The cushions burned me; but I could not leave them.

She laughed again, well pleased. "There, I have told you what you will not do," she said. "Now I am going to tell you what you will do. In front, I am told, they are very suspicious. The story of Madame Corvas, even if backed by your word, may not suffice. You will say, therefore, that I am your mother, and that Mademoiselle is your sister. She would prefer, I daresay," Madame continued, with a cutting glance at her daughter, "to pass for your wife. But that does not suit me."

I breathed hard; but I was helpless as any prisoner, closely bound to obedience as any slave. I could not denounce them, and I could not leave them; honour and love were alike concerned. Yet I foresaw that I must listen, hour by hour, and mile by mile, to gibes at the girl's expense, to sneers at her modesty, to words that cut like whip-lashes. That was Madame's plan. The girl must travel with me, must breathe the same air with me, must sit for hours with the hem of her skirt touching my boot. It was necessary for the safety of all. But, after this, after what we had both heard, if her eye met mine, it could only fall; if her hand touched mine, she must shrink in shame. Henceforth there was a barrier between us.

As a fact, Mademoiselle's pride came to her aid, and she sat, neither weeping nor protesting, nor seeking to join her forces to mine by a glance; but bearing all with steadfast patience, she looked out of the window when I pretended to sleep, and looked towards her mother when I sat erect. Possibly she found her compensations, and bore her punishment quietly for their sake. But I did not think of that. Possibly, too, she suffered less than I fancied; but I doubt if she would admit that, even to-day.

At any rate she had heard me fight her battle; yet she did not speak to me nor I to her; and under these strange conditions we began and pursued the strangest journey man ever made. We drove through pleasant valleys growing green, over sterile passes, where winter still fringed the rocks with snow, through sunshine, and in the teeth of cold mountain winds; but we scarcely heeded any of these things. Our hearts and thoughts lay inside the carriage, where Madame sat smiling, and we two kept grim silence.

About noon we halted to rest and eat at a little village inn, high up. It seemed to me a place almost at the end of the world, with a chaos of mountains rising tier on tier above it, and slopes of shale below. But the frenzy of the time had reached even this barren nook. Before we had taken two mouthfuls, the Syndic called to see our papers; and--God knows I had no choice--Madame passed for my mother, and Denise for my sister. Then, while the Syndic still stood bowing over my commission, and striving to learn from me what news there was below, a horse halted at the door, and I heard a man's voice, and in a breath M. le Baron de Géol walked in. There was a single decent room in the inn--that in which we sat--and he came into it.

He uncovered, seeing ladies; and recognising me with a start smiled, but a trifle sourly. "You set off early?" he said. "I waited at the east gate, but you did not come, Monsieur."

I coloured, conscience-stricken, and begged a thousand pardons. As a fact, I had clean forgotten him. I had not once thought of the appointment I had made with him at the gate.

"You are not riding?" he said, looking at my companions a little strangely.

"No," I answered. And I could not find another word to say. The Syndic still stood smiling and bowing beside me; and on a sudden I saw the pit on the edge of which I tottered; and my face burned.

"You have met friends?" M. le Baron persisted, looking, hat in hand, at Madame.

"Yes," I muttered. Politeness required that I should introduce him. But I dared not.

However, at that, he at last took the hint; and retired with the Syndic. The moment they were over the threshold Madame flashed out at me, in a passion of anger. "Fool!" she said, without ceremony, "why did you not present him? Don't you know that that is the way to arouse suspicion, and ruin us? A child could see that you had something to hide. If you had presented him at once to your mother----"

"Yes, Madame?"

"He would have gone away satisfied."

"I doubt it, Madame, and for a very good reason," I answered cynically. "Seeing that yesterday I told him, with the utmost particularity, that I had neither mother nor sister."

That afforded me a little revenge. Madame St. Alais went white and red in the same instant, and sat a moment with her lips pressed together, and her eyes on the table. "Who is he? What do you know of him?" she said at last.

"He is a poor gentleman and a bigoted Protestant," I answered drily.

She bit her lip. "*Bon Dieu!*" she muttered. "Who could have foreseen such an accident? Do you think that he suspects anything?"

"Doubtless. To begin, I left early this morning, in breach of an agreement to travel with him. When he learns, in addition, that I am travelling with my mother and sister, whom yesterday I did not possess----"

Madame looked at me, as if she would strike me. "What will you do?" she cried.

"It is for my mother to say," I answered politely. And I helped myself very indifferently to cheese. "She dictated this policy."

She was white with rage, and perhaps alarm; I chuckled secretly, seeing her condition. But rage availed her little; she had to humble herself. "What do you advise?" she said at last.

"There is only one course open," I answered. "We must brazen it out."

She agreed. But this, though a very easy course to advise, was one anything but easy to pursue. I discovered that, a few minutes later, when I went out to see if the carriage was ready, and found De Géol in the doorway with a face as hard as his own hills. "You are starting?" he said.

I muttered that I was.

"I find that I have to congratulate you," he continued, with a smile of unpleasant meaning.

"On what, Monsieur?"

"On finding your family," he answered, looking at me with a bitter sort of humour. "To discover both a mother and a sister in twenty-four hours must be great happiness. But--may I give you a hint, M. le Vicomte?"

"If you please," I said, with desperate coolness.

"Then if--being so happy in making discoveries--you happen to light next on M. Froment--on M. Froment, the firebrand of Nîmes, false Capuchin, and false traitor!--do not adopt him also! That is all."

"I am not acquainted with him," I said coldly. He had spoken with passion and fire.

"Do not become so," he answered.

I shrugged my shoulders, and he said no more; and in a moment Madame and Mademoiselle came out, and took their seats, and I set out to walk up the hill beside the horses.

The ascent was steep and long and toilsome, and a dozen times as we climbed out of the valley we had to halt to breathe the cattle; a dozen times I looked back at the grey mountain inn lying on the desolate grey plateau at our feet. Always I found the Baron looking up at us, stern and gaunt and motionless as the house before which he stood. And I shivered.

CHAPTER XVII
FROMENT OF NÎMES

This encounter served neither to raise my spirits nor to remove the apprehensions with which I looked forward to our arrival in places more populous; places where suspicion, once roused, might be less easily allayed. True, Géol had not betrayed me, but he might have his reasons for that; nor did the fact any the more reconcile me to having on our trail this grim stalking-horse in whose person a fanaticism I had deemed dead lurked behind modern doctrines, and sought under the cloak of a new party to avenge old injuries. The barren slopes and rugged peaks that rose above us, as we plodded toilsomely onward, the windswept passes over which the horses scarce dragged the empty carriage, the melancholy fields of snow that lay to right and left, all tended to deepen the impression made on my mind; so that feeling him one with his native hills, I longed to escape from them, I longed to be clear of this desolation and to see before me the sunshine and olive slopes sweep down to the southern sea.

Yet even here there was a counterpoise. The peril which had startled me had not been lost on Madame St. Alais; it had sensibly lowered her tone, and damped the triumph with which she had been disposed to treat me. She was more quiet; and sitting in her place, or walking beside the labouring carriage, as it slowly wound its way round shoulders, or wearily climbed long *lacets*, she left me to myself. Nay, it did not escape me that distance, far from relieving, seemed to aggravate her anxiety; so that the farther we left the uncouth Baron behind, the more restless she grew, the more keenly she scanned the road behind us, and the less regard she paid to me.

This left me at liberty to use my eyes as I would; and I remember to this day that hour spent under the shoulder of Mont Aigoual. Mademoiselle, worn out by days and nights of exertion, had fallen asleep in her corner, and shaken by the jolting of the coach had let the cloak slip from her face. A faint flush warmed her cheeks, as if even in sleep she felt my eyes upon her; and though a tear presently stole from under her long lashes, a smile almost naïve--a smile that remained while the tear passed--seemed to say that the joys of that strange day surpassed the pains, and that in her sleep

Mademoiselle found nothing to regret. God, how I watched that smile! How I hoped that it was for me, how I prayed for her! Never before had it been my happiness to gaze on her uncontrolled, as I did now; to trace the shadow where the first tendrils of her hair stole up from the smooth, white forehead, to learn the soft curves of lips and chin, and the dainty ear half-hidden; to gaze at the blue-veined eyelids half in fear, half in the hope that they might rise and discover me!

Denise, my Denise! I breathed the word softly, in my heart, and was happy. In spite of all--the cold, the journey, Géol, Madame--I was happy. And then in a moment I fell to earth, as I heard a voice say clearly, "Is that he?"

It was Madame's voice, and I turned to her. I was relieved to find that she was not looking my way, but was on her feet, gazing back the way we had come. And in a moment, whether she gave an order or the driver halted on his own motion, the carriage came to a stand; in a mountain pass, where rocks lay huddled on either side.

"What is it?" I said in wonder.

She did not answer, but on the silence of the road and the mountains rose the thin strain of a whistled air. The air was "O Richard, *O mon Roi!*" In that solitude of rock and fell, it piped high and thin, and had a weird startling effect. I thrust out my head on the other side, and saw a man walking after us at his leisure; as if we had passed him, and then stood to wait for him. He was tall and stout, wore boots and a common-looking cloak; but for all that he had not the air of a man of the country.

"You are going to Ganges?" Madame cried to him, without preface.

"Yes, Madame," he answered, as he came quietly up, and saluted her.

"We can take you on," she said.

"A thousand thanks," he answered, his eyes twinkling. "You are too good. If the gentleman does not object?" And he looked at me, smiling without disguise.

"Oh, no!" Madame said, with a touch of contempt in her voice, "the gentleman will not object."

But that gave me, in the middle of my astonishment, the fillip that I needed. The device of the meeting was so transparent, the appearance of this man, in cloak and boots, on the desolate road far from any habitation, was so clearly a part of an arranged plan, that I could not swallow it; I must either fall in with it, be dupe, and play my *rôle* with my eyes open, or act at once. I awoke from my astonishment. "One moment, Madame," I said. "I do not know who this gentleman is."

She had resumed her seat, and the stranger had come up to the window on her side, and was looking in. He had a face of striking power, large-sized and coarse, but not unpleasant; with quick, bright eyes, and mobile lips that smiled easily. The hand he laid on the carriage door was immense.

I think my words took Madame by surprise. She flashed round on me. "Nonsense," she cried imperiously. And to him, "Get in, Monsieur."

"No," I retorted, half-rising. "Stay, if you please. Stay where you are, until----"

Madame turned to me, furious. "This is my carriage," she said.

"Absolutely," I answered.

"Then what do you mean?"

"Only that if this gentleman enters it, I leave it."

For an instant we looked at one another. Then she saw that I was determined, and, knowing my position, she lowered her tone. "Why?" she said, breathing quickly. "Why, because he enters it, should you leave it?"

"Because, Madame," I answered, "I see no reason for taking in a stranger whom we do not know. This gentleman may be everything that is upright----"

"He is no stranger!" she snapped. "I know him. Will that satisfy you?"

"If he will give me his name," I said.

Hitherto he had stood unmoved by the discussion, looking with a smile from one to the other of us; but at this he struck in. "With pleasure, Monsieur," he said. "My name is Alibon, and I am an advocate of Montauban, who last week had the good fortune----"

"No," I said, interrupting him brusquely, and once for all; "I think not. Not Alibon of Montauban. Froment of Nîmes, I think, Monsieur."

A little tract of snow flushed by the sunset lay behind him, and by contrast darkened his face; I could not see how he took my words. And a few seconds elapsed before he answered. When he did, however, he spoke calmly, and I fancied I detected as much vanity as chagrin in his tone. "Well, Monsieur," he said, "and if I am? What then?"

"If you are," I replied resolutely, meeting his eyes, "I decline to travel with you."

"And therefore," he retorted, "Madame, whose carriage this is, must not travel with me!"

"No, since she cannot travel without me," I answered with spirit.

He frowned at that; but in a moment, "And why?" he said with a sneer. "Am I not good enough for your excellency's company?"

"It is not a question of goodness," I said bluntly, "but of a passport, Monsieur. If you ask me, I do not travel with you because I hold a commission under the present Government, and I believe you to be working against that Government. I have lied for Madame St. Alais and her daughter. She was a woman and I had to save her. But I will not lie for you, nor be your cloak. Is that plain, Monsieur?"

"Quite," he said slowly. "Yet I serve the King. Whom do you serve?"

I was silent.

"Whose is this commission, Monsieur, that must not be contaminated?"

I writhed under the sneer, but I was silent.

"Come, M. le Vicomte," he continued frankly, and in a different tone. "Be yourself, I pray. I am Froment, you have guessed it. I am also a fugitive, and were my name spoken in Villeraugues, a league on, I should hang for it. And in Ganges the like. I am at your mercy, therefore, and I ask you to shelter me. Let me pass through Suméne and Ganges as one of your party; thenceforth onwards," he added with a smile and a gesture of conscious pride, "I can shift for myself."

I do not wonder I hesitated, I wonder I resisted. It seemed so small a thing to ask, so great a thing to refuse, that, though half a minute before my mind had been made up, I wavered; wavered miserably. I felt my face burn, I felt the passionate ardour of Madame's eyes as they devoured it, I felt the call of the silence for my answer. And I was near assenting. But as I turned feverishly in my seat to avoid Madame's look, my hand touched the packet which contained the commission, and the contact wrought a revulsion of feeling. I saw the thing as I had seen it before, and, rightly or wrongly, revolted from that which I had nearly done.

"No," I cried angrily. "I will not! I will not!"

"You coward!" Madame cried with sudden passion. And she sprang up as if to strike me, but sat down again trembling.

"It may be," I said. "But I will not do it."

"Why? Why? Why?" she cried.

"Because I carry that commission; and to use it to shelter M. Froment were a thing M. Froment would not do himself. That is all."

He shrugged his shoulders, and magnanimously kept silence. But she was furious. "Quixote!" she cried. "Oh, you are intolerable! But you shall suffer for it. *Eh, bien,* Monsieur, you shall suffer for it!" she repeated vehemently.

"Nay, Madame, you need not threaten," I retorted.

"For if I would, I could not. You forget that M. de Géol is no more than a league behind us, and bound for Nîmes; he may appear at any moment. At best he is sure to lodge where we do to-night. If he finds," I continued drily, "that I have added a brother to my growing family, I do not think that he will take it lightly."

But this, though she must have seen the sense of it, had no effect upon her. "Oh, you are intolerable!" she cried again. "Let me out! Let me out, Monsieur."

This last to Froment. I did not gainsay her, and he let her out, and the two walked a few paces away, talking rapidly.

I followed them with my eyes; and seeing him now, detached, as it were, and solitary in that dreary landscape--a man alone and in danger--I began to feel some compunction. A moment more, and I might have repented; but a touch fell on my sleeve, and I turned with a start to find Denise leaning towards me, with her face rapt and eager.

"Monsieur," she whispered eagerly; before she could say more I seized the hand with which she had touched me, and kissed it fiercely.

"No, Monsieur, no," she whispered, drawing it from me with her face grown crimson--but her eyes still met mine frankly. "Not now. I want to speak to you, to warn you, to ask you----"

"And I, Mademoiselle," I cried in the same low tone, "want to bless you, to thank you----"

"I want to ask you to take care of yourself," she persisted, shaking her head almost petulantly at me, to silence me. "Listen! Some trap will be laid for you. My mother would not harm you, though she is angry; but that man is desperate, and we are in straits. Be careful, therefore, Monsieur, and----"

"Have no fear," I said.

"Ah, but I have fear," she answered.

And the way in which she said that, and the way in which she looked at me, and looked away again like a startled bird, filled me with happiness--

with intense happiness; so that, though Madame came back at that moment, and no more passed between us, not even a look, but we had to sink back in our seats, and affect indifference, I was a different man for it. Perhaps something of this appeared in my face, for Madame, as she came up to the door, shot a suspicious glance at me, a glance almost of hatred; and from me looked keenly at her daughter. However, nothing was said except by Froment, who came up to the door and closed it, after she had entered. He raised his hat to me.

"M. le Vicomte," he said, with a little bitterness, "if a dog came to my door, as I came to you to-day, I would take him in!"

"You would do as I have done," I said.

"No," he said firmly; "I would take him in. Nevertheless, when we meet at Nîmes, I hope to convert you."

"To what?" I said coldly.

"To having a little faith," he answered, with dryness. "To having a little faith in something--and risking somewhat for it, Monsieur. I stand here," he went on, with a gesture that was not without grandeur, "alone and homeless, to-day; I do not know where I shall lie to-night. And why, M. le Vicomte? Because I alone in France have faith! Because I alone believe in anything! Because I alone believe even in myself! Do you think," he continued with rising scorn, "that if you nobles believed in your nobility, you could be unseated? Never! Or that if you, who say 'Long live the King!' believed in your King, he could be unseated? Never! Or that if you who profess to obey the Church believed in her, she could be uprooted? Never! But you believe in nothing, you admire nothing, you reverence nothing--and therefore you are doomed! Yes, doomed; for even the men with whom you have linked yourself have a sort of bastard faith in their theories, their philosophy, their reforms, that are to regenerate the world. But you--you believe in nothing; and you shall pass, as you pass from me now!"

He waved his hand with a gesture of menace, and before I could answer, the carriage rolled on, and left him standing there; the grey landscape, cold and barren, took the place of his face at the door. The light was beginning to fail; we were still a league from Villeraugues. I was glad to feel the carriage moving, and to be free from him; my heart, too, was warm because Denise sat opposite me, and I loved her. But for all that--and though Madame, glowering at me from her corner, troubled me little--the thought that I had deserted him--that, and his words, and one word in particular, hummed in my head, and oppressed me with a sense of coming ill. "Doomed! Doomed!"

He had said it as if he meant it. I could no longer question his eloquence. I could no longer be ignorant why they called him the firebrand of Nîmes. The hot breath of the southern city had come from him; the passion of world-old strifes had spoken in his voice. Uneasily I pondered over what he had said, and recalled the words spoken by Father Benôit, even by Géol, to the same effect; and so brooded in my corner, while the carriage jolted on and darkness fell, until presently we stopped in the village street.

I offered Madame St. Alais my arm to descend. "No, Monsieur," she said, repelling me with passion; "I will not touch you."

She meant, I think, to seclude herself and Mademoiselle, and leave me to sup alone. But in the inn there was only one great room for parlour, and kitchen, and all; and a little cupboard, veiled by a dingy curtain, in which the women might sleep if they pleased, but in which they could not possibly eat. The inn was, in fact, the worst in which I had stopped--the maid draggled and dirty, and smelling of the stable; the company three boors; the floor of earth; the windows unglazed. Madame, accustomed to travel, and supported by her anger, took all with the ease of a fine lady; but Denise, fresh from her convent, winced at the brawling and oaths that rose round her, and cowered, pale and frightened, on her stool.

A hundred times I was on the point of interfering to protect her from these outrages; but her eyes, when they made me happy by timidly seeking mine for an instant, seemed to pray me to abstain; and the men, as their senseless tirades showed, were delegates from Castres, who at a word would have raised the cry of "Aristocrats!" I refrained, therefore, and doubtless with wisdom; but even the arrival of Géol would have been a welcome interruption.

I have said that Madame heeded them little; but it presently appeared that I was mistaken. After we had supped, and when the noise was at its height, she came to me, where I sat a little apart, and, throwing into her tone all the anger and disgust which her face so well masked, she cried in my ear that we must start at daybreak.

"At daybreak--or before!" she whispered fiercely. "This is horrible! horrible!" she continued. "This place is killing me! I would start now, cold and dark as it is, if----"

"I will speak to them," I said, taking a step towards the table.

She clutched my sleeve, and pinched me until I winced. "Fool!" she said. "Would you ruin us all? A word, and we are betrayed. No; but at daybreak we go. We shall not sleep; and the moment it is light we go!"

I consented, of course; and, going to the driver, who had taken our place at the table, she whispered him also, and then came back to me, and bade me call him if he did not rise. This settled, she went towards the closet, whither Mademoiselle had already retired; but unfortunately her movements had drawn on her the attention of the clowns at the table, and one of these, rising suddenly as she passed, intercepted her.

"A toast, Madame! a toast!" he cried, with a gross hiccough; and reeling on his feet, he thrust a cup of wine in front of her. "A toast; and one that every man, woman, and child in France must drink, or be d----d! And that is the Tricolour! The Tricolour; and down with Madame Veto! The Tricolour, Madame! Drink to it!"

The drunken wretch pressed the cup on her, while his comrades roared, "Drink! Drink! The Tricolour; and down with Madame Veto!" and added jests and oaths I will not write.

This was too much; I sprang to my feet to chastise the wretches. But Madame, who preserved her presence of mind to a marvel, checked me by a glance. "No," she said, raising her head proudly; "I will not drink!"

"Ah!" he cried with a vile laugh. "An aristocrat, are we? Drink, nevertheless, or we shall show you----"

"I will not drink!" she retorted, facing him with superb courage. "And more, when M. de Géol arrives to-night, you will have to give an account to him."

The man's face fell. "You know the Baron de Géol?" he said in a different tone.

"I left him at the last village, and I expect him here to-night," she answered coolly. "And I would advise you, Monsieur, to drink your own toasts, and let others go! For he is not a man to brook an insult!"

The brawler shrugged his shoulders, to hide his mortification. "Oh! if you are a friend of his," he muttered, preparing to slink back to the table, "I suppose it is all right. He is a good man. No offence. If you are not an aristocrat----"

"I am no more of an aristocrat than is M. de Géol," she answered. And, with a cold bow, she turned, and went to the closet.

The men were a little less noisy after that; for Madame had rightly guessed that Géol's name was known and respected. They presently wrapped themselves in their cloaks, and lay down on the floor; and I did the same, passing the night, in the result, in greater comfort than I expected.

At first, it is true, I did not sleep; but later I fell into an uneasy slumber, and, passing from one troubled dream to another--for which I had, doubtless, to thank the foul air of the room--I awoke at last with a start, to find some one leaning over me. Apparently it was still night, for all was quiet; but the red embers of the fire glowed on the hearth, and dimly lit up the room, enabling me to see that it was Madame St. Alais who had roused me. She pointed to the other men, who still lay snoring.

"Hush!" she whispered, with her finger on her lip. "It is after five. Jules is harnessing the horses. I have paid the woman here, and in five minutes we shall be ready."

"But the sun will not rise for another hour," I answered. This was early starting with a vengeance!

Madame, however, had set her heart upon it. "Do you want to expose us to more of this?" she said, in a furious whisper. "To keep us here until Géol arrives, perhaps?"

"I am ready, Madame," I said.

This satisfied her; she flitted away without any more, and disappeared behind the curtain, and I heard whispering. I put on my boots, and, the room being very cold, stooped a moment over the fire, and drawing the embers together with my foot, warmed myself. Then I put on my cravat and sword, which I had removed, and stood ready to start. It seemed uselessly early; and we had started so early the day before! If Madame wished it, however, it was my place to give way to her.

In a moment she came to me again; and I saw, even by that light, that her face was twitching with eagerness. "Oh!" she said; "will he never come? That man will be all day. Go and hasten him, Monsieur! If Géol comes? Go, for pity's sake, and hasten him!"

I wondered, thinking such haste utterly vain and foolish--it was not likely that Géol would arrive at this hour; but, concluding that Madame's nerves had failed at last, I thought it proper to comply, and, stepping carefully over the sleepers, reached the door. I raised the latch, and in a moment was outside, and had closed the door behind me. The bitter dawn wind, laden with a fine snow, lashed my cheeks, and bit through my cloak, and made me shiver. In the east the daybreak was only faintly apparent; in every other quarter it was still night, and, for all I could see, might be midnight.

Very little in charity with Madame, I picked my way, shivering, to the door of the stable--a mean hovel, in a line with the house, and set in a sea of mud. It was closed, but a dim yellow light, proceeding from a window towards the farther end, showed me where Jules was at work; and I raised the latch, and called him. He did not answer, and I had to go in to him, passing behind three or four wretched nags--some on their legs and some lying down--until I came to our horses, which stood side by side at the end, with the lantern hung on a hook near them.

Still I did not see Jules, and I was standing wondering where he was-- for he did not answer--when, with a whish, something black struck me in the face. It blinded me; in a moment I found myself struggling in the folds of a cloak, that completely enveloped my face, while a grip of iron seized my arms and bound them to my sides. Taken completely by surprise, I tried to shout, but the heavy cloak stifled me; when, struggling desperately, I succeeded in uttering a half-choked cry, other hands than those which held me pressed the cloak more tightly over my face. In vain I writhed and twisted, and, half-suffocated, tried to free myself. I felt hands pass deftly over me, and knew that I was being robbed. Then, as I still resisted, the man who held me from behind tripped me up, and I fell, still in his grasp, on my face on the ground.

Fortunately I fell on some litter; but, even so, the shock drove the breath out of me; and what with that and the cloak, which in this new position threatened to strangle me outright, I lay a moment helpless, while the wretches bound my hands behind me, and tied my ankles together. Thus secured, I felt myself taken up, and carried a little way, and flung roughly down on a soft bed--of hay, as I knew by the scent. Then some one threw a truss of hay on me, and more and more hay, until I thought that I should be stifled, and tried frantically to shout. But the cloak was wound two or three times round my head, and, strive as I would, I could only, with all my efforts, force out a dull cry, that died, smothered in its folds.

CHAPTER XVIII
A POOR FIGURE

I did not struggle long. The efforts I had made to free myself from the men, and this last exertion of striving to shout, brought the blood to my head; and so exhausted me that I lay inert, my heart panting as if it would suffocate me, and my lungs craving more air. I was in danger of being stifled in earnest, and knew it; but, fortunately, the horror of this fate, which a minute before had driven me to frantic efforts, now gave me the supreme courage to lie still, and, collecting myself, do all I could to get air.

It was time I did. I was hot as fire, and sweating at every pore; however the dreadful sensation of choking went off somewhat when I had lain a while motionless, and by turning my head and chest a little to the side--which I succeeded in doing, though I could not raise myself--I breathed more freely. Still, my position was horrible. Helpless as I was, with the trusses of hay pressing on me, fresh pains soon rose to take the place of those allayed. The bonds on my wrists began to burn into my flesh, the hilt of my sword forced itself into my side, my back seemed to be breaking under the burden, my shoulders ached intolerably. I was being slowly, slowly pressed to death, in darkness, and when a cry--a single cry, if I could raise my voice--would bring relief and succour!

The thought so maddened me that, fancying after an age of this suffering that I heard a faint sound as of some one moving in the stable, I lost control of myself, and fell to struggling again; while groans broke from me instead of cries, and the bonds cut into my arms. But the paroxysm only added to my misery; the person, whoever he was, did not hear me, and made no further noise; or, if he did, the blood coursing to my head, and swelling the veins of my neck almost to bursting, deafened me to the sound. The horrible weight that I had raised for a moment sank again. I gave up, I despaired; and lay in a kind of swoon, unable to think, unable to remember, no longer hoping for relief, or planning escape, but enduring.

I must have lain thus some time, when a noise loud enough to reach my dulled ears roused me afresh; I listened, at first with half a heart. The noise was repeated; then, without further warning, a sharp pain darted through the calf of my leg. I screamed out; and, though the cloak and the hay over my head choked the cry, I caught a kind of echo of it. Then silence.

Stupid as a in an awakened from sleep, I thought for a moment that I had dreamed both the cry and the pain; and groaned in my misery. The next moment I felt the hay that lay on me move; then the truss that pressed most heavily on me was lifted, and I heard voices and cries, and saw a faint light, and knew I was freed. In a twinkling I felt myself seized and drawn out, amid a murmur of cries and exclamations. The cloak was plucked from my head, and, dazzled and half blind, I found half a dozen faces gaping and staring at me.

"Why, *mon Dieu!* it is the gentleman who departed this morning!" cried a woman. And she threw up her hands in astonishment.

I looked at her. She was the woman of the house.

My throat was dry and parched, my lips were swollen; but at the second attempt I managed to tell her to untie me.

She complied, amid fresh exclamations of surprise and astonishment; then, as I was so stiff and benumbed as to be powerless, they lifted me to the door of the stable, where one set a stool, and another brought a cup of water. This and the cold air restored me, and in a minute or two I was able to stand. Meanwhile they pressed me with questions; but I was giddy and confused, and could not for a few minutes collect myself. By-and-by, however, a person who came up with an air of importance, and pushed aside the crowd of clowns and stable-helpers that surrounded me, helped me to find my voice.

"What is it?" he said. "What is it, Monsieur? What brought you in the stable?"

The woman who kept the inn answered for me that she did not know; that one of the men going to get hay had struck his fork into my leg, and so found me.

"But who is he?" the new-comer asked imperatively. He was a tall, thin man, with a sour face and small, suspicious eyes.

"I am the Vicomte de Saux," I answered.

"Eh!" he said, prolonging the syllable. "And how came you, M. le Vicomte--if that be your name--in the stable?"

"I have been robbed," I muttered.

"Bobbed!" he answered with a sniff. "Bah! Monsieur; in this commune we have no robbers."

"Still, I have been robbed," I answered stupidly.

For answer, before I knew what he was about, he plunged his hand, without ceremony or leave, into the pocket of my coat, and brought out a purse. He held it up for all to see. "Robbed?" he said in a tone of irony. "I think not, Monsieur; I think not!"

I looked at the purse in astonishment; then, mechanically putting my hand into my pocket, I produced first one thing, and then another, and stared at them. He was right. I had not been robbed. Snuff-box, handkerchief, my watch and seals, my knife, and a little mirror, and book--all were there!

"And now I come to think of it," the woman said, speaking suddenly, "there are a pair of saddle-bags in the house that must belong to the gentleman! I was wondering a while ago whose they were."

"They are mine!" I cried, memory and sense returning. "They are mine! But the ladies who were with me? They have not started?"

"They went these three hours back," the woman answered, staring at me. "And I could have sworn that Monsieur went with them! But, to be sure, it was only just light, and a mistake is soon made."

A thought that should have occurred to me before--a horrible thought--darted its sting into my heart. I plunged my hand into the inner pocket of my coat, and drew it out empty. The commission--the commission to which I had trusted was gone!

I uttered a cry of rage and glared round me. "What is it?" said the sour man, meeting my eyes.

"My papers!" I answered, almost gnashing my teeth, as I thought how I had been tricked and treated. I saw it all now. "My papers!"

"Well?" he said.

"They are gone! I have been robbed of them!"

"Indeed!" he said drily. "That remains to be proved, Monsieur."

I thought that he meant that I might be mistaken, as I had been mistaken before; and, to make certain, I turned out the pocket.

"No," he said, as drily as before. "I see that they are not there. But the point is, Monsieur, were they ever there?"

I looked at him.

"Yes," he said, "that is the point, Monsieur. Where are your papers?"

"I tell you I have been robbed of them!" I cried, in a rage.

"And I say, that remains to be proved," he answered. "And until it is proved, you do not leave here. That is all, Monsieur, and it is simple."

"And who," I said indignantly, "are you, I should like to know, Monsieur, who stop travellers on the highway, and ask for papers?"

"Merely the President of the Local Committee," he replied.

"And do you suppose," I said, fuming at his folly, "that I bound my hands, and stifled myself under that hay, on purpose? On purpose to pass through your wretched village?"

"I suppose nothing, Monsieur," he answered coolly. "But this is the road to Turin, where M. d'Artois is said to be collecting the disaffected; and to Nîmes, where mischievous persons are flaunting the red cockade. And without papers, no one passes."

"But what will you do with me?" I asked, seeing that the clowns, who gaped round us, regarded him as nothing less than a Solomon.

"Detain you, M. le Vicomte, until you procure papers," he answered.

"But, *mon Dieu!*" I said. "That is not so easily done here. Who is likely to know me?"

He shrugged his shoulders. "Monsieur does not leave without the papers," he said. "That is all."

And he spoke truly, that was all. In vain I laid the facts before him, and asked if any one would voluntarily suffer, merely to hide his lack of papers, what I had undergone; in vain I asked if the state in which I had been found was not itself proof that I had been robbed; if a man could tie his own hands, and pile hay on himself. In vain even that I said I knew who had robbed me; the last statement only made matters worse.

"Indeed!" he said ironically. "Then, pray, who was it?"

"The rogue Froment! Froment of Nîmes!"

"He is not in this country."

"Indeed! I saw him yesterday," I answered.

"Then that settles the matter," the Committee-man answered, with a grim smile; and his little court smiled too. "After that, we certainly cannot lose sight of M. le Vicomte."

And so well did he keep his word, that when, to avoid the cold that began to pierce me, I went into the wretched inn, and sat down on the hearth to think over the position, two of the yokels accompanied me; and when I went out again, and stood looking distrustfully up and down the road, two more were at my elbow, as by magic. Whether I turned this way or that, one was sure to spring up, and, if I walked too far from the house, would touch me on the arm, and gruffly order me back. Mont Aigoual itself, lifting its crest, bleak, and stern, and cold, above the valley, was not more sure than their attendance, or more immovable.

This added to my irritation, and for a time I was like a madman. Deluded by Madame St. Alais, and robbed by Froment--who, I felt sure, had taken my place, and was now rolling at his ease through Suméne and Ganges with my commission in his pocket--I strode up and down the road, the road that was my prison, in a fever of rage and chagrin. Madame's ingratitude, my own easiness, the villagers' stupidity, I execrated all in turn; but most, perhaps, the inaction to which they condemned me. I had escaped with my life, and for that should have been thankful; but no man cares to be duped. And one day, two days, three days passed; it froze and thawed, snowed and was fine; still, while the carriage bowled along the road to Nîmes, and carried my mistress farther and farther from me, I lay a prisoner in this wretched hamlet. I grew to loathe the squalid inn, in which I kicked my heels through the cold hours, the muddy road that ran by it, the mean row of hovels they called the village. All day, and whenever I went abroad, the clowns dogged and flouted me, thinking it sport; each evening the Committee came to stare and question. A house this way, a house that way, were my boundaries, while the world moved beyond the mountains, and France throbbed; and I knew not what might be in hand to separate Denise from me. No wonder that I almost chafed myself into madness.

I had left my horse at Milhau, whence the landlord had undertaken to forward it to Ganges within a couple of days, by the hand of an acquaintance who would be going that way. I expected it every hour, therefore, and my only hope was that its conductor might be able to identify me, since half a hundred at Milhau had seen my commission, or heard it read. But the horse did not arrive, nor any one from Milhau, and fearing that the release of the two ladies had caused trouble there, my heart sank still lower. I could not easily communicate with Cahors, and the Committee, with rustic independence and obstinacy, would neither let me go nor send me to Nîmes, where I could be identified. It was in vain I pressed them.

"No, no," the sour-faced Committee-man answered, the first time I raised the question. "Presently some one who knows you will come by. In the meantime have patience."

"M. le Vicomte is a gentleman many would know," the woman of the house chimed in; looking at me with her arms wrapped up in her apron and her head on one side.

"To be sure! To be sure," the crowd agreed, and, rubbing their calves, the members of the Committee followed her lead, and looked at me with satisfaction, as at something that did them credit.

Their stupid complacency nearly drove me mad; but to what purpose? "After all, you are very well here," the first speaker would say, shrugging his shoulders. "You are very well here."

"Better than under the hay!" the man who had pricked my leg was wont to answer.

And on that--this was a nightly joke--a general laugh would follow, and with another admonition to be patient, the Committee would take its leave.

Or sometimes the argument in the kitchen took a harsher and more dangerous turn; and one and another would recall for my benefit old tales of the dragooning, and Villars, and Berwick; tales, at which the blood crept, of horrible cruelties done and suffered, of stern mountain men and brave women who faced the worst that Kings could do, for the fate that they had chosen; of a great cause crushed but not destroyed, of a whole people trodden down in dust and blood, and yet living and growing strong.

"And do you think that after this," the speaker would cry when he had told me these things with flashing eyes, these things that his grandfathers had done and suffered--"do you think that after this we are not concerned in this business? Do you think that now, Monsieur, when, after all these years, vengeance is in our hand and our persecutors are tottering, we will sit still and see them set up again? Bishops and captains, canons and cardinals, where are they now? Where are the lands they stole from us? Gone from them! Where are the tithes they took with blood? Taken from them! Where is St. Etienne, whose father they persecuted? With his foot on their necks! And, after this, do you think that with all their processions and their idols and their Corpus Christi, they shall defy us and set up their rule again? No, Monsieur, no."

"But there is no question of that!" I said mildly.

"There is great question of that," was the stern answer. "In Nîmes and Montauban, at Avignon, and at Arles! We who live in the mountains have too often heard the storm gathering in the plain to be mistaken. These preachings and processions, and weeping virgins, this cry of Blasphemy--

what do they mean, Monsieur? Blood! Blood! Blood! It has been so a score of times, it is so now! But this time blood will not be shed on one side only!"

And I listened and marvelled. I began to understand that the same word meant one thing in one man's mouth, and in another man's mouth another thing; and that that which worked easily and smoothly in the north might in the south roll hideously through fire and blood. In Quercy we had lost two or three châteaux, and a handful of lives, and for a few hours the mob had got out of hand--all with little enthusiasm. But here--here I seemed to stand on the brink of a great furnace under which the fires of persecution still smouldered; I felt the scorching breath of passion on my cheek, and saw through the white-hot scum old enmities seething with new and fiercer ambitions, old factions with new bigotries. I had heard Froment, now I heard these; it remained only to be seen whether Froment had his followers.

In the meantime, pent up in this place, I found little comfort in such predictions; I lived on my heart, and the better part of a fortnight went by. The woman at the inn was well satisfied to keep me; I paid, and guests were rare. And the Committee took pride in me; I was a living, walking token of their powers, and of the importance of their village. Now to the mingled misery and absurdity of my position, the anxiety on Mademoiselle's account, which this news of Nîmes caused me, added the last intolerable touch, and I determined at all risks to escape.

That I had no horse, and that at Suméne or Ganges I should inevitably be detained, had hitherto held me back from the attempt; now I could bear the position no longer, and after weighing all the chances, I determined to slip away some evening at sunset, and make my way on foot to Milhau. The villagers would be sure to pursue me in the direction of Nîmes, whither they knew that I was bound; and even if a party took the other road, I should have many chances of escape in the darkness. I counted on reaching Milhau soon after daybreak, and there, if the Mayor stood my friend, I might regain my horse, and with credentials travel to Nîmes by the same or another road.

It seemed feasible, and that very evening fortune favoured me. The man who should have kept me company, upset a pot of boiling water over his foot, and without giving a thought to me or his duty went off groaning to his house. A moment later the woman of the inn was called out by a neighbour, and at the very hour I would have chosen, I found myself alone. Still I knew that I had not a moment to lose; instantly, therefore, I put on my cloak, and reaching down my pistols from a shelf on which they had been placed, I put a little food in my pocket and sneaked out at the rear of the house. A dog was kennelled there, but it knew me and wagged its tail; and in two minutes, after warily skirting the backs of the houses, I gained the road to Milhau, and stood free and alone.

Night had fallen, but it was not quite dark; and dreading every eye, I hurried on through the dusk, now peering anxiously forward, and now looking and listening for the first sounds of pursuit. For a few minutes the fear of that took up all my thoughts; later, when the one twinkling light that marked the village had set behind me, and night and the silent waste of mountains had swallowed me up, a sense of eeriness, of loneliness, very depressing, took possession of me. Denise was at Nîmes, and I was moving the other way; what accidents might not befall me, how many things might not happen to postpone my return? In the meantime she lay at the mercy of her mother and brothers, with all the traditions of her family, all the prejudices of maidenhood and her education against my suit. To what use in this imbroglio might not her hand be put? Or, if that were not in question, what in that city of strife, in that fierce struggle, of which the peasants had forewarned me, might not be the fate of a young girl?

Spurred by these thoughts, I pressed on feverishly, and had gone, perhaps, a league, when a sharp sound made by a horse's shoe striking a stone, caught my ear. It came from the front, and I drew to the side of the road, and crouched low to let the traveller go by. I fancied that I could distinguish the tramp of three horses, but when the men loomed darkly into sight, I could see only two figures.

Perhaps I rose a little too high in my anxiety to see. At any rate I had not counted on the horses, the nearer of which, as it passed me, swerved violently from me. The rider was almost dismounted by the violence of the movement, but in a twinkling had his horse again in hand, and before I knew what I was doing, was urging it upon me. I dared not move, for to move was to betray my presence, but this did not avail, for in a minute the rider made out the outline of my figure.

"Hola," he cried sharply. "Who are you there, who lie in wait to break men's necks? Speak, man, or----"

But I caught his bridle. "M. de Géol!" I cried, my heart beating against my ribs.

"Stand back!" he cried, peering at me. He did not know my voice. "Who are you? Who is it?"

"It is I, M. de Saux," I answered joyfully.

"Why, man, I thought that you were at Nîmes," he exclaimed in a tone of great astonishment, "these ten days past! We have your horse here."

"Here? My horse?"

"To be sure. Your good friend here has it in charge from Milhau. But where have you been? And what are you doing here?" he continued suspiciously.

"I lost my passport. It was stolen by Froment."

He whistled.

"And at Villeraugues they stopped me," I continued. "I have been there since."

"Ah," he said drily. "That comes of travelling in bad company, M. le Vicomte. And to-night I suppose you were----"

"Going to get away," I answered bluntly. "But you--I thought that you had passed long ago?"

"No," he said. "I was detained. Now we have met, I would advise you to mount and return with me."

"I will," I said briskly, "with the greatest pleasure. And you will be able to tell them who I am."

"I?" he answered. "No, indeed. I do not know. I only know who you told me you were."

I fell to earth again, and for a moment stood staring through the darkness at him. A moment only. For then out of the darkness came a voice. "Have no fear, M. le Vicomte, I will speak for you."

I started and stared. *Mon Dieu!*" I said, trembling. "Who spoke?"

"It is I--Buton," came the answer. "I have your horse, M. le Vicomte."

It was Buton, the blacksmith; Captain Buton, of the Committee.

This for the time cut the thread of my difficulties. When we rode into the village ten minutes later, the Committee, awed by the credentials which Buton carried, accepted his explanation at once, and raised no further objection to my journey. So twelve hours afterwards we three, thus strangely thrown together, passed through Suméne. We slept at Sauve, and presently leaving behind us the late winter of the mountains, with its frost and snow, began to descend in sunshine the western slope of the Rhone valley. All day we rode through balmy air, between fields and gardens and olive groves; the white dust, the white houses, the white cliffs eloquent of the south. And a little before sunset we came in sight of Nîmes, and hailed the end of a journey that, for me, had not been without its adventures.

CHAPTER XIX
AT NÎMES

It will be believed that I looked on the city with no common emotions. I had heard enough at Villeraugues--and to that enough M. de Géol had added by the way a thousand details--to satisfy me that here and not in the north, here in the Gard, and the Bouches du Rhone, among the olive groves and white dust of the south, and not among the wheatfields and pastures of the north, the fate of the nation hung in the balance; and that not in Paris--where men would and yet would not, where Mirabeau and Lafayette, in fear of the mob, took one day a step towards the King, and the next, fearful lest restored he should punish, retraced it--could the convulsion be arrested, but here! Here, where the warm imagination of the Provençal still saw something holy in things once holy, and faction bound men to faith.

Hitherto the stream of revolution had met with no check. Obstacles apparently the strongest, the King, the nobles, had crumbled and sunk before it, almost without a struggle; it remained to be seen whether the third and last of the governing powers, the Church, would fare better. Clearly, if Froment were right, and faith must be met by faith, and bigotry of one kind be opposed by bigotry of another kind, here in the valley of the Rhone, where the Church still kept its hold, lay the materials nearest to the enthusiast's hand. In that case--and with this in my mind, I took my first long look at the city, and the wide low plain that lay beyond it, bathed in the sunset light--in that case, from this spot might fly a torch to kindle France! Hence might start within the next few days a conflagration as wide as the land; that taken up, and roaring ever higher and higher through all La Vendée, and Brittany, and the Côtes du Nord, might swiftly ring round Paris with a circle of flame.

Once get it fairly alight. But there lay the doubt; and I looked again, and looked with eager curiosity, at this city from which so much was expected; this far-stretching city of flat roofs and white houses, trending gently down from the last spurs of the Cevennes to the Rhone plain. North of it, in the outskirts rose three low hills, the midmost crowned with a tower, the eastern-most casting a shadow almost to the distant river; and from these, eastward and southward, the city sloped. And these hills, and the roads near us, and the plain already verdant, and the great workshops that here and there rose in the faubourgs, all, as we approached, seemed to teem with life and people; with people coming and going, alone and in groups, sauntering beyond the walls for pleasure, or hastening on business.

Of these, I noticed all wore a badge of some kind; many the tricolour, but more a red ribbon, a red tuft, a red cockade--emblems at sight of which my companions' faces grew darker, and ever darker. Another thing characteristic of the place, the tinkling of many bells, calling to vespers-- though I found the sound fall pleasantly on the evening air--was as little to their taste. They growled together, and increased their pace; the result of which was that insensibly I fell to the rear. As we entered the streets, the traffic that met us, and the keenness with which I looked about me, increased the distance between us; presently, a long line of carts and a company of National Guards intervening, I found myself riding alone, a hundred paces behind them.

I was not sorry; the novelty of the shifting crowd, the changing faces, the southern patois, the moving string of soldiers, peasants, workmen, women, amused me. I was less sorry when by-and-by something--something which I had dimly imagined might happen when I reached Nîmes--took real shape, there, in the crooked street; and struck me, as it were, in the face. As I passed under a barred window a little above the roadway, a window on which my eyes alighted for an instant, a white hand waved a handkerchief-- for an instant only, just long enough for me to take in the action and think of Denise! Then, as I jerked the reins, the handkerchief was gone, the window was empty, on either side of me the crowd chattered, and jostled on its way.

I pulled up mechanically, and looked round, my heart beating. I could see no one near me for whom the signal could be intended; and yet-- it seemed odd. I could hardly believe in such good fortune; or that I had found Denise so soon. However, as my eyes returned doubtfully to the window, the handkerchief flickered in it again; and this time the signal was so unmistakably meant for me that, shamed out of my prudence, I pushed my horse through the crowd to the door, and hastily dismounting, threw the rein to an urchin who stood near. I was shy of asking him who lived in the house; and with a single glance at the dull white front, and the row of barred windows that ran below the balcony, I resigned myself to fortune, and knocked.

On the instant the door flew open, and a servant appeared. I had not considered what I would say, and for a moment I stared at him foolishly. Then, at a venture, on the spur of the moment, I asked if Madame received.

He answered very civilly that she did, and held the door open for me to enter.

I did so, confused and wondering; none the less when, having crossed a spacious hall, paved with black and white marble, and followed him up a staircase, I found everything I saw round me, from the man's quiet livery to the mouldings of the ceiling, wearing the stamp of elegance and refinement. Pedestals, supporting marble busts, stood in the angles of the staircase; there were orange trees in jars in the hall, and antique fragments adorned the walls. However, I saw these only in passing; in a moment I reached the head of the stairs, and the man opening a door, stood aside.

I entered the room, my eyes shining; in a dream, an impossible dream, that held possession of me for one moment, that Denise--not Mademoiselle de St. Alais, but Denise, the girl who loved me and with whom I had never been alone, might be there to receive me. Instead, a stranger rose slowly from a seat in one of the window bays, and, after a moment's hesitation, came forward to meet me; a strange lady, tall, grave, and very handsome, whose dark eyes scanned me seriously, while the blood rose a little to her pure olive cheek.

Seeing that she was a stranger, I began to stammer an apology for my intrusion. She curtsied. "Monsieur need not excuse himself," she said, smiling. "He was expected, and a meal is ready. If you will allow Gervais," she continued, "he will take you to a room, where you can remove the dust of the road."

"But, Madame," I stammered, still hesitating. "I am afraid that I am trespassing."

She shook her head, smiling. "Be so good," she said; and waved her hand towards the door.

"But my horse," I answered, standing bewildered. "I have left it in the street."

"It will be cared for," she said. "Will you be so kind?" And she pointed with a little imperious gesture to the door.

I went then in utter amazement. The man who had led me upstairs was outside. He preceded me along a wide airy passage to a bedroom, in which I found all that I needed to refresh my toilet. He took my coat and hat, and attended me with the skill of one trained to such offices; and in a state of desperate bewilderment, I suffered it. But when, recovering a little from my confusion, I opened my mouth to ask a question, he begged me to excuse him; Madame would explain.

"Madame----?" I said; and looked at him interrogatively, and waited for him to fill the blank.

"Yes, Monsieur, Madame will explain," he answered glibly, and without a smile; and then, seeing that I was ready, he led me back, not to the room I had left, but to another.

I went in, like a man in a dream; not doubting, however, that now I should have an answer to the riddle. But I found none. The room was spacious, and parquet-floored, with three high narrow windows, of which one, partly open, let in the murmur of the street. A small wood fire burned on a wide hearth between carved marble pillars; and in one corner of the room stood a harpsichord, harp, and music-stand. Nearer the fire a small round table, daintily laid for supper, and lighted by candles, placed in old silver sconces, presented a charming picture; and by it stood the lady I had seen.

"Are you cold?" she said, coming forward frankly, as I advanced.

"No, Madame."

"Then we will sit down at once," she answered. And she pointed to the table.

I took the seat she indicated, and saw with astonishment that covers were laid for two only. She caught the look, and blushed faintly, and her lip trembled as if with the effort to suppress a smile. But she said nothing, and any thought to her disadvantage which might have entered my mind was anticipated, not only by the sedate courtesy of her manner, but by the appearance of the room, the show of wealth and ease that surrounded her, and the very respectability of the butler who waited on us.

"Have you ridden far to-day?" she said, crumbling a roll with her fingers as if she were not quite free from nervousness; and looking now at the table and now again at me in a way almost appealing.

"From Sauve, Madame," I answered.

"Ah! And you propose to go?"

"No farther."

"I am glad to hear it," she said, with a charming smile. "You are a stranger in Nîmes?"

"I was. I do not feel so now."

"Thank you," she answered, her eyes meeting mine without reserve. "That you may feel more at home, I am going presently to tell you my name. Yours I do not ask."

"You do not know it?" I cried.

"No," she said, laughing; and I saw, as she laughed, that she was younger than I had thought; that she was little more than a girl. "Of course, you can tell it me if you please," she added lightly.

"Then, Madame, I do please," I answered gallantly. "I am the Vicomte de Saux, of Saux by Cahors, and am very much at your service."

She held her hand suspended, and stared at me a moment in undisguised astonishment. I even thought that I read something like terror in her eyes. Then she said: "Of Saux by Cahors?"

"Yes, Madame. And I am driven to fear," I continued, seeing the effect my words produced, "that I am here in the place of some one else."

"Oh, no!" she said. Then, her feelings seeming to find sudden vent, she laughed and clapped her hands. "No, Monsieur," she cried gaily, "there is no error, I assure you. On the contrary, now I know who you are, I will give you a toast. Alphonse! Fill M. le Vicomte's glass, and then leave us! So! Now, M. le Vicomte," she continued, "you must drink with me, *à l'Anglaise*, to----"

She paused and looked at me slily. "I am all attention, Madame," I said, bowing.

"To *la belle* Denise!" she said.

It was my turn to start and stare now; in confusion as well as surprise. But she only laughed the more, and, clapping her hands with childish abandon, bade me, "Drink, Monsieur, drink!"

I did so bravely, though I coloured under her eyes.

"That is well," she said, as I set down the glass. "Now, Monsieur, I shall be able--in the proper quarter--to report you no recreant."

"But, Madame," I said, "how do you know the proper quarter?"

"How do I know?" she answered naïvely. "Ah, that is the question."

But she did not answer it; though I remarked that from this moment she took a different tone with me. She dropped much of the reserve which she had hitherto maintained, and began to pour upon me a fire of wit and badinage, merriment and *plaisanterie*, against which I defended myself as well as I could, where all the advantage of knowledge lay with her. Such a duel with so fair an antagonist had its charms, the more as Denise and my relations to her formed the main objects of her raillery: yet I was not sorry when a clock, striking eight, produced a sudden silence and a change in her, as great as that which had preceded it. Her face grew almost sombre, she sighed, and sat looking gravely before her. I ventured to ask if anything ailed her.

"Only this, Monsieur," she answered. "That I must now put you to the test; and you may fail me."

"You wish me to do something?"

"I wish you to give me your escort," she answered, "to a place and back again."

"I am ready," I cried, rising gaily. "If I were not I should be a recreant indeed. But I think, Madame, that you were going to tell me your name."

"I am Madame Catinot," she answered. And then--I do not know what she read in my face, "I am a widow," she added, blushing deeply. "For the rest you are no wiser."

"But always at your service, Madame."

"So be it," she answered quietly. "I will meet you, M. le Vicomte, in the hall, if you will presently descend thither."

I held the door for her to go out, and she went; and wondering, and inexpressibly puzzled by the strangeness of the adventure, I paced up and down the room a minute, and then followed her. A hanging lamp which lit the hall showed her to me standing at the foot of the stairs; her hair hidden by a black lace mantilla, her dress under a cloak of the same dark colour. The man who had admitted me gave me in silence my cloak and hat; and without a word Madame led the way along a passage.

Over a door at the end of the passage was a second light. It fell on my hat--as I was about to put it on--and I started and stood. Instead of the tricolour I had been wearing in the hat, I saw a small red cockade!

Madame heard me stop, and turning, discovered what was the matter. She laid her hand on my arm; and the hand trembled. "For an hour, Monsieur, only for an hour," she breathed in my ear. "Give me your arm."

Somewhat agitated--I began to scent danger and complications--I put on the hat and gave her my arm, and in a moment we stood in the open air in a dark, narrow passage between high walls. She turned at once to the left, and we walked in silence a hundred, or a hundred and fifty, paces, which brought us to a low-browed doorway on the same side, through which a light poured out. Madame guiding me by a slight pressure, we passed through this, and a narrow vestibule beyond it; and in a moment I found myself, to my astonishment, in a church, half full of silent worshippers.

Madame enjoined silence by laying her finger on her lip, and led the way along one of the dim aisles, until we came to a vacant chair beside a pillar. She signed to me to stand by the pillar, and herself knelt down.

Left at liberty to survey the scene, and form my conclusions, I looked about me like a man in a dream. The body of the church, faintly lit, was rendered more gloomy by the black cloaks and veils of the vast kneeling crowd that filled the nave and grew each moment more dense. The men for the most part stood beside pillars, or at the back of the church; and from these parts came now and then a low stern muttering, the only sound that broke the heavy silence. A red lamp burning before the altar added one touch of sombre colour to the scene.

I had not stood long before I felt the silence, and the crowd, and the empty vastnesses above us, begin to weigh me down; before my heart began to beat quickly in expectation of I knew not what. And then at last, when this feeling had grown almost intolerable, out of the silence about the altar came the first melancholy notes, the wailing refrain of the psalm, *Miserere Domine!*

It had a solemn and wondrous effect as it rose and fell, in the gloom, in the silence, above the heads of the kneeling multitude, who one moment were there and the next, as the lights sank, were gone, leaving only blackness and emptiness and space--and that spasmodic wailing. As the pleading, almost desperate notes, floated down the long aisles, borne on the palpitating hearts of the listeners, a hand seemed to grasp the throat, the eyes grew dim, strong men's heads bowed lower, and strong men's hands trembled. *Miserere mei Deus! Miserere Domine!*

At last it came to an end. The psalm died down, and on the darkness and dead silence that succeeded, a light flared up suddenly in one place, and showed a pale, keen face and eyes that burned, as they gazed, not at the dim crowd, but into the empty space above them, whence grim, carved visages peered vaguely out of fretted vaults. And the preacher began to preach.

In a low voice at first, and with little emotion, he spoke of the ways of God with His creatures, of the immensity of the past and the littleness of the present, of the Omnipotence before which time and space and men were nothing; of the certainty that as God, the Almighty, the Everlasting, the Ever-present decreed, it *was*. And then, in fuller tones, he went on to speak of the Church, God's agent on earth, and of the work which it had done in past ages, converting, protecting, shielding the weak, staying the strong, baptising, marrying, burying. God's handmaid, God's vicegerent. "Of whom alone it comes," the preacher continued, raising his hand now, and speaking in a voice that throbbed louder and fuller through the spaces of the church, "that we are more than animals, that knowing who is behind the veil we fear not temporal things, nor think of death as the worst possible, as do the unbelieving; but having that on which we rest, outside and beyond the world, can view unmoved the worst that the world can do to us. We believe; therefore, we are strong. We believe in God; therefore, we are stronger than the world. We believe in God; therefore, we are of God, and not of the world. We are above the world! we are about the world, and in the strength of God, who is the God of Hosts, shall subdue the world."

He paused, holding the crowd breathless; then in a lower tone he continued: "Yet how do the heathen rage and the people imagine a vain thing? They trample on God! They say this exists, I see it. That exists, I hear it. The other exists, I touch it. And that is all--that is all. But does it come of what we see and hear and feel that a man will die for his brother? Does it come of what we see and hear and feel that a man will die for a thought? That he will die for a creed? That he will die for honour? That, withal, he will die for anything--for anything, while he may live? I trow not. It comes of God! Of God only.

"And they trample on Him. In the streets, in the senate, in high places. And He says, 'Who is on My side?' My children, my brethren, we have lived long in a time of ease and safety; we have been long untried by aught but the ordinary troubles of life, untrained by the imminent issues of life and death. Now, in these late years of the world, it has pleased the Almighty to try us; and who is on His side? Who is prepared to put the unseen before the seen, honour before life, God before man, chivalry before baseness, the Church before the world? Who is on His side? Spurned in this little corner of His creation, bruised and bleeding and trampled under foot, yet ruler of earth and heaven, life and death, judgment and eternity, ruler of all the countless worlds of space, He comes! He comes! He comes, God Almighty, which was, and is, and is to be! And who is on His side?"

As the last word fell from his lips, and the light above his head went suddenly out, and darkness fell on the breathless hush, the listening hundreds, an indescribable wave of emotion passed through the crowd. Men stirred their feet with a strange, stern sound, that spreading, passed in muttered thunder to the vaults; while women sobbed, and here and there shrieked and prayed aloud. From the altar a priest in a voice that shook with feeling blessed the congregation; then, even as I awoke from a trance of attention, Madame touched my arm, and signed to me to follow her, and gliding quickly from her place, led the way down the aisle. Before the preacher's last words had ceased to ring in my ears or my heart had forgotten to be moved, we were walking under the stars with the night air cooling our faces; a moment, and we were in the house and stood again in the lighted salon where I had first found Madame Catinot.

Before I knew what she was going to do, she turned to me with a swift movement, and laid both her bare hands on my arm; and I saw that the tears were running down her face. "Who is on My side?" she cried, in a voice that thrilled me to the soul, so that I started where I stood. "Who is on My side? Oh, surely you! Surely you, Monsieur, whose fathers' swords were drawn for God and the King! Who, born to guide, are surely on the side of light! Who, noble, will never leave the task of government to the base! O----" and there, breaking off before I could answer, she turned from me with her hands clasped to her face. "O God!" she cried with sobs, "give me this man for Thy service."

I stood inexpressibly troubled; moved by the sight of this woman in tears, shaken by the conflict in my own soul, somewhat unmanned, perhaps, by what I had seen. For a moment I could not speak; when I did, "Madame," I said unsteadily, "if I had known that it was for this! You have been kind to me, and I--I can make no return."

"Don't say it!" she cried, turning to me and pleading with me. "Don't say it!" And she laid her clasped hands on my arm and looked at me, and then in a moment smiled through her tears. "Forgive me," she said humbly, "forgive me. I went about it wrongly. I feel--too much. I asked too quickly. But you will? You will, Monsieur? You will be worthy of yourself?"

I groaned. "I hold their commission," I said.

"Return it!"

"But that will not acquit me!"

"Who is on My side?" she said softly. "Who is on My side?"

I drew a deep breath. In the silence of the room, the wood-ashes on the hearth settled down, and a clock ticked. "For God! For God and the King!" she said, looking up at me with shining eyes, with clasped hands.

I could have sworn in my pain. "To what purpose?" I cried almost rudely. "If I were to say, yes, to what purpose, Madame? What could I do that would help you? What could I do that would avail?"

"Everything! Everything! You are one man more!" she cried. "One man more for the right. Listen, Monsieur. You do not know what is afoot, or how we are pressed, or----"

She stopped suddenly, abruptly; and looked at me, listening; listening with a new expression on her face. The door was not closed, and the voice of a man, speaking in the hall below, came up the staircase; another instant, and a quick foot crossed the hall, and sounded on the stairs. The man was coming up.

Madame, face to face with me, dumb and listening with distended eyes, stood a moment, as if taken by surprise. At the last moment, warning me by a gesture to be silent, she swept to the door and went out, closing it--not quite closing it behind her.

I judged that the man had almost reached it, for I heard him exclaim in surprise at her sudden appearance; then he said something in a tone which did not reach me. I lost her answer too, but his next words were audible enough.

"You will not open the door?" he cried.

"Not of that room," she replied bravely. "You can see me in the other, my friend."

Then silence. I could almost hear them breathing. I could picture them looking defiance at one another. I grew hot.

"Oh, this is intolerable!" he cried at last. "This is not to be borne. Are you to receive every stranger that comes to town? Are you to be closeted with them, and sup with them, and sit with them, while I eat my heart out outside? Am I--I *will* go in!"

"You shall not!" she cried; but I thought that the indignation in her voice rang false; that laughter underlay it. "It is enough that you insult me," she continued proudly. "But if you dare to touch me, or if you insult him----"

"Him!" he cried fiercely. "Him, indeed! Madame, I tell you at once, I have borne enough. I have suffered this more than once, but----"

But I had no longer any doubt, and before he could add the next word I was at the door--I had snatched it open, and stood before him. Madame fell back with a cry between tears and laughter, and we stood, looking at one another.

The man was Louis St. Alais.

CHAPTER XX
THE SEARCH

I had not seen Louis since the day of the duel at Cahors, when, parting from him at the door in the passage by the Cathedral, I had refused to take his hand. Then I had been sorely angry with him. But time and old memories and crowding events had long softened the feeling; and in the joy of meeting him again, of finding him in this unexpected stranger, nothing was further from my thoughts than to rake up old grudges. I held out my hand, therefore, with a laughing word. *"Voilà l'Inconnu,* Monsieur!" I said with a bow. "I am here to find you, and I find you!"

He stared at me a moment in the utmost astonishment, and then impulsively grasping my hand he held it, and stood looking at me, with the old affection in his eyes. "Adrien! Adrien!" he said, much moved. "Is it really you?"

"Even so, Monsieur."

"And here?"

"Here," I said.

Then, to my astonishment, he slowly dropped my hand; and his manner and his face changed--as a house changes when the shutters are closed. "I am sorry for it," he said slowly, and after a long pause. And then, with an unmistakable flash of anger, "My God, Monsieur! Why have you come?" he cried.

"Why have I come?"

"Ay, why?" he repeated bitterly. "Why? Why have you come--to trouble us? You do not know what evil you are doing! You do not know, man!"

"I know at least what good I am seeking," I answered, purely astounded by this sudden and inexplicable change. "I have made no secret of that, and I make no secret of it now. No man was ever worse treated than I have been by your family. Your attitude now impels me to say that. But when I see Madame la Marquise, to-morrow, I shall tell her that it will take more than this to change me. I shall tell her----"

"You will not see her!" he answered.

"But I shall!"

"You will not!" he retorted.

Before I could answer, Madame Catinot interposed. "Oh, no more!" she cried in a voice which sufficiently evinced her distress. "I thought that you and he were friends, M. Louis? And now--now that fortune has brought you together again----"

"Would to heaven it had not!" he cried, dropping his hand like a man in despair. And he took a turn this way and that on the floor.

She looked at him. "I do not think that you have ever spoken to me in that tone before, Monsieur," she said in a tone of keen reproach. "If it is due--if, I mean," she continued quietly, but with a sparkling eye, "it is because you found M. le Vicomte with me, you infer something unworthy of us. You insult me as well as your friend!"

"Heaven forbid!" he exclaimed.

But she was roused. "That is not enough," she answered firmly and proudly. "For one week more, this is my house, M. Louis. After that it will be yours. Perhaps then--perhaps then," she continued, with a pitiful break in her voice, "I shall think of to-night, and wonder I took no warning! Perhaps then, Monsieur, a word of kindness from you may be as rare as a rough word now!"

He was not proof against that, and the sadness in her voice. He threw himself on his knees before her and seized her hands. "Madame! Catherine! forgive me!" he cried passionately, kissing her hands again and again, and taking no heed of me at all. "Forgive me!" he continued, "I am miserable! You are my only comfort, my only compensation. I do not know, since I saw him, what I am saying. Forgive me!"

"I do!" she said hastily. "Rise, Monsieur!" and she furtively wiped away a tear, then looked at me, blushing but happy. "I do," she continued. "But, *mon cher*, I do not understand you. The other day you spoke so kindly of M. de Saux; and of--pardon me--your sister, and of other things. To-day M. de Saux is here, and you are unhappy."

"I am!" he said, casting a haggard, miserable look at me.

I shrugged my shoulders and spoke up. "So be it," I said proudly. "But because I have lost a friend, Monsieur, it does not follow that I need lose a mistress. I have come to Nîmes to win Mademoiselle de St. Alais' hand. I shall not leave until I have won it."

"This is madness!" he said, with a groan. "Why?"

"Because you talk of the impossible," he answered. "Because Madame de St. Alais is not at Nîmes--for you."

"She is at Nîmes!"

"You will have to find her."

"That is childishness!" I said. "Do you mean to say that at the first hotel I enter I shall not be told where Madame has her lodging?"

"Neither at the first, nor at the last."

"She is in retreat?"

"I shall not tell you."

With that we stood facing one another; Madame Catinot watching us a little aside. Clearly the events of the last few months, which had so changed, so hardened Madame St. Alais, had not been lost on Louis. I could fancy, as I confronted him, that it was M. le Marquis, the elder, and not the younger brother, who withstood me; only--only from under Louis' mask of defiance, there peeped, I still fancied, the old Louis' face, doubting and miserable.

I tried that chord. "Come," I said, making an effort to swallow my wrath, and speak reasonably, "I think that you are not in earnest, M. le Comte, in what you say, and that we are both heated. Time was when we agreed well enough, and you were not unwilling to have me for your brother-in-law. Are we, because of these miserable differences----"

"Differences!" he cried, interrupting me harshly. "My mother's house in Cahors is an empty shell. My brother's house at St. Alais is a heap of ashes. And you talk of differences!"

"Well, call them what you like!"

"Besides," Madame Catinot interposed quickly, "pardon me, Monsieur--besides, M. St. Alais, you know our need of converts. M. le Vicomte is a gentleman, and a man of sense and religion. It needs but a little--a very little," she continued, smiling faintly at me, "to persuade him. And if your sister's hand would do that little, and Madame were agreeable?"

"He could not have it!" he answered sullenly, looking away from me.

"But a week ago," Madame Catinot answered in a startled tone, "you told me----"

"A week ago is not now," he said. "For the rest, I have only this to say. I am sorry to see you here, M. le Vicomte, and I beg you to return. You can do no good, and you may do and suffer harm. By no possibility can you gain what you seek."

"That remains to be seen," I answered stubbornly, roused in my turn. "To begin with, since you say that I cannot find Mademoiselle, I shall adopt a very simple plan. I shall wait here until you leave, Monsieur, and then accompany you home."

"You will not!" he said.

"You may depend upon it I shall!" I answered defiantly.

But Madame interposed. "No, M. de Saux," she said with dignity. "You will not do that; I am sure that you will not; it would be an abuse of my hospitality."

"If you forbid it?"

"I do," she answered.

"Then, Madame, I cannot," I replied. "But----"

"But nothing! Let there be a truce now, if you please," she said firmly. "If it is to be war between you, it shall not begin here. I think, too--I think that I had better ask you to retire," she continued, with an appealing glance at me.

I looked at Louis. But he had turned away, and affected to ignore me. And on that I succumbed. It was impossible to answer Madame, when she spoke to me in that way; and equally impossible to remain in the house, against her will. I bowed, therefore, in silence; and with the best grace I could, though I was sore and angry, I took my cloak and hat, which I had laid on a chair.

"I am sorry," Madame said kindly. And she held out her hand.

I raised it to my lips. "To-morrow--at twelve--here!" she breathed.

I started. I rather guessed than heard the words, so softly were they spoken; but her eyes made up for the lack of sound, and I understood. The next moment she turned from me, and with a last reluctant glance at Louis, who still had his back to me, I went out.

The man who had admitted me was in the hall. "You will find your horse at the Louvre, Monsieur," he said, as he opened the door.

I rewarded him, and going out, without a thought whither I was going, walked along the street, plunged in reflection; until marching on blindly I came against a man. That awoke me, and I looked round. I had been in the house little more than three hours, and in Nîmes scarcely longer; yet so much had happened in the time that it seemed strange to me to find the streets unfamiliar, to find myself alone in them, at a loss which way to turn. Though it was hard on ten o'clock, and only a swaying lantern here and there made a ring of smoky light at the meeting of four ways, there were numbers of people still abroad; a few standing, but the majority going one way, the men with cloaks about their necks, the women with muffled heads.

Feeling the necessity, since I must get myself a lodging, of putting away for the moment my one absorbing thought--the question of Louis' behaviour--I stopped a man who was not going with the stream, and asked him the way to the Hôtel de Louvre. I learned not only that but the cause of the concourse.

"There has been a procession," he answered gruffly. "I should have thought that you would know that!" he added, with a glance at my hat. And he turned on his heel.

I remembered the red cockade I wore, and before I went farther paused to take it out. As I moved on again, a man came quickly up behind me, and as he passed thrust a paper into my hand. Before I could speak he was gone; but the incident and the bustle of the streets, strange at this late hour, helped to divert my thoughts; and I was not surprised when, on reaching the inn, I was told that every room was full.

"My horse is here," I said, thinking that the landlord, seeing me walk in on foot, might distrust the weight of my purse.

"Yes, Monsieur; and if you like you can lie in the eating-room," he answered very civilly. "You are welcome, and you will do no better elsewhere. It is as if the fair were being held at Beaucaire. The city is full of strangers. Almost as full as it is of those things!" he continued querulously, and he pointed to the paper in my hand.

I looked at it, and saw that it was a manifesto headed "*Sacrilege! Mary Weeps!*" "It was thrust into my hand a minute ago," I said.

"To be sure," he answered. "One morning we got up and found the walls white with them. Another day they were flying loose about the streets."

"Do you know," I asked, seeing that he had been supping, and was inclined to talk, "where the Marquis de St. Alais is living?"

"No, Monsieur," he said. "I do not know the gentleman."

"But he is here with his family."

"Who is not here," he answered, shrugging his shoulders. Then in a lower tone, "Is he red, or--or the other thing, Monsieur?"

"Red," I said boldly.

"Ah! Well, there have been two or three gentlemen going to and fro between our M. Froment, and Turin and Montpellier. It is said that our Mayor would have arrested them long ago if he had done his duty. But he is red too, and most of the councillors. And I don't know, for I take no side. Perhaps the gentleman you want is one of these?"

"Very likely," I said. "So M. Froment is here?"

"Monsieur knows him?"

"Yes," I said drily, "a little."

"Well, he is here, or he is not," the landlord answered, shaking his head. "It is impossible to say."

"Why?" I asked. "Does he not live here?"

"Yes, he lives here; at the Port d'Auguste on the old wall near the Capuchins. But----" he looked round and then continued mysteriously, "he goes out, where he has never gone in, Monsieur! And he has a house in the Amphitheatre, and it is the same there. And some say that the Capuchins is only another house of his. And if you go to the Cabaret de la Vierge, and give his name--you pay nothing."

He said this with many nods, and then seemed on a sudden to think that he had said too much, and hurried away. Asking for them, I learned that M. de Géol and Buton, failing to get a room there, had gone to the Ecu de France; but I was not very sorry to be rid of them for the time, and accepting the host's offer, I went to the eating-room, and there made myself as comfortable as two hard chairs and the excitement of my thoughts permitted.

The one thing, the one subject that absorbed me was Louis' behaviour, and the strange and abrupt change I had marked in it. He had been glad to see me, his hand had leaped to meet mine, I had read the old affection in his eyes; and then--then on a sudden, in a moment he had frozen into surly, churlish antagonism, an antagonism that had taken Madame Catinot by surprise, and was not without a touch of remorse, almost of horror. It could not be that she was dead? It could not be that Denise--no, my mind failed to entertain it. But I rose, trembling at the thought, and paced the room until daylight; listening to the watchman's cry, and the mournful hours, and the occasional rush of hurrying feet, that spoke of the perturbed city. What to me were Froment, or the red or the white or the tricolour, veto or no veto, endowment or disendowment, in comparison to that?

The house stirred at last, but I had still to wait till noon before I could see Madame Catinot. I spent the interval in an aimless walk through the town. At another time the things I saw must have filled me with wonder; at another time the hoary, gloomy ring of the Arènes, rising in tiers of frowning arches, high above the squalid roofs that leaned against it--and choked within by a Ghetto of the like, huddled where prefects once sat, and the Emperor's colours flew victorious round the circle--must have won my admiration by its vastness; the Maison Carrée by its fair proportions; the streets by the teeming crowds that filled them, and stood about the cabarets, and read the placards on the walls. But I had only thought for Louis, and my love, and the lagging minutes. At the first stroke of twelve I knocked at Madame Catinot's door; the last saw me in her presence.

It needed but a look at her face, and my heart sank; the thanks I was preparing to utter died on my lips as I gazed at her. She on her part was agitated. For a moment we were both silent.

At last, "I see that you have bad news for me, Madame," I said, striving to smile, and bear myself bravely.

"The worst, I fear," she said pitifully, smoothing her skirt. "For I have none, Monsieur."

"Yet I have heard it said that no news is good news?" I said, wondering.

Her lip trembled, but she did not look at me.

"Come, Madame," I persisted, though I was sick at heart. "Surely you are going to tell me more than that? At least you can tell me where I can see Madame St. Alais."

"No, Monsieur, I cannot tell you," she said in a low voice.

"Nor why M. Louis has so suddenly become hostile to me?"

"No, Monsieur, nor that. And I beg--as you are a gentleman," she continued hurriedly, "that you will spare me questions! I thought that I could help you, and I asked you to see me to-day. I find that I can only give you pain."

"And that is all, Madame?"

"That is all," she said, with a gesture that told more than her words.

I looked round the silent room, I walked half way to the door. And then I turned back. I could not go. "No!" I cried vehemently, "I will not go so! What is it you have learned, that has closed your lips, Madame? What are they plotting against her--that you fear to tell me? Speak, Madame! You did not bring me here to hear this! That I know."

But she only looked at me, her face full of reproach. "Monsieur," she said, "I meant kindly. Is this my reward?"

And that was too much for me. I turned without a word, and went out--of the room and the house.

Outside I felt like a child in darkness, on whom the one door leading to life and liberty had closed, as his hand touched it. I felt a dead, numbing disappointment that at any moment might develop into sharp pain. This change in Madame Catinot, resembling so exactly the change in Louis St. Alais, what could be the cause of it? What had been revealed to her? What was the mystery, the plot, the danger that made them all turn from me, as if I had the plague?

For awhile I was in the depths of despair. Then the warm sunshine that filled the streets, and spoke of coming summer, kindled lighter thoughts. After all it could not be hard to find a person in Nîmes! I had soon found M. Louis. And this was the eighteenth century and not the sixteenth. Women were no longer exposed to the pressure that had once been brought to bear on them; nor men to the violence natural in old feuds.

And then--as I thought of that and strove to comfort myself with it--I heard a noise burst into the street behind me, a roar of voices and a sudden trampling of hundreds of feet; and turning I saw a dense press of men coming towards me, waving aloft blue banners, and crucifixes, and flags with the Five Wounds. Some were singing and some shouting, all were brandishing clubs and weapons. They came along at a good pace, filling the street from wall to wall; and to avoid them I stepped into an archway, that opportunely presented itself.

They came up in a moment, and swept past me with deafening shouts. It was difficult to see more than a forest of waving arms and staves over swart excited faces; but through a break in the ranks I caught a glimpse of three men walking in the heart of the crowd, quiet themselves, yet the cause and centre of all; and the middle man of the three was Froment. One of the others wore a cassock, and the third had a reckless air, and a hat cocked in the military fashion. So much I saw, then only rank upon rank of hurrying shouting men. After these again followed three or four hundred of the scum of the city, beggars and broken rascals and homeless men.

As I turned from staring after them I found a man at my elbow; by a strange coincidence the very same man who, the night before, had directed me to the Hôtel de Louvre. I asked him if that was not M. Froment.

"Yes," he said with a sneer. "And his brother."

"Oh, his brother! What is his name, Monsieur?"

"Bully Froment, some call him."

"And what are they going to do?"

"Groan outside a Protestant church to-day," he answered pithily. "To-morrow break the windows. The next day, or as soon as they can get their courage to the sticking point, fire on the worshippers, and call in the garrison from Montpellier. After that the refugees from Turin will come, we shall be in revolt, and there will be dragoonings. And then--if the Cevennols don't step in--Monsieur will see strange things."

"But the Mayor?" I said. "And the National Guards? Will they suffer it?"

"The first is red," the man answered curtly. "And two-thirds of the last. Monsieur will see."

And with a cool nod he went on his way; while I stood a moment looking idly after the procession. On a sudden, as I stood, it occurred to me that where Froment was, the St. Alais might be; and snatching at the idea, wondering hugely that I had not had it before, I started recklessly in pursuit of the mob. The last broken wave of the crowd was still visible, eddying round a distant corner; and even after that disappeared, it was easy to trace the course it had taken by closed shutters and scared faces peeping from windows. I heard the mob stop once, and groan and howl; but before I came up with it it was on again, and when I at last overtook it, where one of the streets, before narrowing to an old gateway, opened out into a little square--with high dingy buildings on this side and that, and a meshwork of alleys running into it--the nucleus of the crowd had vanished, and the fringe was melting this way and that.

My aim was Froment, and I had missed him. But I was at a loss only for a moment, for as I stood and scanned the people trooping back into the town, my eye alighted on a lean figure with stooping head and a scanty cassock, that, wishing to cross the street, paused a moment striving to pass athwart the crowd. It needed a glance only; then, with a cry of joy, I was through the press, and at the man's side.

It was Father Benôit! For a moment we could not speak. Then, as we looked at one another, the first hasty joyful words spoken, I saw the very expression of dismay and discomfiture, which I had read on Louis St. Alais' face, dawn on his! He muttered, "O mon Dieu! mon Dieu!" under his breath, and wrung his hands stealthily.

But I was sick of this mystery, and I said so in hot words. "You at any rate shall tell me, father!" I cried.

Two or three of the passers-by heard me, and looked at us curiously. He drew me, to escape these, into a doorway; but still a man stood peering in at us. "Come upstairs," the father muttered, "we shall be quiet there." And he led the way up a stone staircase, ancient and sordid, serving many and cleaned by none.

"Do you live here?" I said.

"Yes," he answered; and then stopped short, and turned to me with an air of confusion. "But it is a poor place, M. le Vicomte," he continued, and he even made as if he would descend again, "and perhaps we should be wise to go----"

"No, no!" I said, burning with impatience. "To your room, man! To your room, if you live here! I cannot wait. I have found you, and I will not let another minute pass before I have learned the truth."

He still hesitated, and even began to mutter another objection. But I had only mind for one thing, and giving way to me, he preceded me slowly to the top of the house; where under the tiles he had a little room with a mattress and a chair, two or three books and a crucifix. A small square dormer-window admitted the light--and something else; for as we entered a pigeon rose from the floor and flew out by it.

He uttered an exclamation of annoyance, and explained that he fed them sometimes. "They are company," he said sadly. "And I have found little here."

"Yet you came of your own accord," I retorted brutally. I was choking with anxiety, and it took that form.

"To lose one more illusion," he answered. "For years--you know it, M. le Vicomte--I looked forward to reform, to liberty, to freedom. And I taught others to look forward also. Well, we gained these--you know it, and the first use the people made of their liberty was to attack religion. Then I came here, because I was told that here the defenders of the Church would make a stand; that here the Church was strong, religion respected, faith still vigorous. I came to gain a little hope from others' hope. And I find pretended miracles, I find imposture, I find lies and trickery and chicanery used on one side and the other. And violence everywhere."

"Then in heaven's name, man, why did you not go home again?" I cried.

"I was going a week ago," he answered. "And then I did not go. And----"

"Never mind that now!" I cried harshly. "It is not that I want. I have seen Louis St. Alais, and I know that there is something amiss. He will not face me. He will not tell me where Madame is. He will have nothing to do with me. He looks at me as if I were a death's head! Now what is it? You know and I must know. Tell me."

"*Mon Dieu!*" he answered. And he looked at me with tears in his eyes. Then, "This is what I feared," he said.

"Feared? Feared what?" I cried.

"That your heart was in it, M. le Vicomte."

"In what? In what? Speak plainly, man."

"Mademoiselle de St. Alais'--engagement," he said.

I stood a moment staring at him. "Her engagement?" I whispered. "To whom?"

"To M. Froment," he answered.

CHAPTER XXI
RIVALS

"It is impossible!" I said slowly. "Froment! It is impossible!"

But even while I said it, I knew that I lied; and I turned to the window that Benôit might not see my face. Froment! The name alone, now that the hint was supplied, let in the light. Fellow-traveller, fellow-conspirator, in turn protected and protector, his face as I had seen it at the carriage door in the pass by Villeraugues, rose up before me, and I marvelled that I had not guessed the secret earlier. A bourgeois and ambitious, thrown into Mademoiselle's company, what could be more certain than that, sooner or later, he would lift his eyes to her? What more likely than that Madame St. Alais, impoverished and embittered, afloat on the whirlpool of agitation, would be willing to reward his daring even with her daughter's hand? Rich already, success would ennoble him; for the rest I knew how the man, strong where so many were weak, resolute where a hundred faltered, assured of his purpose and steadfast in pursuing it, where others knew none, must loom in a woman's eyes. And I gnashed my teeth.

I had my eyes fixed, as I thought these thoughts, on a little dingy, well-like court that lay below his window, and on the farther side of which, but far below me, a monastic-looking porch surmounted by a carved figure, formed the centre of vision. Mechanically, though I could have sworn that my whole mind was otherwise engaged, I watched two men come into the court, and go to this porch. They did not knock or call, but one of them struck his stick twice on the pavement; in a second or two the door opened, as of itself, and the men disappeared.

I saw and noted this unconsciously; yet, in all probability, it was the closing of the door roused me from my thoughts. "Froment!" I said, "Froment!" And then I turned from the window. "Where is she?" I said hoarsely.

Father Benôit shook his head.

"You must know!" I cried--indeed I saw that he did. "You must know!"

"I do know," he answered slowly, his eyes on mine. "But I cannot tell you. I could not, were it to save your life, M. le Vicomte. I had it in confession."

I stared at him baffled; and my heart sank at that answer, as it would have sunk at no other. I knew that on this door, this iron door without a key, I might beat my hands and spend my fury until the end of time and go no farther. At length, "Then why--why have you told me so much?" I cried, with a harsh laugh. "Why tell me anything?"

"Because I would have you leave Nîmes," Father Benôit answered gently, laying his hand on my arm, his eyes full of entreaty. "Mademoiselle is contracted, and beyond your reach. Within a few hours, certainly as soon as the elections come on, there will be a rising here. I know you," he continued, "and your feelings, and I know that your sympathies will be with neither party. Why stay then, M. le Vicomte?"

"Why?" I said, so quickly that his hand fell from my arm as if I had struck him. "Because until Mademoiselle is married I follow her, if it be to Turin! Because M. Froment is unwise to mingle love and war, and my sympathies are now with one side, and it is not his! It is not his! Why, you ask? Because--you cannot tell me, but there are those who can, and I go to them!"

And without waiting to hear answer or remonstrance--though he cried to me and tried to detain me--I caught up my hat, and flew down the stairs; and once out of the house and in the street hastened back at the top of my speed to the quarter of the town I had left. The streets through which I passed were still crowded, but wore an air not so much of disorder as of expectation, as if the procession I had followed had left a trail behind it. Here and there I saw soldiers patrolling, and warning the people to be quiet; and everywhere knots of townsmen, whispering and scowling, who stared at me as I passed. Every tenth male I saw was a monk, Dominican or Capuchin, and though my whole mind was bent on finding M. de Géol and Buton, and learning from them what they knew, as enemies, of Froment's plans and strength, I felt that the city was in an abnormal state; and that if I would do anything before the convulsion took place, I must act quickly.

I was fortunate enough to find M. de Géol and Buton at their lodgings. The former, whom I had not seen since our arrival, and who doubtless had his opinion of the cause of my sudden disappearance in the street, greeted me with a scowl and a bitter sarcasm, but when I had put a few questions, and he found that I was in earnest, his manner changed. "You may tell him," he said, nodding to Buton.

Then I saw that they too were excited, though they would fain hide it. "What is it?" I asked.

"Froment's party rose at Avignon yesterday," he answered eagerly. "Prematurely; and were crushed--crushed with heavy loss. The news has just arrived. It may hasten his plans."

"I saw soldiers in the street," I said.

"Yes, the Calvinists have asked for protection. But, that, and the patrols," De Géol answered with a grim smile, "are equally a farce. The regiment of Guienne, which is patriotic and would assist us, and even be some protection, is kept within barracks by its officers; the mayor and municipals are red, and whatever happens will not hoist the flag or call out the troops. The Catholic cabarets are alive with armed men; in a word, my friend, if Froment succeeds in mastering the town, and holding it three days, M. d'Artois, governor of Montpellier, will be here with his garrison, and----"

"Yes!"

"And what was a riot will be a revolt," he said pithily. "But there is many a slip between the cup and the lip, and there are more than sheep in the Cevennes Mountains!"

The words had scarcely passed from his lips, when a man ran into the room, looked at us, and raised his hand in a peculiar way. "Pardon me," said M. de Géol quickly; and with a muttered word he followed the man out. Buton was not a whit behind. In a moment I was alone.

I supposed they would return, and I waited impatiently; but a minute or two passed, and they did not appear. At length, tired of waiting, and wondering what was afoot, I went into the yard of the inn, and thence into the street. Still I did not find them; but collected before the inn I found a group of servants and others belonging to the place. They were all standing silent, listening, and as I joined them one looked round peevishly, and raised his hand as a warning to me to be quiet.

Before I could ask what it meant, the distant report of a gun, followed quickly by a second and a third, made my heart beat. A dull sound, made, it might be, by men shouting, or the passage of a heavy waggon over pavement, ensued; then more firing, each report short, sharp, and decisive.

While we listened, and as the last red glow of sunset faded on the eaves above us, leaving the street cold and grey, a bell somewhere began to toll hurriedly, stroke upon stroke; and a man, dashing round a corner not far away, made towards us.

But the landlord of the Ecu did not wait for him. "All in!" he cried to his people, "and close the great gates! And do you, Pierre, bar the shutters. And you, Monsieur," he continued hurriedly, turning to me, "will do well to come in also. The town is up, and the streets will not be safe for strangers."

But I was already half-way down the street. I met the fugitive, and he cried to me, as I passed, that the mob were coming. I met a frightened, riderless horse, galloping madly along the kennel; it swerved from me, and almost fell on the slippery pavement. But I took no heed of either. I ran on until two hundred paces before me I saw smoke and dust, and dimly through it a row of soldiers, who, with their backs to me, were slowly giving way before a dense crowd that pressed upon them. Even as I came in sight of them, they seemed to break and melt away, and with a roar of triumph the mob swept over the place on which they had stood.

I had the wit to see that to force my way past the crowd was impossible; and I darted aside into a narrow passage darkened by wide flat eaves that almost hid the pale evening sky. This brought me to a lane, full of women, standing listening with scared faces. I hurried through them, and when I had gone, as I judged, far enough to outflank the mob, chose a lane that appeared to lead in the direction of Father Benôit's house. Fortunately, the crowd was engaged in the main streets, the byways were comparatively deserted, and without accident I reached the little square by the gate.

Probably the attack on the soldiers had begun therse, or in that neighbourhood, for a broken musket lay in two pieces on the pavement, and pale faces at upper windows followed me in a strange unwinking silence as I crossed the square. But no man was to be seen, and unmolested I reached the door of Father Benôit's staircase, and entered.

In the open the light was still good, but within doors it was dusk, and I had not taken two steps before I tripped and fell headlong over some object that lay in my way. I struck the foot of the stairs heavily, and got up groaning; but ceased to groan and held my breath, as peering through the half light of the entry, I saw over what I had fallen. It was a man's body.

The man was a monk, in the black and white robe of his order; and he was quite dead. It took me an instant to overcome the horror of the discovery, but that done, I saw easily enough how the corpse came to be there. Doubtless the man had been shot in the street at the beginning of the riot--perhaps he had been the first to attack the patrol; and the body had been dragged into shelter here, while his party swept on to vengeance.

I stooped and reverently adjusted the cowl which my foot had dragged away; and that done--it was no time for sentiment--I turned from him, and hurried up the stairs. Alas, when I reached Father Benôit's room it was empty.

Wondering what I should do next, I stood a moment in the failing light. What could I do? Then I walked aimlessly to the casement and looked out. In the dull, almost blind wall which met my eyes across the court, was one window on a level with that at which I stood, but a little to the side. On a sudden, as I stared stupidly at the wall near it, a bright light shone out in this window. A lamp had been kindled in the room; and darkly outlined against the glow I saw the head and shoulders of a woman.

I almost screamed a name. It was Denise!

Even while I held my breath she moved from the window, a curtain was drawn and all was dark. Only the plain lines of the window--and those fast fading in the gloom--remained; only those and the gloomy, well-like court, that separated me from her.

I leaned a moment on the sill, my heart bounding quickly, my thoughts working with inconceivable rapidity. She was there, in the house opposite! It seemed too wonderful; it seemed inexplicable. Then I reflected that the house stood next to the old gate I had seen from the street; and had not some one told me that Froment lived in the Port d'Auguste?

Doubtless this was it; and she lay in his power in this house that adjoined it and was one with it. I leaned farther out, partly that I might cool my burning face, partly to see more; my eyes, greedily scanning the front of the house, traced the line of arrow-slits that marked the ascent of the staircase. I followed the line downwards; it ended beside the porch surmounted by a little statue, at which I had seen the two men enter.

They were still fighting in the town. I could hear the dull sound of distant volleys, and the tolling of bells, and now and then a wave of noise, of screams and yells, that rose and sank on the evening air. But my eyes were on the porch below; and suddenly I had a thought. I followed the line of arrow-slits up again--it was too dark in the sombre court to see them well--and marked the position of the window at which Denise had appeared. Then I turned, and passing through the room, I groped my way downstairs.

I had no light, and I had to go carefully with one hand on the grimy wall; but I knew now where the monk's body lay, and I stepped over it safely, and to the door, and putting out my head, looked up and down.

Two men, as I did so, passed hurriedly through the little square, and, before reaching the gate, dived into an entry on the right, and disappeared. About the eaves of the highest house, that towered high and black above me, a faint ruddy light was beginning to dance. I heard voices, that came, I thought, from the tower of the gateway; and there, too, I thought that I saw a figure outlined against the sky. But otherwise, all was quiet in the neighbourhood; and I went in again.

No matter what I did in the darkness at the foot of the stairs; I hate to recall it. But in a minute or two I came out a monk in cowl and girdle. Then I, too, dived into the entry, and in a trice found myself in the court. Before me was the porch, and with the barrel of the broken musket, which I had snatched up as I passed, I struck twice on the pavement.

I had no time to think what would happen next, or what I was going to confront. The door opened instantly, and I went in; as by magic the door closed silently behind me.

I found myself in a long, bare hall or corridor, plain and unfurnished, that had once perhaps been a cloister. A lighted lamp hung against a wall, and opposite me, on a stone seat sat two persons talking; three or four others were walking up and down. All paused at my entrance, however, and looked at me eagerly. "Whence are you, brother?" said one of them, advancing to me.

"The Cabaret Vierge," I answered at a venture. The light dazzled me, and I raised my hand to ward it off.

"For the Chief?"

"Yes."

"Come, quickly then," the man said, "he is on the roof. It goes well?" he continued, looking with a smile at my weapon.

"It goes," I answered, holding my head low, so that my face was lost in the cowl.

"They are beginning to light up, I am told?"

"Yes."

He took up a small lamp, and opening a door in a kind of buttress that strengthened one of the arches, he led the way through it, and up a narrow winding staircase made in the thickness of the wall. Presently we passed an open door, and I ticked it off in my mind. It led to the rooms on the first floor from the ground. Twenty steps higher we passed another door--closed this time. Again fifteen steps and we came to a third. That floor held my heart, and I looked round greedily, desperately, for some way of evading my guide and so reaching it. But I saw only the smooth stones of the wall; and he continued to climb.

I halted half a dozen steps higher. "What is it?" he asked, looking down at me.

"I have dropped a note," I said; and I began to grope about the steps.

"For the Chief?"

"Yes."

"Here, take the light!" he answered impatiently. "And be quick! if your news is worth the telling, it is worth telling quickly. *Sacré!* man, what have you done?"

I had let the lamp fall on the steps, extinguishing it; and we were in darkness. In the moment of silence which followed, before he recovered from his surprise, I could hear the voices of men above us, and the tramp of their feet on the roof; and a cold draught of air met me. He swore another oath. "Get down, get down!" he cried angrily, "and let me pass you! You are a pretty messenger to--there wait; wait until I fetch another light."

He squeezed by me, and left me standing in the very place I would have chosen, in the angle of the doorway we had just passed; before he had clattered down half a dozen steps I had my finger on the latch. To my joy the door--which might so easily have been locked--yielded to my knee, and passing through it, I closed it behind me. Then turning to the right--all was still dark--I groped my way along the wall through which I had entered. I knew it to be the outside wall, and dimly in front I discerned the faint radiance of a window. Now that the moment had come to put all to the test I was as calm as I could wish to be. I counted ten paces, and came, as I expected, to the window; ten paces farther and I felt my way barred by a door. This should be the room--the last that way; listening intently for the first sounds of pursuit or alarm, I felt about for a latch, found it, and tried the door. Again fortune favoured me, it came to my hand; but instead of light I found all dark as before; and then understood, as I struck with some violence against a second door.

A stifled cry in a woman's voice came from beyond it: and some one asked sharply, "Who is that?"

I gave no answer, but searched for the latch, found it, and in a moment the door was opened. The light which poured out dazzled me for a second or two; but while I stood blinking, under the lamp I had a vision of two girls standing at bay, one behind the other, and the nearer was Denise!

I stepped towards her with a cry of joy; she retreated with terror written on her face. "What do you want?" she stammered as she retreated. "You have made some mistake. We----"

Then I remembered the guise in which I stood, and the gun-barrel in my hand, and I dashed back the cowl from my face; and in a moment--it was of all surprises the most joyous, for I had not seen her since we sat opposite one another in the carriage, and then only a word had passed between us--in a moment she was in my arms, on my breast, and sobbing with her head hidden, and my lips on her hair.

"They told me you were dead!" she cried. "They told me you were dead!"

Then I understood; and I held her to me, held her to me more and more closely, and said--God knows what I said. And for the moment she let me, and we forgot all else, our danger, the dark future, even the woman who stood by. We had been plighted before, and it had been nothing to us; now, with my lips on hers, and her arms clinging, I knew that it was once for all, and that only death, if death, could part us.

Alas! that was not so far from us that we could long ignore it. In a minute or two she freed herself, and thrust me from her, her face pale and red by turns, her eyes soft and shining in the lamplight. "How do you come here, Monsieur?" she cried. "And in that dress?"

"To see you," I answered. And at the word, I stepped forward and would have taken her in my arms again.

But she waved me back. "Oh, no, no!" she cried, shuddering. "Not now! Do you know that they will kill you? Do you know that they will kill you if they find you here? Go! Go! I beg of you, while you can."

"And leave you?"

"Yes, and leave me," she answered, with a gesture of despair. "I implore you to do so."

"And leave you to Froment?" I cried again.

She looked at me in a different way, and with a little start. "You know that?" she said.

"Yes," I answered.

"Then know this too, Monsieur," she replied, raising her head, and meeting my eyes with the bravest look. "Know this too: that whatever betide, I shall not, after this, marry him, nor any man but you!"

I would have fallen on my knees and kissed the hem of her gown for that word, but she drew back, and passionately begged me to begone. "This house is not safe for you," she said. "It is death, it is death, Monsieur! My mother is merciless, my brother is here; and *he*--the house is full of his sworn creatures. You escaped him hardly before; if he finds you here now he will kill you."

"But if I need fear him so," I answered grimly,--for I saw, now that she had ceased to blush, how pale and wan she was, and what dark marks fear had painted under her eyes--child's eyes no longer, but a woman's--"if I need fear him so, what of you? What of you, Mademoiselle? Am I to leave you at his mercy?"

She looked at me with a strange gravity in her face; and answered me so that I never forgot her answer. "Monsieur," she said, "was I afraid on the roof of the house at St. Alais? And I have more to guard now. Have no fear. There is a roof here, too, and I walk on it; nor shall my husband ever have cause to blush for me."

"But I was there," I said quickly. Heaven knows why; it was a strange thing to say. Yet she did not find it so.

"Yes," she said--and smiled; and with the smile, her face burned again and her eyes grew soft, and all her dignity fled in a moment, and she looked at me, drooping. And in an instant she was in my arms.

But only for a few seconds. Then she tore herself away almost in anger. "Oh, go, go!" she cried. "If you love me, go, Monsieur."

"Swear," I said, "to put a handkerchief in your window if you want help!"

"In my window?"

"I can see it from Father Benôit's."

A gleam of joy lit up her face. "I will," she said. "Oh, God be thanked that you are so near! I will. But I have Françoise, too, and she is true to me. As long as I have her----"

She stopped with her lips apart, and the blood gone suddenly from her cheeks; and we looked at one another. Alas, I had stayed too long! There was a noise of feet coming along the passage, and a hubbub of voices outside, and the clatter of a door hastily closed. I think for a moment we scarcely breathed; and even after that it was her woman who was the first to move. She sprang to the door and softly locked it.

"It is vain!" Denise said in a harsh whisper; she leaned against the table, her face as white as snow. "They will fetch my mother, and they will kill you."

"There is no other door?" I muttered, staring round with hunted eyes, and feeling for the first time the full danger of the course I had taken.

She shook her head.

"What is that?" I cried, pointing to the farther end of the chamber, where a bed stood in the alcove.

"A closet," the woman answered, almost with a sob. "Yes, yes, Monsieur, they may not search. Quick, and I can lock it."

In such a case man acts on instinct. I heard the latch of the door tried, and then some one knocked peremptorily; and so long I hesitated. But a second knock followed on the first, and a voice I knew cried imperatively: "Open, open, Françoise!" and I moved towards the closet. The girl, distracted by the repeated summons and her terror, hung a moment between me and the door of the room; but in the end had to go to the latter, so that I drew the closet door upon myself.

Then in a moment it came upon me that if, hiding there, I was found, I should shame Denise; it darted through my brain that if, lurking there behind the closed doors among her woman's things, I was caught, I should harm her a hundred times more than if I stood out in the middle of the floor and faced the worst. And with my face on fire at the mere thought, I opened the door again, and stepped out; and was just in time. For as the door of the room flew open, and M. de St. Alais strode in and looked round, I was the first person he saw.

There were three or four men behind him; and among them the man whom I had cheated on the stairs. But M. St. Alais' eyes blazing with wrath caught mine, and held them; and the others were nothing to me.

CHAPTER XXII
NOBLESSE OBLIGE

Yet he was not the first to speak. One of the men behind him took a step forward, and cried, "That is the man! See, he still has the gun barrel."

"Seize him, then," M. de St. Alais replied. "And take him from here! Monsieur," he continued, addressing me grimly, and with a grim eye, "whoever you are, when you undertook to be a spy you counted the cost, I suppose? Take him away, my men!"

Two of the fellows strode forward, and in a moment seized my arms; and in the surprise of M. de St. Alais' appearance and the astonishment his words caused me, I made no resistance. But in such emergencies the mind works quickly, and in a trice I recovered myself. "This is nonsense, M. de St. Alais!" I said. "You know well that I am no spy. You know why I am here. And for the matter of that----"

"I know nothing!" he answered.

"But----"

"I know nothing, I say!" he repeated, with a mocking gesture. "Except, Monsieur, that we find you here in a monk's dress, when you are clearly no monk. You had better have tried to swim the Rhone at flood, than entered this house to-night--I tell you that! Now away with him! His case will be dealt with below."

But this was too much. I wrested my hands from the men who held me, and sprang back. "You lie!" I cried. "You know who I am, and why I am here!"

"I do not know you," he answered stubbornly. "Nor do I know why you are here. I once knew a man like you; that is true. But he was a gentleman, and would have died before he would have saved himself by a lie--by a trumped-up tale. Take him away. He has frightened Mademoiselle to death. I suppose he found the door open, and slipped in, and thought himself safe."

At last I understood what he meant, and that in his passion he would sacrifice one rather than bring in his sister's name. Nay, I saw more; that he viewed with a cruel exultation the dilemma in which he had placed me; and my brow grew damp, as I looked round wildly, trying to solve the question. I had the sounds of street fighting still in my ears; I knew that men staking all in such a strife owned few scruples and scant mercy. I could see that this man in particular was maddened by the losses and humiliations which he had suffered; and I stood in the way of his schemes. The risk existed, therefore, and was no mere threat; it seemed foolish quixotism to run it.

And yet--and yet I hesitated. I even let the men urge me half-way to the door; and then--heaven knows what I should have done or whether I could have seen my way plainly--the knot was cut for me. With a scream, Denise, who since her brother's entrance had leaned, half-fainting, against the wall, sprang forward, and seized him by the arm.

"No, no!" she cried in a choked voice. "No! You will not, you will not do this! Have pity, have mercy! I----"

"Mademoiselle!" he said, cutting her short quietly, but with a gleam of rage in his eyes. "You are overwrought, and forget yourself. The scene has been too much for you. Here!" he continued sharply to the maid, "take care of your mistress. The man is a spy, and not worthy of her pity."

But Denise clung to him. "He is no spy!" she cried, in a voice that went to my heart. "He is no spy, and you know it!"

"Hush, girl! Be silent!" he answered furiously.

But he had not counted on a change in her, beside which the change in him was petty. "I will not!" she answered, "I will not!" and to my astonishment, releasing the arm to which she had hitherto clung, and shaking back from her face the hair which her violent movements had loosened, she stood out and defied him. "I will not!" she cried. "He is no spy, and you know it, Monsieur! He is my lover," she continued, with a superb gesture, "and he came to see me. Do you understand? He was contracted to me, and he came to see me!"

"Girl, are you mad?" he snarled in the breathless hush of the room, the hush that followed as all looked at her.

"I am not mad," she answered, her eyes burning in her white face.

"Then if you feel no shame do you feel no fear?" he retorted in a terrible voice.

"No!" she cried. "For I love! And I love him."

I will not say what I felt when I heard that, myself helpless. For one thing, I was in so great a rage I scarcely knew what I felt; and for another, the words were barely spoken before M. le Marquis seized the girl roughly by the waist, and dragged her, screaming and resisting, to the other end of the room.

This was the signal for a scene indescribable. I sprang forward to protect her; in an instant the three men flung themselves upon me, and bore me by sheer weight towards the door. St. Alais, foaming with rage, shouted to them to remove me, while I called him coward, and cursed him and strove desperately to get at him. For a moment I made head against them all, though they were three to one; the maid's screaming added to the uproar. Then the odds prevailed; and in a minute they had me out, and had closed the door on her and her cries.

I was panting, breathless, furious. But the moment it was done and the door shut, a kind of calm fell upon us. The men relaxed their hold on me, and stood looking at me quietly; while I leaned against the wall, and glowered at them. Then, "There, Monsieur, have no more of that!" one of them said civilly enough. "Go peaceably, and we will be easy with you; otherwise----"

"He is a cowardly hound!" I cried with a sob.

"Softly, Monsieur, softly."

There were five of them, for two had remained at the door. The passage was dark, but they had a lantern, and we waited in silence two or three minutes. Then the door opened a few inches, and the man who seemed to be the leader went to it, and having received his orders, returned.

"Forward!" he said. "In No. 6. And do you, Petitot, fetch the key."

The man named went off quickly, and we followed more slowly along the corridor; the steady tramp of my guards, as they marched beside me, awaking sullen echoes that rolled away before us. The yellow light of the lantern showed a white-washed wall on either side, broken on the right hand by a dull line of doors, as of cells. We halted presently before one of these, and I thought that I was to be confined there; and my courage rose, for I should still be near Denise. But the door, when opened, disclosed only a little staircase which we descended in single file, and so reached a bare corridor similar to that above. Half-way along this we stopped again, beside an open window, through which the night wind came in so strongly as to stir the hair, and force the man who carried the lantern to shield the light under his skirts. And not the night wind only; with it entered all the noises of the night and the disturbed city; hoarse cries and cheers, and the shrill monotonous jangle of bells, and now and then a pistol-shot--noises that told only too eloquently what was passing under the black veil that hid the chaos of streets and houses below us. Nay, in one place the veil was rent, and through the gap a ruddy column poured up from the roofs, dispersing sparks--the hot glare of some great fire, that blazing in the heart of the city, seemed to make the sky sharer in the deeds and horrors that lay beneath it.

The men with me pressed to the window, and peered through it, and strained eyes and ears; and little wonder. Little wonder, too, that the man who was responsible for all, and had staked all, walked the roof above with tireless steps. For the struggle below was the one great struggle of the world, the struggle that never ceases between the old and the new: and it was being fought as it had been fought in Nîmes for centuries, savagely, ruthlessly, over kennels running with blood. Nor could the issue be told; only, that as it was here, it was likely to be through half of France. We who stood at that window, looked into the darkness with actual eyes; but across the border at Turin, and nearer at Sommières and Montpellier, thousands of Frenchmen bearing the greatest names of France, watched also--watched with faces turned to Nîmes, and hearts as anxious as ours.

I gathered from the talk of those round me, that M. Froment had seized the Arènes, and garrisoned it, and that the flames we saw were those of one of the Protestant churches; that as yet the patriots, taken by surprise, made little resistance, and that if the Reds could hold for twenty-four hours longer what they had seized, the arrival of the troops from Montpellier would then secure all, and at the same time stamp the movement with the approval of the highest parties.

"But it was a near thing," one of the men muttered. "If we had not been at their throats to-night, they would have been at ours to-morrow!"

"And now, not half the companies have turned out."

"But the villages will come in in the morning," a third cried eagerly. "They are to toll all the bells from here to the Rhone."

"Ay, but what if the Cevennols come in first? What then, man?"

No one had an answer to this, and all stood watching eagerly, until the sound of footsteps approaching along the passage caused the men to draw in their heads. "Here is the key," said the leader. "Now, Monsieur!"

But it was not the key that disturbed us, nor Petitot, who had been sent for it, but a very tall man, cloaked, and wearing his hat, who came hastily along the corridor with three or four behind him. As he approached he called out, "Is Buzeaud here?"

The man who had spoken before stood out respectfully. "Yes, Monsieur."

"Take half a dozen men, the stoutest you have downstairs," the new comer answered--it was Froment himself--"and get as many more from the Vierge, and barricade the street leading beside the barracks to the Arsenal. You will find plenty of helpers. And occupy some of the houses so as to command the street. And--But what is this?" he continued, breaking off sharply, as his eyes, passing over the group, stopped at me. "How does this gentleman come here? And in this dress?"

"M. le Marquis arrested him--upstairs."

"M. le Marquis?"

"Yes, Monsieur, and ordered him to be confined in No. 6 for the present."

"Ah!"

"As a spy."

M. Froment whistled softly, and for a moment we looked at one another. The wavering light of the lanterns, and perhaps the tension of the man's feelings, deepened the harsh lines of his massive features, and darkened the shadows about his eyes and mouth; but presently he drew a deep breath, and smiled, as if something whimsical in the situation struck him. "So we meet again, M. le Vicomte," he said with that. "I remember now that I have something of yours. You have come for it, I suppose?"

"Yes, Monsieur, I have come for it," I said defiantly, giving him back look for look; and I saw that he understood.

"And M. le Marquis found you upstairs?"

"Yes."

"Ah!" For a moment he seemed to reflect. Then, turning to the men. "Well, you can go, Buzeaud. I will be answerable for this gentleman--who had better remove that masquerade. And do you," he continued, addressing the two or three who had come with him, "wait for me above. Tell M. Flandrin--it is my last word--that whatever happens the Mayor must not raise the flag for the troops. He may tell him what he pleases from me--that I will hang him from the highest window of the tower, if he likes--but it must not be done. You understand?"

"Yes, Monsieur."

"Then go. I will be with you presently."

They went, leaving a lantern on the floor; and in a moment Froment and I were alone. I stood expectant, but he did not look at me. Instead, he turned to the open window, and leaning on the sill, gazed into the night, and so remained for some time silent; whether the orders he had just given had really diverted his thoughts into another channel, or he had not made up his mind how to treat me, I cannot determine. More than once I heard him sigh, however; and at last he said abruptly, "Only three companies have risen?"

I do not know what moved me, but I answered in the same spirit. "Out of how many?" I said coolly.

"Thirteen," he answered. "We are out-numbered. But we moved first, we have the upper hand, and we must keep it. And if the villagers come in to-morrow----"

"And the Cevennols do not."

"Yes; and if the officers can hold the Guienne regiment within barracks, and the Mayor does not hoist the flag, calling them out, and the Calvinists do not surprise the Arsenal--I think we may be able to do so."

"But the chances are?"

"Against us. The more need, Monsieur"--for the first time he turned and looked at me with a sort of dark pride glowing in his face--"of a man! For--do you know what we are fighting for down there? France! France!" he continued bitterly, and letting his emotion appear, "and I have a few hundred cutthroats and rascals and shavelings to do the work, while all the time your fine gentlemen lie safe and warm across the frontier, waiting to see what will happen! And I run risks, and they hold the stakes! I kill the bear, and they take the skin. They are safe, and if I fail I hang like Favras! Faugh! It is enough to make a man turn patriot and cry '*Vive la Nation!*'"

He did not wait for my answer, but impatiently snatching up the lantern, he made a sign to me to follow him, and led the way down the passage. He had said not a word of my presence in the house, of my position, of Mademoiselle St. Alais, or how he meant to deal with me; and at the door, not knowing what was in his mind, I touched his shoulder and stopped him.

"Pardon me," I said, with as much dignity as I could assume, "but I should like to know what you are going to do with me, Monsieur. I need not tell you that I did not enter this house as a spy----"

"You need tell me nothing," he answered, cutting me short with rudeness. "And for what I am going to do with you, it can be told in half a dozen words. I am going to keep you by me, that if the worst comes of this--in which event I am not likely to see the week out--you may protect Mademoiselle de St. Alais and convey her to a place of safety. To that end your commission shall be restored to you; I have it safe. If, on the other hand, we hold our own, and light the fire that shall burn up these cold-blooded *pedants là bas*, then, M. le Vicomte--I shall have a word to say to you. And we will talk of the matter as gentlemen."

For a moment I stood dumb with astonishment. We were at the door of the little staircase--by which I had descended--when he said this; and as he spoke the last word, he turned, as expecting no answer, and opened it, and set his foot on the lowest stair, casting the light of the lantern before him. I plucked him by the sleeve, and he turned, and faced me.

"M. Froment!" I muttered. And then for the life of me I could say no more.

"There is no need for words," he said grandly.

"Are you sure--that you know all!" I muttered.

"I am sure that she loves you, and that she does not love me," he answered with a curling lip and a ring of scorn in his voice. "And besides that, I am sure of one thing only."

"Yes?"

"That within forty-eight hours blood will flow in every street of Nîmes, and Froment, the bourgeois, will be Froment le Baron--or nothing! In the former case, we will talk. In the latter," and he shrugged his shoulders with a gesture a little theatrical, "it will not matter."

With the word he turned to the stairs, and I followed him up them and across the upper corridor, and by the outer staircase, where I had evaded my guide, and so to the roof, and from it by a short wooden ladder to the leads of a tower; whence we overlooked, lying below us, all the dim black chaos of Nîmes, here rising in giant forms, rather felt than seen, there a medley of hot lights and deep shadows, thrown into relief by the glare of the burning church. In three places I picked out a cresset shining, high up in the sky, as it were; one on the rim of the Arènes, another on the roof of a distant church, a third on a tower beyond the town. But for the most part the town was now at rest. The riot had died down, the bells were silent, the wind blew salt from the sea and cooled our faces.

There were a dozen cloaked figures on the leads, some gazing down in silence, others walking to and fro, talking together; but in the darkness it was impossible to recognise any one. Froment, after receiving one or two reports, withdrew to the outer side of the tower overlooking the country, and walked there alone, his head bowed, and his hands behind him, a desire to preserve his dignity having more to do with this, or I was mistaken, than any longing for solitude. Still, the others respected his wishes, and following their example I seated myself in an embrasure of the battlements, whence the fire, now growing pale, could be seen.

What were the others' thoughts I cannot say. A muttered word apprised me that Louis St. Alais was in command at the Arènes; and that M. le Marquis waited only until success was assured to start for Sommières, whence the commandant had promised a regiment of horse should Froment be able to hold his own without them. The arrangement seemed to me to be of the strangest; but the Emigrés, fearful of compromising the King, and warned by the fate of Favras--who, deserted by his party, had suffered for a similar conspiracy a few months before--were nothing if not timid. And if those round me felt any indignation, they did not express it.

The majority, however, were silent, or spoke only when some movement in the town, some outcry or alarm, drew from them a few eager words; and for myself, my thoughts were neither of the struggle below--where both parties lay watching each other and waiting for the day--nor of the morrow, nor even of Denise, but of Froment himself. If the aim of the man had been to impress me, he had succeeded. Seated there in the darkness, I felt his influence strong upon me; I felt the crisis as and because he felt it. I thrilled with the excitement of the gambler's last stake, because he had thrown the dice. I stood on the giddy point on which he stood, and looked into the dark future, and trembled for and with him. My eyes turned from others, and involuntarily sought his tall figure where he walked alone; with as little will on my part I paid him the homage due to the man who stands unmoved on the brink, master of his soul, though death yawns for him.

About midnight there was a general movement to descend. I had eaten nothing for twelve hours, and I had done much; and, notwithstanding the dubious position in which I stood, appetite bade me go with the rest. I went, therefore; and, following the stream, found myself a minute later on the threshold of a long room, brilliantly lit with lamps, and displaying tables laid with covers for sixty or more. I fancied that at the farther end of the apartment, and through an interval in the crowd of men before me, I caught a glimpse of women, of jewels, of flashing eyes, and a waving fan; and if anything could have added to the bewildering abruptness of the change from the dark, wind-swept leads above to the gay and splendid scene before me it was this. But I had scant time for reflection. Though I did not advance far, the press, which separated me from the upper end of the room, melted quickly, as one after another took his seat amid a hum of conversation; and in a moment I found myself gazing straight at Denise, who, white and wan, with a pitiful look in her eyes, sat beside her mother at the uppermost table, a picture of silent woe. Madame Catinot and two or three gentlemen and as many ladies were seated with them.

Whether my eyes drew hers to me, or she glanced that way by chance, in a moment she looked at me, and rose to her feet with a low gasping cry, that I felt rather than heard. It was enough to lead Madame St. Alais' eyes to me, and she too cried out; and in a trice, while a few between us still talked unconscious, and the servants glided about, I found all at that farther table staring at me, and myself the focus of the room. Just then, unluckily, M. St. Alais, rather late, came in; of course, he too saw me. I heard an oath behind me, but I was intent on the farther table and Mademoiselle, and it was not until he laid his hand on my arm that I turned sharply and saw him.

"Monsieur!" he cried, with another oath--and I saw that he was almost choking with rage--with rage and surprise. "This is too much."

I looked at him in silence. The position was so perplexing that I could not grasp it.

"How do I find you here?" he continued with violence and in a voice that drew every eye in the room to me. He was white with anger. He had left me a prisoner, he found me a guest.

"I hardly know myself," I answered. "But----"

"I do," said a voice behind M. St. Alais. "If you wish to know, Marquis, M. de Saux is here at my invitation."

The speaker was Froment, who had just entered the room. St. Alais turned, as if he had been stabbed. "Then I am not!" he cried.

"That is as you please," Froment said steadfastly.

"It is--and I do not please!" the Marquis retorted, with a scornful glance, and in a tone that rang through the room. "I do not please!"

As I heard him, and felt myself the centre, under the lights, of all those eyes, I could have fancied that I was again in the St. Alais' *salon*, listening to the futile oath of the sword; and that three-quarters of a year had not elapsed since that beginning of all our troubles, But in a moment Froment's voice roused me from the dream.

"Very well," he said gravely. "But I think that you forget----"

"It is you who forget," St. Alais cried wildly. "Or you do not understand--or know--that this gentleman----"

"I forget nothing!" Froment replied with a darkening face. "Nothing, except that we are keeping my guests waiting. Least of all, do I forget the aid, Monsieur, which you have hitherto rendered me. But, M. le Marquis," he continued, with dignity, "it is mine to command to-night, and it is for me to make dispositions. I have made them, and I must ask you to comply with them. I know that you will not fail me at a pinch. I know, and these gentlemen know, that in misfortune you would be my helper; but I believe also that, all going well, as it does, you will not throw unnecessary obstacles in my way. Come, Monsieur; this gentleman will not refuse to sit here. And we will sit at Madame's table. Oblige me."

M. St. Alais' face was like night, but the other was a man, and his tone was strenuous as well as courteous; and slowly and haughtily M. le Marquis, who, I think, had never before in his life given way, followed him to the farther end of the room. Left alone, I sat down where I was, eyed curiously by those round me; and myself, finding something still more curious in this strange banquet while Nîmes watched; this midnight merriment, while the dead still lay in the streets, and the air quivered, and all the world of night hung, listening for that which was to come.

CHAPTER XXIII
THE CRISIS

When the grey dawn, to which so many looked forward, broke slowly over the waking city, it found on the leads of Froment's tower some pale faces; perhaps some sinking hearts. That hour, when all life lacks colour, and all things, the sky excepted, are black to the eye, tries a man's courage to the uttermost; as the cold wind that blows with it searches his body. Eyes that an hour before had sparkled over the wine--for we had sat late and drunk to the King, the Church, the Red Cockade, and M. d'Artois--grew thoughtful; men who, a little before, had shown flushed faces, shivered as they peered into the mist, and drew their cloaks more closely round them; and if the man was there, who regarded the issue of the day with perfect indifference, he was not of those near me.

Froment had preached faith, but the faith for the most part was down in the street. There, I have no doubt, were many who believed, and were ready to rush on death, or slay without pity. And there may have been one or two of these with us. But in the main, the men who looked down with me on Nîmes that morning were hardy adventurers, or local followers of Froment, or officers whose regiments had dismissed them, or--but these were few--gentlemen, like St. Alais. All brave men, and some heated with wine; but not Froment only had heard of Favras hanged, of De Launay massacred, of Provost Flesselles shot in cold blood! Others beside him could make a guess at the kind of vengeance this strange new creature, La Nation, might take, being outraged: and so, when the long-expected dawn appeared at last, and warmed the eastern clouds, and leaping across the sea of mist which filled the Rhone valley, tinged the western peaks with rosy light, and found us watching, I saw no face among all the light fell on, that was not serious, not one but had some haggard, wan, or careworn touch to mark it mortal.

Save only Froment's. He, be the reason what it might, showed as the light rose a countenance not merely resolute, but cheerful. Abandoning the solitary habit he had maintained all night, he came forward to the battlements overlooking the town, and talked and even jested, rallying the faint-hearted, and taking success for granted. I have heard his enemies say that he did this because it was his nature, because he could not help it;

because his vanity raised him, not only above the ordinary passions of men, but above fear; because in the conceit of acting his part to the admiration of all, he forgot that it was more than a part, and tried all fortunes and ran all risks with as little emotion as the actor who portrays the Cid, or takes poison in the part of Mithridates.

But this seems to me to amount to no more than saying that he was not only a very vain, but a very brave man. Which I admit. No one, indeed, who saw him that morning could doubt it; or that, of a million, he was the man best fitted to command in such an emergency; resolute, undoubting, even gay, he reversed no orders, expressed no fears. When the mist rolled away--a little after four--and let the smiling plain be seen, and the city and the hills, and when from the direction of the Rhone the first harsh jangle of bells smote the ear and stilled the lark's song, he turned to his following with an air almost joyous.

"Come, gentlemen," he said gaily, and with head erect. "Let us be stirring! They must not say that we lie close and fear to show our heads abroad; or, having set others moving, are backward ourselves--like the tonguesters and dreamers of their knavish assembly, who, when they would take their King, set women in the front rank to take the danger also! *Allons*, Messieurs! They brought him from Versailles to Paris. We will escort him back! And to-day we take the first step!"

Enthusiasm is of all things the most contagious. A murmur of assent greeted his words; eyes that a moment before had been dull enough, grew bright. "*A bas les Traîtres!*" cried one. "*A bas le Tricolor!*" cried another.

Froment raised his hand for silence. "No, Monsieur," he said quickly. "On the contrary, we will have a tricolour of our own. *Vive le Roi! Vive la Foi! Vive la Loi! Vivent les Trois!*"

The conceit took. A hundred voices shouted, "*Vivent les Trois!*" in chorus. The words were taken up on lower roofs and at windows, and in the streets below; until they passed noisily away, after the manner of file-firing, into the distance.

Froment raised his hat gallantly. "Thank you, gentlemen," he said. "In the King's name, in his Majesty's name, I thank you. Before we have done, the Atlantic shall hear that cry, and La Manche re-echo it! And the Rhone shall release what the Seine has taken! To Nîmes and to you, all France looks this day. For freedom! For freedom to live--shall knaves and scriveners strangle her? For freedom to pray--they rob God, and defile His temples! For freedom to walk abroad--the King of France is a captive. Need I say more?"

"No! No!" they cried, waving hats and swords. "No! No!"

"Then I will not," he answered hardily. "I will use no more words! But I will show that here at least, at Nîmes at least, God and the King are honoured, and their servants are free! Give me your escort, gentlemen, and we will walk through the town and visit the King's posts, and see if any here dare cry, 'A bas le Roi!'"

They answered with a roar of assent and menace that shook the very tower; and instantly trooping to the ladder, began to descend by it to the roof of the house, and so to the staircase. Sitting on the battlements of the tower, I watched them pass in a long stream across the leads below, their hilts and buckles glittering in the sunshine, their ribbons waving in the breeze, their voices sharp and high. I thought them, as I watched, a gallant company; the greater part were young, and all had a fine air; not without sympathy I saw them vanish one by one in the head of the staircase, by which I had ascended. One half had disappeared when I felt a touch on my arm, and found Froment, the last to leave, standing by my side.

"You will stay here, Monsieur," he said, in an undertone of meaning, his eyes lowered to meet mine; "if the worst happens, I need not charge you to look to Mademoiselle."

"Worst or best, I will look to her," I answered.

"Thanks," he said, his lip curling, and an ugly light for an instant flashing in his eyes. "But in the latter case I will look to her myself. Don't forget, that if I win, we have still to talk, Monsieur!"

"Yet, God grant you may win!" I exclaimed involuntarily.

"You have faith in your swordsmanship?" he answered, with a slight sneer; and then, in a different tone, he went on: "No, Monsieur, it is not that. It is that you are a French gentleman. And as such I leave Mademoiselle to your care without a qualm. God keep you!"

"And you," I said. And I saw him go after the others.

It was then about five o'clock. The sun was up, and the tower-roof, left silent and in my sole possession, seemed so near the sky, seemed so bright and peaceful and still, with the stillness of the early morning which is akin to innocence, that I looked about me dazed. I stood on a different plane from that of the world below, whence the roar of greeting that hailed Froment's appearance came up harshly. Another shout followed and another, that drove the affrighted pigeons in a circling cloud high above the roofs; and then the wave of sound began to roll away, moving with an indescribable note of menace southward through the city. And I remained alone on my tower, raised high above the strife.

Alone, with time to think; and to think some grim thoughts. Where now was the sweet union of which half the nation had been dreaming for weeks? Where the millennium of peace and fraternity to which Father Benôit, and the Syndics of Giron and Vlais, had looked forward? And the abolition of divisions? And the rights of man? And the other ten thousand blessings that philosophers and theorists had undertaken to create--the nature of man notwithstanding--their systems once adopted? Ay, where? From all the smiling country round came, for answer, the clanging of importunate bells. From the streets below rose for answer the sounds of riot and triumph. Along this or that road, winding ribbon-like across the plain, hurried little flocks of men--now seen for the first time--with glittering arms; and last and worst--when some half-hour had elapsed, and I still watched--from a distant suburb westward boomed out a sudden volley, and then dropping shots. The pigeons still wheeled, in a shining, shifting cloud, above the roofs, and the sparrows twittered round me, and on the tower, and on the roof below, where a few domestics clustered, all was sunshine and quiet and peace. But down in the streets, there, I knew that death was at work.

Still, for a time, I felt little excitement. It was early in the day; I expected no immediate issue; and I listened almost carelessly, following the train of thought I have traced, and gloomily comparing this scene of strife with the brilliant promises of a few months before. But little by little the anxiety of the servants who stood on the roof below, infected me. I began to listen more acutely; and to fancy that the tide of conflict was rolling nearer, that the cries and shots came more quickly and sharply to the ear. At last, in a place near the barracks, and not far off, I distinguished little puffs of thin white smoke rising above the roofs, and twice a rattling volley in the same quarter shook the windows. Then in one of the streets immediately below me, the whole length of which was visible, I saw people running--running towards me.

I called to the servants to know what it was.

"They are attacking the arsenal, Monsieur," one answered, shading his eyes.

"Who?" I said.

But he only shrugged his shoulders and looked out more intently. I followed his example, but for a time nothing happened; then on a sudden, as if a door were opened that hitherto had shut off the noise, a babel of shouts burst out and a great crowd entered the nearer end of the street below me, and pouring along it with loud cries and brandished arms--and a crucifix and a little body of monks in the middle--swirled away round the farthest corner, and were gone. For some time, however, I could still hear the burthen of their cries, and trace it towards the barracks, whence the crackle of musketry came at intervals; and I concluded that it was a reinforcement, and that Froment had sent for it. After that, chancing to look down, I saw that half the servants, below me, had vanished, and that figures were beginning to skulk about the streets hitherto deserted; and I began to tremble. The crisis had come sooner than I had thought.

I called to one of the men and asked him where the ladies were.

He looked up at me with a pale face. "I don't know, Monsieur," he answered rapidly; and he looked away again.

"They are below?"

But he was watching too intently to answer, and only shook his head impatiently. I was unwilling to leave my place on the roof, and I called to him to take my compliments to Madame St. Alais and ask her to ascend. It seemed strange that she had not done so, for women are not generally lacking in the desire to see.

But the man was too frightened to think of any one but himself--I fancy he was one of the cooks--and he did not move; while his companions only cried: "Presently, presently, Monsieur!"

At that, however, I lost my temper; and, going to the ladder, I ran down it, and strode towards them. "You rascals!" I cried. "Where are the ladies?"

One or two turned to me with a start. "Pardon, Monsieur?"

"Where are the ladies?" I repeated impatiently.

"Ah! I did not understand!" the nearest answered glibly. "Gone to the church to pray, Monsieur."

"To the church?"

"To be sure. By the Capuchins."

"And they are not here?"

"No, Monsieur," he answered, his eyes straying. "But--what is that?"

And, diverted by something, he skipped nimbly from me, his cheek a shade paler. I followed him to the parapet, and looked over. The view was not so wide as from the tower above, but the main street leading southward could be seen, and it was full of people; of scattered groups and handfuls, all coming towards us, some running, at an easy pace, while others walked quickly, four or five abreast, and often looked behind them.

The servants never doubted what it meant. In a trice the group broke up. With a muttered, "We are beaten!" they ran pell-mell across the sunny leads to the head of the staircase, and began to descend. I waited awhile, looking and fearing; but the stream of fugitives ever continued and increased, the pace grew quicker, the last comers looked more frequently behind them and handled their arms; the din of conflict, of yells, and cries, and shots, seemed to be approaching; and in a moment I made up my mind to act. The staircase was clear now; I ran quickly down it as far as the door on the upper floor, by which I had entered the house that evening before. I tried this, but recoiled; the door was locked. With a cry of vexation, my haste growing feverish--for now, in the darkness of the staircase, I was in ignorance what was happening, and pictured the worst--I went on, descending round and round, until I reached the cloister-like hall, at the bottom.

I found this choked with men, armed, grim-faced, and furious; and beset by other men who still continued to pour in from the street. A moment later and I should have found the staircase stopped by the stream of people ascending; and I must have remained on the roof. As it was, I could not for a minute or two force myself through the press, but was thrust against a wall, and pinned there by the rush inwards. Next me, however, I found one of the servants in like case, and I seized him by the sleeve. "Where are the ladies?" I said. "Have they returned? Are they here?"

"I don't know," he said, his eyes roving.

"Are they still at the church?"

"Monsieur, I don't know," he answered impatiently; and then seeing, I think, the man for whom he was searching, he shook me off, with the churlishness of fear, and, flinging himself into the crowd, was gone.

All the place was such a hurly-burly of men entering and leaving, shouting orders, or forcing themselves through the press, that I doubted what to do. Some were crying for Froment, others to close the doors; one that all was lost, another to bring up the powder. The disorder was enough to turn the brain, and for a minute I stood in the heart of it, elbowed and pushed, and tossed this way and that. Where were the women? Where were the women? The doubt distracted me. I seized half a dozen of the nearest men, and asked them; but they only cried out fiercely that they did not know--how should they?--and shook me off savagely and escaped as the servant had. For all here, with a few exceptions, were of the commoner sort. I could see nothing of Froment, nothing of St. Alais or the leaders, and only one or two of the gallants who had gone with them.

I do not think that I was ever in a more trying position. Denise might be still at the church and in peril there; or she might be in the streets exposed to dangers on which I dare not dwell; or, on the other hand, she might be safe in the next room, or upstairs; or on the roof. In the unutterable confusion, it was impossible to know or learn, or even move quickly; my only hope seemed to be in Froment's return, but after waiting a minute, which seemed a lifetime, in the hope of seeing him, I lost patience and battled my way through the press to a door, which appeared to lead to the main part of the house.

Passing through it, I found the same disorder ruling; here men, bringing up powder from the cellars, blocked the passage; there others appeared to be rifling the house. I had little hope of finding those whom I sought below stairs; and after glancing this way and that without result, I lighted on a staircase, and ascending quickly to the second floor, hastened to Denise's room. The door was locked.

I hammered on it madly and called, and waited, and listened, and called again; but I heard no sound from within; convinced at last. I left it and tried the nearest doors. The two first were locked also, and the rooms as silent; the third and fourth were open and empty. The last I entered was a man's.

The task was no long one, and occupied less than a minute. But all the time, while I rapped and listened and called, though the corridor in which I moved was quiet as death and echoed my footsteps, the house below rang with cries and shouts and hurrying feet; and I was in a fever. Madame might be on the roof. I turned that way meaning to ascend. Then I reflected that if I climbed to it I might find the staircase blocked when I came to descend again; and, cursing my folly for leaving the hall--simply because my quest had failed--I hurried back to the stairs, and dashed recklessly down them, and, stemming as well as I could the tide of people that surged and ebbed about the lower floor, I fought my way back to the hall.

I was just in time. As I entered by one door Froment entered by the other, with a little band of his braves; of whom several, I now observed, wore green ribbons--the Artois colours. His great stature raising him above the crowd of heads, I saw that he was wounded; a little blood was running down his cheek, and his eyes shone with a brilliance almost of madness. But he was still cool; he had still so much the command, not only of himself, but of those round him, that the commotion grew still and abated under his eye. In a moment men who before had only tumbled over and embarrassed one another, flew to their places; and, though the howling of a hostile mob could plainly be heard at the end of the street, and it was clear that he had fallen back before an overwhelming force, resolution seemed in a moment to take the place of panic, and hope of despair.

Standing on the threshold, and pointing this way, and that, with a discharged pistol which he held in his hand, he gave a few short, sharp orders for the barricading of the door, and saw them carried out, and sent this man to one post, and that man to another. Then, the crowd, which had before cumbered the place, melting as if by magic, he saw me forcing my way to him. And he beckoned to me.

If he played a part, then let me say, once for all, he played it nobly. Even now, when I guessed that all was lost, I read no fear and no envy in his face; and in what he said there was no ostentation.

"Get out quickly," he muttered, in an undertone, forestalling by a hasty gesture the excited questions I had on my lips, "through yonder door, and by the little postern at the foot of the other staircase. Go by the east gate, and you will find horses at the St. Geneviève outside. It is all over here!" he added, wringing my hand hard, and pushing me towards the door.

"But Mademoiselle?" I cried; and I told him that she was not in the house.

"What?" he said, pausing and looking at me, with his face grown suddenly dark. "Are you mad? Do you mean that she has gone out?"

"She is not here," I answered. "I am told that she went to the church with Madame St. Alais, and has not returned."

"That beldam!" he exclaimed, with a terrible oath, and then, "God help them!" he said--twice. And after a moment of silence, meeting my eyes and reading the horror in them, he laughed harshly. "After all, what matter?" he said recklessly. "We shall all go together! Let us go like gentlemen. I did what I could. Do you hear that?"

He held up his hand, as a roar of musketry shook the house; and he gave an order. The small windows had been stopped with paving stones, the door made solid with the wall behind it; and daylight being shut out, lamps had been lighted, which gave the long whitewashed, stone-groined room a strange sombre look. Or it was the grim faces I saw round me had that effect.

"I am afraid that the St. Alais are cut off in the Arènes," he said coolly. "And they are not enough to man the walls. Those cursed Cevennols have been too many for us. As for our friends--it is as I expected; they have left me to die like a bull in the ring. Well, we must die goring."

But in the midst of my admiration of his courage a kind of revulsion seized me. "And Denise?" I said, grasping his arm fiercely. "Are we to leave her to perish?"

He looked at me, his lip curling. "True," he said, with a sneering smile. "I forgot. You are not of us."

"I am thinking of her!" I cried, raging. And in that moment I hated him.

But his mood changed while he looked at me. "You are right, Monsieur," he said, in a different tone. "Go! There may be a chance; but the church is by the Capuchins, and those dogs were baying round it when we fell back. They are ten to one, or--still there may be a chance," he continued with decision. "Go, and if you find her, and escape, do not forget Froment of Nîmes."

"By the postern?" I said.

"Yes--take this," he answered; and abruptly drawing a pistol from his pocket, he forced it on me. "Go, and I must go too. Good fortune, Monsieur, and farewell. And you, bark away, you dogs!" he continued bitterly, addressing the unconscious mob. "The bull is on foot yet, and will toss some of you before the ring closes!"

CHAPTER XXIV
THE MILLENNIUM

With that word he thrust me towards the door that led to the inner hall and the postern; and, knowing, as I did, that every moment I delayed might stand for a life, and that within a minute or two at most the rear of the building would be beset, and my chance of egress lost, it was to be expected that I should not hesitate.

Yet I did. The main body of Froment's followers had flocked upstairs, whence they could be heard firing from the roof and windows. He stood almost alone in the middle of the floor; in the attitude of one listening and thinking, while a group of green ribbons, who seemed to be the most determined of his followers, hung growling about the barricaded door. Something in the gloomy brightness of the room, and the disorder of the barricaded windows, something in the loneliness of his figure as he stood there, appealed to me; I even took one step towards him. But at that moment he looked up, his face grown dark; and he waved me off with a gesture almost of rage. I knew then that I had but a small part of his thoughts; and that at this moment, while the edifice he had built up with so much care and so much risk was crumbling about him, he was thinking not of us, but of those who had promised and failed him; who had given good words, and left him to perish. And I went.

Yet even for that moment of delay it seemed that I might pay too dearly. A dozen steps brought me to the low-browed door he had indicated, in the thickness of the wall at the foot of the main staircase. But already a man was adjusting the last bar. I cried to him to open. "Open! I must go out!" I cried.

"*Dieu!* It is too late!" he said, with a dark glance at me.

My heart sank; I feared he was right. Still he began to unbar, though grudgingly, and in half a minute we had the door loose. With a pistol in his hand, he opened it on the chain and looked out. It opened on a narrow passage--which, God be thanked, was still empty. He dropped the chain, and almost thrust me out, cried, "To the left!" and then, as dazzled by the sunlight I turned that way, I heard the door slam behind me and the chain rattle as it was linked again.

The houses that rose on each side somewhat deadened the noise of the mob and the firing; but as I hurried down the alley, bareheaded and with the pistol which Froment had given me firmly clutched in my hand, I heard a fresh spirt of noise behind me, and knew that the assailants had entered the passage by the farther end; and that had I waited a moment longer I should have been too late.

As it was, my position was sufficiently forlorn, if it was not hopeless. Alone and a stranger, without hat or badge, knowing little of the streets, I might blunder at any corner into the arms of one of the parties--and be massacred. I had a notion that the church of the Capuchins was that which I had visited near Madame Catinot's; and my first thought was to gain the main street leading in that direction. This was not so easy, however; the alley in which I found myself led only into a second passage equally strait and gloomy. Entering this, I turned after a moment's hesitation to the left, but before I had gone a dozen paces I heard shouting in front of me; and I halted and retraced my steps. Hurrying in the other direction, I found myself in a minute in a little gloomy well-like court, with no second outlet that I could see, where I stood a moment panting and at a loss, rendered frantic and almost desperate by the thought that, while I hovered there uncertain, the die might be cast, and those whom I sought perish for lack of my aid.

I was about to return, resolved to face at all risks the party of rioters whom I heard behind me, when an open window in the lowest floor of one of the houses that stood round the court caught my eye. It was not far from the ground, and to see was to determine; the house must have an outlet on the street. In a dozen strides I crossed the court, and resting one hand on the sill of the window, vaulted into the room, alighted sideways on a stool, and fell heavily to the floor.

I was up in a moment unhurt, but with a woman's scream ringing in my ears, and a woman, a girl, cowering from me, white-faced, her back to the door. She had been kneeling, praying probably, by the bed; and I had almost fallen on her. When I looked she screamed again; I called to her in heaven's name to be silent.

"The door! Only the door!" I cried. "Show it me. I will hurt no one."

"Who are you?" she muttered. And still shrinking from me, she stared at me with distended eyes.

"*Mon Dieu!* What does it matter?" I answered fiercely. "The door, woman! The door into the street!"

I advanced upon her, and the same fear which had paralysed her gave her sense again. She opened the door beside her, and pointed dumbly down a passage. I hurried through the passage, rejoicing at my success, but before I could unbar the door that I found facing me a second woman came out of a room at the side, and saw me, and threw up her hands with a cry of terror.

"Which is the way to the church of the Capuchins?" I said.

She clapped one hand to her side, but she answered. "To the left!" she gasped. "And then to the right! Are they coming?"

I did not stay to ask whom she meant, but getting the door open at last I sprang through the doorway. One look up and down the street, however, and I was in again, and the door closed behind me. My eyes met the woman's, and without a word she snatched up the bar I had dropped and set it in the sockets. Then she turned and ran up the stairs, and I followed her, the girl into whose room I had leapt, and whose scared face showed for a second at the end of the passage, disappearing like a rabbit, as we passed her.

I followed the woman to the window of an upper room, and we looked out, standing back and peering fearfully over the sill. No need, now, to ask why I had returned so quickly. The roar of many voices seemed in a moment to fill all the street, while the casement shook with the tread of thousands and thousands of advancing feet, as, rank after rank, stretching from wall to wall, the mob, or one section of it, swept by, the foremost marching in order, shoulder to shoulder, armed with muskets, and in some kind of uniform, the rearmost a savage rabble with naked arms and pikes and axes, who looked up at the windows, and shook their fists and danced and leapt as they went by, with a great shout of *"Aux Arènes! Aux Arènes!"*

In themselves they were a sight to make a quiet man's blood run chill; but they had that in their midst, seeing which the woman beside me clutched my arm and screamed aloud. On six long pikes, raised high above the mob, moved six severed heads--one, the foremost, bald and large, and hideously leering. They lifted these to the windows, and shook their gory locks in sport; and so went by, and in a moment the street was quiet again.

The woman, trembling in a chair, muttered that they had sacked La Vierge, the red cabaret, and that the bald head was a town-councillor's, her neighbour's. But I did not stay to listen. I left her where she was, and, hurrying down again, unbarred the door and went out. All was strangely quiet again. The morning sun shone bright and warm on the long empty street, and seemed to give the lie to the thing I had seen. Not a living creature was visible this way or that; not a face at the window. I stood a moment in the middle of the road, disconcerted; puzzled by the bright stillness, and uncertain which way I had been going. At last I remembered the woman's directions, and set off on the heels of the mob, until I reached the first turning on the right. I took this, and had not gone a hundred yards before I recognised, a little in front of me, Madame Catinot's house.

It showed to the sunshine a wide blind front, long rows of shuttered windows, and not a sign of life. Nevertheless, here was something I knew, something which wore a semblance of familiarity, and I hailed it with hope; and, flinging myself on the door, knocked long and recklessly. The noise seemed fit to wake the dead; it boomed and echoed in every doorway of the empty street, that on the evening of my arrival had teemed with traffic; I shivered at the sound--I shivered standing conspicuous on the steps of the house, expecting a score of windows to be opened and heads thrust out.

But I had not yet learned how the extremity of panic benumbs; or how strong is the cowardly instinct that binds the peaceful man to his hearth when blood flows in the streets. Not a face showed at a casement, not a door opened; worse, though I knocked again and again, the house I would awaken remained dead and silent. I stood back and gazed at it, and returned, and hammered again, thinking this time nothing of myself.

But without result. Or not quite. Far away at the end of the street the echo of my knocking dwelt a little, then grew into a fuller, deeper sound--a sound I knew. The mob was returning.

I cursed my folly then for lingering; thought of the passage in the rear of the house that led to the church, found the entrance to it, and in a moment was speeding through it. The distant roar grew nearer and louder, but now I could see the low door of the church, and I slackened my pace a little. As I did so the door before me opened, and a man looked out. I saw his face before he saw me, and read it; saw terror, shame, and rage written on its mean features; and in some strange way I knew what he was going to do before he did it. A moment he glared abroad, blinking and shading his eyes in the sunshine, then he spied me, slid out, and with an indescribable Judas look at me, fled away.

He left the door ajar--I knew him in some way for the door-keeper, deserting his post; and in a moment I was in the church and face to face with a sight I shall remember while I live; for that which was passing outside, that which I had seen during the last few minutes, gave it a solemnity exceeding even that of the strange service I had witnessed there before.

The sun shut out, a few red altar lamps shed a sombre light on the pillars and the dim pictures and the vanishing spaces; above all, on a vast crowd of kneeling women, whose bowed heads and wailing voices as they chanted the Litany of the Virgin, filled the nave.

There were some, principally on the fringe of the assembly, who rocked themselves to and fro, weeping silently, or lay still as statues with their foreheads pressed to the cold stones; whilst others glanced this way and that with staring eyes, and started at the slightest sound, and moaned prayers with white lips. But more and more, the passionate utterance of the braver souls laid bonds on the others; louder and louder the measured rhythm of *"Ora pro nobis! Ora pro nobis!"* rose and swelled through the vaults of the roof; more and more fervent it grew, more and more importunate, wilder the abandonment of supplication, until--until I felt the tears rise in my throat, and my breast swell with pity and admiration--and then I saw Denise.

She knelt between her mother and Madame Catinot, nearly in the front row of those who faced the high altar. Whence I stood, I had a side view of her face as she looked upward in rapt adoration--that face which I had once deemed so childish. Now at the thought that she prayed, perhaps for me--at the thought that this woman so pure and brave, that though little more than a child, and soft, and gentle, and maidenly, she could bear herself with no shadow of quailing in this stress of death--at the thought that she loved me, and prayed for me, I felt myself more or less than a man. I felt tears rising, I felt my breast heaving, and then--and then as I went to drop on my knees, against the great doors on the farther side of the church, came a thunderous shock, followed by a shower of blows and loud cries for admittance.

A horrible kind of shudder ran through the kneeling crowd, and here and there a woman screamed and sprang up and looked wildly round. But for a few moments the chant still rose monotonously and filled the building; louder and louder the measured rhythm of *"Ora pro nobis! Ora pro nobis!"* still rose and fell and rose again with an intensity of supplication, a pathos of repetition that told of bursting hearts. At length, however, one of the leaves of the door flew open, and that proved too much; the sound sent three parts of the congregation shrieking to their feet--though a few still sang. By this time I was half way through the crowd, pressing to Denise's side; before I could reach her the other door gave way, and a dozen men flocked in tumultuously. I had a glimpse of a priest--afterwards I learnt that it was Father Benôit--standing to oppose them with a cross upraised; and then, by the dim light, which to them was darkness, I saw--unspeakable relief--that the intruders were not the leaders of the mob, but foremost the two St. Alais, blood-stained and black with powder, with drawn swords and clothes torn; and behind them a score of their followers.

In their relief women flung themselves on the men's necks, and those who stood farther away burst into loud sobbing and weeping. But the men themselves, after securing the doors behind them, began immediately to move across the church to the smaller exit on the alley; one crying that all was lost, and another that the east gate was open, while a third adjured the women to separate--adding that in the neighbouring houses they would be safe, but that the church would be sacked; and that even now the Calvinists were bursting in the gates of the monastery through which the fugitives had retreated, after being driven out of the Arènes.

All, on the instant, was panic and wailing and confusion. I have heard it said since that the worst thing the men could have done was to take the church in their flight, and that had they kept aloof the women would not have been disturbed; that, as a fact, and in the event, the church was not sacked. But in such a hell as was Nîmes that morning, with the kennels running blood, and men's souls surprised by sudden defeat, it was hard to decide what was best; and I blame no one.

A rush for the door followed the man's words. It drove me a little farther from Denise; but as she and the group round her held back and let the more timid or selfish go first, I had time to gain her side. She had drawn the hood of her cloak close round her face, and until I touched her arm did not see me. Then, without a word, she clung to me--she clung to me, looking up; I saw her face under the hood, and it was happy. God! It was happy, even in that scene of terror!

After that, Madame St. Alais, though she greeted me with a bitter smile, had no power to repel me. "You are quick, Monsieur, to profit by your victory," she said, in a scathing tone. And that was all. Unrebuked, I passed my arm round Denise, and followed close on Louis and Madame Catinot; while Monsieur le Marquis, after speaking with his mother, followed. As he did so his eye fell on me, but he only smiled, and to something Madame said, answered aloud, "*Mon Dieu*, Madame; what does it matter? We have thrown the last stake and lost. Let us leave the table!"

She dropped her hood over her face; and even in that moment of fear and excitement I found something tragic in the act, and on a sudden pitied her. But it was no time for sentiment or pity; the pursuers were not far behind the pursued. We were still in the church and some paces from the threshold giving on the alley, when a rush of footsteps outside the great door behind us made itself heard, and the next instant the doors creaked under the blows hailed upon them. It was a question whether they would stand until we were out, and I felt the slender figure within my arm quiver and press more closely to me. But they held--they held, and an instant later the crowd before us gave way, and we were outside in the daylight, in the alley, hurrying quickly down it towards Madame Catinot's house.

It seemed to me that we were safe then, or nearly safe; so glad was I to find myself in the open air and out of the church. The ground fell away a little towards Madame Catinot's, and I could see the line of hastening heads bobbing along before us, and here and there white faces turned to look back. The high walls on either hand softened the noise of the riot. Behind me were M. le Marquis and Madame; and again behind them three or four of M. le Marquis' followers brought up the rear. I looked back beyond these and saw that the alley opposite the church was still clear, and that the pursuers had not yet passed through the church; and I stooped to whisper a word of comfort to Denise. I stooped perhaps longer than was necessary, for before I was aware of it I found myself stumbling over Louis' heels. A backward wave sweeping up the alley had brought him up short and flung him against me. With the movement, as we all jostled one another, there arose far in front and rolled up the passage between the high walls a sound of misery; a mingling of groans and screams and wailing such as I hope I may never hear again. Some strove furiously to push their way back towards the church, and some, not understanding what was amiss, to go forwards, and some fell, and were trodden under foot; and for a few seconds the long narrow alley heaved and seethed in an agony of panic.

Engaged in saving Denise from the crush and keeping her on her feet, I did not, for a moment, understand. The first thought I had was that the women--three out of four were women--had gone mad or given way to a shameful, selfish terror. Then, as our company staggering and screaming rolled back upon us, until it filled but half the length of the passage, I heard in front a roar of cruel laughter, and saw over the intervening heads a serried mass of pike-points filling the end of the passage opposite Madame Catinot's house. Then I understood. The Calvinists had cut us off; and my heart stood still.

For there was no retreat. I looked behind me, and saw the alley by the church-porch choked with men who had reached it through the church; alive with harsh mocking faces, and scowling eyes, and cruel thirsty pikes. We were hemmed in; in the long high walls, which it was impossible to scale, was no door or outlet short of Madame Catinot's house--and that was guarded. And before and behind us were the pikes.

I dream of that scene sometimes; of the sunshine, hot and bright, that lay ghastly on white faces distorted with fear; of women fallen on their knees and lifting hands this way and that; of others screaming and uttering frenzied prayers, or hanging on men's necks; of the long writhing line of humanity, wherein fear, showing itself in every shape, had its way; above all of the fiendish jeers and laughter of the victors, as they cried to the men to step out, or hurled vile words at the women.

Even Nîmes, mother of factions, parent of a hundred quarterless brawls, never saw a worse scene, or one more devilish. For a few seconds in the surprise of this trap, in the sudden horror of finding ourselves, when all seemed well, at grips with death, I could only clutch Denise to me tighter and tighter, and hide her eyes on my breast, as I leaned against the wall and groaned with white lips. O God, I thought, the women! The women! At such a time a man would give all the world that there might be none, or that he had never loved one.

St. Alais was the first to recover his presence of mind and act--if that could be called action which was no more than speech, since we were hopelessly enmeshed and outnumbered. Putting Madame behind him he waved a white kerchief to the men by the door of the church--who stood about thirty paces from us--and adjured them to let the women pass; even taunting them when they refused, and gibing at them as cowards, who dared not face the men unencumbered. But they only answered with jeers and threats, and savage laughter. "No, no, M. le Prêtre!" they cried. "No, no! Come out and taste steel! Then, perhaps, we will let the women go! Or perhaps not!"

"You cowards!" he cried.

But they only brandished their arms and laughed, shrieking: "*A bas les traîtres! A bas les prêtres!* Stand out! Stand out, Messieurs!" they continued, "or we will come and pluck you from the women's skirts!"

He glowered at them in unspeakable rage. Then a man on their side stepped out and stilled the tumult. "Now listen!" said this fellow, a giant, with long black hair falling over a tallowy face. "We will give you three minutes to come out and be piked. Then the women shall go. Skulk there behind them, and we fire on all, and their blood be on your heads."

St. Alais stood speechless. At last, "You are fiends!" he cried in a voice of horror. "Would you kill us before their eyes?"

"Ay, or in their laps!" the man retorted, amid a roar of laughter. "So decide, decide!" he continued, dancing a clumsy step and tossing a half-pike round his head. "Three minutes by the clock there! Come out, or we fire on all! It will be a dainty pie! A dainty Catholic pie, Messieurs!"

St. Alais turned to me, his face white, his eyes staring; and he tried to speak. But his voice failed.

And then, of what happened next I cannot tell; for, for a minute, all was blurred. I remember only how the sun lay hot on the wall beyond his face, and how black the lines of mortar showed between the old thin Roman bricks. We were about twenty men and perhaps fifty women, huddled together in a space some forty yards long. Groans burst from the men's lips, and such as had women in their arms--and they were many--leaned against the wall and tried to comfort them, and tried to put them from them. One man cried curses on the dogs who would murder us, and shook his fists at them; and some rained kisses on the pale senseless faces that lay on their breasts--for, thank God, many of the women had fainted; while others, like St. Alais, looked mute agony into eyes that told it again, or clasped a neighbour's hand, and looked up into a sky piteously blue and bright. And I--I do not know what I did, save look into Denise's eyes and look and look! There was no senselessness in them.

Remember that the sun shone on all this, and the birds twittered and chirped in the gardens beyond the walls; that it wanted an hour or two of high noon, a southern noon; that in the crease of the valley the Rhone sparkled between its banks, and not far off the sea broke rippling and creaming on the shore of Les Bouches; that all nature rejoiced, and only we--we, pent between those dreadful walls, those scowling faces, saw death imminent--black death shutting out all things.

A hand touched me; it was St. Alais' hand. I think, nay, I know, for I read it in his face, that he meant to be reconciled to me. But when I turned to him--or it may be it was the sight of his sister's speechless misery moved him--he had another thought. As the black-haired giant called "One minute gone!" and his following howled, M. le Marquis threw up his hand.

"Stay!" he cried, with the old gesture of command. "Stay! There is one man here who is not of us! Let him pass first, and go!" And he pointed to me. "He has no part with us! I swear it!"

A roar of cruel laughter was the answer. Then, "He that is not with me is against me!" the giant quoted impiously. And they jeered again.

On that, I take no credit for what I did. In such moments of exaltation men are not accountable, and, for another thing, I knew that they would not listen, that I risked nothing. And trembling with rage I flung back their words. "I am against you!" I cried. "I would rather die here with these, than live with you! You stain the earth! You pollute the air! You are fiends----"

No more, for with a shrill laugh the man next me, a mere lad, half-witted, I think, and the same who had cursed them, sprang by me and rushed on the pike-points. Half a dozen met in his breast before our eyes--before our eyes--and with a wild scream he flung up his arms and was borne back against the side-wall dead and gushing blood.

Instinctively I had covered Denise's face that she might not see. And it was well; for at that--there was a kind of mercy in it, and let me tell it quickly--the wretches tasting blood broke loose, and rushed on us. I saw St. Alais thrust his mother behind him, and almost with the same movement fling himself on the pikes; and I, pushing Denise down into the angle of the wall--though she clung to me and prayed to me--killed the first that came at me with Froment's pistol, and the next also, with the other barrel at point blank distance--feeling no fear, but only passion and rage. The third bore me down with his pike fixed in my shoulder, and for a moment I saw only the sky, and his scowling face black against it; and shut my eyes, expecting the blow that must follow.

But none did follow. Instead a weight fell on me, and I began to struggle, and a whole battle, it seemed to me, was fought over me--in that horrible slaughterhouse alley, where they dragged men from women's arms, and forced them, screaming, to the wall, and stabbed them to death without pity; and things were done of which I dare not tell!

CHAPTER XXV
BEYOND THE SHADOW

I thank Heaven that I saw little more than I have told. A score of feet trampled on me as the murderers stumbled this way and that, and bruised me and covered me with blood that was not my own. And I heard screams of men in the death-throe, ear-piercing shrieks of women--shrieks that chilled the blood and stopped the breath--mad laughter, sounds of the pit. But to rise was to court instant death, and, though I had no hope and no looking forward, my momentary passion had spent itself and I lay quiet. Resistance was useless.

At last I thought the end had come. The body that pressed on me, and partly hid me, was abruptly dragged away; the light came to my eyes, and a voice cried, briskly: "Here is another! He is alive!"

I staggered to my feet, stupidly willing to die with some sort of dignity. The speaker was a stranger, but by his side was Buton, and beyond him stood De Géol; and there were others, all staring at me, face beyond face. Still, I could not believe that I was saved. "If you are going to do it, do it quickly," I muttered; and I opened my arms.

"God forbid!" Buton answered hurriedly. "Enough has been done already, and too much! M. le Vicomte, lean on me! Lean on me, and come this way. *Mon Dieu*, I was only just in time. If they had killed you----"

"That is the fifth," said De Géol.

Buton did not answer, but taking my arm, gently urged me along, and De Géol taking the other side, I walked between them, through a lane of people who stared at me with a sort of brutish wonder--a lane of people with faces that looked strangely white in the sunshine. I was bareheaded, and the sun dazzled and confused me, but obeying the pressure of Buton's hand I swerved and passed through a door that seemed to open in the wall. As I did so I dropped a kerchief which some one had given me to bind up my shoulder. A man standing beside the door, the last man on the right-hand side of the lane of people, picked it up and gave it to me with a kindly alacrity. He had a pike, and his hands were covered with blood, and I do not doubt that he was one of the murderers!

Two men were carrying some one into the house before us, and at the sight of the helpless body and hanging head, sense and memory returned to me with a rush. I caught Buton by the breast of his coat and shook him-- shook him savagely. "Mademoiselle de St. Alais!" I cried. "What have you done to her, wretch? If you have----"

"Hush, Monsieur, hush," he answered reproachfully. "And be yourself. She is safe, and here, I give you my word. She was carried in among the first. I don't think a hair of her head is injured."

"She was carried in here?" I said.

"Yes, M. le Vicomte."

"And safe?"

"Yes, yes."

I believe that at that I burst into tears not altogether unmanly; for they were tears of thankfulness and gratitude. I had gone through very much, and, though the wound in my arm was a trifle, I had lost some blood; and the tears may be forgiven me. Nor indeed was I alone in weeping that day. I learned afterwards that one of the very murderers, a man who had been foremost in the work, cried bitterly when he came to himself and saw what he had done.

They killed in Nîmes on that day and the two next, about three hundred men, principally in the Capuchin convent--which Froment had used as a printing-office, and made the headquarters of his propaganda--in the Cabaret Rouge, and in Froment's own house, which held out until they brought cannon to bear on it. Not more than one-half of these fell in actual conflict or hot blood; the remainder were hunted down in lanes and houses and hiding-places, and killed where they were found, or, surrendering at discretion, were led to the nearest wall, and there shot.

Later, both in Paris and the provinces, this severity was commended, and held up to admiration as the truest mercy; on the ground that it stamped out the fire of revolt which was on the point of blazing up and prevented it spreading to the rest of France. But, looking back, I find in it another thing; I find in it not mercy, but the first, or nearly the first, instance of that strange contempt of human life which marked the Revolution in its later stages; of that extravagance of cruelty which three years afterwards paralysed society and astounded the world, and, by the horrible excesses into which it occasionally led men, proved to the philosophers of the Human Race that France in the last days of the eighteenth century could do in the daylight, at Arras and Nantes and Paris, deeds which the tyrants of old confined to the dark recesses of their torture-chambers: deeds--I blush to say it--that no other polite country has matched in this age.

But with these crimes--and be it understood I do not refer here to the work of the guillotine--I thank God that I have at this time nothing to do. They left their traces on later pages of my life--as on the life of what Frenchman have they not?--and some day I may revert to them. But my task here barely touches them. It is enough for me to say that of eighteen men who shared with me the horrors of the alley by the Capuchins, four only lived to tell the tale, and look back on the walls of Nîmes; they and I owing our lives in part to the timely arrival of Buton and some foreign representatives, who did not share the Cevennols' fanaticism, and partly to the late relenting of the murderers themselves.

Of the four, Father Benôit and Louis St. Alais were two, and strange was the meeting, when we three, so wonderfully preserved, with clothes still torn and disordered, and faces splashed with blood, came together in the upstairs *salon* at Madame Catinot's. The shutters of the room, with the exception of one high corner shutter, were still closed; dead ashes lay white and cold in the empty fire-place, that had blazed so cheerfully in my honour the night I supped with Madame Catinot. The whole room was gloomy and chill, the furniture cast long shadows, and up the stairs came the clamour of the mob, that having seen us into the house eddied curiously round the scene of the murder, and could not have enough of it.

A strange meeting, for we three had all loved one another, and by stress of the times had been separated. Now we met as from the grave, ghostly figures, livid, trembling, with shaking hands and eyes burning with the light of fever; but with all differences purged away. "My Brother!" "Your Brother!" and Louis' hands met mine, as if the dead man who had died with the courage of his race joined them; while Father Benôit wrung his hands in uncontrollable grief or walked the room, crying: "My poor children! Oh, my poor children! God have mercy on this land!"

A low sound of women's voices, and weeping, with the hurrying of feet going softly to and fro, came from the next room: and that it was, I think, that presently calmed us, so that except for an occasional burst of grief on Louis' part we could talk quietly. I learned that Madame St. Alais lay there, sadly injured in the *mêlée*, either by her fall or a blow from a foot; and that Denise and Madame Catinot and a surgeon were with her. The very room in its gloom was funereal, and we talked in whispers--and then sank into silence; or again one or other would rise with a shudder of remembrance, and walk the room with heaving breast. Presently, the sound of guns coming to our ears, we forgot ourselves for a while and talked of Froment, and what chance of escape he had, and listened and heard the mob raving and howling as it surged by; and then talked again. But always as men who were no longer concerned; as men whom death had released from the common obligations.

Presently they came and called Louis, who went to his mother; and then after another interval Father Benôit was summoned, and I walked the room alone. Silence after so great commotion, solitude, when an hour before I had dealt death and faced it in that inferno, safety after danger so imminent, all stirred the depths of my heart. When, in addition, I thought of St. Alais' death, and recalled the brilliant promise, the daring, the brightness of that haughty spirit now for ever quenched, I felt the tears rise again. I paced the room in uncontrollable emotion, and was thankful for the gloom that allowed me to give it vent. Old times, old scenes, old affections rose up, and my boyhood; I remembered that we had played together, I forgot that we had gone different ways.

After a long time, a long, long time, when evening had nearly come, Louis came in to me. "Will you come?" he said abruptly.

"To Madame St. Alais?"

"Yes, she wants to see you," he replied, holding the door open, and speaking in the dull even tone of one who knows all.

After such a scene as we had passed through comes reaction; I was worn out and I went with him mechanically, thinking rather of the past than the present. But no sooner was I over the threshold of the next room, which, unlike that I had left, was brilliantly lit by candles set in sconces, the shutters being closed, than I came to myself with a shock. Propped up with pillows on a bed opposite the door, so that I met her eyes and had a full view of her face as I entered, lay Madame St. Alais; and I stood. Her face was white with a red spot burning in each cheek; her eyes matched the colour in brilliance; but it was neither of these things that brought me up suddenly, nor--though I noticed it with foreboding--the way in which she plucked at the coverlet when she spoke. It was something in her expression; something so unfitting the occasion, so bizarre and light that I stood appalled.

She saw my hesitation, and in a gay and slightly affected tone, that in a moment told the story, a tone more dreadful under the circumstances than the most pathetic outbursts, she reproached me with it. "Welcome, M. le Vicomte," she said. "And yet I am glad to see that you have some modesty. We will not be hard on you, however. A late repentance is better than none, and--where is my fan, Denise? Child, my fan!"

Denise rose with a choking sound from her seat by the bed, and must, I think, have broken down; we had all nerves worn to the last thread. But Madame Catinot saved the situation. Hastily reaching a fan from a side table she laid a firm hand on the younger woman's shoulder as she passed, and gently pressed her back into her seat.

"Thank you, my dear," Madame St. Alais said, playing an instant with the fan, and smiling from side to side, as I had seen her smile a hundred times in her *salon*. "And now, M. le Vicomte," she continued with ghastly archness, "I think that you will have the grace to say that I was a true prophet?"

I muttered something, heaven knows what; the scene, with Madame's smiling face, and the others' bowed shoulders and averted eyes, was dreadful.

"I never doubted that you would have to join us," she went on, with complacency. "And if I were cruel, I should have much to say. But as you have returned to your allegiance before it was too late, we will let bygones be bygones. His Majesty is so good that--but where are the others? We cannot proceed without them."

She looked round with a touch of her native peremptoriness. "Where is M. de Gontaut?" she said. "Louis, has not M. de Gontaut arrived? He promised to be here to witness the contract."

Louis, from his place by one of the closed windows, where he stood with Father Benôit and the surgeon, answered in a strained voice that he had not yet arrived.

Madame seemed to find something unnatural in his tone and our attitude, she looked uneasily from one to the other of us. "There is nothing the matter, is there?" she said, flirting her fan more vigorously. "Nothing has happened?"

"No, no, Madame," Louis answered, striving to soothe her. "Doubtless he will be here by-and-by."

But a shadow of anxiety still clouded Madame's face. "And Victor?" she said. "He has not come either? Louis, are you sure that there is nothing the matter?"

"Madame, Madame, you will see him presently," he answered with a half-stifled sob; and he turned away with a gesture of horror, which, but for one of the curtains of the alcove, she must have seen.

She did not, though there was enough in this to arouse a sane person's suspicions. As he spoke, however, Madame's eyes fell on me, and the piteous anxiety which had for the moment darkened her face, passed away as quickly as the shadow of a cloud passes on an April morning. She took up her fan again, and looked at me gaily. "Do you know," she said, "I had the strangest dream last night, M. le Vicomte--or was it when I was ill, Denise? Never mind. But I dreamed all sorts of horrors; that our house here was burned, and the house at Cahors, and that we had to fly and take refuge at Montauban, and then--I think it was at Nîmes. And that M. de Gontaut was murdered, and all the *canaille* were up in arms! As if--as if," she continued, with a little laugh, cut short by a gasp of pain, "the King would permit such things, or they were possible. And there was something--something still more absurd about the Church." She paused, knitting her brows; and then with a touch of her fan dismissing the subject: "But I forget--I forget. And just when it was most horrible I awoke. It was all absurd. So extravagant you would all be ill with laughing if I could remember it. I fancied that a pair of red-heeled shoes were as good as a death warrant, and powder and patches condemned you at once."

She paused. The fan dropped from her hand, and she looked round uneasily. "I think--I think I am not quite well yet," she said in a different tone, and a spasm crossed her face--it was plain that she was in pain. "Louis!" she continued petulantly, "where is the notary? He might read the contract. Doubtless Victor and M. de Gontaut will be here before long. Where is he?" she continued sharply.

It is easy to say that we might have played our parts; but the pity and the horror of it, falling on hearts already tortured by the scenes of the day, fairly unmanned us. Denise hid her face, and trembled so that the chair on which she sat shook; and Louis turned away shuddering, while I stood near the foot of the bed, frozen into silence. This time it was the surgeon, a thin young man of dark complexion, who put himself forward.

"The papers are in the next room, Madame," he said gravely.

"But you are not M. Pettifer?" she answered querulously.

"No, Madame, he was so unwell as to be unable to leave the house."

"He has no right to be unwell," Madame retorted severely. "Pettifer unwell, and Mademoiselle St. Alais' contract to be signed! But you have the papers?"

"In the next room, Madame."

"Fetch them! Fetch them!" she answered, her eyes wandering uneasily from one to another. And she moved in the bed and sighed as one in pain. Then, "Where is Victor? Why does he not come?" she asked impatiently.

"I think I hear him," Louis said suddenly. It was the first time he had spoken of his own free will, and I caught a new sound in his voice. "I will see," he went on, and moving to the door he gave me a sign, as he passed, to follow him.

I muttered something, and did so. In the room in which I had waited, the half-shuttered room of gloom and shadows, from which Louis had fetched me, we found the surgeon groping hastily about. "Some paper, Monsieur," he said, looking up impatiently as we entered. "Some paper! Almost anything should do."

"Stay!" Louis said, his voice harsh with pain. "We have had too much of this--this mockery. I will have no more."

"Monsieur?"

"I say I will have no more!" Louis answered fiercely, a sob in his throat. "Tell her the truth."

"She would not believe it."

"At any rate, anything is better than this."

"Do you mean it, Monsieur?" the surgeon asked slowly, and he looked at him.

"I do."

"Then I will have no part in it," the man answered with gravity. "I acquit myself of all responsibility. Nor shall you do it, Monsieur, until you have heard what the inevitable result will be."

"My mother cannot recover," Louis said stubbornly.

"No, Monsieur, nor will she live, in my opinion, more than a few hours. When the fever that now supports her begins to wane she will collapse, and die. It depends on you whether she closes her eyes, knowing none of the evil that has happened, or her son's death; or dies----"

"It is horrible!"

"It is for you to choose," the surgeon answered inexorably.

Louis looked round. "There is paper there," he said suddenly.

I suppose that we had been absent from the room no more than a couple of minutes, but when we returned we found Madame St. Alais calling impatiently for us and for Victor. "Where is he? Where is he?" she repeated feverishly. "Why is he late to-day of all days? There is no--no quarrel between you?" And she looked jealously at me.

"None, Madame," I said, with tears in my voice. "That I swear!"

"Then why is he not here? And M. de Gontaut?" Her eyes were still bright; the red spot burned still in her cheeks; but her features had taken a pinched look, she was changed, and her fingers were never still. Her voice had grown harsh and unnatural, and from time to time she looked round with a piteous expression as if something puzzled her. "I am not well to-day," she muttered presently, with a painful effort to be herself. "And I forget to be as gay as I should be. Mademoiselle, go to M. le Vicomte, and say something pretty to amuse us while we wait. And you, M. le Vicomte! In my young days it was usual for the *fiancé* to salute his mistress on these occasions. Fie on you! For shame, Monsieur! I am afraid that you are a laggard in love."

Denise rose, and came slowly to me before them all, but no word passed her pale lips, and she did not raise her eyes to mine. She remained passive when in accordance with Madame's permission I stooped and kissed her cold cheek; it grew no warmer, her eyes did not kindle. Yet I was satisfied, more than satisfied; for as I leant over her I felt her little hands--little hands I longed to take in mine and shelter and protect--I felt them clutch and hold the front of my coat, as the child clings to its mother's neck. I passed my arm round her before them all, and so we stood at the foot of Madame's bed, and she looked at us.

She laughed gaily. "Poor little mouse!" she said. "She is shy yet. Be good to her, *mon cher*, she is a tender morsel, and--I don't feel well! I don't feel well," Madame repeated, abruptly breaking off, and lifting herself in bed, while one hand went with difficulty to her head. "I don't--what is it?" she continued, the colour visibly fading from her face and leaving it white and drawn, while fear leapt into her staring eyes. "What is it? Fetch--fetch some one, will you? The--the doctor! And Victor."

Denise slipped from my arm, and flew to her side. I stood a moment, then the surgeon touched my arm. "Go!" he muttered. "Go. Leave her to the women. It will be quickly over."

And so Madame St. Alais gave Mademoiselle to me at last; and the compact for our marriage, into which she had entered so many years before with my dead father, was fulfilled.

Madame died next morning, being taken not only from the evil to come, but from that which was then present, and roared and eddied through the streets of Nîmes round the unburied body of her son; for she died without awaking from the delirium which followed her hurt. I went in to see her lying dead and little changed; and in the quiet decorum of the lighted chamber I thought reverently of the change which one year--one brief year had made, coming at the end of fifty years of prosperity. It seemed pitiful to me then, as I stooped and kissed the waxen hand--very pitiful; now, knowing what the future had in store, remembering the twenty years of exile and poverty and tedium and hope deferred, that were to be the lot of so many of her friends, of so many of those who had graced her *salons* at St. Alais and Cahors, I think her happy. Possessed of energy as well as pride, a rare combination in our order, she and hers dared greatly and greatly lost; staked all and lost all. Yet better that, than the prison or the guillotine; or growing old and decrepit in a strange land, to return to a *patrie* that had long forgotten them; that stood in the roads and jeered at the old berlins and petticoats and headgear that were the fashion in the days of the Polignacs.

I have said that the riots in Nîmes lasted three days. On the last Buton came to me and told us we must go; that to avoid worse things we must leave the city without delay, or he and the more moderate party who had saved us would no longer be responsible. On this, Louis was for retiring to Montpellier, and thence to the *émigrés* at Turin; and for a few hours I was of the same mind, desiring most of all to place the women in safety.

I owe it to Buton that I did not take a step hard to recall, and of which I am sure that I should have repented later. He asked me bluntly whither I was going, and when I told him, set his back against the door. "God forbid!" he said. "Who go, go. Few will return."

I answered him with heat. "Nonsense!" I cried. "I tell you, within a year you will be on your knees to us to come back."

"Why?" he said.

"You cannot keep order without us!"

"With ease," he answered coolly.

"Look at the state of things here!"

"It will pass."

"But who will govern?"

"The fittest," he replied doggedly. "For do you still think, M. le Vicomte--after all that has happened--that a man to make laws must have a title--saving your presence? Do you still think that the wheat will not grow, nor the hens lay eggs, unless the Seigneur's shadow falls on them? Do you think that to fight, a man must have powder on his head as well as in his musket?"

"I think," I retorted, "that when a man who does not know the sea turns pilot it is time to leave the vessel!"

"The pilot will learn," he answered. "And for quitting the vessel, let those go who have no business on board. Be guided, Monseigneur," he continued in a different tone. "Be guided. They have killed in Nîmes three hundred in three days."

"And you say, stay?"

"Ay, for there is blood between us," he answered grimly. "That has been done now which will not easily be forgiven; that has been done which will abide. Go abroad after this--and stay abroad! Or rather do not--do not, but be guided," he continued, with rough emotion in his voice. "Go home to the Château, and be quiet, Monsieur, and no one will harm you."

There was much in what he said. At any rate, I thought the advice so good that, after some hesitation, I not only determined to follow it, but I gave it to the others. But Louis would not change his mind. A horror of the country had seized him since his escape; and he would go. He raised no opposition, however, when I asked him to give me Denise; and within twenty-four hours of her mother's death she became my wife, in that dark-shuttered house by the Capuchins' alley, Father Benôit performing the service. Louis was at the same time married to Madame Catinot, who was to share his exile. Needless to say there were no rejoicings at these weddings; no *fête* and no joy-bells, and no bride-clothes, but sobs and wailings, and cold lips and passive hands.

But a bright day has sometimes a weeping dawn, and though for three years or more our life knew perils enough and some sorrows--the story of which I may one day tell--and we shared the lot of all Frenchmen in those times of shame and stress, I had never, no, not for a day or an hour, cause to repent the deed done so hurriedly at Nîmes. Clinging hands and warm lips, eyes that shone as brightly in a prison as a palace, cheered me, when things were worst; and when better days came, and with them grey hairs and a new France, my wife found means still to grace, and ever more and more to share my life.

One word of the man to whom under God I owe it that I won her. He survived, but I never saw Froment of Nîmes again. On the third day of the riots cannon were brought to bear on his tower, it was stormed, and the garrison were put to the sword, one man only, I believe, escaping with his life. That man was Froment, the indomitable, the most capable leader that the Royalists of France ever boasted. He got safely to the frontier and thence to Turin, where he was received with honour by those whose aid might a little earlier have saved all. Who fails must expect buffets, however; the cold shoulder was presently turned to him; he was slighted, and as the years went on his complaints grew louder. Once I sought to find and assist him, but he was then engaged in some enterprise on the African coast, and my circumstances were such that I could have done little had I found him. Soon afterwards, I believe, he died, though certain information never reached me. But dead or alive I owe him gratitude, respect, and other things, among which I count the greatest happiness of my life.